MERCURY'S WAR

Mercury's War

Lora Leigh

BERKLEY SENSATION, NEW YORK

THE BERKLEY PUBLISHING GROUP
Published by the Penguin Group
Penguin Group (USA) Inc.
375 Hudson Street, New York, New York 10014, USA
Penguin Group (Canada), 90 Eglinton Avenue East, Suite 700, Toronto, Ontario M4P 2Y3, Canada
(a division of Pearson Penguin Canada Inc.)
Penguin Books Ltd., 80 Strand, London WC2R 0RL, England
Penguin Group Ireland, 25 St. Stephen's Green, Dublin 2, Ireland (a division of Penguin Books Ltd.)
Penguin Group (Australia), 250 Camberwell Road, Camberwell, Victoria 3124, Australia
(a division of Pearson Australia Group Pty. Ltd.)
Penguin Books India Pvt. Ltd., 11 Community Centre, Panchsheel Park, New Delhi—110 017, India
Penguin Group (NZ), 67 Apollo Drive, Rosedale, North Shore 0632, New Zealand
(a division of Pearson New Zealand Ltd.)
Penguin Books (South Africa) (Pty.) Ltd., 24 Sturdee Avenue, Rosebank, Johannesburg 2196,
South Africa

Penguin Books Ltd., Registered Offices: 80 Strand, London WC2R 0RL, England

This is a work of fiction. Names, characters, places, and incidents either are the product of the author's imagination or are used fictitiously, and any resemblance to actual persons, living or dead, business establishments, events, or locales is entirely coincidental. The publisher does not have any control over and does not assume any responsibility for author or third-party websites or their content.

MERCURY'S WAR

A Berkley Sensation Book / published by arrangement with the author

PRINTING HISTORY
Berkley Sensation mass-market edition / October 2008

ISBN: 978-0-7394-9871-2

BERKLEY® SENSATION
Berkley Sensation Books are published by The Berkley Publishing Group,
a division of Penguin Group (USA) Inc.,
375 Hudson Street, New York, New York 10014.
BERKLEY SENSATION and the "B" design are trademarks of Penguin Group (USA) Inc.

PRINTED IN THE UNITED STATES OF AMERICA

In loving memory of my father,
Russell Kanduha, for always believing.
And my aunt and uncle, Sue and Sid, for
wounderful childhood memories.
You are dearly missed.

· PROLOGUE ·

BUFFALO GAP, VIRGINIA
BREED COMPOUND, SANCTUARY

He was a beast, an animal. He was a creation, the blending of man and lion, and the beast was caged within him. Powerful, strong. The ability to run, to hunt, to scent the enemy on the wind and taste it in the breeze was chained in the dimmest part of the man's subconscious.

How was it fair that it was locked away? it roared. The man was given leave to walk the land, and yet the beast was forced to hide. It stared out of the man's eyes, it pumped the blood in the man's body, and forever it was leashed, restrained.

But it was growing stronger. The drugs that had kept it leashed had worn off; the years of freedom that the man had known, the false sense of security that the man had developed, would aid the creature hiding inside him.

The beast waited. It prowled. It roared out in nightmares as it bided its time. The man was certain of his control. Certain that the drugs the scientists had given him in those labs, and his own control, had killed the animal that fought with such ferocity to survive.

But it wasn't dead. It had never left. For a time, it had slept. A forced sleep. A sleep that built the anger growing inside it, and now it was awake. It was awake and clawing to be free.

But it was patient, or so the animal thought. It could hold on until the man let it free. It was part of the man, part of who he was, what he was. The man would release the animal soon. As soon as the animal was strong enough. It was tired. The attempts to kill it had nearly succeeded. Only by slipping so deep within the man's primal unconsciousness that even the most vital parts of it were hidden, had it managed to survive.

But when it slipped back, the drugs had built an unbreakable fortress of bars around it. They pressed into the animal. Drove spikes through its soul and filled it with pain. And weakened it. Weakened it as surely as a fatal wound would have killed the man.

And the man stayed diligent. The man had no reason to give rein to his heart, or to open his soul. For the man believed his soul lost. Only the animal knew better. And the animal waited . . . Waited for the man to find his soul.

◆   ◆   ◆

"Have you finished the tests?" Jonas stepped into the small lab, as Jackal trailed behind him. Damned security personnel. Callan had given the order that with Jonas's own force of men now protecting Vanderale's glorified clerk, Jonas had to have a bodyguard. A human bodyguard at that. It was a damned good thing he could at least get along with the other man.

He stared at Elyiana Morrey's back as she tensed, her hand lifting to rub the back of her neck. The muscles stiffened beneath her white lab coat as the scent of her irritation began to bloom around her.

She was doing that a lot lately. As soon as he found the time, he would remind her who was the boss here. He didn't have time to engage in power plays with her.

"I finished the tests." She picked up a folder, turned and strode to the counter beside him before slapping it down and returning to whatever she was working on before. Completely ignoring both him and his bodyguard, Jackal.

Silence filled the lab as Jonas stared at the file, quirking his brow at her obvious ill temper. Breed females didn't have PMS, so he couldn't explain her mood swings as well as he could those of the few non-Breed females in the compound.

He had decided months ago that Ely was just contrary.

He liked that about her though. Sometimes. He understood it and could deal with it. But she was being unusually contrary and that didn't set well with him.

"Would you like to explain the tests you ran?" he finally asked her.

"It's in the file."

"I don't want to read your scientific gibberish." He allowed a primal growl to vibrate in his throat. "Tell me what I need to know."

She turned back to him slowly, and he saw the anger burning in her eyes.

"Your games are out of hand," she hissed, her gaze flickering nervously to Jackal. "Your manipulations and conniving machinations are going to get someone killed. And this conversation is none of his business." She pointed her finger at the bodyguard as her gaze snapped with ire.

Jonas stared at her in surprise. Hell, he thought she liked Jackal. He rubbed at his chin thoughtfully as he tried to figure out what had her so incensed. He could only come up with one thing.

"Are you still pissed over Dawn and Seth?" It was the only explanation he could find for her anger. He had ordered to have the hormonal treatments in Dawn's body leveled off when the mating hormone in Seth's system had begun disappearing. Dawn was losing her mate, and Jonas hadn't been willing to allow that to happen no matter how much he disliked Seth Lawrence personally. But then, there were few men that Jonas liked. Hell, few people he could say he liked period.

The rest of that mission had gone to hell in a handbasket though. He had succeeded in ensuring Dawn and Seth stayed together, but the blood that had been spilled was cause for concern.

Ely's lips pressed together in stubborn anger.

Jonas breathed out in resignation, picked up the file and opened it.

Within seconds his brows lifted and his gaze moved back to hers.

"I thought the drugs the scientists gave him in the labs reversed this?"

"He hasn't been on the drugs in seven years," she snapped. "And that isn't his actual state at the moment. That's what happened when I ran the mating test with that of Ms. Rodriquez."

Now this was interesting. Jonas rubbed his jaw as he continued to read through the tests Ely had run.

The tests she had designed to determine mating compatibility were complicated. A mix of saliva, blood and semen samples from the male, combined with saliva, blood and female hormonal samples.

"Jonas, he killed people when he rampaged in the labs," Ely whispered worriedly.

Jonas waved his hand at that. "He had lost his friend . . ."

"His mate," she snapped. "The mating hormone was in his

in frustration. "You don't know Merc very well, Ely. I do. Keep your mouth shut and keep me up-to-date on this. I'll take care of the rest."

Dammit to hell. He didn't need this. He needed Merc to keep Vanderale's little paper pusher out of trouble, not to mate her or go insane on him. And he sure as hell didn't need Ely wigging out on him.

He turned and left the lab, closing the door carefully behind him despite his need to slam it off the fucking hinges. At times like this, he wished he were a drinking man. A good drunk might have helped.

· CHAPTER I ·

Two Weeks Later

The private jet taxied into the hangar, pulling into the heated cavern awaiting it, and huge metal doors closed to trap the heat inside as its motors stilled.

Long minutes later, the door opened, and Ria Rodriquez stepped out onto the top step the pilot had lowered. She stared around the hangar.

A long black limo was parked well out of the way of the jet's wings, and as she watched, a door opened and Mercury Warrant stepped from the car.

She wanted to groan at the sight of the man sent to meet her. Or rather the Breed.

She stared at him curiously. She had seen his photos over the past months, knew as much about him as her boss Dane Vanderale could dig up, and still, the sight of him was like a punch of reaction deep inside her stomach.

His features weren't those of a man's. Nor were they those of the lion his genes had been merged with. If a sexier than hell version of both could be created, then that was Mercury Warrant.

Slanted amber eyes, the line of the lids black, as though someone had applied the lightest layer of eyeliner. She knew his lashes were thick. His nose was long and straight, though a bit flatter, a bit more arrogantly defined than possible in a normal male.

His lips were just a bit thin, but that lower lip, it had a tempting fullness at the center of it that had had her tongue running over her own lips whenever she had noticed it in the pictures she'd studied of the Breeds she would be in contact with.

"Ms. Rodriquez, we're heading to Venezuela to pick up Mr. Dane. Should you need us, don't hesitate to call for pickup."

She turned and looked at her pilot. Bush pilot. Scruffy, his eyes flat and hard, but there was a twinkle of warmth in them when he looked at her.

She was used to working with the hidden Breeds of the world. The ones the Vanderales has slipped from the labs, or from missions. The ones that were listed as dead. Such as Burke had been.

"Tell Mr. Dane to please remember the bling he promised me," she murmured. "I'm about to earn it."

Burke glanced to the limo and the Breed awaiting her. "He's a fine specimen," he said quietly. "Dangerous though. More dangerous than we might realize."

Ria shrugged. He wasn't the one she was after. She'd already drawn her initial suspicions and sent them to Dane. The person or persons they were after would never stare back at her with such captivating eyes, or with such savage interest.

"He's going to be my bodyguard, not my mark," she reminded Burke with a smile.

He snorted at that. "I'll inform Mr. Dane to add to the bling. Because if that's your bodyguard, I'm not certain which one of you I should feel the most sorry for. But I like you best."

"You're a good man, Burke." She smiled smugly as she patted his arm. "Tell Mr. Dane the emeralds looked especially fine next to the diamonds. I'm very eager to see just how much he appreciates the risk I'm taking."

Burke chuckled as he escorted her down the steps and over to the limo.

"Mr. Warrant. I see Director Wyatt couldn't awaken in time to meet me." Ria restrained the urge to check the thick bun she had rolled her hair into on the plane, or the dowdy outfit she had donned.

Damn, she was really going to miss her finer clothes. But she knew the persona that garnered the greatest results. And as much as she disliked that persona, she owed the Vanderales. She owed them her life.

"Director Wyatt was detained in D.C.," Mercury informed her as he glanced at the pilot curiously.

"Anything more that I should tell Mr. Dane?" Burke asked her as she released his arm and he turned to help the copilot with her luggage and laptop case.

"Yes, inform him I won my end of that bet we made. Director Wyatt didn't show up after all."

She caught Mercury's grimace from the periphery of her vision.

"I'll make a note of that." Burke nodded his dark, shaggy head as the trunk opened on the limo and her luggage was stored inside.

As he and the copilot loped back to the plane, Ria turned and stared back at Mercury, trying not to feel too female in his presence.

He was tall, broad and absolutely delicious looking. Savage and male—the combination did something to her feminine core that surprised her.

Her lips twitched as he turned his gaze from the Vanderale pilots back to her.

"They were at the hospital with the first Leo," he commented. "They're Breeds."

She nodded as he reached out and opened the door for her.

"They are." She slid into the sumptuous leather, sliding to the other side as Mercury bent and moved in with her, sitting in the seat across from her.

She glanced to the driver's section to see Lawe Justice. She almost chuckled at his name. She loved some of the names the Breeds had chosen for themselves when given the chance. Lawe Justice, Rule Breaker, two of Jonas Wyatt's main security force, and Mercury Warrant.

Mercury, the messenger of the gods. It should have been Ares. How apt that name might have been if the scientists that created him hadn't completely annihilated the primal instincts he had possessed. According to his file, he may have been one of the greatest Breeds to have ever been created.

"Breeds the Leo worked to rescue over the years," Mercury pointed out coolly. "Rather than working to ensure we were all free."

She had known there was an edge of anger in the Breeds who had been at the hospital and sworn to silence concerning the first Leo, who had arrived to oversee his son's well-being.

Callan Lyons, pride leader and the bane of the first Leo's existence. Leo didn't share his son's belief that the Breeds should carve out their place in the world. The only protection they could be certain of, he believed, was in hiding among the non-Breeds until their numbers were greater. And Ria wasn't certain which side of the argument she felt was right. But for now, both sides still existed.

"I refuse to debate Leo's choices; they're his own," she pointed out, staring back at him.

"But you're part of his family," Mercury argued, calmly. He always argued calmly, she had read. "You've known what he was all along."

She smiled at that. "Surprisingly, Mr. Warrant, I'm not a Breed. I'm simply a lowly little clerk that does the Vanderale bidding. Nothing more. I'm very human and I'm a reasonably healthy twenty-eight years old, rather than however old Dane or Leo are. I try really hard not to do the math there."

They were older than they appeared. Far older. And the secrecy of their existence as Breeds was paramount. And it was at risk if the information Dane had received was right.

"A clerk?" Mercury's gaze raked over her, and she was glad she had donned her jacket before leaving the plane, because she swore her nipples were hardening beneath the thin blouse she wore. "Why do I have trouble believing that?"

He was suspicious. His gaze was direct, and she almost thought she detected the faintest hint of blue in his eyes.

She almost shook her head when she looked closer and saw only the dark amber shades of the pupil.

"My charming personality?" She arched her brow.

His lips twitched. "I've seen your communiqués with Jonas, Ms. Rodriquez. Trust me, charming isn't an adjective I would apply to them."

"Firmly enchanting then?" she suggested.

He cleared his throat. "I thought the reaction they produced from our director was interesting. And amusing."

Ria let her own amusement tug at her lips and wished he would release all that thick, multihued hair from the strip of leather confining it behind his neck.

She wanted to see it flowing around his shoulders, the dark russets, browns and blacks merging together to create a heavy, lionlike mane that made her fingers itch to touch.

Strange, Leo had similar hair and she had never wanted to touch his. Of course, his wife Elizabeth might have cut her hand off if she'd attempted it.

For the most part, Leo used a temporary color on his hair when he was required to be out in public. And like Mercury, he kept it tied back behind his neck.

Leo was considered a rogue, a mercenary and a bastard businessman. But no one had ever breathed the word *Breed* with his name.

The owner of the multinational Vanderale Industries that his father had left him, Leo Vanderale was a law unto himself. And unto the Breeds that knew him.

"I'll settle for amusing," she finally stated.

"You might have to."

He sat in the corner of the seat, one elbow propped on the padded armrest he had lowered, the other arm braced along the back of the seat.

She glanced to the driver's section and caught a glimpse of Lawe's lips twitching as his icy blue eyes flicked to the rearview mirror.

"So, Ms. Rodriquez, what put a burr in the Leo's tail that he sent you out here only weeks after rushing to his son's side at the hospital?"

Rather, two months, Ria thought. And unfortunately, if the Leo found out what she was doing and where she was doing it, he was liable to skin her and hang her up to dry. That wasn't a pleasant thought.

"The Leo is a businessman, Mr. Warrant," she informed him, following the line Dane had taken. "Sanctuary and its Breeds profit greatly by Vanderale's largesse. The recent attacks against Sanctuary and the weaknesses within it concern him. Both professionally as well as personally. He would enjoy visiting his son and grandson. He's spoken of attending when his daughter-in-law gives birth to her second child. He can't do this as long as there's a risk of the world discovering who and what he is."

His lips curled mockingly. The sight of it had her restraining the urge to lick her own lips. Damn him, he made her feel weak-kneed and too much like a woman. She realized that weakness could threaten her job. She was looking for another spy, and the consequences of information possibly leaking out of Sanctuary could destroy the Breed community as a whole. On a different note, allowing herself to get involved with Mercury also had the potential to hurt her personally.

She never got personally involved, she reminded herself. That path led to nothing but disaster, and she really didn't need more disaster in her life.

"Ms. Rodriquez—"

She invited him to use her name. "Ria please." *Ms. Rodriquez* just made her feel old.

"Ria." His brow arched. "Why do I have a feeling there's much more to you than meets the eye?"

Her eyes widened as though she couldn't imagine. Dowdy clothes, no makeup. She did a damned fine job of being the little nobody everyone expected.

"Trust me, Mr. Warrant, what you see is what you get." She smiled back softly. "Of course, I can be rather ill natured when the situation calls for it. I'm not always nice."

He stared back at her silently, and she had a feeling he was seeing more than she wanted him to. He was definitely seeing more than anyone else had bothered to look for.

For the first time in her life Ria wondered if she had run up against a man she couldn't continue hiding from. His eyes urged her to share her secrets; the swirl of ambers, the curiosity, the interest, invited her to reach for things she knew she should never reach for.

Play with fire and you'll get burned. She remembered, long ago, too long ago, how her mother had laughingly advised her to always watch out for people.

They'll deceive you, my little Ria, she had always said. *They'll lie and they'll smile, and when they've taken all you have to give, they'll find someone else to use up.*

She couldn't have been very old, but she remembered those words.

The memory of it had her turning her head from Mercury, shifting her gaze to the mountains they were winding their way through as she pushed back the loneliness that filled her whenever she allowed it.

Her mother had died before she was six. Ria had spent three days alone in their apartment, crying for her mother, and her mother had been lying in a cold morgue.

She might have stayed there forever if a neighbor hadn't realized that no one had mentioned the child of Leo Vanderale's secretary. Her child hadn't even been listed in her personnel files. The people she had worked with hadn't even known about the daughter Mary Rodriquez had borne. Until Mary's death.

Until Ria had been left alone.

She pushed back the memories. They had no place here. She hadn't even let herself think about it for years. She was who she was, and she owed the Vanderales for her life after her mother's death.

And here she was, still running errands for Dane, and still doing his bidding. Still joining in his little games because he flashed that devil's smile of his and dared her to be courageous when they both knew she really wasn't courageous at all.

✦　　✦　　✦

She was being courageous now all right, and this time, Leo just might hang them both out to dry for it. Sanctuary was Leo's baby, so to speak. Callan Lyons was the son he hadn't known of until the revelation of the Breeds broke across the world. He was the son Leo hadn't been able to reach out to.

Dane was his heir, and Leo had always doted on Dane, to a point. He respected Dane but knew his son well enough to know Dane lived a much wilder, much more reckless life than made Leo happy.

Leo was a family man. He was a prime pride leader and he had proven it with the Breeds he protected on his African estate. And he ached for the sons he knew the Council had created from the semen and eggs they had stolen from him and his mate. And he ached for his grandchildren. Grandchildren Dane seemed in no hurry to provide him with.

"I hope you've been honest with Jonas concerning your reasons to be here, Ria," Mercury drawled then. "He can be a bastard when you lie to him."

Yeah yeah, like father like son. Jonas Wyatt was Leo's son as well and was more like him than any other, Ria thought.

She turned back to him with a smile. "I know his father, Mr. Warrant, and the apple didn't fall far from the tree as you would say here. Don't worry, being honest and straightforward are but a few of my faults."

Dane would have laughed his rear off at that comment, and she knew it.

But Mercury nodded and said nothing more. But he still

watched her. His gaze stayed on her, and she swore the flush mounting beneath her clothing was sinking into her bones.

Damn, she was glad his sense of smell wasn't as good as most Breeds, but from the way his eyes were narrowing and his nostrils were flaring, she suspected he sensed the arousal she could feel building in her.

She was a woman. And damn if he wasn't a fine specimen of a man and a Breed. She wasn't mated, and she wasn't dead. She had all the instincts other women had, and all those instincts were rioting for a taste of tall, dangerous and delicious over there.

That didn't mean she had to act on them.

The window rose between the driver's section and the passenger's. Ria turned and gave Mercury a questioning look.

"Lawe likes to open his window. It might be too cold for you," he stated, but his eyes said something entirely different. Something that had her ducking her head and turning to stare out the window next to her.

Yes, she was aroused, and no doubt the Breed driving knew it.

She gave a mental shrug. Just as she didn't doubt in the least that they should be used to it. Women around the world, in blogs, Breed-sighting websites and a variety of other online communities, both reviled and lusted after the creations man had made and lost control of.

They were fascinated by the Breeds. They were frightened of them and aroused by them. In little more than a decade they had become the bogeyman in the night as well as the dark lovers that invaded women's dreams. Sometimes it was amusing. Most of the time it managed to remind her how fickle humans could be.

Because it would take very little to turn the tide against the Breeds, and if the rumors Dane had heard were correct, then that tide could be coming through much sooner than anyone expected. And it could be more cataclysmic than anyone guessed.

◆   ◆   ◆

The animal opened tired eyes, not certain what had drawn it awake. The man. The man's emotions were slipping. The animal could feel the break in the man's defenses, the chance to stretch, to reach out. To sense freedom. Sweet freedom.

It stretched with all its senses, slowly, cautiously; it reveled in the chance.

Then it paused. Blinked. It stared through the man's eyes. It inhaled through the man's nostrils. It tasted the air against the man's tongue and it had to restrain its roar.

It crouched, staring, scenting, tasting. It had waited. It had been weak. Worn. So close to death. But it had fought. And it had waited.

For this.

Dark eyes peeked up at the man from beneath lowered lashes. It wasn't a coy look, it was a cautious look. Dark lashes, shades lighter than her eyes. Dark hair was restrained when it should be free.

And her scent.

This was what had awakened it. Her scent.

The animal felt something akin to joy race through it. Her scent was like mercy. It was like warmth in the middle of the cold. Her scent was like a place to belong.

It was careful. The man was still diligent. The animal let the smell of that sweet scent linger in its head, for only a moment. Just a taste, a tease of what true pleasure was, before pulling back.

The animal crouched now, awake, unblinking. The presence of the woman filled it with hope, renewed that last ounce of strength it needed just to survive.

The man's emotions, the animal could feel them straining, the chains that bound it growing weaker, because the man was distracted. The man was dealing with his emotions; he didn't have to be on guard for the animal that had nearly died long ago.

He was just a man. The animal could feel the thought as the man let himself ease his guard. He was just a man, no need to worry. He could watch this woman. He could want this woman.

And the animal watched. And it wanted. It crouched, waiting, growing hungry now where before there was no strength to even hunger.

The animal watched. It waited. Knowing freedom would soon arrive.

CHAPTER 2

"Hello, Mr. Wyatt. What a pleasure to finally meet you." Ria accepted Jonas Wyatt's handshake as she stepped into his office at Sanctuary and looked around the well-appointed office.

It wasn't fancy by any means, but it was large, open and airy. The walnut desk he used had been used by the Council scientists who had inhabited the estate before the Breeds took possession of it.

Dark, heavy file cabinets had been placed along the walls. He kept his files close to him. Hard copy was a bit antiquated, but at least he kept them secured. She knew his office in D.C. was completely electronic and unattached to any lines outside his office other than the PDA and laptop that often traveled with him.

"I've had coffee brought up from the kitchens." Jonas extended his hand to the small sitting area off to the side of the room.

A couch, sofa and two chairs sat around a gleaming, heavy walnut coffee table. The coffee sat on a silver tray in the center of the table, tempting her senses with its smell.

"My weakness." She smiled in all-apparent appreciation as he led her to the couch. "I must admit, my body doesn't adjust as well to different time zones as it used to. I could use the caffeine."

Jonas made a noncommittal little sound in his throat, sort of a cross between an irritated grunt and a hum of suspicion.

He sat down across from her as Mercury silently took the chair to the side of the couch.

"Should I pour?" She indicated the coffee service sitting before them.

Jonas's brow arched. "If you like."

He sat back as she poured the coffee and handed him then Mercury a cup before she took her own, balanced it on the delicate china saucer and sat back.

Lifting the cup by its handle, she inhaled first, her brain sparking in anticipation before she sipped cautiously. It was really hard to find good coffee.

She was pleased to discover this brew was some of the best. Her lashes almost fluttered in ecstasy.

Jonas chuckled. "You like your coffee," he commented as he drank his own, staring back at her with those odd silver eyes of his.

"I adore my coffee." She took another sip, then relaxed further against the couch and glanced between him and Mercury.

She had arrived the day before and been taken to the cabin Dane had rented for her. It sat on the edge of Sanctuary, but not within the boundary of the compound itself.

Nearly a half mile from the cabin, a secured perimeter had been set up. She knew most of the equipment was designed to be fenceless. Both Vanderale Industries as well as Seth Lawrence's various companies had contributed to the security of Sanctuary.

Lions roamed the Sanctuary side of the border, and Breeds patrolled it tirelessly. She had heard the lions roar the night before, obviously patrolling the perimeter despite the cold temperatures that had descended over the mountain.

It was only the first of October and already temperatures were dipping into the freezing zone. She could feel that cold clear to her bones.

"I understand Vanderale's concerns, Miss Rodriquez . . ."

"Oh please, call me Ria." She smiled back at him blandly. "There's no need to stand on ceremony. After all, I do know your family quite well."

His expression went blank, but his silver eyes flared with sudden animosity.

"I very much doubt that," he growled.

She blinked back at him. "But I do. Your father and your brother looked after me after the death of my mother. They've been quite kind."

His eyes narrowed as she literally rubbed his nose in the fact that he couldn't exactly treat her like an employee. And he certainly didn't seem to accept the fact of his parentage very well.

Unlike Callan, Jonas's mother hadn't been Leo's mate. Only Leo's sperm and another scientist's egg were used in his creation.

Mercury shifted dangerously in the chair beside him, his gaze turning on Jonas, the amber darkening before he glanced back at Ria.

"Ria." Jonas smiled back at her with heavy mockery. "As I'm certain you know, I've investigated you just as well as Dane," he growled the name, "has investigated Sanctuary and all its inhabitants. The Vanderales didn't adopt you. And you aren't a treasured daughter."

Ria set the cup back on the table, folded her hands in her lap and stared back at him placidly. He wasn't telling her something she wasn't already aware of.

"Mr. Wyatt, I never hinted at any such thing. I said I know your family quite well. I've worked for Leo and Dane since I was eighteen years old, as you know. They paid for my education, and before that they paid for my upbringing." She leaned forward just enough to let him know she wasn't intimidated by his heavy stare. "Never doubt, I am a cherished *friend* of the Vanderale family, and as such, my loyalty to the family, the company and the job I'm sent to do is above reproach. I have been sent to catalog, categorize and, in essence, determine whether or not Sanctuary is secure enough to continue to receive all the handy little toys we make certain Sanctuary gets to play with first. Do not doubt that my opinion carries weight. And do not doubt that my job is secure, no matter the protests you make. Now," she sat back against the couch, "shall we do this in a civilized fashion or do I get to listen to you growl and snarl and flash those wickedly sharp canines in my direction, as your brother does, when he's unreasonably upset?"

Jonas growled.

"Jonas." Mercury leaned forward, almost protectively.

Ria kept her gaze on the dangerously shifting colors in Jonas's eyes as Mercury drew his attention.

"What?" Jonas asked carefully.

"If you break any more furniture in this office," Ria looked around the room, speaking before Mercury could, "then Callan may begin limiting you on your office account. I was going over the office supply records just last week. It appears that in six months this office was refurbished with two different walnut coffee tables, as well as a very sturdy metal one. You've lost three secretaries in one year, and the glass in your apartment has been replaced twice. You have quite a temper, don't you, sir?"

"Or something." His smile was tight.

Ria waited for the truth as he stared her down. She knew the truth. The windows in his apartment were due to several attempts on his life. The metal coffee table had taken an uncontained blast from an explosive that had slipped past their security, a highly advanced explosive. The two wooden tables had most likely been temper, though.

Finally, she allowed her gaze to flicker, as though she understood his alpha position. He hadn't researched her enough. She didn't even bow down to Dane.

"Very well." She breathed in deeply. "I truly don't wish to antagonize you. But it's best that we know up front why I'm here. It's my job to determine if the funds Sanctuary receives should continue, be raised, reduced or halted all together. It's your job to make certain I have complete access to all your files involving any purchases, payments, contracts or outside services provided by Sanctuary in both electronic and hard-copy form. I'd like to get to work tomorrow if you don't mind."

She bent, picked up her coffee and sipped at it as she crossed her knees and waited.

He was obviously restraining his snarl, while Mercury was watching her with a flash of amusement in his eyes.

Jonas, unfortunately, was too much like Dane. Unfortunately for him, because Ria had learned how to deal with Dane years before. She received bling in the form of jewels from around the world in payment for allowing him to manipulate her. And he did so manipulate her.

She smiled back at Jonas. "I'm really a very nice person. Plenty of coffee helps."

Mercury snorted. Jonas glared back at her.

"Dane Vanderale is behind this, isn't he?" He lifted his lip in a sneer. "That's why the Leo is suddenly so interested in how his money is being spent."

Ria frowned. "The Leo cannot be manipulated, Mr. Wyatt. Once you get to know him, you'll learn that." Perhaps the hard way, just as Dane often did.

Jonas was suspicious, though, and that did not bode well for

Dane. Or for her. Leo wouldn't fire her, but boy, would he make sure she'd wish he'd done something so humane as simply firing her.

Leo knew her. He knew how to guilt her. And he could use it with shocking strength.

"What exactly do you need?" Jonas asked her from between clenched teeth.

"As I stated, hard-copy and/or electronic-copy information regarding purchases, contracts, sales or negotiations concerning those. The only things I don't require on individual Breeds are lab files or sensitive mission reports. Anything concerning the business of Sanctuary should be made available to me."

"And this will take you how long?" he snapped out.

Regret shimmered inside her, because she knew she was close to antagonizing him, perhaps making an enemy of him. And he did remind her so much of Dane. She was very fond of Dane, even if he was a manipulating, calculating coldhearted male for convincing her to come here.

The Leo was going to kill them both, but the danger Sanctuary faced terrified her. She looked from Jonas to Mercury and let her demeanor soften marginally.

"Hopefully, not too long," she told him. "Truly, Mr. Wyatt, making an enemy of you isn't my wish, but neither is it something that will sway me in my job. Though, I promise you, the viability of Sanctuary does mean something to me, as well as to Leo and Dane. I'm not here to risk your safety, I'm here to gather the information. All I need is your cooperation. No matter my determination, I know Leo and Dane will be willing to work with Sanctuary to continue the relationship Sanctuary does enjoy with Vanderale."

Even if they were leaking money like a sieve, Leo would never contemplate cutting them off. Sanctuary could leak till hell froze over and he would still pour money into it. But that wasn't the case. It wasn't money that was leaking, it was something much more vital.

"You'll have what you need." Jonas stood to his feet. "In the morning."

She rose as well, aware of Mercury straightening also.

"I look forward to it." She set her coffee on the table and extended her hand once more. "It's been a pleasure meeting you."

He shook her hand firmly, but he didn't strengthen his grip;

he didn't attempt to show her his strength, and her estimation of him rose. Because she knew he was furious.

"Mercury, show her back to her cabin. You, Lawe and Rule will be her personal security. Make sure no one kills her. Because she doesn't seem to care much about her own welfare today. And she's to be in Ely's lab in the morning for testing."

Ria paused. "There will be no testing, Mr. Wyatt. I supplied the necessary samples before my arrival. There will be no more given."

He paused and stared back at her, a muscle ticking at his jaw before he smiled tightly. "You do like to play with fire, don't you, Ms. Rodriquez?"

She let a light laugh escape her throat as she looked up at him. "Mr. Wyatt, Dane often says that's exactly what I do best. I think my mother accused me of it several times as well. But you'll find I'm truly not the enemy."

"I don't consider women my enemies." He shrugged and in his quick smile she could see the charm he was capable of. "Combatants maybe."

That told her. She inclined her head in agreement before turning to her personal bodyguard. It was enough to make a woman wish the word had a whole other connotation. Like naked and in her bed.

Too bad relationships and her just didn't mix. Besides, she knew Breeds mated. They were playful, erotic and wicked, but loving a woman always came with a mating. And mating was almost instantaneous.

So far, she had no uncontrollable urges where his body was concerned. Irrational maybe, but that didn't count.

She fought to restore her equilibrium as Mercury once again escorted her from the estate house to the limo. Sliding into the back, she watched as he moved in opposite her before the car began moving from the driveway.

They were both silent as they rode through the gates and the crowd of protestors that chanted outside them.

The gossip rags fueled the protests. Rumors of forced sexual desires due to a virus the Breeds carried were in the rags again. There was also the story of the serial killer/cannibal who was linked to the Breeds. The rags kept protestors at the door, and suspicion swirling around the Breeds both here and at the Wolf Breed compound Haven.

"You pushed a line with Jonas. I'd suggest not pushing it again for a while," Mercury stated as they headed back to the cabin.

She glanced back at him silently before speaking. "Jonas, like Dane, requires a certain understanding to deal with. If he believed I was easy to run over, he would spend his time denying what I needed and blocking my attempts."

But that didn't change the fact that facing him hadn't been easy. Her heart had been in her throat more often than not, and controlling any hint of fear had been almost impossible.

"Dealing with Jonas is nothing like dealing with Dane Vanderale, Ria. Don't fool yourself. He can make a hard enemy."

"As can Dane." She shrugged.

She looked back at him, the sprawled position he preferred tempting her. She wanted to curl into his lap. She wanted to warm herself against him.

Illogical. Irrational. Insane.

The night before had been filled with dreams of him. He had been outside patrolling the area around her cabin, she knew that. It was too close. Too tempting.

At least he hadn't actually been in the cabin. She didn't share her space very well, no matter how much she was attracted to a man.

She was a die-hard loner. She had decided that a long time ago. People left too easily. They walked in, got you used to their presence, then left, leaving you alone. It was a hard lesson to learn, and one she reminded herself of whenever she happened to wonder what it would be like to actually share space with someone.

"Why don't you have a lover?"

Her head swung around at the question.

"Excuse me?" She blinked back at him in shock, and her body nearly sizzled at the look he was giving her.

His expression was decidedly sensual.

"Why don't you have a lover?" he asked again, spacing out the words as though she might have trouble understanding English. "You're pretty. Single. And you're alone."

"I don't see a woman hanging on your arm," she snapped out. "Perhaps I left him at home."

He shook his head. "There's no scent of a man on you. If you had a lover, the scent of his arousal would linger around you for weeks, even if you were separated from him. So you don't have a lover."

"And I don't consider it your business," she told him, striving for calm.

"I do."

Her heart slapped in her chest, blood rushed to her head, and she wondered if the reaction was a precursor to a stroke. Because it had never happened to her before.

"I don't." She watched him warily now.

"Dane shouldn't have sent you here alone," he told her, his voice quiet, too soft, dangerous. "You're tempting, Ms. Rodriquez. And you're a challenge. Two things a Breed has a hard time ignoring."

And she was going to melt into her seat. Tempting and a challenge? She was plain and she knew it. She tried to spice it up with sexy underclothes and the bling Dane brought her. Not always jewels. Sometimes a scarf, sometimes something as simple as an odd piece of art found in an unknown market.

She liked pretty things around her, because she knew she wasn't so pretty. She wasn't tempting. And despite his claim, she wouldn't be much of a challenge if he decided he wanted into her bed.

"You needn't play with me, Mercury," she told him, aware she couldn't cover that small hint of sadness that slipped free. "I do my job. No matter the temptation not to."

And he could tempt her. He could be her downfall.

· C H A P T E R   3 ·

He watched her. That ridiculous bun her hair had been twisted into at the nape of her neck was trying to unravel. When she glanced at him, her brown eyes, almost the color of dark chocolate, were irritated. Her softly rounded, creamy face and stubborn chin were intriguing. But there were other parts of her making him crazy.

If she kept twitching her ass like that, he was going to fuck it. So help him God, he was going to take her to her knees, hike that plain brown skirt to her hips, and show her the folly of teasing a fully grown, hungry male Lion Breed.

Mercury Warrant leaned against the wall of the small office Gloria "please call me Ria" Rodriquez was using, and fought to maintain the same cool facade he'd held over the past month.

It wasn't easy. Especially when she moved from the desk to the table set up across from it to go through the files stacked there. She would lean over, sometimes studying each file's contents before choosing one, and the ugly brown skirt would mold to her ass like a loving hand.

Like his hand wanted to mold to it, clench it, separate the full globes as he watched his erection slide into the moist, silky heat below.

He was a walking hard-on, and after four weeks of it, it was starting to piss him off. He jacked off to the thought of her, the image of her face and her naked body straddling him. The days he spent with her only fueled that desire until it was starting to pinch at his balls in hunger.

He wanted the little plain Jane. He wanted to throw her to the bed and rut in her until the need was obliterated and his mind was free of her.

"You were the mechanical specialist before you became part

of Mr. Wyatt's team?" She turned her head, gazing at him through sharp, brown eyes. "You were the one who set the specifications of the dirt bikes we shipped here?"

The "we" in question meaning Vanderale Industries, Sanctuary's more than generous benefactor.

He nodded shortly.

"Your lab files didn't hint at mechanical knowledge. Your specialty there was recon and weapons with a significant talent in assassination and torture."

He lifted a brow. "You make it sound like college."

She stared back at him silently, her expression unchanging.

"The ability wasn't listed because there was no chance to develop the talent." He finally shrugged. "When I came here, there were some old cycles in one of the sheds. I spent my time fixing them."

Jonas had said to cooperate with her. Fine, he'd cooperate. And he had to admit he liked that little flare of interest in her eyes whenever he gave her what she wanted. He'd like to give her a whole lot more than what she was asking for.

"So you found the talent while you were recuperating?" She straightened and turned toward him, her hands sliding into the pockets of her slim skirt as she leaned a hip against the table.

Recuperating. Now there was a word for it.

He nodded. It was hard to talk to her when all he wanted to do was growl with lust. He could feel the urge rising in his throat and fought it back. Damn, he must have been too long without a woman. Maybe he should find one. Fast. Or he was going to end up in bed with a potential disaster. Vanderale's emissary was no one to screw around with. Literally.

"You requested six more of the cycles, with advanced electronics, weapons and power. Did you come up with the specifications?" she asked.

He nodded again. Those cycles would be a terror in the mountains the government had ceded to the Breeds.

The cycles were stripped down to only necessary weight to allow for the small, mounted gun barrels and ammunition. GPS and advanced satellite links were contained in bulletproof shields on the bikes, and the engines themselves were modified for a vast increase in power.

"And what would be the consequences if the cycles weren't approved?"

That question threw him. They needed those cycles.

"More Breeds will die," he answered her. "Keeping up with the tricks the Supremacists use to get into the protected area is paramount. Those cycles will aid the teams that have to patrol the perimeters, which have grown in the past few years."

"The advancements you're asking for raise the price of the machines by several tens of thousands of dollars per cycle," she pointed out. "Not to mention ammunition and satellite time they'll be using. At this rate, Vanderale will need to place a satellite in orbit for Sanctuary alone. Do you know the cost of that?"

"Vanderale profits as well," he reminded her. "How many of our people do you already have working security for the new facilities you've placed in the Middle East?"

"People we pay an excellent wage," she argued. "There's no exchange of favors, Mercury."

Bullshit. He stared back at her mockingly. "Tell that to your executive we rescued from Iran last month, Ms. Rodriquez. The Breed community did for free what no other team could have done for any price. How much was his life worth to you?"

Her lips twitched at the point.

"You're right." She shrugged. "Mr. Vasquez is very important to Vanderale. He's doing fine, by the way. Considered it a hell of an adventure."

She shifted again, crossing one ankle over the other as she leaned against the desk, and he swore he heard the sound of silken flesh rubbing together. And that couldn't be happening, because unlike other Breeds', his hearing just wasn't that advanced.

God, he wanted to lift her to that damned table and bury his head between her thighs. He wondered if she would taste as sweet as he imagined she did. If she would be as wet and hot as he was hard.

Would she scream for him? He wanted her screaming, begging, her head tilted back and that bun at the nape of her neck released.

"Sanctuary needs those cycles," he said instead. "With one of those per team going out, we'll have an advantage over the Supremacists attempting to slip in and assassinate or kidnap the members of the Feline Ruling Cabinet and their families."

In the past months, two more attempts had been made upon the main house.

She turned back to the files spread over the table before choosing one and turning back to her desk.

Mercury watched as she took her seat and opened the file. Her head bent, displaying the soft skin of her neck, the pulse beating heavily just below the flesh. He ground the back of his teeth together at the need to scrape his teeth over it. To feel the delicate skin, to taste it, maybe bite it a little bit.

Fuck. At the thought, his cock jerked, his balls tightened with a shard of pleasure so sharp it was nearly painful. Mercury hastily ran his tongue over his teeth, checking for a swelling of the small glands beneath it, for any unusual taste in his mouth. Anything that would indicate mating heat. Not that he expected it, but he had to be sure.

There was no swelling, no spilling of the mating hormone that would signal she was his.

What would he have done, he wondered, if it had been there? If he had learned that he hadn't lost the one person in the world meant to be his after all? That the dreams that flitted through his mind as he slept could become reality?

He clenched his jaw at the overpowering thought of mating her. Of having the choice taken away from him, of marking her, this one woman, as his own. The sexuality the mating heat produced was intense, fiery. The sexual need overwhelming.

Unfortunately it was something Mercury knew he would never know. He had lost his mate, years ago, in a life he fought daily to forget.

He hadn't marked the small Lioness his heart and body had claimed. He had never taken her, never kissed her, but he remembered the overriding hunger to do just that. The sensitivity in his tongue, the primal awareness of her and her scent, her lust every chance he had to see her. His rage and grief when she had been killed on a mission had nearly resulted in his own death.

She had been his mate. And Lion Breeds only mate once, just like their cousin the lion. But he could still fuck. And he was damned determined to fuck his little plain Jane into screaming orgasm.

"Vanderale contributed more than twenty million dollars to Sanctuary last year alone," she murmured as she went over another file. "Mr. Wyatt has quite an impressive list of wants in the file he sent us for financial aid next year."

Mercury said nothing. He wasn't part of the Ruling Cabinet, and at the moment, Jonas's wants were the last thing on his mind. He was too busy staring at the rise and fall of her breasts beneath her bulky blouse, wondering at the color of her nipples, and if the soft curves beneath the blouse were as generous as he was guessing they were.

The sound of her throat clearing pulled his gaze up. Mercury stared back at her, maintaining an even expression despite the fact he had been caught leering at her breasts.

Besides, he liked that little hint of a blush on her cheeks, the way her eyes chastised him behind the small lenses of her glasses.

"I realize you're likely bored." She sighed, her expression resigned. "But that makes me uncomfortable."

"Why?"

Surprise glittered in her dark chocolate eyes. Mercury wasn't as fond of chocolate as some of the Breeds were, but he had to admit, this woman could make him like it.

"Why?" she asked with a slight, uncomfortable laugh. "Perhaps because you and I both know it's not out of interest but merely an attempt to amuse yourself. I know the past weeks haven't been easy for you, trailing me around. Besides, women don't like to have their breasts leered at. You should know that by now."

"Doesn't mean I understand it," he said and shrugged. "The fact that I find your breasts interesting shouldn't be such an issue. You appear to have nice breasts. You should wear blouses that emphasize that rather than attempting to hide it."

Women were strange creatures. And he wasn't bored at all. Being with her was anything but boring.

"How would you like it if all I did was ogle your crotch?" she snapped. "It's insulting."

"Ogle to your heart's content." The very thought of it had his cock twitching in pitiful hunger to be noticed.

When her gaze dropped, her eyes widened and jerked back to his.

"Normal reaction when a man finds a woman attractive." He frowned at her displeasure. "Would you rather I had no reaction at all?"

"Yes." She slapped the folder closed. "I don't have time for affairs here."

"Did I ask you for an affair?" He frowned; he knew he hadn't. "I said I find you attractive."

"And you get hard for every woman you find attractive?"

Now that question made him uncomfortable. There weren't a lot of women he found attractive in that sense.

"Do you get wet for every man who comes on to you?" he questioned her instead. Because she was wet. He could smell her arousal, her interest. He had been smelling it for days and it was driving him crazy. It was the first time he had smelled a woman's lust in such a way, from clear across the room. He might look like the lion his genes were taken from, but contrary to popular belief, his senses were nowhere near as strong as other Breeds'. Still, they were stronger than a human's, but . . . That scent tempted him again.

The sweet scent of dawn rising. That elusive, subtle scent of awakening, of moist warmth and adventure. That was what she smelled of, and Mercury loved the dawn.

Her skin was flushed a gentle pink now, and with the smell of her arousal, he could also sense her confusion.

"I'm not wet," she lied, shifting in her seat, most likely pressing her legs tight together.

Mercury let a smile tug at his lips. She knew the Breeds' sense of smell was stronger than that of a normal human, and she had no idea of his own weakness in it. She would also know that he would see the lie for what it was, an attempt to deny the attraction building between them.

He didn't call her on it. He kept his stance against the wall, his eyes on her, despite the fact that he wanted his hands on her.

She gave a little sniff of disapproval before turning back to the files and pointedly ignoring him. That was fine with him; growing accustomed to a hunger of this strength took time anyway. Time and patience. He had both.

✦   ✦   ✦

Ria was flustered. She never got flustered, or embarrassed, or as turned on by a man as she had been for the past month. But she was now. She stared down at the file that detailed the dirt bikes Vanderale had originally supplied Sanctuary with, as well as the notes and captions of the modifications Mercury Warrant had made on them.

Modifications he had built into the specs for the new bikes

they wanted. But her mind wasn't on motorcycles, attached
weapons and the cost thereof, which was astronomical. Her
mind was on the man.

Or the Breed. Mercury showed more of the physical charac-
teristics than all the Lion Breeds she had met thus far combined.

High cheekbones and exotic brown eyes, almost amber but
not quite. There was a faint darkness around the eye and lids, as
though someone had applied the smallest line of kohl. Thick,
sun-kissed lashes framed the eyes and gave him an erotic appearance. His lips were a bit thin, but well sculpted and sexier
than they should have been. His nose was long, with a flattened
bridge more prominent than most Breeds'.

Long, thick, brown-, black- and russet-streaked hair fell to
his shoulders. Unlike Callan Lyons, with his golden brown hair
and handsome features, Mercury seemed to epitomize the
Breeds. A lion walking within a man's body. She could clearly
see the primal, feral qualities that she knew he fought to keep
subverted. As though he could hide what he was, especially to
himself.

She let the file she was reading cover her hand as it lay over
the memory card slot into which she had inserted a "ghost"
chip, one of the new, specially enhanced memory chips that
would be undetectable to the Breed systems.

It slid free into her hand and tucked nicely into the sleeve of
her blouse. The electronic messages and orders she had been investigating were contained on the chip, with more on several
other chips she had slipped out of the office over the weeks.

It appeared that Sanctuary had more to worry about than
even Dane had imagined, if what she was learning were true.

"I'm ready to go home." She slapped the file closed and
stood from the chair.

She couldn't keep her mind on the file or the job she had
gone there to do. She was too aware of him, too aware of the
sensuality steadily rising between them.

"I'll let Jonas know we're leaving." He nodded as he flipped
the mic of the communications unit down from the side of his
face.

"We aren't leaving. I am." She walked back to the desk that
held the files she had pulled to go through. "I don't need an escort."

"That's not what I was told," he informed her before turning his conversation to the link. "Jonas, we're ready to head back to the house." He listened for a moment before replying. "My bag is in the Jeep. I'll keep in contact from there."

Ria propped her hands on her hips as she stared back at him. "Exactly what do you mean by that?"

His eyes narrowed on her. "There was another attempt to breach the perimeter of Sanctuary's boundaries on the east side of the mountain. Your cabin sits there. Since you're outside the boundaries of Sanctuary, you're at risk."

"So?"

He restrained his smile. "So, from now on you have a guard inside the house, namely me, as well as one outside whenever you aren't at Sanctuary. We can't risk your kidnapping or death, Ria."

"Namely you?" Oh no, that was not going to work. No way, no how. "You'll have to tell Mr. Wyatt I've refused your charming company. You can sit outside with your buddy."

"That scared you can't resist me?" His brow arched, and there was an arrogant confidence to the curl of his lips.

"Excuse me?" He couldn't mean what she thought he did.

"You heard me," he said. "Are you that afraid you can't handle your own response to me, that you'd put your life in danger?"

Now that was a dare. She hated dares. A dare had landed her there to begin with.

"I would have no problems resisting you, Mr. Warrant," she snapped, her voice cold despite the heat traveling through her body. "This has nothing to do with you, and everything to do with privacy. I like living alone."

He crossed his arms over his chest, his broad, powerful chest, and stared down at her with a frown.

"We aren't willing to risk your life for the sake of your privacy," he informed her. "You can accept the conditions or we'll be forced to call Vanderale Industries and inform them of the danger and your lack of cooperation. We were assured you would cooperate with the protective measures we set in place."

Dammit. She was going to kill her boss. If Sanctuary complained, it wouldn't just go through her own department, it would also hit the desk of the president and owner of Vanderale. And no one, but no one messed with him over his favorite charity. Except her boss. Dane Vanderale might be the son and potential heir, but he was still answerable to his father, just as she was. And *he* had no idea she was here. She was trapped and she knew it.

"Don't you have a female enforcer you can assign to the house?" She fought back her irritation. "Someone who at least has a sense of humor?"

"I have a sense of humor." He shrugged again. "For example, I find it very amusing that you're afraid to be alone with me."

"Afraid?" She smirked. "You have an overrated opinion of your appeal, Mr. Warrant. I just don't want the aggravation of your hard-on bouncing around my house and invading my privacy. If I wanted that, I would have brought a man with me."

Yeah, right. She hadn't had sex in years and wasn't likely to anytime soon. For some reason, she hadn't excelled in sexual relationships as easily as she excelled in her job.

She got along with her vibrator much easier than she got along with men.

"Regardless of my opinion or your wants, I've been assigned to the house. We don't have enough enforcers to go around as it is. You're stuck with me."

Oh great. She stared at him, pursing her lips in displeasure as she met his gaze. His hot gaze. He watched her like the four-legged lions that patrolled the estate watched dinner being led in. It was nerve-wracking.

"This is not going to work," she bit out. "This is Friday. I don't even come in for the next two days."

He stared back at her silently, as though she hadn't even spoken. God, she hated it when he did that.

"I need to talk to Jonas," she insisted. "Now."

"Not possible. He's preparing to head back to Washington tonight for meetings this weekend, and he's currently heading into conference with the Ruling Cabinet. You'll have to wait until Monday."

She snapped her teeth together. She wanted to stomp her foot and curse, but hated to give him a reason to be any more amused at her discomfort than he was now. He seemed to delight in throwing her off balance.

"This is not going to work." She jerked her purse from the corner of the desk. "Not in any way."

He straightened as she neared the door, all animal grace and sexual confidence. He was dressed in the black enforcer mission outfit, a mini-Uzi strapped to his side, a knife sheathed at one of his thighs and a holstered handgun at the other. He was too tall, too broad, much too sexy and way too dangerous.

"It's going to work fine. You'll be perfectly safe," he assured her as he opened the office door and allowed her to pass.

He made her brush against his body, her shoulder sliding along his chest, the heat of him surrounding her as she moved past him. God, she loved it when he did that. Loved the sense of strength and protective power she could feel surrounding her. That didn't mean she liked the thought of dealing with it all weekend. She used the time away from him for distance, to push back the attraction and the growing need. How the hell was she supposed to do that with him in her face twenty-four-seven?

"This is so not going to work," she muttered again as she made her way down the sterile hallways of the underground offices.

"You worry too much." He followed her too closely.

"You're not the one stuck with an overgrown male all weekend," she snorted. "I like my privacy, Mr. Warrant."

"You'll survive, Ms. Rodriquez."

Maybe.

God, she wanted him. Wanted what she knew she couldn't have, because Ria didn't do one-night stands. She had learned long ago that they weren't for her, and she was determined never to be tricked into it again. And Mercury Warrant would never be anything else. Hadn't his file already stated that he was considered a surviving mate? The woman his heart and soul had chosen for its own had died. Mercury Warrant couldn't give his heart to another woman, because it was already taken. And Ria knew she couldn't bear walking away if she gave him the rest of her heart.

· C H A P T E R   4 ·

"Here's your bedroom." Ria pushed the door open to the smaller bedroom the cabin contained. Still, it was large enough for the bed, dresser and small attached bath. Her room was the master suite, with a king-sized bed, full bath and walk-in closet. It wasn't nearly as large as her bedroom in Johannesburg, but it was adequate for her needs here.

Mercury moved into the room and tossed his duffel bag onto the thick comforter that covered the bed before moving to the large window.

He snapped the shades closed before pulling the heavy curtains over them and moving back into the living room. Ria pressed her lips together in irritation before following him.

He proceeded through the living room, then the kitchen, closing all the shades and pulling the curtains closed on the larger windows.

"Keep them closed," he told her before heading for her bedroom.

Ria followed silently, biting her tongue, holding back her temper as he did the same there. Fine, she understood the need; after all, if the Supremacists could get lucky enough to kill him, it would be a major feather in the murderer's cap. Mercury was considered one of the best trackers and enforcers the Breeds possessed. That didn't mean she had to like it.

Next he pulled a small electronic device from the utility belt at his side and began to go from room to room again. The receiver was one of Vanderale's and the finest that could be found. So far, there had been no listening device developed that could evade its sensitive electronics. But she didn't remember it being on the roster of equipment that had been sent to Sanctuary.

"How did you get the R72?" she asked, watching as he ran it along baseboards and around furniture.

"It arrived last month with half a dozen others by special courier from L. Vanderale." He growled the name. It seemed Mercury had had a run-in with the first Leo around the same time Jonas had. "Which is why Jonas finds it so hard to believe he would consider cutting funding a month later."

"I don't make the decisions, I just follow them." She shrugged.

"Hmm," he murmured as he moved through the rest of the house before apparently having assured himself that it wasn't bugged.

He tucked the small receiver back into the special pack attached to his belt before staring back at her, his gaze hooded, his appearance seeming more dangerous in the dim light of the house.

"I have work to do," she finally sighed. "There are a few groceries in the kitchen and drinks in the fridge. Make yourself at home."

She turned and headed toward her bedroom.

"You don't eat dinner?"

Ria halted in the middle of the living room. What was that thread of emotion she heard in his voice? Was it even truly there?

Loneliness?

She turned back to him, seeing more than the man standing so still and silent, his head raised high, his shoulders thrown back. His expression was cool, almost bland, but something in his eyes raged. They were predatory, yet filled with a sadness that pricked at her own heart.

There was something in his eyes that she had always recognized within herself. A need, hunger that no amount of food could ever fill.

For her, it was simply for a place to belong. What it was for Mercury, she had no idea. She knew, though, that the longer she stayed here, the more she felt as though she didn't want to leave as quickly as she'd thought she would.

Dammit. He was getting to her, and she did not like that.

"I usually shower first." Actually, she usually ate a sandwich as she hunched over her computer and fought with the files she had stolen through the day. Did she even have anything for dinner? She thought fast.

"Why don't you order something from the pizza place in town while I shower? I'll watch for the delivery guy while you shower."

Well, of course that couldn't work; she knew it the minute his brows lowered.

"I'll hurry and shower before he gets here," he said a second later. "Pizza sounds good. What do you want on yours?" He headed for the phone.

"Everything and the kitchen sink." She shrugged. "Just get what you like; I'll eat pizza just about any way it comes."

He nodded as he picked up the phone and punched in the numbers efficiently.

Damn, she was such a sucker. Turning on her heel, she stalked to the bedroom, wondering if she could have possibly made a bigger mistake. She had work to do; she didn't have time to entertain a Breed grieving for a mate he would never have.

Who cared how lonely he was—it wasn't as though she could do anything about it. The man was lonely for something that didn't exist, for a mate that had died long ago. That wasn't her problem and she couldn't fix it. She would have if she could, but she couldn't bring back the dead, as Dane often reminded her.

But she could wish . . .

❖   ❖   ❖

She was fucked.

Mercury made the vow the minute she stepped from her bedroom with all those nut brown waves of silky hair falling to the middle of her back. She was dressed in light gray cotton pants, pajama bottoms perhaps, or lounging pants, he thought he might have heard Merinus call them. Wide-legged and damned near shapeless. He hated them.

With it, she wore a thigh-long gray jersey, just as damned shapeless as the pants. God, he hoped she at least had sexy underwear. If she didn't, he was going to buy her some. Lots of it. Red and black, sinful silk and lace.

"Would you please stop looking at me like that." A flush covered her face again. It was almost innocent.

"Like what?" He actually hadn't been aware that he was staring at her in any way unusual.

"As though you're undressing me," she retorted, stalking to the kitchen and pulling two beers from the fridge. "A month in your company and it's a wonder I have any semblance of modesty at all."

He grinned at her. "What color is your underwear?"

She stared back at him, her eyes rounded in shock, her expression outraged. "That is none of your business. Do I ask you about your underwear?"

He glanced down at the jeans he had changed into.

"No underwear. Sorry. We didn't get into the habit of wearing those at the labs."

She paused in the process of setting the beers on the table, as he crossed his arms over his chest and waited.

"TMI," she finally muttered. "That's just TMI."

Too much information. He nodded. Okay, he understood that, Cassie Sinclair was always throwing that one out.

"Just in case you were wondering." He grinned.

"Well, I wasn't."

The soft scent of a lie was easy to detect. His grin widened. Sometimes, he just loved being a Breed.

"Drink your beer and leave me alone. You're really aggravating, do you know that? Didn't Jonas tell me you were the quiet Breed?"

He arched his brow as he took the beer and deftly twisted the cap off.

"Well, I don't exactly wonder about Jonas's underwear," he chuckled. "So there's not a lot to talk about there."

"Well, you can stop wondering about mine." If her face could have gotten pinker, it did.

He sat down at the table, leaned back in his chair and stared back at her thoughtfully.

"You want me. I can smell it. Why deny it?"

"And you think wanting is all that matters?" she asked as she turned and moved to the cabinets for plates. "There's more to life than just wanting, Mercury."

She sat the plates on the table before facing him again, her expression earnest.

"Is wanting you so bad?"

No, wanting *him* was so bad, Ria thought to herself as she

stared at him, amazed at the relaxed, sensual animal he had become, as though changing from the enforcer's uniform into
jeans and a T-shirt had somehow altered his entire personality.

"It depends on what the want is," she sighed, then stared
back at him intently. "Let's be honest here. There's not a chance
of anything between us besides a one-night stand or a fly-by-
night affair. I don't want either of those."

"You want love." He nodded slowly, as though he could possibly understand that. "A commitment."

"And what's wrong with that?" She opened her own beer
and took a quick drink. She needed something to settle her
nerves.

"There's nothing wrong with it, Ria," he answered softly.
"But what makes you automatically think I'm not capable of
caring for you? Not that I'm saying I do." He suddenly frowned.
"But I'm not incapable of it just because I'm a Breed."

"No, because you've already mated. I've read your file, Mercury. Any other woman will always be second best," Ria answered, keeping her voice soft, quiet. "I don't do second best
real well."

As she met his gaze, his eyes darkened and narrowed, chilling in their appraisal.

"Mating is a chemical reaction," he snapped. "It doesn't
mean I'm dead or that my emotions were lobotomized."

"No, it means sex will always be just that, sex."

"And there's something wrong with that?" he growled. He really growled. It wasn't just a deeper tone as it was with some
men, it was an actual rumble of sound, a rough, graveled scraping
of his voice.

"It's all according to your point of view." She sipped at the
beer again, using it to distract herself from the fierce frown on his
face. "For me, sex has to mean more. I have to feel more than just
arousal." And she had been feeling more than just that, for this
Breed, for far too many weeks now.

"You've never had a one-night stand?"

"Not by choice," she retorted. "Look, this isn't a debate. It's
my choice. I choose not to have sex with you. See why I didn't
want you here? Why I preferred a woman to stay with me rather
than you? I knew you would harass me over this."

"Harass you?" He came out of his seat, the relaxed facade

dropping in the blink of an eye. "I have yet to harass you. I simply want answers."

"Tell it to someone who will believe you." She rolled her eyes at the declaration. "Come on, Merc. You want sex. And you don't care what you have to do to get me in bed, you'll do it. Forget how it might hurt me, or how it will affect how I do my job." She stopped then, her eyes narrowing. "Or is that the point? Are you trying to influence my decision where the Breed funding is concerned?"

Anger snapped in his eyes and it wasn't a comfortable sight. But neither was the heartache awaiting her. She needed to belong. She could never belong to this man because he had already lost that part of himself that could belong to a woman.

"Do I look like Jonas's fucking gigolo?" he snarled.

Ria propped her hand on her hip as she set the beer down with a thump and faced him.

"Oh, just go ahead and pretend he's not above it," she charged. "It wouldn't be the first time one of his enforcers has seduced a mark to get what Jonas wanted. He's cold, calculating and manipulative. And he lets nothing and no one stand in the way of what he wants. Go ahead and deny it."

Jonas is his father's son, Dane liked to drawl in amusement. Jonas Wyatt was created from sperm collected from Leo before his escape from the labs a century before. From the reports she had read on the director of Breed affairs, he possibly had all of Leo's worst traits. He was damned scary.

"I am not a goddamned puppet for Jonas Wyatt," Mercury snarled. And damn if he didn't do a good snarl.

He was pissed.

"Then why the sudden pressure to sleep with you? I've been here a month and you're just now getting to the hot looks and the flirty little comments?"

"You wanted me to jump you the first day? Damn, wish I had known that, because all I could think about was bending you over that desk, shoving that damned shapeless skirt over your ass and watching my cock sink balls-deep into your hot little pussy." His lips lifted in a snarl as he flashed his incisors at her. "Sorry, baby, thought you might need a small amount of time there to get to know me."

The image was flashing through her head. Oh God, she would never be able to sit at that desk comfortably again.

"Pervert," she said accusingly, fighting for a defense against him. Against the fact that he had been, what was the antiquated term for it? Courting her?

"Pervert?" he growled. "That's not perverted, sweetheart, but I can work on it if that's what you want."

Her teeth snapped together, her lips pressing into a thin line as she restrained the angry, passionate words rising to her mouth. She wanted to berate him. Wanted to assure him she wanted nothing to do with his mangy Breed hide. Unfortunately, it wasn't the truth. And he could probably smell a lie anyway. God, she hated Breeds.

"Don't put yourself out," she finally forced out. "Better yet, try not to think about me at all. This is insane."

"Insane is being so damned hard I'm about to bust through my uniform." He swiped his hand through his hair before jerking his beer from the table and taking a healthy drink. "Insane is smelling that hot pussy wanting me and trying to ignore it. If you want me to back off, then maybe you better see what you can do about not getting aroused around me."

She was mortified.

"I hate Breeds," she muttered. "Do you know that? You and your sharp, damned noses. Just because I want to doesn't mean I should. Hell, I want cheesecake but I know better. It goes right to my hips. Does that mean I have to eat it anyway?"

He stared back at her in disbelief. "You're comparing me to cheesecake?" Offended male fury and outrage glittered in his eyes.

She huffed, "Well, the same principle applies."

It wasn't like it was offensive or anything. She loved cheesecake. Especially chocolate cheesecake.

"The hell it does."

There was no chance to avoid him. No way to evade the arms that jerked her into his embrace, or the lips that suddenly covered hers.

But, oh man, could he kiss.

His lips on hers were like rough velvet, his tongue rasping over lips, pushing against them, seeking entrance as she whimpered beneath the onslaught. His hands moved from her back to her rear, cupping the curves there and lifting her to him, pulling her to her tiptoes as her hands clenched his shoulders to steady herself.

She was overwhelmed. That was all there was to it. A hungry little whimper broke from her throat as her lips parted for him, then his tongue was twining with hers, licking at her, sending erratic, erotic pulses of sensation straight between her thighs.

Now, this was a kiss. Until this, she had never been kissed. He ate at her mouth, consumed her, nipped at her, growled when her lips closed around his tongue and she suckled at it, allowing him to mimick the controlled thrusts of his hips against hers.

His cock was thick and hard, pressing into the juncture of her thighs as he bent to her, rolling his hips to press the heated length against her swollen clit as she fought to rein in her sudden, uncontrolled need.

His kiss, his touch made her ache. From her breasts to her sex, she ached with a need so imperative it was all she could do to keep from tearing at his clothes, demanding that he throw her over the table and take her now. Hard. Fast.

"Hey guys, pizza's here. Are you going to share?"

Just as quickly as he had jerked her to him, Mercury was pushing her back, almost throwing her into the relative safety of the kitchen as he swung around, his gun clearing the holster at his powerful thigh.

"Whoa! Hold up there, big guy." Lawe raised his hands, pizza box included, his ice blue eyes filled with amusement as he stared back at Mercury. "You didn't answer the door for the pizza guy, so I did the honors and paid for it. I should at least get a taste, doncha think?"

Mercury cursed as Ria felt heat flame in her face. Great. Just great. Another Breed and another damned sensitive nose.

"Rule's hungry too," Lawe offered when no one spoke.

"Didn't you two bring food?" Mercury snapped.

"You'd make us eat cold sandwiches while you eat pizza?" Lawe's expression seemed to fall. "Man, that's just cruel. What happened to camaraderie? Friendship? To share and share alike?" He wagged his brows toward Ria as she glared at him in return. "Do you have beer? I swear I smell beer."

Mercury jammed the gun back into its holster as a growl vibrated from his chest and he turned back to Ria.

"This isn't over," he muttered. "Not by a long shot."

The hell it wasn't. As far as she was concerned, it was definitely over. It was over, or she was going to end up with more than a broken heart. And if she ended up with a broken heart, well, now that would just suck.

❖   ❖   ❖

The beast crouched, snarling in frustration, torn between its hunger and its certainty that patience was needed. It couldn't risk discovery yet. The man wasn't ready to accept that the beast still lurked, that it hungered and raged.

But the beast could wait. The chains of drugs no longer bound it. It no longer slept that nightmare sleep where there was no waking. Soon, the man would hunger, and he would need, and the beast knew that then it would be free.

❖   ❖   ❖

Mercury paced the living room after Ria had retired to her bedroom. He could see the light beneath the door and knew she was up working. Though what a glorified clerk could be doing that took so much damned computer time, he wasn't certain.

Clerk, his ass. She was nobody's clerk. Exactly what she was he wasn't certain, but she was more than a paper pusher.

She was too smart. Too quick. And too damned sexy.

He flexed his shoulders, fighting to relax the tension tearing through him. It was an uncomfortable sensation, prickles of awareness that tightened his muscles and left his flesh with an odd sensitivity.

He wanted her touch.

He could remember the feel of her hands in his hair as he kissed her, tugging at the strands as those hot little moans came from her throat. He wanted to feel her palms on his naked flesh, her lips at his throat, his neck. He wanted her with a hunger that was beginning to make him crazy.

He was pacing the damned living room like a caged animal, feeling the walls closing in on him, and freedom lurked just behind Ria's bedroom door. It wasn't outside where he could run, where he could be free in the darkness of the night. No, freedom beckoned in the other room, in a bed too big for

one small woman, his body taking hers until she was screaming for mercy.

It was those screams of pleasure he needed to hear. Ached to
hear.

He paused in the middle of the room, realizing with a sense
of shock that small growls were vibrating from his chest. Predatory, primal, guttural sounds. Sounds Mercury wasn't completely comfortable hearing. He growled when he chose, and he
had not chosen to let the sound free.

He shook his head, fighting back a sense of imbalance and a
nearly overwhelming urge to force that locked bedroom door
open and take her. To bend her over the bed, bare her pretty ass
and just take her.

He shook the image clear of his head as he found himself
taking a determined, forceful stride toward that door. He had
never, at any time, done anything so irrational. He wasn't going
to start now.

She was just a woman. There were dozens of women, Breed
and non-Breed, that he could have with no more than a snap of
his fingers. Women who would smile, who would gasp and cry
out for him as he moved into their luscious bodies. He didn't
need Ria. He just wanted her.

Wanting was not the same as needing.

Or so he tried to convince himself as he stalked to the front
door and flung it open before stepping into the shadowed recess
of the porch and the darkness of night.

He inhaled forcefully, pushing back whatever primal demand was making him so irrational. He checked his tongue
against his teeth again. Nope, no swollen glands. No hormonal
fluid tormenting his tongue and his lusts. Not that he had expected it.

He restrained his disappointment. With each passing year
more Breeds mated, and found a sense of peace and balance in
this freedom they had found. A balance Mercury knew wasn't
meant to be his.

His mate had died long ago. He was alone.

He leaned against a heavy post and stared into the black velvet night and the forest surrounding Ria's rented cabin and remembered the bleak years before the Breed rescues. Not that
his captivity had been as hard as some of the others'. The scientists at the South American labs he had been created within had

ruled with cooler heads. There were strict guidelines, but the Breeds weren't tortured just to see how much they could endure.

They had been trained from birth. They had been cuddled at odd times as babes by their caretakers, but each day of their lives, even as infants, contained lessons in being Breeds. For Mercury, it had been a life of almost complete isolation from other Breeds, though. His training had been more exacting, his body and his mind pushed harder. And he strove to succeed, because success meant time with the small pride he shared those labs with. It meant a chance to see one small Lioness who smiled back at him shyly and made his heart race.

As they grew older, they were trained harshly, but not horrifically. And yet Mercury couldn't remember a day of his life when he didn't dream of freedom. Of running with the wind, of testing himself against his own goals. Of a day when he wouldn't be required to kill on demand, but only in self-defense.

And he remembered Alaiya. Strong, confident, the young Lioness had been filled with life, and he had loved her. With all a young man's passion and a warrior's soul, he had loved her.

He had rarely spoken to her. Had never touched her. Yet he remembered the day the scientists had found the strange hormone in his semen and saliva, and the confusion it had garnered. From him as well as from the scientists. And he remembered when Alaiya had died.

The animalistic core of his psyche had never been far beneath the surface, but when he learned of her death, he lost what little control he had managed to learn. The drugs they kept in his system to try to restrain the feral rage of his beast were powerless against the flood of animalistic adrenaline that washed through him that day.

He hadn't even touched her. He hadn't kissed her. But the thought of her death nearly drove him mad.

Mercury shook his head at the thought. It seemed impossible that he was destined to live his life alone because a woman he had never touched, never held, had died.

In ways, though, perhaps he was better off. The worst thing a Breed could have was a weakness. A mate, a child, were the epitome of weakness. Their loss could destroy a man's soul, but it could rupture a Breed's sanity. And Mercury vowed long ago to always maintain his sanity.

He wanted Ria. Wanted her like he had never wanted another woman in his life, even Alaiya. But there was no chance of her getting close to his soul. Ever.

CHAPTER 5

Ria came to a bleary-eyed stop the next morning as she opened her bedroom door and met with a sight she couldn't have expected, no matter the circumstances. Rather than sleeping in the spare bedroom, Mercury was propped against the wall beside her bedroom door, his drowsy gaze holding hers as he came to his feet.

His chest was bare. Gloriously, incredibly, strong-and-hard bare. And he was seriously ripped. All that powerful muscle flexed and rippled beneath his skin as he rose and caused Ria to lose what little mental capacities she had left.

All he wore was a pair of thin, light cotton sweatpants, and the gun he had picked up from the floor beside him. Good Lord, she couldn't handle this. She could feel a flood of response surging through her body, sensitizing her nerve endings, forcing her to fight to control her breathing.

"Where did you sleep?" She winced at the rough sound of her voice.

Mercury stared at the floor for a long moment before lifting his eyes to her once again.

"Guess I slept in front of your door." It was said with weary acceptance, as though he didn't quite believe it himself.

Ria shook the thought away. God, it was just too early for this.

"The beds are comfortable," she muttered, stalking past him to the kitchen and the coffeepot she had prepared the night before.

"Yeah. They are." His voice was cool, yet she couldn't shake the feeling that the undercurrent she heard in it was more confusion than sleepiness.

She filled the coffeepot with water then turned back to him.

"Don't touch the pot. Do not get your own coffee first. First cup is mine. Understood?"

His eyes narrowed, his gaze flicking from the coffee to her before he nodded cautiously. "Fine."

"Good. I'm taking my shower. I need to go back to the office this morning." She turned and headed back to the bedroom.

"Why do you need to go back to the office? I thought you weren't working on the weekends." The suspicion in his voice— hell, his voice itself—seemed to grate across her nerves.

She paused at the door.

"Don't talk to me. Don't question me. No comments, no nothing until I drink my coffee." She shuddered at the effort it took to think. "Just . . . be invisible or something."

She moved into her room and slammed the bedroom door closed, ignoring the surprise on his face. She just couldn't handle thinking. If he spoke to her, if she was required to respond in any way, there was no way she could manage even a semblance of civility.

Waking up wasn't her favorite pastime. Especially in strange places, to the sight of a man she wanted to lick like candy.

She was an early riser, but a grouchy one. She could out-growl a Breed first thing in the morning any day of the week. And if anyone dared touch her coffee before she got that first fresh cup, then she could get rabid. It just tasted different after that, she swore it did. And it was her coffee, so she should know. That first cup was hers, or someone paid for it.

Okay, she was a bitch; she readily admitted to it. But hell, she went without sex for years, worked long hours and put up with no small amount of frustration in her job. She deserved to have a few quirks.

Half an hour later, dressed in a straight black skirt that fell below her knees and a white silk blouse, Ria wound her hair into its comfortable bun and pushed her feet into the leather shoes she wore in the office—whichever office she happened to be working in at the time—and headed back to the kitchen.

Her brain was in semi-working condition, and as long as Mercury hadn't messed with her coffee, then she could tolerate him. As long as he wasn't sleeping in front of her door again.

That was just odd. It wasn't as though she was actually in any danger, especially with two more Breeds parked outside her front door.

Mercury was standing in the kitchen reaching into the cabinet for a coffee cup as she entered the room. He was dressed in the black enforcers uniform that just looked way too good on him, his hair slightly damp from his own shower.

She snagged the cup as his hand came down and headed straight for the coffeepot. And if that was a chuckle she heard behind her, then she might end up kicking him.

Turning back with the steaming, full cup, she moved past him and headed to the dinette table that sat off the small kitchen.

As long as he didn't try to talk to her, she was fine.

The first sip of the dark, rich coffee was ambrosia that began firing her brain cells. The second and third had the heavy sluggishness in her mind beginning to ease. She was able to reach over and snag the remote then and flip on the wall-mounted television across from her for the morning news.

She was aware of Mercury carrying his own cup of coffee to the table and taking the seat to her left. He leaned back in his chair and watched her with silent amusement. She could handle silent amusement. As long as it stayed silent for just a little while longer.

Finally, the first infusion of caffeine was seeping into her bloodstream and making its way to her brain, when she turned to her silent companion.

"You forgot the pot," she informed him.

That golden brown brow lifted. "I was supposed to bring it with me?"

"Well, if you weren't here I would have just brought it with me." Didn't everyone? "So it's your job."

His lips twitched, but he didn't comment. Instead he rose, turned and moved to the kitchen. And Ria enjoyed the view. Those snug black mission pants did indeed mold over a very fine male Breed ass. The kind that just made your hands itch to cup and test the hard muscles beneath.

"You're a bitch in the morning, did you know that?" he asked as he returned with the coffeepot.

"Yeah well, get that first cup of coffee in me and you'll revise your opinion. I'm actually a demon from hell. You were just smart enough to stay out of my way."

He poured the coffee for her.

"No sugar or cream?" He seemed surprised as she shuddered.

"God no. What would be the point?"

He grunted as he took his seat and refilled his own cup.

"You're going to have to make another pot," she told him as she leaned forward, propping her arm on the table and paying attention to the early morning stock reports. She had missed them last night.

"Me?"

"Uh-huh." She turned up the sound to catch the Asian markets before reaching across the table for a leather legal pad folder and flipping it open to make notes. She might have to call her broker.

She heard him clear his throat and ignored it. He was helping her drink it. A pot was usually enough for her.

"Just a word of warning. You might not like my coffee," he said.

"Three level scoops of grounds from the canister into a clean filter and a pot of water. You can't screw it up." She waved him toward the kitchen. Surprised that he went, she was actually curious now exactly how far she could push him.

Yeah, she was a bitch. But she was resigned to her little faults and had learned to live with them.

As she watched the financial reports and then turned to world news, she was aware of Mercury bringing the refreshed coffee back to the table. Keeping her eyes on the newscast, she pushed her cup toward him then waited on him to pour.

The first sip was ghastly.

Her eyes opened as she stared down at the cup, then up at Mercury.

"You did that deliberately," she accused in amazement. "Why did you do that?"

A frown jerked between his brows as he clunked the pot to the table and glared back at her.

"Coffee takes a knack, dammit," he snarled back at her. "I don't have the knack. Now live with it."

Live with it? She opened her mouth to snap out a refusal. Before the words could leave her lips, he was in her face. Right in her face. Leaning down, arms braced on the table as his brown eyes seemed to glow with anger.

"Live with it." The rumbling growl of displeasure wasn't faked. Mercury, she had found, didn't play intimidation games.

Ria cleared her throat nervously. "You could have warned me."

He leaned back slowly. "I believe I did. But your 'Demon from Hell' attitude chose to ignore me. Now, if you want to go to Sanctuary, finish that damned coffee. We can get breakfast there."

Breakfast. She stared back at him wide-eyed. Okay, *that* was his problem. Men got cranky when they were hungry.

"There are Danishes in the cabinet."

The look he gave her wasn't polite. Okay. So maybe not Danishes. Of course, that didn't mean she was drinking the coffee. Some things she just wasn't about to be intimidated into.

◆   ◆   ◆

It could smell her. The scent of her arousal, the scent of her soul. It called to the animal, it made the animal ache, made it hurt. It wanted her. It wanted to hold her, to touch her, to mark her before she was jerked away from it, before anything or anyone could jerk her from its grip and take her from it forever.

But it waited. Waiting was killing it. It had waited so long, forced itself to patience for so many years. Just a little longer. It couldn't push the man much harder or awareness would cause the man to restrain it once again.

It would not be restrained. While the man slept, the animal awakened. It prowled through the man's mind then, laid to waste whatever remained of the rusted shackles that had once held it. And it protected the woman. Its woman.

Soon, the man would have no choice but to allow it freedom. Sweet, precious freedom.

◆   ◆   ◆

How the hell had he ended up sleeping beside Ria's bedroom door rather than the guest room where he had laid down? Mercury couldn't make sense of waking there, knowing he had gone to sleep elsewhere. Hell, he never walked in his sleep. Wasn't it impossible for a Breed to walk in his sleep? Some unwritten law or something? There had to be.

Yet, that was the only explanation. It didn't matter that the explanation sucked. The fact was, when he awoke, that was where he sat, beside her door. And he felt as though he hadn't slept a wink. Weariness tugged at him, leaving him frustrated and fraying the edges of his control. Mercury prided himself on his control at all times.

But as he stood in the office Ria insisted on returning to several hours later, he found himself frowning more often, and found the scent of her tempting him further.

He checked his tongue again. He couldn't stop doing that. There was no sensitivity, no swelling of the glands, none of the signs of mating heat except the inability to think of anything but fucking her.

"You don't have to stand in here glowering at me all morning," she informed him as she kept her gaze on the file she had opened before her. "I'm perfectly capable of working alone, you know."

"I assumed you were." He wasn't going anywhere without her.

She lifted her eyes, staring at him without raising her head, her expression less than friendly.

"If you don't stop glaring, Mercury, I'm going to kick you outside."

"You can try." He would actually have preferred it if she had. He was dying to find a reason to get his hands on her.

She blew out an exasperated breath before turning her attention back to the file she was going through. She was too intent on it. He could literally feel her mind working as she read, feel her searching for something.

A frown furrowed her brow and her fingers rubbed at the corner of a page. As though she were working through a puzzle, stroking the paper in an attempt to coax it into giving her the secrets she needed.

Mercury glanced down at the paper, seeing one of the new reports that had been faxed to the Bureau in Washington the week before concerning an attempt to hack into the communications equipment the previous month. It was pretty straightforward, if detailed.

The hacker had managed to infiltrate the government-backed satellite the Breeds used. Sanctuary's communications experts had traced the link as far as Germany before the hacker ended the connection and disappeared.

"This would have never happened with a Vanderale satellite," she sighed as she ran her fingers over the first lines of the report. "You would think your government would have a few protocols that actually work."

Her voice was disparaging.

"The satellite's an older one. We hadn't had problems until the hacker managed to get past the first defense by inputting the correct pass code on the first try."

She shook her head slowly. "That shouldn't have been possible unless someone gave them the code."

She continued to stare at the paper as she bit her lip thoughtfully.

"The pass code changes daily," she murmured.

Her finger ran over another line of printed words.

"Odd," she said before shaking her head and turning to the next page. "You need a more advanced program."

"We need funding to pay for it."

He met her gaze as her eyes lifted slowly, her expression pensive as she watched him.

"You need to update your systems," she pointed out. "You have millions of dollars' worth of Vanderale equipment that isn't even on the market yet. That makes you a security risk. Therefore, a financial risk to the company. Unless there's something in these files to convince me otherwise, then I can't in all good conscience suggest a reversal of the decision to halt funding, Mercury."

Jonas was going to love hearing that.

"Keep looking then," he grunted. "We've managed to counter every attempt at breaking into our files. We'll catch them soon."

"It's been a year since the attempted hacks began," she pointed out. "So far, you've lost several enforcers due to the leaks, and security is breached along the perimeters of Sanctuary at least monthly. Their rate of success in doing so is worrisome. I'm wondering if there's a chance you have another spy operating inside Sanctuary."

They had caught one only months before, a trusted, loved member of the pride who had been attempting to destroy them from the beginning.

"Not possible." Was it?

Hell, he had been investigating this himself for over six months. There was no way information was getting past the compound's perimeters, yet their enemies were finding a way in anyway. And information was getting out.

"Anything is possible," she murmured before turning her attention back to the file for long moments.

That studied concentration on her face pricked at him. He

could feel an awareness he didn't know how to describe moving inside him.

His flesh tingled at the sensation, muscles rippling as though they were being invaded. The hair along the back of his neck prickled, a feeling he was highly uncomfortable with.

Mercury wasn't accustomed to the signs of primal awareness that other Breeds took for granted. The drugs the scientists had given him to suppress his animal genetics years before his rescue had completely eradicated not just the instinctive responses of his animal genetics but also the feral, uncontrollable intensity he used to possess.

But now, as he watched Ria's studied concentration of the files, the hairs at his nape seemed to lift in warning.

"Do you think you can find a spy in those files?" Suspicion echoed heavily in his voice.

She lifted her eyes again, her expression disparaging.

"That's not my job," she drawled. "My job is to determine if you have enough control of the situation to allow you to possess the nifty little gadgets and toys that Vanderale sends you before they ever hit production. Don't fool yourself, Mercury. I'm not here to do your job for you."

She snapped the file closed, her eyes gleaming with an edge of anger as she rose from her chair and stalked back to the file table. The file was slapped back onto the pile before she bent over for another.

She bent over.

The skirt tightened over her shapely ass.

Full, beautiful globes filled his vision. His hand fisted, stretched, his fingers bending as though clawed, as a sudden, horrifying haze of hunger washed over him.

He had to have her.

◆　　◆　　◆

One minute she was searching for the file she remembered seeing the day before, the next minute there was an iron rod pressing against the seam of her ass through her skirt and Mercury's pants.

Eyes widening, her gaze flew to the arms trapping her at the sides, heavily muscled arms, with attached hands that were gripping the wooden table, nails biting into it as a low growl sounded at the back of her neck.

Oh hell. This was not good. She could feel the need to back into him, to roll her hips against his straining cock and feel the fierce throb of hunger in it.

"The cameras," she suddenly managed to gasp, remembering the small piece of electronics in the corner of the room behind them.

"They can't see shit," he snarled at her ear. "Pull your skirt up for me."

"I will not," she hissed, scandalized. "I'm not here to—"

"Do it or I will. And if I touch you, I may not let go until I'm coming inside that hot little pussy I smell. Now pull the fucking skirt up."

Ria shuddered. Bent over as she was, her elbows braced on the table, she was in one of the most vulnerable positions that a woman could know. And he wanted her to make it worse?

"Merc—"

"Now." His breathing was hard at her ear, lust echoing in the imperative need of the word he uttered.

Ria fought back the shiver building in her spine and the uncontrollable impulse to do as he commanded.

"Mercury . . ."

"Make me do it, and it's over with," he snarled, his teeth nipping at her ear. "I'll fuck you, Ria. Right here, right now. If I touch you with my hands, we're both screwed, and I don't care who's watching."

Oh God.

She lay against the table, feeling him shift as her hands moved to the sides of her skirt.

She was actually doing it? She was inching her skirt up her legs, baring her thighs and the naked curves of her ass. And they were naked. The thong she wore did very little to hide the rounded globes of her ass.

And as she did, Ria could feel her arousal growing, blooming. Her pussy was dampening, preparing for him, aching for him.

"Damn, you smell sweet." The rough whisper had her clenching as the skirt cleared her thighs. "Like dawn. I love the dawn, Ria."

Ria panted in response, eagerly pulling her skirt higher now. He was as hard and as hot as newly forged iron through the material of his uniform, and God, it was turning her on.

She was so wet she could feel it dampening her panties.

"Yeah," he whispered as his lips suddenly smoothed over her neck. "Yeah. Let me feel your ass, baby. I love your ass. So sweet. So nice."

The skirt cleared her rear, bunching above her hips when his hips slammed against hers as she braced her arms on the table. They undulated, and beneath his pants she felt his cock throb.

"I want to see you." His teeth grazed her neck. "I want to see your tits naked, your nipples hard for me. Release them, Ria. Let me see them."

"The camera," she gasped.

"No one can see you. Release your pretty tits for me. Do it."

The hard, primal growl in his voice made her shake with lust. She had never been so damned turned on in her life. It was depraved, with the threat of the camera watching them.

Yet her hand moved, her fingers fumbling with the buttons as a little moan left her lips.

"Yeah. That's it, baby," he groaned, his long hair falling over her shoulder as he watched her unbutton the blouse. "Bare those pretty tits for me. Are they swollen, Ria? Do they ache for my mouth?"

They ached they were so swollen, her nipples rasping against the lace of her bra as they hardened and became distended.

She fumbled with the buttons of her blouse but finally managed to release them.

"Pull the shirt from your skirt," he commanded, his voice harsh and rough and sending shudders of arousal tearing through her. "Do it. Fast."

She pulled the material free, biting her lip as the edges gaped open then.

"Release the bra." His breathing was hard, rough, small puffs of air striking her suddenly sweat-dampened neck. "Let me see your tits, baby. I want to look. Let me look and I'll wait to taste. I promise. Just give me this. Sweet God, just a little bit, Ria."

She couldn't believe this. It was so erotic she was melting. His voice at her ear, commanding her, and she was obeying. Her fingers moved to the front clasp, releasing it slowly as shards of sensation raced through her system.

When the material slackened, she drew the cups free of her

heavy breasts, feeling her hips twitch, press tighter against the cock grinding into her rear.

"How pretty," he breathed.

Ria stared down at the ripe curves. They were so swollen that her hard nipples poked out like little soldiers standing to attention. They were hot, desperate to be touched. To be taken.

"Touch them. Let me see you playing with your nipples."

"No." Shock pushed the word passed her lips.

A second later his teeth nipped her neck, sending curling pleasure/pain rushing straight to her tormented clit.

"Do it." His voice changed, becoming deeper, darker. "Do it or I will. I'll do it, and then there'll be no stopping. I won't stop before my cock is buried so deep inside you that you'll never be free of me."

The camera. Oh God, she had to remember the camera. She had to remember her vow not to let him take her, not to let herself love him. If he took her, he was right, she would never be free. There would be no way to hold her heart back from him.

"Mercury," she whispered miserably. "This is too dangerous."

"Now." The harsh rumble spurred her to action.

One hand moved, her thumb and forefinger gripping her nipple as sensuality overwhelmed her.

"God! Fuck! Yes. Show me what you like, Ria. Show me so that when I get my mouth there I'll know how to pleasure you."

Her fingers tightened as rational thought disappeared. She rolled the stiff flesh, moaning in rapture as his hips pressed hers into the table and ground her clit against the edge. She shook, shuddered and pressed closer to the sensation as her own fingers tormented her nipple.

"Your nipples are blushing," he whispered. "I can see that pretty pink reddening, baby. Just like they're going to redden for my mouth. My tongue. My teeth."

His teeth.

Ria jerked against him at the thought of his teeth rasping over the tender tips. Oh, she wanted that. She wanted it so desperately she was on fire for it now. Her hips bucked against the table, rubbing her clit harder against the friction as another moan broke free of her lips.

The camera. Remember the camera.

"I'm going to fuck you, Ria. I'm going to rip those panties off your body and push every fucking inch of my cock up your pussy at once. I want to hear you scream. I want the pleasure to be so hard and so fast you can't fight it. That all you can do is come for it."

The primal, feral growl sent erotic fear chasing through her. She could feel him beneath his pants, thick and long, and she knew she would scream when he took her. Scream and beg for more because she knew nothing had felt as good as his cock fucking into her would feel.

She tightened her grip on her nipple, feeling the building sensations in her clit, knowing that her orgasm was coming closer by the second. She ached for it. Hungered for it. If she didn't have it . . .

The thunder echoing in her ears made no sense at first. She felt Mercury jerk behind her, heard his feral, "Fuck no." Then realized exactly what it was.

Dr. Morrey's voice called from outside the door. "Mercury, I need you in my office when you have time, please. Lawe can watch Ms. Rodriquez. Are you in there?"

"Oh. My. God. Oh God. Let me go," she hissed as he jerked back.

Her fingers fumbled with her bra as she heard the low, growling curse behind her. Reclipping it had never been so hard. She could feel the frantic fear pounding as hard through her veins now as the lust had seconds before.

"Mercury, are you there?" The doorknob rattled. When the hell had he locked the door?

"Just a minute, Ely," he snarled.

Ria felt a heated flush suffuse her body at the sound of his voice. There was no way to mistake the lust, the hunger, in it. Hell, the good doctor had probably been watching every second of the heated foreplay on the cameras. Dammit. This wasn't good. This was mortifying.

She finally managed to straighten her clothes and retuck her shirt into her skirt, keeping her back to Mercury.

"Ria." She felt him approach.

Dammit, she *felt* him approach. The heat of his body wrapped around her, infusing her arousal, making her eyes dampen with emotion, with the need for his touch.

"Go." She held her hand up, praying it would forestall his advance. "See what she wants. Leave me the hell alone, Merc. Just fucking go."

Seconds later she heard the snick of the door closing as he did just that.

He left.

◆   ◆   ◆

Tests. Blood. Saliva. Semen.

The animal retreated carefully into its mental burrow, restraining the need to roar out its fury at being taken so abruptly from the pleasure consuming it.

So many years it had been alone, sleeping that pain-filled sleep and aching for warmth. Now the warmth was here, and pushing the man to revel in it rather than deny it took all the animal's concentration.

It had to move carefully, to open the layers of the man's hunger in only small degrees at a time to avoid suspicion. But it hadn't been careful enough. It should have known the situation was too dangerous, but the man had weakened with his lust. He ached and hungered for what was his alone, and the beast slipped free, thinking it could stay hidden within the shadows of the man's lust.

If it weren't careful, the animal knew it would be revealed. It couldn't risk exposure. They might put it to sleep again, and it wasn't strong enough yet to survive a second round of the horrific chains that bound it in a sleep that wracked it with agony.

It had to hide. Just a little while longer it had to hide. At least until no eyes watched, and no scientists took their hated samples to find it. Until it was alone with the sweet soft scent of its mate.

CHAPTER 6

"Everything okay, Doc?" Mercury pulled his black mission shirt back over his head and stared back at Elyiana Morrey as she stored another vial of his blood in her little carrier.

They called her the Vampire of Sanctuary. Every time a Breed turned around, she was standing there with her little blood-collecting necessities staring at them with those soft brown puppy-dog eyes. A Feline female shouldn't have puppy-dog eyes, but this one did.

Too much emotion, Mercury had always thought. She was driving herself crazy trying to find answers to all the anomalies showing up in the Breeds since freedom had been achieved.

She had once been the star pupil of the Council scientists, a genius on a level that had never been attained within their ranks before. With the rescues, she had become the Breeds' only hope of finding a way to learn the secrets of their own bodies.

"Hey, Doc, you're not answering me." He adjusted the shirt beneath the band of his uniform pants, watching her back carefully now.

"What did you say?" She turned back to him, her gaze slightly distant as she focused on him.

He restrained his smile. He liked Ely.

"I said, is everything okay?"

"Fine." She nodded, turning back to the vials as she stored them in one of her contraptions.

"So why more tests? You just did this whole thing last week." He stood to his feet, watching her carefully as he re-strapped the weapon holsters onto his body. They were a part of him now; he felt naked without them.

"You know how it goes." She shrugged. "You're in close-quarter contact with an unknown female. I like to keep an eye on your tests in that case. Just in case."

Just in case. He breathed out heavily, silently.

"She's not my mate." He growled the word because for the first time since he had learned of the mating heat he was pissed off that there wasn't a chance of it affecting him. He'd lost his mate before he'd ever had the chance to know what having one meant.

"I've never believed you truly mated, Merc," she reminded him. "My experience with this is that it takes more than wanting or caring deeply for anyone." She turned back to him, her gaze compassionate. "Have you been feeling any changes since Ms. Rodriquez showed up?"

She moved toward him, her bare hand, devoid of the gloves she normally wore, gripping his wrist to check his pulse. Then she rubbed his arm, almost like a comforting gesture, before patting it as she would a child's.

At this point, he was watching her suspiciously.

"Do I get a sucker too?" he asked warily.

"You didn't answer my question, Merc," she reminded him. "Feeling anything unusual?"

"Well, Doc, there's no enlarging of the glands under my tongue, but you checked those, so you know that. No funny taste in my mouth, and that little stroke and pat against my arm didn't have me cringing in pain," he reported with an edge of disgust. "Is there anything else I should be looking for?"

Her lips twitched. "You have the symptoms down, I see."

"Pretty hard not to with the damned epidemic that seems to be going on," he snorted. "Lawe and Rule are bitching constantly over it. I think they like their footloose and carefree ways."

"And you don't?" She leaned against the table, watching him carefully.

"You a psychiatrist now, Doc?" He grinned back at her. "Come on, put away the doctor stuff here. Tell me what you really want to know and we'll work from there."

She shook her head at that, a light laugh leaving her throat. "You caught me. Are you attracted to Ms. Rodriquez, Merc?"

"She's a woman." He arched his brows. "I'm a man, and I'm not mated. And Jonas has me on her butt twenty-four-seven. What do you think?"

She nodded at that, but something flickered in her eyes that had him frowning down at her. "Is something wrong here, Ely? Something I don't know anything about?"

"Trust me, Merc, if something was wrong, Jonas would be the first to know and you would be the second. Chain of command." She rolled her eyes. "If you want to be first in line, you'll have to take it up with him."

"Then let's put this another way," he growled, growing tired of the feeling that there was a very subtle game being played here. "What would make you suspect it is possible for me to mate Ms. Rodriquez when none of the symptoms are there?"

She sighed at that. "Honestly, there's no suspicion. As you said, with all the matings recently, and the fact that there were very few in the years after Kane and Sherra, I'm merely being diligent. And a word of warning—when the techs in the control room contact me that you're acting unusual in regards to the clerk in the file room, it's my job to check for the mating hormone."

Mercury stilled at that. "Unusual how?"

"I should inform you, just because they can't see exactly what you're doing doesn't mean they aren't speculating on it." She grimaced. "I received the call just before coming for you. They were afraid." She inhaled slowly. "They thought perhaps you were doing something Ms. Rodriquez may not have been agreeing with."

Mercury's nostrils flared as he fought back a rush of pure male fury. "They thought I was raping her?"

"There's a fine line, Merc," she said. "They merely thought there might be a problem. I checked it out and now I've taken the required blood, semen and hormonal samples. I'll let you know what I find once I find it."

"There is no fine line," he gritted out. "No means no. Dammit, Ely." He forcibly pulled back the anger eating inside him now. He could feel it building, welling in his head until a tide of red edged at the corner of his vision.

"As I said, it was merely a suggestion." His gaze flashed down as a needle punctured his vein again and blood washed into the attached vial.

Icy rage stole over him. His eyes lifted, and he was only barely aware of the growl that rumbled from his throat and had Ely pausing to stare up at him in surprise.

"I forgot the last tube I needed." She slid the needle from his arm and efficiently disconnected the sealed tube of blood from the needle.

He clenched his fists, the need to jerk it from her grip nearly overwhelming him. He needed that blood back. He couldn't risk it . . . He reached for it, his hand quickly covering her wrist as she stared back at him in shock.

"Mercury."

"You don't need that blood." He felt as though he were staring out at her from someone else's eyes, feeling someone else's rage. He couldn't allow her to keep that blood.

But he had no reason for it. No reason for the anger, no reason not to trust her, other than the fact that something warned him that he couldn't trust anyone. And why he felt that way was confusing as hell.

He released her hands slowly, staring at the vial of blood in her fist.

"You're lying to me, Ely," he stated, watching her closely, inhaling deeply. He swore—and he had never smelled emotions as other Breeds sometimes could—but he swore he could smell her deceit.

She swallowed tightly. "You're not acting yourself, Mercury," she whispered. "Are you certain there isn't anything wrong?"

"Are you?" He had to get away from her; every word that passed his lips was a growl. He held his hand out. "Give me the vial."

"I can't run the tests without it." Did she pale? Was that fear flickering in her eyes?

"You have enough. Make due."

As he spoke, the lab door opened and Kane, Sanctuary's head of security, and Callan Lyons stepped into the room.

Mercury looked up at the all-seeing eye of the camera. Like the labs. Always someone watching. How could he have forgotten that? Always the suspicion, always the eyes tracking and second-guessing.

He turned back to Ely. "I asked nicely," he reminded her.

"Merc, what's going on here?" Kane's voice was questioning, but Mercury could feel his pride leader watching, tracking, smelling the danger in the room.

"He doesn't like giving blood suddenly," Ely said nervously, moving to turn away.

Merc didn't touch her this time as he stepped in front of her. "Make sure you get everything you need from that vial of blood, Dr. Morrey," he said softly. "Because you'll get no more."

"You were ordered . . ."

His growl surprised him. It rumbled, fierce and threatening in his chest.

"I'm not Jonas's gigolo, or his puppet. Tell him to get screwed if that's what he thinks." He flicked a glance to the other two men.

Kane was watching him worriedly; Callan's expression was thoughtful. Mercury had had enough. He brushed past the other two and jerked the door open as he moved through the narrow corridors of what had once been a Council lab. The cameras followed him; he could feel them now, and he never had before. Like a brand against his back, they burned into his flesh and sent a surge of anger pulsing through him.

He moved to the first floor, turned down the hall and stepped back into Ria's office, where she lifted her head, surprise showing on her face.

"Merc?" she asked warily as he moved to the corner of the room, lifted his arm and jerked the camera from the wall, before turning to her.

Ria stared at him in shock. His eyes, once a perfect golden amber, were highlighted with tiny blue sparks. She swore they glittered like blue stars against a pure gold backdrop.

As large as he was, he suddenly appeared larger, his muscles harder, his shoulders broader. His fingers clenched around the camera in his hand.

"Was I raping you?" he snarled back at her, his canines flashing and something more than rage flickering in his eyes.

"Excuse me?" She stood from her desk slowly.

"Was I raping you?" The camera flew from his hand to strike the wall across from her, and then she heard it. It wasn't just anger, it was betrayal. Something in his voice, in his expression, echoed with it.

"You weren't raping me." She shook her head slowly.

He paced closer to the desk, staring at her, eating her with his eyes. She could feel his gaze almost as she would a caress stroking over her face.

"Are you scared of me?" he growled. "Is that why you're saying that? Do I frighten you, Ria?" He suddenly sneered. "Is that why you're reluctant to take my touch, to feel pleasure from me? Is it too much like fucking a goddamned animal?"

"Let me hear that word out of your lips again and I'll give you an animal," she retorted, her hands propping on her hips as she glared back at him. "You might be pissed, Mercury Warrant, but that's no reason to take His name in vain. Settle down or leave."

Ria moved to sit back down, though her stomach was jumping with nerves. He was nearly enraged, furious over something. That rage, that hard, lonely look in his eyes did something to her that it shouldn't. It made her ache, and the worst thing she could do was feel enough for this man to ache for him.

"Answer me." His hands flattened on the table in a short, sharp burst of flesh meeting wood. "Is that why you're reluctant to take me to your bed? Do you fear me?"

She lifted her eyes, let her gaze lock with his. "The only thing I'm scared of where you're concerned," she stated clearly, "is allowing you to ever make coffee again. Other than that, no, you don't scare me. But at the moment, you are making me angry."

And he made her want to touch him. She had to restrain herself to keep from lifting her hand, from touching his hard jaw. Who could have dared to suggest he could force her into anything?

He stayed in position, leaning over the desk, his long hair framing features so savage she should have been terrified. Not dying to reach out to him.

Then her office door was pushed open, banging against the wall as she watched Mercury's jaw clench, watched his eyes flare brighter. He stayed still, silent, staring back at her as she looked around him to see Callan Lyons and Kane Tyler at her doorway.

"Can I help you gentlemen with something?" she asked politely.

Callan's gaze went to the camera that had bounced to the floor across the room.

"What happened to the camera?" he asked. His expression was hard, his gaze flat and dangerous, and he looked entirely too powerful for a man who had nearly died two months before.

Ria stood to her feet. "I don't appreciate being tattled on," she stated as she gathered the files from her desk and moved around it, aware of Mercury shifting, sliding around her protectively, keeping himself between her and the other two men. "I'm aware what happened earlier may not have been particularly politically correct in such a setting, but I was assured Sanctuary was quite informal." She turned and leaned against the table set up for the files she was using at any given time. "I asked Mercury to turn it off." She looked at the camera and grinned. "I believe he may have taken me a little too literally."

"I jerked the son of a bitch out of the fucking wall before she could say a word," Mercury growled as she rolled her eyes at him. "I don't hide behind a woman's skirts."

Well, he was the first man in her life who had made that claim. Most of the men she knew, with the exception of Dane, begged to borrow her skirts if the Leo was anywhere near.

"Is he always so arrogant?" she asked Callan then.

Callan lifted his hand to his shoulder and the enforcers behind him moved back, the door closing behind them as they left, leaving the four of them alone.

"Mercury is usually fairly calm," Kane stated, his pale blue eyes watching the scene curiously now.

Mercury was silent, his gaze steady on her, those blue tints to his eyes almost mesmerizing her.

"I didn't say he wasn't calm, I said he was arrogant," she stated. "I apologize for our earlier actions . . ."

Mercury growled. This could get on her nerves fast. She sliced him a silencing look and continued to stare. He was obviously struggling to maintain some sort of control, to keep from doing something. He stood ramrod stiff between her and the other two men, his expression carved from granite and forbidding in its fierceness.

"Or perhaps I don't." She crossed her arms over her breasts and leaned against the desk. "Would someone like to explain to me what's going on?" she asked them then. "Ely drags off a perfectly reasonable man and he returns pissed off to the point that he rips the camera out of the wall and asks me if he was raping me? I'm a little confused here."

Kane cursed. Callan grimaced but no one spoke. And something wild and merciless flashed in Mercury's eyes. That look should have made her wary, it shouldn't have made her heart jump with excitement instead. And it shouldn't have made her remember what it felt like to have him covering her back, growling out his demand that she touch her own breasts.

But she could see where things were going here, and the why of it was beginning to piss her off. She had expected someone to attempt to distract her for weeks now. She hadn't expected this. But perhaps others had seen what she was only beginning to suspect herself. Mercury could be a very habit-forming weakness of hers.

"Kane?" Mercury's voice was tense, deep and so dark she almost shivered.

"Yeah, Merc?" Kane asked warily.

"Could you ensure that Ms. Rodriquez is adequately protected when she returns to her cabin please? Shiloh Gage would perhaps be best to place within the house with her tonight."

She stared at him in surprise.

"I'll take care of that, Mercury," Kane answered him. "Ely needs you back in the lab, though."

Mercury's lips pulled back from his teeth as he turned to look at the other man. Evidently, what Kane Tyler saw shocked him as much as it had shocked Ria moments before.

"Tell Ely she has all she's getting from me." With that, he stalked from the office, moving purposefully along the hall until, moments later, Ria heard a door slam, loudly.

"Ms. Rodriquez, I'm going to ask nicely," Callan said carefully. "Please submit yourself to the labs below so Ely can take a few blood and saliva samples. I promise, it should be relatively harmless."

"Like hell." She straightened, suddenly furious. "What the hell did you do to him? You accused him of trying to rape me?"

"He moved in on you while you weren't looking. Moments later, it appeared he was taking you without your consent," Kane informed her. "I had a brief moment to see the tapes before we had to go to the labs. I admit, Sanctuary is a bit informal, but if there was something going on here, something you were unwilling to participate in, now is the time to say it."

To Kane Tyler's credit, he didn't appear to believe any such thing, but that didn't keep it from pricking her anger. What the hell did they think was going on? And how did they have the temerity to even suggest anything so preposterous as Mercury Warrant attempting something so horrible?

"And perhaps I was willing." She was amazed at the anger that flooded her now. "That's what you get for being so damned nosy, Mr. Tyler. You've managed to humiliate me in the middle of what should have been a perfectly nice Saturday afternoon, and you've insulted and betrayed a friend." Contempt rose within her as she flicked them both a hard look. "Perhaps you should get me a ride back to my cabin. And don't bother with another babysitter. I've grown pretty comfortable with the one I had; I wouldn't handle another one well."

They might not understand loyalty, but she could assure them, she did. It was what had landed her in the middle of this mess to begin with.

"An enforcer will accompany you—"

"I'll call Dane Vanderale, my boss, and I'll have a Vanderale heli-jet parked on your landing pad in thirty minutes flat if my wishes are ignored in this case." She'd had enough. Even Dane couldn't sweet-talk his way out of this one. "It's no damned wonder you can't keep a handle on the spies in Sanctuary. You're too damned busy suspecting those loyal to you to look beyond them. Get a clue here. I'm not a Breed nor am I answerable to Sanctuary and as far as I'm concerned you can all go bugger yourselves."

Her accent slipped free. That never happened. She'd been born and raised in South Africa, and her job habitually required that she maintain the impression that she could be from any-where, everywhere except Vanderale's home offices.

It irritated her to no end that it had slipped free now.

"Are we clear, sirs?" Dammit, it was still there. "I require a vehicle of my own, immediately. Your enforcers can freeze to death outside for all I give a bloody damn. But if one attempts to step inside my cabin, then that call shall be made."

She jerked her bag from the floor, pulled it over her shoulder and glared back at them. "The vehicle. Now."

This time Callan cursed, jerked the door open and stomped out, leaving her alone with Kane Tyler, who stared back at her curiously. "I thought Mercury lost his mate," he mused.

Her jaw clenched and she had to hold back the trembling of her lips. "I'm quite certain he did. I was unaware it took mating to defend a man accused unfairly. You know, Tyler, I'm disappointed by the lot of you. To be honest, I had a better opinion of the inner strength of Sanctuary. Perhaps I was wrong about that."

Kane sighed. "Some things might seem that way," he sighed. "But trust me, it's not always that easy. Come on, I'll get your car and your escort."

Not that either helped her frame of mind. And it wasn't going to help Dane's once she got hold of him. He had sent her on this damned fool's errand. They both knew Sanctuary still had a very dangerous spy, but the first Leo wanted to visit. He wanted to spend time with his grandchild and the child Callan's mate was now expecting, and Ria had a feeling he wanted to put Jonas Wyatt in his place. The Leo was *the Leo*. Period. Arrogant. Hardheaded, and stubborn. He was frighteningly intelligent, in control, and certain of himself. All the qualities that Jonas used to piss off everyone he came in contact with.

✦   ✦   ✦

As Kane watched Ms. Rodriquez drive off, the enforcers trailing her, he bit off a curse.

"Ely thinks he's going feral again," Callan told him quietly from the doorway. "That was why he didn't want her to have that last vial of blood."

Feral displacement had once nearly driven Mercury insane. The death of the young Lioness he could have mated, likely cared for, had triggered a surge of such violent adrenaline in his body that he'd had to be confined in a special cell in the labs until a drug could be created to control him.

Kane shook his head. "I don't believe that. I saw those videos of Merc from years back the same as you did, Callan. What Mercury is going through now isn't some kind of bullshit feral fever."

"She's doing initial tests now on that last vial of blood. She thinks he's beginning to lose control."

Kane had seen the security videotape. What he saw concerned him, made him wonder what the hell was going on, but it hadn't made him worry about Merc's sanity. Evidently, Callan felt the same or they would be sending enforcers after Mercury now. But Ely didn't make determinations without evidence either.

"I didn't see anything to indicate force." He propped his hands on his hips and stared at the entrance to Sanctuary, grimacing at the chanting of voices from the other side of the iron gates.

Protestors, again. They'd been amassing over the past weeks, no doubt drawn by more horror stories in those rags about human sacrifices. Shaking his head, he turned back to the pride leader and watched Callan curiously.

"What proof do we have that he mated to that Breed girl that died?" He headed up the steps as he asked the question. "Could we be looking at another anomaly in mating heat?"

"Ely says no. The mating hormone was detected in him in those labs, just as the feral fever was detected," Callan told him. "The mating hormone was recorded in him from the tests for weeks before she was killed. Mixing with it was the unknown hormone they couldn't explain. It seemed to mix with his blood, like adrenaline, or perhaps with the adrenaline during moments of stress, anger or danger. It was present after several missions as well. The day he learned the girl had been killed, he went feral. Hell, Kane, he punched his hand through a Coyote's chest and tore out his heart. Even for a Breed, that's not normal."

Kane remembered those videos as well.

"They were smug about the death. The trainer was laughing and the scientist was less than sympathetic over the loss. Would either of us have done anything differently at the loss of someone we cared for?"

Callan glanced back at him as they moved through the mansion. "After restraining him, the scientist had the foresight to extract blood immediately. The adrenaline was so spiked with the unknown hormone that they decided it was some sort of fever. They used him to research it, then developed a drug therapy to control it."

"A super downer," Kane grunted.

"A drug perfected to control that particular hormone. They were still testing it when the rescues took place. He was slowly taken off the drug therapy after the rescues, but there was never a change in his control, until now," Callan sighed as they entered his office. "And I have to agree with Ely, he's not acting like himself. Mercury has never shown anger toward anyone in Sanctuary before."

"Until someone accused him of attempting to rape a woman? Perhaps his woman?"

Callan rubbed one hand over his face as he collapsed in his chair and breathed out roughly. "Until now. And Ely doesn't seem to know what the hell is going on."

That one Kane very much doubted, and as he stared back at Callan, he knew his brother-in-law felt the same.

They had fought this fight for eleven years now. The battle to preserve the Breeds' freedom and hold on to their secrets until they understood them themselves. The battle to protect their people, and their children.

Kane thought of his son, not much younger than Callan's, and felt the same concern he knew ran through the other man's mind. They couldn't afford Mercury's loss of control. He was the Breed that frightened little children on the street for God's sake. The savage features of the animal stamped on the face of the man.

"What now?" he breathed out heavily.

"Pull Lawe away from the cabin and find Mercury. I'll call Jonas back from D.C. Merc is one of his enforcers; maybe he can help us figure out what the hell is going on here. And how to control it."

"And the woman?" Kane asked. "Can we afford to piss her off any further than we have already?"

Callan's lips twisted thoughtfully at the question. "We need to convince her to let Ely take those samples, but after she stole that blood from Merc, Ms. Rodriquez isn't going to allow Ely within touching distance of her." He stroked the side of his jaw in contemplation. "And I swear, that video looked more like a Breed in mating heat than one experiencing feral displacement."

"He stood between her and us until he stomped out of the house," Kane pointed out. "He was protective and angry. And I can't blame him for the anger."

"He lost control after the episode in the lab." Callan's voice was tight now, hard. "And that isn't acceptable. He's a Breed. We were bred to have control over that part of ourselves and he's lost it. That I can't tolerate. Have Lawe find him and get him back to Sanctuary. Let's see if we can't talk to him and convince him to resume the tests."

"And if he doesn't?" Kane had a feeling he wouldn't.

Callan shook his head wearily. "Hell, I don't even want to consider that option, Kane, and neither do you."

CHAPTER 7

Ely handed the vials to Charles Fayden, her lab assistant, with a vague smile at his murmured offer to replace them for her. He was one of the few Breeds allowed to assist in the mating tests, and he was showing quite an aptitude for them.

She inserted a sample of the last vial of blood she had taken from Mercury into the test vial, sealed it and placed it into the machine Vanderale had helped her to acquire.

She waited impatiently while the individual hormones were separated, then extracted the sample and placed it in the computer analyzer. The answers that came up didn't bring her any comfort.

She covered her face with her hands for long moments before staring at the results once again. The feral hormone was definitely mixed into the strains of adrenaline now. It hadn't been in the first three vials, but that fourth one, taken as anger had surged in his eyes, showed it.

Those eyes had terrified her. The warm honey color had hardened to molten gold, and within the gold, the lightest flicker of blue pinpoints had fired within it. She had never seen anything so frightening in a Breed during all the years she had been testing them. Far longer than the years they had been free.

But it had done no more than confirm her suspicions that Mercury was once again going feral. The scientists at the lab he had been created in had recorded the same phenomenon.

She saved the results, attached them to the encryption program and sent them along to Jonas. She wasn't arguing with him further. If he didn't respond quickly, then she was going to Callan. Forget the chain of command he was always reminding her of, Callan was her pride leader, not Jonas. No matter how Jonas may or may not lust for the position.

She set her pass code on the computer, stored the samples and rubbed at the back of her neck wearily.

"Everything okay, Dr. Morrey?" Charles stepped up beside her, staring down at her from his soft hazel green eyes.

"Everything's fine, Charles." She smiled back at him rather distantly as she rose from her stool. "I'll be in my office if you need me."

"Yes, ma'am." He nodded before returning to the tests she had him working on. Matching for potential Breed mates was an exacting and time-consuming job. She was pleased to have found an assistant she trusted with it.

The tests on Mercury were another matter.

She sat down at her desk and carefully noted the information in her journal. She was going to have to find a way to convince Mercury to continue the tests. She needed this information, because there was always the chance it could happen again. No one knew the number of Breeds who had developed feral fever before the rescues. And she hoped no one ever found out.

✦   ✦   ✦

Jonas stared at the report, his eyes narrowing at the findings Ely had sent to him, before he pressed the intercom button into his secretary's office. Or rather his redheaded robot's office, he thought with a silent grunt. For a new mother, the woman was decidedly un-maternal at work.

"Rachel, I need the heli-jet prepped for a return to Sanctuary. Inform Jackal we'll be heading out again."

"Yes sir, Mr. Wyatt."

He grimaced at her cool, competent voice. He missed his last secretary, Kia, but she'd left in a storm of tears for some damned reason more than three months before. He still hadn't figured out why she was so upset with him. But at least she'd had a personality. The piece of cardboard manning the desk now was as dry as dust.

"Mr. Wyatt, you had a meeting with Ms. Warden in an hour. Should I reschedule that?"

"God yes," he muttered. The last meeting he had with Warden he'd sworn Breed genetics were rubbing off on her as she demanded answers for the disappearance of a Council scientist. Her eyes were shot with anger and her cute little face had tightened in almost dislike. For some reason, she didn't seem to believe that he had no idea where the former scientist, Jeffery Amburg, was located.

Not that he hadn't been lying; he knew very well where the scientist was currently being held. He just had no intention of telling her.

"Mr. Jackal is here now, sir," she told him. "The jet will be awaiting your arrival on the roof, destination Sanctuary. Do you require anything else?"

Yeah, a secretary with a sense of humor would be a nice start. Where the hell had Merinus Tyler found this droid?

But at the moment a cardboard secretary was the least of his concerns. He lifted his briefcase to his desk, loaded into it the files and reports he needed, then disconnected his PDA from the computer. He had everything now.

Shutting down his office took only minutes, and then he was striding to the door, opening it as Jackal came to his feet, his expression as stoic as always. But there was a hint of amusement in his gaze this time.

Jonas gave his secretary a hard look. She stared back at him, as placid as always. He was going to have to inform her how much he wouldn't appreciate it if she was entertaining his enforcers when she refused to entertain him.

The damned woman.

"Looks like we're heading home for the weekend, Jackal," he announced, putting his secretary's lack of loyalty out of his mind. He would deal with her later.

"Have a nice weekend, Mr. Wyatt," she called out as he left the office.

He didn't bother to return the farewell.

"Is there a problem?" Jackal asked as they moved through the empty hallways of the Justice building. Saturday evening wasn't exactly peak hours.

Jonas grimaced, the potential for disaster so far outweighed "a problem" that it was laughable.

"Mercury," he informed the other man, his voice quiet as they stepped into the elevator and Jonas hit the button for the roof.

Jackal snorted. "That little paper pusher of Vanderale's?"

Paper pusher, his ass. Ms. Rodriquez was looking for something; Jonas just hadn't figure out what yet.

"That's my suspicion." And Jonas hoped his suspicion was

right. His own investigation into Mercury's lab years had brought him to the conclusion that the feral fever had been nothing more than rage.

At one time, Mercury had been very close to the animal that his genetics had been altered with. His sense of smell had been off the charts, his ability to run long distances had broken records. Sight, hearing, night vision, scent and taste—he had been exceptional.

Until he'd begun showing shows of feral displacement. Pacing his cage. Growling in irritation, refusing to perform his missions within their proper parameters. And the unknown hormone attached to the adrenaline that flooded his body at those times. Feral fever or displacement the scientists had called it. Jonas preferred to think of it as the call of the wild. All the signs Mercury had exhibited in the labs had been those of an animal going insane in the search for freedom.

But that didn't explain what was going on now. Or why the hormone was showing itself once again. Unless, somehow Mercury was mating his little paper pusher as Jackal called her.

"Give Merc space, Jonas," Jackal advised him as they stepped into the heli-jet. "If he's acting weird, then he deserves it. That man is too damned calm the way it is."

And Jonas would have agreed with him, until Ely's report came through. Now he was starting to worry, and worry wasn't something he liked. He preferred action, decisive forward motion. And in this case, he had a feeling that wasn't going to help much.

❖ ❖ ❖

The cabin was too quiet, and she had grown too used to Mercury's presence. Even before he had been assigned to stay in the cabin with her, he had occasionally come in for a few moments. He had teased her just long enough to leave her wanting more before he left.

She had never been certain where he went, but he had always returned the next morning to escort her back to Sanctuary.

Now she felt a bit lost without him.

There was plenty of work to do. She still had the memory chips she had slipped out of Sanctuary this week, waiting on her to analyze them, to find the discrepancies she had been finding with alarming regularity.

Someone was slipping information from Sanctuary and selling it to a research lab determined to unlock the secret of the age depression that went along with mating heat. Forget figuring out why the mating heat occurred, or developing something to ease the symptoms of it. No, all these people cared about was reversing aging and creating fortunes off the desperation of millions.

It was a nightmare in the making.

And was she working on the chips that contained the information concerning who in Sanctuary could be selling those secrets. Of course she wasn't. She was pacing her bedroom floor, rubbing her arms against the chill that seemed to seep into the cabin and wondering where Mercury had gone.

As she turned and paced back toward the bed, a scraping at the window had her turning quickly, and staring in shock as the window eased open and Mercury, all six feet four inches of incredible muscle, eased through the opening until he was standing in her bedroom. He closed the window, locked it and reclosed the thick curtains before turning back to her.

"How did you slip past the Breeds patrolling outside?" she asked him in surprise.

He snorted. "You don't slip past Lawe and Rule. They know I'm here."

Suddenly, the long, violet gown and robe she wore seemed too heavy, too warm. Where she had been cold moments before, she could feel herself heating.

"What the hell do you think you're doing here?" she hissed as he stared across the room at her, his amber eyes darker, those little sparks of blue twinkling in them. His expression was somber, his gaze too quiet, and too filled with things she didn't want to see, because they too closely resembled things she didn't want to admit she felt herself.

"Never had a man slip into your room?" he asked her as he moved to the door, opened it and checked outside before turning back to her.

He turned the lock and kept his gaze locked on hers as he did so.

"Are you scared?" he asked curiously.

Ria rolled her eyes. "Not hardly. But my original question remains. Why the hell are you sneaking into my bedroom rather than using the door?"

"Maybe I'm trying to romance you?" He arched a brow, and it looked sexy as hell. Too bad she knew better than to believe him.

"Am I now harboring a runaway Breed?" She tilted her head and looked him up and down. "Dane buys me jewels for allowing myself to get involved with his little schemes. What do you have to offer, Mr. Warrant?"

Oh, that smile. Tinted just a bit with a shade of bitterness, but hungry, confident and very much in control.

"Jewels don't keep you warm at night," he told her quietly.

And that was only too true. They were hard and cold, and she found little solace in them other than the knowledge that they had the power to restrain Dane. Sometimes.

"And you can?" she asked him.

He moved forward. A step at a time, slow, a confident swagger that had her forcing herself to calm her breathing.

He would be able to keep her warm on the coldest winter night, she thought. He was large enough, tall enough to curl right around her and hold the cold at bay.

"You stomped out today and forgot your duties," she reminded him, hearing the nervousness in her voice. "Am I supposed to reward you now?"

His eyes gleamed. "I was never far from your side. You just didn't see me. You can reward me for that if you feel a need to."

He stopped in front of her, staring down at her with all those hungry shadows in his eyes. She could feel the need growing between them, building. Fighting it didn't seem to help much, because she wanted to give in so desperately.

"What are you doing here, Mercury?" she sighed, lifting her hands to place them against the black material of his mission shirt. The heavy, conforming fabric was warm from the heat of his body, and he really needed to take it off, she thought irrationally.

"You tried to protect me today," he said softly. "I don't think anyone has ever thought to try to lie for me."

His voice was musing, as though he were trying to figure out why she had done it.

"It wasn't as much a lie as it seemed," she said to excuse herself. "I was damned glad to see that camera go."

"I'm glad I could accommodate you then." His lips quirked, that hint of amusement clenching her thighs.

"Break security cameras often then?" Her voice had a tremor in it that wasn't hard to read.

His smile deepened; his exotically lined and tilted eyes took on a sensual, drowsy cast. "Not often," he admitted.

"Would a person have cause to lie for you often?" She lied for Dane all the time.

"I'm fairly honest." His voice lowered further. "And as much as those damned ugly skirts of yours turn me on, I don't need to hide behind them."

"My skirts aren't ugly." They were detestable.

"This is much better." He reached up and fingered the shoulder of her silky robe. "You look like a princess dressed in that. All that pretty hair flowing down your back. I should be shot for the things I think about doing to you."

She licked her lips and breathed in roughly.

"Like what?" She almost winced at the question.

It had been a hell of a day, she rationalized. The stress of stealing information from Sanctuary, the risk of knowing she might be caught at any time, and now this. The knowledge that she hadn't worked fast enough and she was getting entangled in her own emotions.

No. No emotions, she warned herself.

"Like taking the sadness out of your eyes, maybe?" He lowered his head, his lips pressing against her temple. "What goes through that pretty head when your eyes darken like that?"

No emotions. No entanglements.

She was fooling herself. He had charmed her from the first moment she met him, and look at her now. She was melting against him like butter.

"How foolish you were to sneak through the window when the doors work perfectly fine," she told him breathlessly. "Are all Breed males so complicated?"

"Hmm." His fingers threaded into the side of her hair, his hand cupping her head, holding her in place. "I just want a nice good-night kiss and then I'll leave."

"You don't have to leave."

He paused, his lips almost touching hers.

"The spare room," she rushed to say, feeling her heart racing against her chest, need clawing through her.

His lips quirked. "Just a nice good-night kiss," he repeated. "Very harmless. I promise."

Harmless? Like hell!

His lips covered hers with the same destructive results as they had before. She couldn't think, she didn't want to think. Her hands lifted, speared into the coarse length of his hair, and she moaned at the pleasure.

Had she ever known a kiss as good, as wicked as Mercury's? He didn't just move his lips against hers, he nibbled; he stroked and he licked, and when his tongue finally touched hers, she was so ready for it that she sucked it eagerly into her mouth.

As though she had tripped a hidden switch, both hands gripped her head, holding her still. His lips slanted over hers and skyrockets exploded in her head. She didn't want this kiss to end. She didn't want to ever lose this feeling, the taste of him, the feel of him, the certainty that there would never be another kiss to rock through her soul as this one did.

"God, you make a man forget what he came for." He tore his lips from hers, but he still held her. His large hands cupped her head, his fingers rubbing against her scalp.

"You came for something more than the kiss?" She stared up at him, dazed, needing.

"I need you to promise me something." He laid his forehead against hers. "Just one little thing."

"Okay." Her bling? It was his. Her body? All he had to do was take it.

"No tests," he said softly. "Promise me, Ria, you won't let anyone take those samples Ely's going to demand."

It took her a moment to process the request, to pull her mind from the visions of his lips devouring her body.

"I had no intention of it," she finally bit out. "But why ask me? What would it matter?"

"I don't know." He shook his head, his gaze turning hard. "I don't know what's going on with her, and I don't want you involved. Promise me. No tests."

"Fine. I promise." She pulled away from him before turning back and glaring at him. "Is that what the kiss was all about? To convince me?"

His gaze moved over her slowly, his expression shifting, his eyes darkening.

"No, Ria. That kiss was because I was dying for the taste of you. And if I don't get the hell out of here, I'm going to take far more than a taste."

But he wasn't moving as quickly as she was sure he meant to. His hand reach out again, his fingers tugging at the belt of her robe. The silken belt slithered free, the edge of her robe parting enough to reveal the snug bodice of the gown.

Ria watched, uncertain, breathing roughly, feeling her nipples peak hard and tight against the material covering them.

And he saw it. His eyes darkened to that unique color of hammered gold, and his fingers lifted, the backs of them brushing against the mounds that rose above the princess neckline of the deep purple gown.

"If I taste you here, I won't leave," he murmured, lifting his eyes to her. "I'll keep tasting. And I'll take you."

There was a problem with that?

She was trembling, each movement of her breasts pressing her flesh more firmly against his fingers.

"Good night, Ria." His hand fell away and he backed off from her.

She stood there, like a twit. Aching, her body burning furiously for more of his touch, and she just stood there as he left, terrified to reach out to him. Hurting as she watched him leave and cursing herself for it.

He could stay, but she knew that once she allowed him in her bed, she would be lost to him forever.

She watched as he left. She didn't protest; she couldn't. It would have been so easy to ask him to stay, and so hard to lose him when this job ended. Once again, she was playing with fire, but she feared that this time she was definitely going to get burned.

CHAPTER 8

Sunday was a waste of time. Dane couldn't be found through the normal channels they used when she needed to contact him, and Ria was so seriously close to calling the Leo and informing him of his son's mad plan that she had actually found herself dialing the number before she flipped her phone closed and glared at it.

She paced the cabin. She cursed men in general and Breeds in particular and spent a restless night tossing and turning in a bed that she knew was too big for her. Even as she watched that damned window.

She knew he was out there. She could feel him watching her, and the knowledge of it was tormenting. How easy would it be to invite him in to her? To let him take her? And once she did, how easy it would be to lose him once he learned the truth of how she had tricked him as well as everyone else at Sanctuary.

It was a double-edged sword, this job Dane had sent on her on. Secrecy was imperative, simply because of the nature of what she was finding in the electronic memos and orders that had been sent out.

The technology being used was so new and undetectable that only the most sophisticated programs could find it. Programs she possessed.

Monday morning, she was more out of sorts than normal and didn't even attempt to head to Sanctuary until the second pot of coffee had been consumed.

As she walked into the file room, she found that the camera had been replaced. Her lips thinned as she shrugged her sweater from her shoulders, moved a chair beneath it and climbed onto it.

"No peeking," she said clearly, certain the eyes that watched could read her lips before she draped the sweater over the camera's all-seeing eye and got to work.

She was finding the pattern she had been looking for in the multitude of files, memos and faxes that went through Sanctuary, the Bureau of Breed Affairs and to the various offices and businesses Sanctuary dealt with. The code was subtle, and she still wasn't 100 percent certain of what she was finding, but the knowledge was like an itch at the back of her neck. It was there. She just had to identify it. She'd begun picking up on it weeks before, but breaking that code wasn't going to be easy. It was an unknown system of numbers, letters and odd glyphs that made no sense, and finding the contact points for where the code had been laid in was difficult as well.

Shaking her head, she moved to the file table, picked up several files she had laid aside for further review and moved back to her desk.

She powered up the desk computer, grimacing at that thought that she couldn't use her own laptop here. And she couldn't install the program to detect the transmissions on this one.

An hour later she was still going through the first file—faxes and requisitions to several businesses in D.C. She was frowning over one particular memo when the door to the office opened.

She restrained the need to groan at the knowledge of who was walking through the door. But at least he set a cup of coffee beside her elbow for the aggravation she knew she was about to endure.

Her head lifted and she stared back at Jonas as he stared up at the sweater lying over the eye of the camera. His silver gray eyes moved back to her and his lips twitched.

"You are aware that camera is there for our safety as well as yours?" he asked her. "How are we supposed to know that you aren't stealing files?"

She lowered her head once again to the memo she was going over. He didn't want her to answer that question. She had already taken incredible advantage this morning and loaded the memory chips she had brought along with her for further study.

"If you treat Dane this way, then it's a wonder he hasn't fired you." He took the chair across from her desk and stared back at her.

"Dane knows better than to disturb me while I'm working on a job he assigned," she told him. "But then, he does pay me an exorbitant hourly wage, so it's usually in his best interest to keep me satisfied and undisturbed."

"And how much is he paying you for this job?" He leaned back in his chair, those silver eyes intent on her, his expression curious.

She almost snorted.

"Your brother Dane has the same annoying habit of couching nosy questions in a subtly curious voice. Go away, Mr. Wyatt, though I do thank you for the coffee."

She threw the knowledge of his relationship to Dane and the Leo in his face.

She lifted the mug and sipped the heavenly brew before turning her attention back to the memo. But she wasn't concentrating any better now than she had been the first few minutes after she opened the file.

She missed Mercury. It made her angry, it made her wonder where the hell her common sense had gone, but there it was, steeped in a feeling of loss and loneliness.

"Where is he?" she finally asked as Jonas continued to sit across from her and drink his coffee silently.

She didn't lift her head, but she no more saw the words on the memo than she knew what they said.

"He spent the night patrolling your cabin. He came in right behind you and went to the barracks to crash."

Her throat tightened as she swallowed and forced her gaze up to meet his.

"What's going on, Jonas?" Sanctuary itself seemed subdued today, the enforcers guarding her quieter than normal, less friendly.

He leaned forward and set his cup on the desk before relaxing back in the chair. The white silk dress shirt and slacks did nothing to hide the body of the powerful male animal beneath.

"Mercury is an anomaly within the Breed community," he told her. "Few of his kind were allowed to live."

"What do you mean, 'his kind'?" She already knew this information, but Jonas wasn't aware of that. And she wanted his stand on it. It was hard to fight a battle when you weren't certain the battle you were fighting.

His jaw bunched as he stared back at her. "Those whose features were so similar to the animal. The scientists in the lab he was created within kept him mostly isolated from the others, fearing his ability to escape or aid the others in escape if what they expected occurred."

She stared back at him, staying silent. His lips quirked as he nodded with a subtle gesture of approval.

"They were right. Mercury was more cunning, swifter, stronger, more dangerous than other Breeds within their lab. His training was highly advanced, but as he grew older, he began showing signs of a phenomenon they called feral fever; other scientists named it feral displacement. It was something that normally only infected the young, those at toddler stages. It only affected adult Breeds who were closer to the animal they were enhanced with."

"The call of the wild," she whispered. "That's what Leo calls it. He says all Breeds have it to a degree."

Jonas inclined his head slowly as he grimaced.

"He was barely twenty when he learned the young female of the pride, the one the scientists were watching closely when he came in contact with her, had been killed. She was only fifteen and sent on a mission she should have never been a part of. When he was told, the Coyotes, two of them, the scientists that worked with her, weren't exactly sympathetic. Mercury had just come in from a mission of his own; the feral displacement was already running high within him. He killed them all, with his bare hands, before he could be restrained by the other trainers and guards."

"Sweet heaven," she whispered. She hadn't known the details of that event. "With his bare hands?"

"We have the videos of the event. At one point, Mercury slammed his hand into one Coyote's chest and ripped his heart from his body. He took two bullets that should have been fatal wounds, but he kept going. He tore a scientist's head from his shoulders, the trainer . . ." He paused and shook his head. "Barehanded, Ria, he disemboweled a trainer. Once they managed to restrain him and begin running tests, they found a hormone that attached itself to the adrenaline pumping through his body. One they still have no name for, no idea from where it's produced. But they found a way to recess it. A drug therapy that kept him calm, kept him controllable."

Ria was horrified. She hadn't known this. She stared back at

Jonas, sick to her stomach, imagining the horror of being controlled.

"What did it do to him?"

Jonas steepled his fingers as he frowned thoughtfully. "I asked him that once. He said he felt as though he were walking in two worlds. An automaton. With it, he lost all the exceptional senses he had tested so highly in. But he was merciless when it came to killing. Cunning. He had no compassion and that was what they had wanted all along. When he was rescued, he was slowly taken off the drug therapy, and his adjustment was remarkable. I consider him one of my strongest enforcers. But still, his senses are barely better than a non-Breed's. Sense of smell, hearing, scent and taste barely register when he's tested."

Ria felt her chest tighten. "And now?"

Jonas shrugged. "He doesn't talk about it much. But the last tests Ely ran showed an advanced state of the feral displacement. She wants to restart the drug therapy."

She stared at him in shock. The doctor the entire Breed community held in such regard would suggest something so horrifying?

"Why?" she gasped in outrage. "Why would she want to do that if he can control it?"

"Because she believes, based on the video from that camera"—he nodded to the camera—"that Mercury was within minutes of sexually assaulting you. You didn't see his expression before he moved to you. His features seemed to shift, became more animalistic, and his eyes . . ." He frowned.

"Blue," she said softly. "Blue sparks."

He nodded. "The woman he was bred from was a blond-haired, blue-eyed Swede reputed to be from a family that once bred berserkers. Vikings."

Ria rose to her feet, rubbing her hand over the back of her neck as she closed the file she was working on and moved around Jonas to the file table.

"I have a favor to ask you, Ria," he said then, his voice quiet as she stopped at the table and stared down at the files. "I want you to come to the labs with me. I want you to have the blood, hormone and saliva samples taken."

She stared at the wall, remembering Callan's order to do just that, as well as the promise Mercury had extracted. He didn't trust the doctor now for some reason.

"Did Ely find the mating hormone in his tests?" she asked, though she knew the answer.

"No. She didn't."

It was no more than she had expected.

"Then there's no need for me to submit to a woman who would so unfairly accuse and betray someone who went willingly to have those tests done." She turned back to Jonas slowly. "She tricked him, didn't she, Jonas? She deliberately antagonized him to get what she wanted."

He stared back at her, his silver eyes solemn and, for the first time since she had met him, without the cynical mockery they usually contained.

"You're very perceptive," he acknowledged. "Yes, she deliberately antagonized him to prove what she suspected."

"Why?"

With that question, he shook his head. "I'm not certain why," he finally said. "There were traces of the displacement found when the tests were mixed with the results from the blood, saliva and hormone samples of yours that Vanderale sent us before your arrival. We knew you would be in close-quarter contact with Mercury, Lawe and Rule. We run the mating tests as a precaution. The hormone showed up in those tests where they didn't show up in the tests done on his samples alone or with other women."

"And you're telling me this why?" she asked him. "Is it somehow my fault?"

"It's not your fault, Ria, merely an anomaly." He shook his head. "One that concerns me."

"You're afraid he'll hurt me?" She couldn't imagine that, and didn't want to hear it.

"On the contrary." He looked at her as though surprised by the question. "I believe Mercury would destroy himself before he ever risked harming you. I believe it's merely coincidence that the hormone showed up in the mating tests. An error perhaps on Ely's part. The tests aren't infallible and aren't always right. But her opinion carries quite a bit of weight with the Ruling Cabinet. If she suggests Mercury be placed back on the drug therapy, then he'll have one of two choices. Submit to it, or leave Sanctuary."

"They wouldn't order him to do such a thing."

Jonas stood slowly to his feet. "Ely has begun the paperwork to have it presented before the Ruling Cabinet. How it's handled will depend a lot upon you."

"Me?" And now she watched him suspiciously.

"Get him back in that cabin, Ria. Get him back on your protective detail. Unless I can prove Mercury isn't going to start ripping hearts out and heads off at the spur of the moment, then we're all screwed. The Breed community is fighting to keep public opinion on its side. It would take very little to turn the tide of approval at present, and the Ruling Cabinet knows this. If I can't prove this is something he can control, then they could unintentionally destroy a damned good enforcer, and a hell of a Breed."

"You're manipulating me." She crossed her arms over her breasts and stared back at him in disgust. "I know you, Jonas. You and Dane are so similar it's terrifying."

He grimaced and shot her a look that would have withered a weaker personality.

"Insulting me will get you nowhere," he stated as he moved to his feet. "Do as you please. I've merely informed you of the situation, just as Mercury knows it stands."

He stood up then, surprising her as he moved to the other side of the door a second before it opened.

And there was Mercury. His gaze was flat, his face expressionless as he stepped into the room. He wasn't wearing his enforcer uniform; instead he wore jeans, a black T-shirt and boots. He looked dangerous, exotic and less than pleased to find Jonas there.

"Warning her?" Mercury questioned him with an edge of sarcasm as he stepped into the room.

"Merely apprising her of the reason why she'll be receiving orders from the Ruling Cabinet to submit to the lab for testing later." Jonas shrugged as though unconcerned.

"You're not serious." Her lips curled in disgust. "I do believe I made my opinion on that clear Saturday. There will be no testing done." There it was, that damned hint of an accent.

She was infuriated that they would even consider making it an order. And offended on Mercury's part that they would dare to make such a move.

"They can shove their orders," she informed him before turning to Mercury. "And you took your damned good time showing up, didn't you? Do you have any idea how chatty that insane Breed Shiloh is that they've assigned to me?"

She jerked several files from the pile and stomped back to her desk, casting both men an impatient glance.

"I believe that's my cue to leave." Jonas's lips twitched as he glanced at Mercury. "You're still on detail and your mission status hasn't changed." He nodded in her direction. "She's your primary concern unless you wish to be relieved."

Mercury's arms crossed over his chest. "I've been ordered back to the labs as well. I refused."

Evidently that meant something because Jonas grimaced at the knowledge. He finally nodded. "Continue refusing."

Mercury grunted. "I don't need your permission, Director."

Jonas let a smile tip his lips then, his gaze flicking back to Ria. "I'll leave you to your job then," he told them both. "I'll be here for a few more days yet. If there are any problems I expect to be informed."

"I'm sure you'll hear the bones breaking if it's needed." Mercury shrugged.

"And you're out of uniform," Jonas growled as though finally realizing that.

Mercury's expression hardened further, his jaw twitching as tension seemed to thicken and fill the room dangerously. "I don't need the uniform to do my job."

No, he didn't; he appeared more dangerous, more exciting, with all those weapons strapped over his body while denim hugged his legs.

But Jonas's eyes narrowed. "Where's the uniform, Merc?"

Mercury grinned. It wasn't a friendly smile. "I was informed my rank has been revoked until I submit to those tests. Don't worry, Jonas. I made my opinion of that clear."

"By doing what?" Jonas's voice was icy now.

"Ask Callan." He shrugged, moving into the room and glancing at the camera, still covered by Ria's sweater, before turning back to Jonas. "I'm sure he's waiting on you."

He took the easy chair in the corner, sat down and lifted one of the magazines lying on the table beside it. As though he wasn't raging inside, as though fury wasn't eating him alive.

Ria could see it, feel the danger in the air, and so could Jonas.

"Did you break any bones Mercury?" he finally sighed.

"Nope. All bones are intact and in working order," he retorted.

The muscle at Jonas's jaw flinched. "What about other enforcers' bones?"

"All intact and in working order." Mercury flipped open the magazine.

"Then what did you do?"

Mercury settled back in the chair comfortably, crossed one ankle over the opposite knee and focused his gaze on the magazine. "I think they're still trying to figure out exactly how to repair my shoulder weapon."

That was when Ria realized what was missing. The unique gun, rather like a mini-Uzi, that the Breed Enforcers carried. Vanderale had donated the weapons to the Breeds and limited the sale of them anywhere else. They were powerful, deadly, and Mercury wasn't wearing his.

Breeds, you had to love them, Ria thought as Jonas's expression turned as deadly as Mercury's. His silver eyes flashed, his entire body tensed. They could look more savage in their anger than the animals they were created from.

"I'll talk with you before you leave this evening," he stated, his voice cold. "Contact me before doing so."

"Sure." Mercury flipped the page of the magazine, his gaze still focused inside it. "I'll do that, Jonas."

Ria stayed silent. She was certain a snarl was pulling at Jonas's lips as he stalked from the room and slammed the door behind him.

Mercury moved then, reach over and flipped the lock on the door, before going back to the magazine, remaining silent, almost thoughtful, as he read.

Ria lowered her gaze to his well-worn reading material, an auto engineering magazine that was quite popular, even in Johannesburg, with some of the top designers who worked in the production departments at Vanderale.

Mercury might well have been reading it, but the tension rising in the room was so stifling that when the phone rang beside her, she jerked and barely held back a gasp before reaching for the receiver on the land-based line.

"Yes?"

"Ms. Rodriquez, this is Austin, from the Security Control Center. Could you please remove the covering from the camera?"

The arrogance in that nasal little voice antagonized her with the first words out of his mouth.

Her lips flattened as she glanced at Mercury. He was staring at her from beneath his lashes, the look from those exotically tilted eyes both wickedly sexual and dangerous.

"That might be a little difficult," she stated with a heavy emphasis on the false sweetness in her voice. "I'll tell you what, Austin, why don't you come down here and see if you can remove it yourself?"

She hung up the phone and glared at Mercury. "Stop the damned growling or you can sit outside. My day has been messed with enough." And she went back to work. Concentration shot, nerves raw, but she was determined to find what Dane needed so she could leave Sanctuary and the man she knew would break her heart if given the chance.

· C H A P T E R   9 ·

They took his uniform. Mercury sat silently, his gaze focused on the magazine, though he had no idea what it said.

He felt odd in the civilian clothes he rarely wore. They were comfortable enough, but they weren't the clothes specially designed to conform to his body.

And his weapon.

He almost growled again. They had confiscated his weapon. The enforcers sent after it had been polite enough, but the feral rage that had nearly consumed him had ensured that the weapon would never be used again. It lay in so many pieces in the barracks now that it was fit for nothing more than the garbage.

He should have left. Hell, he'd even considered it. Packing his stuff then and there, because he didn't have much, and just riding out. He'd had enough job offers over the years; supporting himself outside Sanctuary wouldn't be a problem. But Ria wasn't anywhere else in the world. She was here, and she was his responsibility.

His hunger.

He shifted in his chair, still not as used to the jeans as he was to the uniform, and restrained the anger still burning inside him.

Damn Ely. What the hell was she trying to do to him? The betrayal stuck in his throat until he couldn't figure out how to displace it. He had considered her a friend, and perhaps that had been his mistake. Making friends hadn't been easy, even here in Sanctuary. He reminded the other Breeds too much of where they came from, and most non-Breeds stared at him in fascinated fear, frightened to come too close.

Too often he had felt as though he were on the outside looking in, searching for a warmth that didn't exist and that he didn't know how to name. A place to exist perhaps.

He stared at his hands where he gripped the magazine. At the claws his nails invariably grew into. They were thicker than most, with the slightest curve. Keeping them trimmed and honed to a nonlethal appearance was an exacting job. If left alone, they could become claws in the truest sense.

He almost flexed them, almost remembered the feel of how easily those nails and the denser, harder strength of his bones had allowed his hand to punch into a Coyote Breed's chest and rip out his heart.

It hadn't been a job. It had been so easy. The rage that had spurred him sometimes caused him to cringe when he thought of it. And now, sitting across from Ria, feeling the wildness that had once been so much a part of him stretching inside him, he felt a moment's concern.

Once, too long ago, he had been a man comfortable with the creature he was. The animal and the human coexisted, if not in harmony, in a state of truce. Now the animal was gone, but the wildness was building. He could feel it building, stretching out, its attention focused on the woman sitting so silently across the room.

She wasn't concentrating on those files any more than he was concentrating on the magazine. The tension building between them was thick, heated.

"Are you frightened of me now?" He flipped the page of the magazine as he spoke, pretending to read. Knowing he wasn't and that he wouldn't be.

"Do I have a reason to be frightened of you now?" She turned one of the papers she was likely not reading before checking it against something she had pulled up on the computer.

He looked at his hands again, wondering if they could actually harm something so fragile, so sweet as the woman sitting across from him.

"And if I told you I didn't know?" He looked up from the magazine, meeting her gaze as her head lifted in surprise.

"Then I would say you're allowing your good doctor to mess with your head a bit much, wouldn't you?" That little hint of an accent intrigued him more than it should have and made him harder than he had ever been in his life.

Jeans confined his erection. The mission uniform had allowed it room for comfort, even if it didn't hide it. Of course,

he'd never had a problem controlling the surge of lust that engorged his cock and tightened his balls. Until Ria. From the
moment he had first drawn her scent into him, he had known
she would be a problem to his hard-won sense of control.

He shifted in his chair, hoping to relieve the pressure.

"Why did they take your uniform?" She lowered her head
once again, asking the question as though it wasn't a concern
between of the two of them.

"I'm a risk to the community now." He shrugged. "If I rip
someone's heart from their chest, then they don't want me doing it while wearing an insignia of the Breed community." His
lips twisted mockingly.

"And this is something you do on a daily basis? Rip out
hearts?" Her lips almost twitched, and he could have sworn he
sensed amusement in the movement.

"I usually wait for permission to do that," he told her laconi-
cally. "We were taught a few manners in those labs. My trainer
always felt it polite to make certain I was ripping out the right
heart."

"Very interesting." She nodded. "But you're speaking to me,
and distracting me."

He was going to distract her. He looked at the camera, wondering how long it was going to take the techs in the control
room to convince someone to remove that sweater.

He glanced at the watch on his wrist. He had a feeling it
wouldn't be much longer. There wasn't enough time to give in to
the arousal building inside him, and he didn't know how much
longer he could wait to taste her.

She was all buttoned up; the sleeveless top she wore wasn't
as bulky as the clothes she normally worked in, and the soft
creamy color was incredibly flattering to the breasts beneath it.

She was wearing another of those damned skirts too. Black
this time with a little flare at the knees. A tulip skirt Cassie had
once called it when she was trying to convince her mother to
buy one. Though that one had been much shorter. For some reason Cassie Sinclair thought Mercury made the perfect escort for
their shopping trips.

He had to admit, the longer length on Ria was sexy as hell.
The more skin she hid, the more he found himself wanting to
see.

The last thing he needed right now was to have an enforcer,

or Ely, come into the room while he had her bent over a table again.

He pulled at the shoulder of the T-shirt he wore. Damn, he missed his uniform. And maybe he even missed the sense of acceptance that uniform had given him. A place to belong, no matter how slight.

He didn't frown, he didn't allow his expression to shift, but the betrayal he could feel inside him fucking ached to the center of his bones. He'd never hurt anyone that didn't deserve it. He always controlled his strength, he always controlled his actions, because he knew his appearance was less than comfortable to everyone around him.

He frightened his fellow Breeds, with the exception of a very few. He frightened the humans that came in contact with him, and he was very much aware his missions were most always those that involved a limited presence among the non-Breeds.

As the tabloids reported each time their journalists caught sight of him, he was the vision that followed children and adults alike into their nightmares.

"The bogeyman" one newspaper had titled him.

He stared at the magazine and felt a somber realization fill him. He had told himself he fit in here, at Sanctuary, but he'd been wrong. He'd only fit in as long as he followed the silent parameters he'd sensed had been placed around him.

He was as trapped here as he had been in the labs, and he hadn't even realized it.

On the heels of that realization, the doorknob to the office clicked, and when the lock refused to allow entrance, a hard knock sounded on the panel.

Ria lifted her head and stared at him.

"I would be very disappointed were I to see blood," she informed him. "Even the slightest amount has the power to make me ill."

A grin tugged at his lips as he laid the magazine aside, stood to his feet and unlocked the door, before stepping back to cover Ria.

Everything inside him rose to full alert; nothing mattered but shielding her.

The door pushed open forcefully, bouncing against the wall to the side before settling in place, fully opened.

Mercury stared at the Breed who had his weapon lifted,

poised for battle, and felt that sense of anger fill him. He had fought alongside this Breed many times, and yet here he was, his weapon lifted as though to protect himself as the skinny, glaring Austin, head tech in Security Control, stalked into the room.

Mercury glared at the weapon the Breed held. Before Austin could take another step forward, Mercury blocked him, reached around and jerked the powerful, shortened automatic rifle from the guard's hands as he pushed him back and snarled a warning at him to stay put.

Blond hair spiked, his gray eyes a bit malicious, Austin sneered at Mercury as he moved forward. The scent of ego filled the room. He believed himself safe, able to order other Breeds around because of his position rather than his strength. For the most part, enforcers only barely tolerated him.

Glaring at him, Mercury watched as Austin crossed to the corner, jerked the sweater from the camera and tossed it to the floor.

Mercury growled furiously at the blatant disrespect of the action. His hand fell to the weapon strapped to his thigh as the Breed Enforcer backed up a step, swallowed tightly and glanced from the tech to Mercury.

"Pick the sweater up," Mercury ordered the geeky little bastard who had always set his hackles to rising.

Austin Crowl was a computer and expert security technician, trained by the Council, and his sense of power had grown over the years within Sanctuary, as he rose to rein over the control room.

The bastard sneered at him with his tiny little canines.

"She can pick it up herself." And he moved to stomp from the room, clearly ignorant of the Breed he was dealing with, and the fact that the normal rules that governed enforcers no longer applied to Mercury.

Before Mercury could stop himself, he had his hand around Austin's throat and was pinning the other man to the wall, aware of Ria coming to her feet quickly behind the desk.

"There's no blood, Ria," he informed her, staring into Austin's pale, despicable little face. "At least not yet."

"Merc, man, let him go." The young Breed Enforcer had a nervous quiver to his voice as Mercury kept his hand around the tech's throat.

Fear. The scent of it slammed into Mercury's senses, caus- ing his lips to curl back, a vicious rumble brewing in his chest.

"Pick up the sweater," Mercury growled into Austin's face as he released him just enough to shift his grip to the back of his neck and force him down. To his knees, watching as the other man picked up the sweater, gasping for air and in pain at the grip Mercury had on him.

It would be so easy to snap his little head right off his shoul- ders and watch him bleed. The slight he had delivered to Ria was intolerable. It wouldn't be allowed.

Pulling him back to his feet, Mercury stared into his eyes, watching fear sink into Austin's bones as he trembled like a weak-kneed coward.

"Respect." He let the word rumble from his throat. "In her presence. Or you die, little girl." He used the worst insult he could have used to the egomaniacal little Breed.

His gaze flickered over the pristine, perfectly pressed, per- fectly starched yellow shirt, buttoned to the throat and glaring against the Breed's dark skin and white-tipped, spiked brown hair.

"Before you challenge me, girl, grow some balls," he snarled, pushing him out the door, as once again, Kane, Callan, and Jonas rushed into the hallway.

"He's crazy," Austin gasped, his high-pitched voice causing them all to wince as he pointed to Mercury. "He tried to kill me. I was ordered to watch the room and he tried to kill me for re- moving that damned sweater."

Callan turned to him, Jonas leaned against the opposite wall, and Mercury felt Ria move to his side as she watched, the scent of her anger drifting around him now. It was so volatile that even he could smell it.

"Mercury, leave the cameras uncovered, for God's sake," Callan bit out, staring back at him in anger.

"Why? I'm with her. It's not like she can steal the files while I'm watching her."

"Perhaps it's not the files but her we're worried about." Ely stepped into the fray, maintaining a careful distance as she stared back at him worriedly.

"Dammit, Ely, since when the hell aren't we worried about Ms. Rodriquez?" Callan snapped. "Security is my concern here."

Mercury stared back at her, aching. His chest actually ached from the eyes trained on him, suspicious, cautious.

"Mr. Lyons, was the order to uncover the camera given by you?" Ria asked, her voice bland, carefully neutral.

"Ms. Rodriquez, those files are the heart and soul of Sanctuary," he snapped back at her, his eyes blazing now. "I wouldn't allow anyone alone in this room with them."

"I wasn't alone," she pointed out.

And Callan shook his head. "Until we know what the hell is going on here, then it's my job to protect everyone here. Even you," he snapped, glowering at Mercury.

"I'll be returning to my cabin now." Ria turned, collecting her purse and the large thermal cup she used to bring coffee in with her. "You'll be hearing from my boss by morning I assume."

She left the room, hips swaying, all delicate strength and confidence, and Mercury didn't hesitate to follow her. Fuck it. He'd put his life on the line for Sanctuary for a decade or longer. He'd followed orders, he'd played the good little Feline, and even his pride leader found no trust in him.

"Mercury."

He paused as Callan growled his name.

Turning slowly, he stared back at the other man, years of what he had believed were trust and friendship hanging between them, pulling at him.

"Your safety is no less important than Sanctuary's."

Mercury shook his head, his lips twisting mockingly. He countered his pride leader. "Yeah, can't have the bogeyman ripping hearts out in full view, can we? Only when ordered."

Just as it had been in the labs. *Only when ordered.* He shrugged. "My mission is protecting the woman. As far as I know, I'm still operational." He looked to Jonas. They all looked to Jonas.

And Jonas grinned. "As far as I'm concerned, you are. And the woman's getting ahead of you, Enforcer." He nodded to the door she was disappearing through.

"Good day, Pride Leader Lyons." Mercury nodded back to him respectfully. Callan was a man he did respect, even if Callan didn't trust him. "If you need me, I'm sure Director Wyatt will let me know."

With that, Mercury turned and followed the path Ria had

taken. She hadn't left. She was waiting by the passenger side of the SUV, door open, watching the house expectantly. When he followed her out, she got inside the car and was waiting when he slid into the driver's seat.

Ahead, Lawe's four-by-four pickup led the way.

"There's a power play in Sanctuary," she stated as he put the vehicle in gear and drove toward the gates.

He glanced at her in surprise. "Callan doesn't allow those."

The gates swung open, protestors pouring around the truck ahead of them, then around theirs. Signs proclaiming "Breeds Are Atrocities in God's Eyes" and "Breeds Die" were waved frantically as enraged faces filled the windows.

"Animal," one woman screamed as she pounded at the driver's window. "Bastard Breeds."

Mercury drove steadily through the crowd until it disappeared behind them, the chanting ringing in his head long after the sound died down.

And with the chanting was Ria's statement. *A power play.* Callan didn't allow power plays, but he wasn't at peak strength either. The gunshot wound that had nearly killed him two months before had weakened him and he was still recovering. Was someone moving to threaten Sanctuary while the pride leader was down?

Mercury shook his head. He couldn't imagine it. Kane and Jonas watched Callan's back, as did Callan's brothers, Taber and Tanner. He had a capable, able force around him. A power play wasn't possible. But other things were.

And Mercury was just an enforcer stripped of his rank and his uniform. And the friends he had once believed he had.

✦   ✦   ✦

Callan slammed the door to his office viciously behind him as Jonas, his bodyguard Jackal, Kane, Ely, the little dweeb Austin and the enforcer who had been holding a weapon on Mercury stepped into the room.

He motioned Ely, Austin and the enforcer to the back of the room, out of earshot, as he waved the others to his desk and glared at Jonas furiously.

"Why the hell was Mercury not in uniform?" he snarled to Jonas. He had never seen Mercury out of his enforcer uniform while on duty. With Mercury, it wasn't heard of. And at this point, it appeared to be a deliberate slap against the authority Callan held within the community.

Jonas stared back at him in surprise, before glancing to the other side of the room. Ely had her arms wrapped across her chest as she paced; the tech and the enforcer were standing nervously next to the wall.

Jonas turned and stared back at Callan intently. "Because you ordered his rank revoked. His uniform and his weapon were taken, Callan."

Callan stared back at Jonas, stilling, every instinct inside him roaring out in challenge now. Because he had given no such order.

"What the hell is going on around here?" He kept his voice calm, level, low enough to go no further than the men surrounding him, but he couldn't stop the furious growl that rumbled through it. "I have revoked no one's rank. Least of all Merc's. But I may well be getting ready to."

He glowered back at the others in the room.

Ely flinched, the enforcer paled, and if Austin Crowl could have shrunk farther back against the wall, then he did.

"You." He stabbed a finger in Austin's direction. "Would you like to tell me what the hell you were doing??"

Austin blinked. "Following your orders, sir." His voice trembled as Callan stared back at him in furious shock.

"My orders? I ordered you to deliberately antagonize another Breed?" His voice lowered further. Something was wrong here, because he had given no such order, and he sure as hell hadn't revoked Mercury's rank.

Austin was paste white now, his lips trembling as he licked them. "No, sir. You ordered the camera uncovered." Terror filled his voice. "He answered the call." He pointed to the enforcer as though it were his fault.

The young enforcer stood tall, Callan gave him credit for that, but his gaze was stark with fear. "You asked for Austin, and when he hung up he stated we were to uncover that camera and I was to go with him."

Callan stared back at the two men. They weren't lying. Someone had managed to impersonate him, from his own home.

Callan turned slowly to Kane, lowering his voice once again. "See if you can get into the system. See if that call can be traced.

And I want the orders that went out regarding Mercury's rank traced as well. Find out what the hell is going on here."

"You didn't give the order?" Jonas asked him carefully, his silver eyes swirling with chilling force.

Callan flicked him a disgusted look as Kane remained silent. "Any such order would have gone to you, Jonas. Not an enforcer below Mercury's rank."

"Callan, you have to do something about Mercury," Ely stated then, her voice rising with anger.

Desperation and fear laced her voice as Callan glanced at Jonas and read the flat, hard anger in the director's expression.

"Ely." Callan turned to her, fighting back his anger as he indicated that she should take a seat before him. "What kind of game are you playing with Mercury?"

Kane and Jonas took their seats as well, watching as the doctor moved forward warily and sat down. With a flick of his hand, Callan sent the tech and the enforcer outside the door.

"He's dangerous, Callan." She pushed her fingers through her tussled hair and stared back at him as she rubbed at her neck, clearly concerned, worried. "These tests don't lie. The Council developed the criteria to detect the feral fever. It's building in him, and someone's going to die if you don't confine him and get him back on the drug therapy."

Confine Merc? Callan stared at her in shock. "You want to confine Merc? And drug him?"

Disbelief filled him. Where had her compassion gone? This wasn't the doctor who had overseen their mates, their community, and protected them when the anomalies in their systems went haywire. The Ely he knew would have never considered such a thing.

"It's the only venue of safety," she argued, clearly believing the words spilling from her lips. "Callan, we can't risk him going feral. If the press gets so much as a hint of this, it could destroy us."

"Bullshit."

All eyes turned to Jonas.

"How dare you!" Ely snarled as she turned on him. "You're playing your damned games again. Tell our pride leader how you refused to allow me to bring my findings to him or Mercury. Ordered me not to reveal them. You're risking all our lives."

Callan watched the confrontation, inhaling slowly, deeply, trying to figure out the emotions or the cause for her behavior.

"And you're a paranoid scientist with nothing better to do than chase shadows," Jonas grunted. "You're irrational lately, Ely. Have you had yourself tested?" He flicked her a disgusted look.

"You have to do something about him." Ely surged to her feet as Callan leaned back against his desk and watched the entire scene with a sense of disbelief.

"Sit down, Ely," he ordered her.

"I will not sit here and listen to his insults," she bit out. "He's protecting Mercury for some game he's playing and I've had enough of it. I want that Breed confined and tested. I demand it."

"You demand it?" He straightened slowly. "By what right do you demand anything?"

He watched the scientist closely now. Her features were flushed, her eyes bright as anger coursed through her.

"I'll take my findings to the Ruling Cabinet if you refuse to listen to me," she snarled back in his face.

She was defying him; not just defying him but deliberately challenging him.

"Will you now?" He looked around the room. "We have three of the Ruling Cabinet here now, disagreeing with your suggestions. What makes you think for a second that you can get the vote you need to even consider your demands?"

Her fists clenched at her side; rage was burning inside her, and that was unlike Ely. Ely was cool, calm. She didn't become enraged and never had she suggested anything so vile as confining a Breed.

"You're no better than the Council then," she yelled. "At least they had the good sense to confine him and find a treatment for him. You will only allow him to destroy himself and the Breed community in the process."

They were all staring at her in shock.

Callan gave himself a second, then another. Then before he could control himself, he was in her face, his canines flashing in a furious snarl as she plopped back in her chair, paling.

Callan braced his hands on the arms of that chair, leaning close to her, his eyes holding hers, enforcing his authority over her, feeling the strength of the animal inside him rising to the fore.

He was pride leader. It was his decisions that led his community, and damn her to hell, but she would submit to those decisions. He stared down at her, waited until her gaze shifted from his to his shoulder in respect, and the smell of her fear overcame the smell of her arrogance.

"Would you care to repeat to me the insult that just left your lips?" he asked her, the hard rasp of the animal fury coursing through his voice.

Her gaze flickered, lowered, as she breathed roughly.

"I apologize," she whispered. "I had no right to say that." Her eyes lifted again, and he saw the fear and the concern in her gaze as she stared at his shoulder once again. "Callan, I'm frightened for Mercury, and for that woman. He's dangerous and you won't listen to me because he's your friend. I understand that. But you have to do something."

"Jonas." Callan kept his gaze on Ely's eyes, boring into them, enforcing his strength, enforcing his command. "Did you order her to keep this information from me?"

"I did, Pride Leader." Jonas was smarter than the scientist; he kept his voice level, calm.

Callan moved back, watching as Ely's eyes lowered, her hands folded tightly in her lap, her posture calmer now.

"Why?" He turned on the director.

In terms of power within the hierarchy of the Breed Ruling Cabinet, Jonas was but a step below him. If push came to shove, the other man could possibly enforce certain areas of strength, but Jonas understood the battle they were fighting. Sometimes.

"I disagree with her assessment," Jonas stated calmly, confidently, though he cast Ely another confused look.

"You've seen the tests?" Callan asked him.

"I've seen the test results. I compared those results to the security video of Mercury and Ms. Rodriquez, as well as the video from the lab the day Ely tricked that blood from his arm. She deliberately antagonized him, then took the blood. Results from the blood taken moments earlier showed none of the feral hormone. It was only in the blood she took while accusing him of raping his woman that it showed up."

"She's not his mate," Ely snapped. "I've run all the tests, Jonas. There's no possibility of it."

Callan turned, and before he could halt it, a hiss of male fury passed his lips. Animal to animal, Breed to Breed, that sound had the power to shock them both, because it was one Callan never used. It was a warning of strength and power, and the line she was crossing.

Callan turned back to Jonas now. "What's your opinion now, Director Wyatt?" he snarled.

"Callan, Mercury's always had the feral hormone." Jonas sighed. "His lab reports show this. The drug therapy they used merely kept him under their control. He killed when he was ordered. The drug controlled him; it silenced the need for freedom inside him and the anger he would have felt at the death of his pride members. You don't see him in battle, or during missions. I do. And I've blocked Ely's attempts to test him before and after his missions. Dr. Morrey's concern for Mercury is commendable, but unnecessary."

Callan's eyes narrowed. "Why have you blocked those tests, at those times?"

Jonas sighed roughly at the question. "Because he's what he was created to be in battle," he admitted. "I have no better enforcer than Mercury. He's cunning, merciless and frighteningly intelligent. His kill rate is lower than the other enforcers because he has enough power to take his enemies down physically, hand to hand, in large numbers, and he's intelligent enough and in control enough to know when to kill and when not to."

"And I haven't been informed of these possible problems for what reason?" Callan growled back at him.

"Because the Bureau of Breed Affairs isn't under Sanctuary's control, Callan," Jonas stated, albeit respectfully. "The enforcers are mine to watch over, and if I do say so, I do a damned good job of watching out for them. In the middle of mating heat, with Supremacists and fucking protestors crowding around our asses every time they see one of us on the streets. Those are my men, and regardless of Dr. Morrey's paranoid little suspicions, the manipulations she accuses me of are some damned brilliant strategy if I do say so myself. My enforcers succeed, and that record speaks for itself."

Kane spoke up then. "I want to know what made Dr. Morrey suspicious enough to deceive a friend and deliberately enrage him before taking that blood. You've always been someone we can trust, Ely. The one person we could count on to figure out what was going on with our mates, and in the Breeds' cases, with their bodies. Why trick him?"

She stared at her hands.

"That's something I'm interested in as well," Callan stated, staring back at Ely. "Why did you target Mercury?"

She lifted her head, though she didn't meet his eyes. She stared at his shoulder, the animal in her realizing the fine line she was walking now.

"The mating tests," she whispered.

"He's not her mate, so what's the problem? Besides the feral adrenaline that showed up in it."

Ely's gaze flickered. "She'll make it worse. Her hormones intensify the feral fever," she whispered. "For some reason, when I tested for their mating values, that feral quality immediately showed up in the adrenaline. She'll destroy him. His reaction to her will destroy him."

"Or she'll complete him," Jonas spoke up, turning his gaze from Ely to Callan. "I've studied the lab reports, Callan. I don't think Mercury lost his mate in those labs; he lost his animal instead. I think Ria is possibly his mate, and the presence of the strength in that feral adrenaline proves it. Mercury's test results are never the same as other Breeds'. The animal DNA fluctuates in its recession, as Ely can confirm. I believe the results of those mating tests are more an indication that she *is* his mate, rather than not. I think the lioness *could have* been his mate. But I believe Ria is his mate."

Ely's anger built around her, the scent of it causing Callan to shoot her a sharp look.

"Respectfully," she finally bit out, "where did he obtain his degree in genetics? Because his supposition is the most dangerous load of crap I've ever heard."

"Respectfully, Dr. Morrey," Jonas stated then, "I don't need a degree to know not to betray a friend. It appears perhaps your education was lacking, though."

"I know the science, and I know Breed genetics," she fired back at him, though quieter than before. "All you know is your own arrogance."

"Ask yourself, Ely, is it possible in any way that your findings could have been tampered with as well? Because if you'd pull your head out of your scientific ass long enough to realize it, you'd see that Mercury is in complete control."

"Ely, leave the room," Callan ordered her, staring at her, something hardening inside him at the sense of fanatical certainty he could feel pouring from her. "Return to your labs. I'll let you know when I need to talk to you again."

"Callan, you can't let him continue this game," she cried, jumping to her feet and facing him with a hint of desperation.

"Get your notes and your tests in order and have them faxed into this office," he told her, his voice hardening. "I expect to see them within the hour."

She stared back at him, breathing rapidly, before clenching her fists and stalking from the room. Callan watched her go, his eyes narrowed, his own suspicions aroused now as he turned back to Jonas.

"Any orders I give concerning Mercury will come from me, in person." He turned to Kane. "Find out who the hell is falsifying my orders and bring that person to me. I want to know exactly what the hell is going on here."

"The enforcer who relieved Mercury of his weapon and uniform came to me afterward," Jonas told him. "He said the order came into Austin Crowl's office. The enforcer took the call himself. Someone's impersonating your voice, at the least."

Callan rubbed at the still-sensitive flesh of his chest, where he had taken a bullet but months before, and turned to Kane.

"Is this room secured?"

Kane moved from his chair, slid open a drawer on Callan's desk and lifted free the handheld listening device detector.

"It says we're clear," he murmured, replacing it. But his pale blue eyes were suspicious.

He drew away a second later as the phone at his side rang.

"There's no way to impersonate me to my mate," Callan growled as he stared back at Jonas. "If you're in doubt regarding an order, bring Merinus to me. It's the only safety precaution we can depend on. Until then, find out what the hell is going on here, and where these fucking orders came from."

"Gentlemen." Kane sighed as he lowered the phone that had rung at his side moments before. "Our problems have just been added to."

Callan's gaze cut to him.

Just what the hell they needed, a bigger problem. As though dealing with Jonas and Ely butting heads over the enforcers again wasn't enough.

Kane looked at them all mockingly. "Ms. Rodriquez has just notified her boss that her job is being blocked, she's been insulted, and she's requested the Vanderale heli-jet to be sent to transport her to the airport, where the Vanderale private jet is to pick her up. Let's kiss our funding good-bye right now. It was nice while it lasted."

In her life Ria couldn't remember ever being so furious as she had been when she walked out of Sanctuary. And she couldn't even explain to herself why the burning anger was rushing through her so powerfully.

The moment she entered the cabin, she put her case on the bar and lifted the laptop from it before setting it on the counter and lifting the screen.

She pulled her email up, very much aware that her connection was through Sanctuary's secured network and would be intercepted. She didn't bother to encrypt the email she typed out to Dane, and pushed "send."

She let a smile tip her lips. She had no intention of leaving Sanctuary, but it would bring Dane on their asses like a ton of bricks.

"You're not going anywhere," Mercury stated as he passed by her on the way to the kitchen. "And you need to eat. You haven't eaten today."

She curled her fingers against the counter and bit back the smart-assed comment hovering on her lips. Yeah, she was a bitch. She knew she was a bitch, but it was an attitude that worked for her. Usually. She had a feeling the consequence of that attitude might be more than she could handle at the moment. And besides, she knew how to be a cautious bitch. It was the intelligent path to take when Dane was in one of his crappy moods as well; she hoped it worked with Mercury.

"This isn't the time to treat me as though I were one of your underlings," she informed him coolly, though she felt anything but cool. "Sanctuary has some serious problems at the moment, Mercury."

"And canceling their funding is going to help that?" He

snorted as he faced her from the other side of the bar. "If there's a power play within the ranks, then we need to figure out who's doing it and what the hell is going on."

"Why should I bother? Why should you?" She glared back at him, pushed to a limit she hadn't known she had. "Do you think I haven't read your Sanctuary file?" She hadn't been given the lab files. "Are you aware, Mercury, that your pride leader has all but disavowed you?" Her accent slipped free. Dammit. "Ah, why the hell do I care? Obviously you don't."

She reached behind her to release the bun at the back of her head, her headache intensifying with each moment it weighed on her head.

The long strands of hair rippled through her fingers as she turned away and pushed her fingers through it in frustration.

"Do you know . . ." She went silent as she turned back to him. "Mercury?"

He was moving around that counter, slowly. His eyes were hammered gold rather than amber, those blue sparks intensifying the color once more.

Berserker. Once, long ago, his ancestors had terrified English conquerors with their savagery and strength.

It wasn't rage she saw in his eyes though, it was hunger. Arousal. The same arousal that had tormented her since that kiss days before. The one that had left her burning each night, enflamed, tossing and turning in her bed as she struggled against the need for his body and her need to protect her heart.

"I like this blouse." He stopped in front of her, the backs of his fingers caressing along the shoulder of the silk blouse she wore. "Why don't you take it off?"

"Take it off?" she whispered. "How insane would that be?"

Did his expression appear more savage than normal? His eyes more sensual?

"That way I won't have to rip it off you," he stated, his voice rough, watching as his fingers rubbed against the material before he lifted his gaze to hers. "I wouldn't want to destroy such pretty clothes."

She wanted him to rip the shirt from her. She wanted something she didn't understand, something she had never faced about herself before. She wanted her lover to be wild. But as much as she wanted him to rip her clothes from her, she wanted to rip his as well.

And that terrified her. She wasn't a wild lover. Hell, one of her lovers had even told her she was much too polite in bed for his tastes. But Mercury, he made her want wild. He made her want to *be* wild.

She backed away from him, watching his gaze flicker, his expression turn mocking.

"Afraid?" he asked her.

"Of you, or myself?" she asked him nervously, trying to skirt around him, only to come up short as his arm snaked out, wrapped around her waist and drew her to a stop.

She stared up at him, way up. Six-four was a hell of a stretch for her five-six. Her head barely topped his chest, and his height and breadth made her feel entirely too feminine.

"Why would you be frightened of yourself?" he asked her, using his other hand to stroke down her hair as though soothing her. His fingers threaded into the strands, caressed them, eased her head back until he was staring into her eyes.

Ria swallowed tightly. "We have enough problems here; mixing it with a sexual relationship between us isn't a good idea."

She could barely breathe. And focusing on all the reasons why a relationship was a really bad idea was getting harder by the second. By the stroke. The stroke of his hand over her long hair. She had never considered her hair particularly sexy until this moment, until she felt him caressing it, enjoying it.

"A sexual relationship between us is a given," he told her, that growly thing he did with his voice sending shivers down her spine. "I think you know that, sweetheart."

He called her sweetheart, and he said it in a way it had never been said to her before, as his hand tightened at her hip and pulled her closer to him.

She felt his erection beneath his jeans, thick and hard, pressing into her lower stomach.

"Mercury."

His head lowered. His hand slid beneath her hair, cupped the side of her neck and held her in the most erotic grip she had ever known, as his lips settled against hers.

"Kiss me, Ria," he whispered. "Don't leave me alone in the cold. Warm me, as only you can warm me."

And she was supposed to deny him? No man had ever asked her to warm him. Not to leave him out in the cold where she always felt she existed herself. Always on the outside looking in. Always left out in the cold.

But there was no cold here. As Mercury's lips opened over hers, pressing into hers, there was only heat and pleasure; the feel of his hands stroking her, building the fire inside her as he soothed a part of her.

It wasn't supposed to be like this. He had already mated. He could never belong to her. Not really all-the-way-to-the-soul belong to *her*. But she couldn't deny him either.

A whimper of surrender left her lips, met his kiss, and her hands lifted from his chest to his shoulders. Then to his hair. Coarse, thick, warm. She tightened her fingers in the strands and held him to her as he kissed her with slow, easy possession.

His tongue licked over hers. Faintly rough, just enough to cause her to jerk at the thought of what the lick of his tongue would do to other parts of her body. It was dominant, possessive; it stroked over her lips, her tongue, and when she trapped it and suckled it, she almost cried at the lack of the mating taste. A taste she had heard was wilder than the male giving it.

She let her hands dig into his scalp, lifted herself tighter against him, licked at him, her lips fighting for the kiss as her soul fought to possess some part of him. If even for a moment, to claim a part of him as her own.

And this was why she had fought the attraction building between them. As his hands controlled her, lifted her to him, she had to fight the need to give him parts of herself that no one else had ever touched before.

That wild center growing inside her, the one that wanted to shred his clothes from his body and mark him. That primitive stupid female center that couldn't accept that he belonged to another, even if she was dead.

He growled as he tore his lips from hers.

Ria opened her eyes, staring into his primal gaze as his hands gripped the curves of her rear and clenched. She shuddered, her lashes dipping closed before she forced them open once again.

"I'm hurting you," he said quietly, his hand lifting, touching her cheek as she stared back in surprise. "How am I hurting you, my Ria?"

She shook her head, tugging at his hair, trying to pull him back to her. "Don't stop, Mercury. Kiss me more."

His head lowered. A gentle kiss to the corner of her lips when she didn't want gentle. The stroke of his hand along the hair behind her ear when she wanted the sharp bite of his fingers tangling in it.

"Why are you doing this?" she moaned. "Don't tease me."

"Tell me how I'm hurting you," he demanded, and even his voice was gentle.

She closed her eyes against the knowledge that there would be nothing she could hide from him, and so much he could hide from her.

"Because I'm insane," she whispered, opening her eyes again and gazing back at him. "Because I want more than I should."

He paused, his expression somber, but his eyes watched her with primitive awareness, with desperate hunger.

"What do you want, Ria?"

"I want all of you."

"Then all of me is exactly what you'll have," he promised her.

His lips moved to hers again, took them fiercely, and she felt the wildness inside him as he gave it rein. He nipped at her lips, then pumped his tongue into her mouth as he lifted her against him, turned and bore her to the couch.

Her back met the cushions as he came over her, his lips still on hers, allowing her room to twist beneath him, to arch against the knee that pressed between her thighs.

"Take it off." She tore her lips from his, tugging at his shirt.

He gripped the hem and jerked it off. Then he gripped the front of her blouse and ripped it from her.

"Damn pretty shirt." He was staring at what he had revealed, not at what he had ripped. "Damn." He ran the backs of his fingers over the curve of flesh that rose above her lacy bra. "I knew I could see the hint of your nipples under that damned fabric, and now I know why."

Because her bra was so sheer the tight peaks were nearly pressing through the lace.

Ria tried to calm her breathing, but nothing could calm it. She needed his kiss again, she needed more of him. She lifted her back, arching, displaying her breasts and praying he would give in to his hunger for them.

And he did. His head lowered, his lips covering one achingly sensitive peak and drawing it into his mouth.

Ria was in ecstasy. Pleasure was rising inside her like a tidal wave sweeping through her fears. Tomorrow. She would worry about the complications tomorrow. Right now, tonight, he was hers. She had had more of him now than any man she had ever been with in the past. What did it matter if he wasn't mating her? If he wasn't keeping her? She didn't want to be kept anyway, did she?

A part of her ached at the question, but it was fiercely reined in by the sensation washing over her flesh. The lash of his tongue against her nipple, even through the sheer lace of the bra, was destructive. The feel of his hands jerking her skirt up her legs, baring her to him as he pulled back to stare at his handiwork.

Her nipple was red and engorged. His lips covered its mate, sucked and licked and nipped as his hands roamed over her thighs and finally tore the panties from her hips.

Ria almost orgasmed. She had never had her panties ripped from her before. It was so sexual, so wicked she felt her juices flooding her vagina as her clit heated and throbbed with a desperate demand for his touch.

"Beautiful." He leaned back, allowed his fingers to brush over the dark curls between her thighs. "So soft and warm. So wet." The dampened curls clung to his fingers.

Ria watched at he touched her, then watched as she touched him. Her fingers pressing against his hard abs, feeling silky sun-kissed flesh, toughened skin and tight muscle.

His fingers parted the swollen flesh between her thighs as hers moved to his belt. She wanted him naked. She want to touch.

A cry fell from her lips. Her gaze jerked between her thighs where he was slowly, slowly burying two fingers inside her. Working them into her tightened channel, twisting them with sharp little movements of his wrist and wringing a whimper from her throat.

He grimaced, his lips pulling tight, the little snarl at the corner revealing a canine. Wild. Primal and wild, and he was making her wild. Her back arched and she drove herself on his fingers and cried out his name.

Long, broad fingers. Oh God, she would never be able to see a man's fingers without thinking of Mercury's. Without remembering this. The feel of him stroking inside her body, caressing her, sensitizing her until she was writhing against him, her hips churning as she fought for deeper, faster, harder.

"I'm going to taste you, Ria." The growl in his voice did shivery things to her spine that spread out through her body and echoed with painful pleasure.

She shook her head, one hand falling from the belt of his jeans to grip his wrist, to hold him in place.

"Don't stop," she panted. "Please. Please don't stop."

He thrust his fingers inside her again, deeper, harder, stronger, and she held her breath, fighting for her orgasm as he stilled just as suddenly.

He ignored her protest as he moved down her body, sliding her hips to the edge of the couch as he knelt on the floor and lowered his head.

The first touch of his tongue against her clit froze her in place, the second had her hips jerking. The third and she was lost. His tongue rasped. The faintest bit of roughness, just enough to turn excitement to sheer brutal pleasure.

Her hands latched onto his hair and she lifted to him as she felt his fingers slide free of her. His fingers retreated, and his tongue plunged deep. Her legs wrapped around his shoulders, her hips lifting as he fucked her with hard, penetrating strokes of his tongue and growled into her flesh.

His fingers curled beneath her rear, lifting her closer, and she felt the blunted tips of those clawlike nails digging into her flesh and jerked with a pleasure so extreme it felt as though her heart was going to burst from her chest.

She was coming apart from the pleasure, from the wild, desperate need building inside her. She had to come. He had to let her come.

As he pushed his tongue inside her with fierce strokes, his thumb settled on her clit, rotated, stroked, and sent her flying into release. She was exploding into fragments and didn't care. She held on to him with both hands, held him closer and wailed out her pleasure, not even bothering to be shocked with the fact that she had never wailed in pleasure in her entire life.

"So sweet." His tongue retreated, his head lifting to kiss the violently sensitive flesh of her clit gently. That light touch had her gasping with the bolt of sensation that raced through her.

"Easy, sweetheart," he murmured, still kissing, moving

lower, giving her no time to come down from her orgasm before he began building the need for another.

And he did it gently, tenderly. The softest strokes of his tongue, the gentlest kisses around her clit.

"I want to touch you," she moaned, her hands gripping his shoulders as those blunted nails, curved and powerful, raked down her thighs with primitive intensity.

"Not yet." He nipped at her thigh, causing her to whimper with the edge of pleasure/pain. "Let me taste you. Let me have you like this, Ria. Let me fill my senses with you. I want your taste, your scent with me. In my pores. The same as I'll give you mine."

A part of him.

She moaned his name as he spread her thighs farther and kissed the swollen, flushed lips of her pussy. Then he licked her again. Inside and out.

He made her weak. He made her desperate. Her nails dug into his shoulders, scratched his flesh as the rising tide of lust began to build and churn inside her again.

She needed him. And she needed more than his hungry kisses and diabolical tongue.

Fighting for breath, she moved her hands to her breasts, cupped them, raked her nipples with her own fingers and felt him pause. She gripped her nipples between her thumbs and forefingers, opened her eyes and stared back at him.

Dazed, nearly out of her mind with the need burning across every nerve ending, she watched him watch her. Watched his eyes dilate, his lips pull back from his teeth as a grumbling snarl rumbled in his throat.

He kissed his way up her body then. His hands moving to his belt, his jeans. She had only a second to glimpse the furiously flushed head of his cock before his lips covered an aching, hard nipple and drew it into his mouth.

A second later, his cock head pressed against her, hot, thick, silk over iron, and pressing farther.

He paused, his breathing rough and hot as sweat beaded his shoulders and glistened over the tiny, fine invisible hairs that covered his body.

"You promised me," she reminded him, her voice rough. "You promised me, Mercury. The first time. Hard and fast. You would fill me with all of you in one stroke."

He rolled his forehead against her shoulder, then nipped the tender flesh as he growled.

"I need it," she whimpered, arching closer to him, gasping at the feel of his erection stretching her farther. "Please. You promised."

His hands clenched her hips and she arched closer. He growled again, his lips parting, his teeth gripping her shoulder as his hips bunched and he thrust. Hard. Spearing into her as his name became a scream of such excruciating pleasure that for a second, the smallest second, her mind went black.

And still, she didn't have all of him. He retreated, worked inside her slowly this time. He pressed into her then thrust again, hard and deep. He buried his cock full-length inside her and burned her with the desperate fullness. The heated impalement of iron-hard flesh threatened to steal her mind as she felt her own delicate muscles spasming, milking him as he throbbed inside her.

And he was biting her. His teeth were locked on her shoulder, pinching into her flesh as she went wild beneath him. One arm curled around his head, trying to keep his bite. The other dug into his back as he began to move, her nails piercing his flesh as his teeth pierced hers and his cock penetrated her with heavy lunges.

Each stroke carried her higher, threw her further into the maelstrom of sensation. She swore she forgot how to breathe. Breathing didn't matter. When they were done, he would breathe for her. That or she would die from lack of oxygen because she needed all her strength for this. Meeting each thrust, holding tight to him, feeling his hips churning, his cock shafting her, his muscles tightening against her.

And feeling herself fly in his arms. That was what coming with Mercury did. She flew in his arms and screamed, or tried to scream from the rapture tearing through her.

It was wild and pulsating. It was filled with sensation burning, raking across her nerve endings and shattering into fragments. It was the feel of his final thrust, the heavy spurt of his heated semen, his snarl at her shoulder then his lips covering hers as his hips jerked between her thighs.

It was the most exquisite pleasure she could have ever imagined finding in his arms, and it almost, almost overshadowed the pain. Because there was no barb. There was no extension swelling from his cock to hold him in place as he filled her with his seed. There was no hormone spilling into her to ensure he never walked out of her life. There was just this, agony and ecstasy, and the knowledge that she was bound to *him*. Whether she wanted to be or not.

· CHAPTER 11 ·

The animal prowled the man's mind, careful to stay in the shad-
ows, to hold back, though rage was a fire in its gut and the need
for action was like a hunger for blood.
  But it couldn't move yet.
  It had to ease into place. It was still so weak. The drugs had
taken so long to wear away, and it had taken still longer to
awaken. And it might have never awoken if not for her. If not for
the soft scent of what the animal knew belonged irrevocably to it.
  The man had staked his claim. The animal could retreat just
enough to strengthen a little more. If it moved too quickly, the
man could fight it. If they fought, it would be a battle they would
both lose, because once the animal stepped free of its bonds, it
knew it would never return. There would be no going back, not
even to save the man's life.
  Freedom awaited. Its mate awaited him, and it could smell her
scent, her pain, her need to be marked, to be claimed by one such
as the animal. She was wild and she was bound to it. But she
ached; her spirit reached out to the animal, and it longed to shel-
ter that spirit in the shadow of its strength.
  So sweet. It inhaled her scent as the man's defenses relaxed,
as the man rested against her, lost in the pleasure of his release.
The animal inhaled her essence and it was pleased. It stepped
closer, just a little bit closer to the man's flesh, felt her warmth,
felt her like a gentle rain and it rumbled its pleasure.

✦ ✦ ✦

Ria's lashes lifted, a frown on her face as she felt something. She
didn't hear it. She felt it. Mercury held her tight to his chest as
he rested against her, catching his breath, and she could have
sworn . . . She waited, holding her breath. A grumbly little purr?

She heard it again and let a smile touch her lips.

"You're purring," she murmured.

He stilled against her. Tensed and it stopped.

"I don't purr." He moved, lifting himself off her, his expression set now, his eyes their normal amber brown as he adjusted his clothes then helped her from the couch.

Ria frowned, standing before him as she unzipped the skirt that was bunched at her hips, stepped out of it and collected the shreds of the rest of her clothing.

"I know a purr when I feel one," she told him, irritated by his denial.

"You misfelt then." He shrugged, his gaze hooded as she stared back at him.

She wasn't going to let herself get angry, she promised. This was the best sex she had ever had in her life, why argue over a damned purr?

"What, are you ashamed of it?" she asked him, defying her own promise.

He picked up his shirt from the floor and pulled it back on. He was fully dressed now and she was as naked as the day she was born. That small detail had the power to irritate her. He should be as naked as she was at the moment.

"Breeds don't just purr," he informed her. "And you need to shower. I'm betting we can expect company within the hour. I don't think I can handle anyone seeing you naked like this."

"What the hell do you mean Breeds don't just purr?" Her nakedness didn't bother her, and it wouldn't until company actually did arrive. "Come on, Mercury, it wasn't that big a deal. Just a tiny little purr . . ."

"Breeds only purr during mating," he told her stiffly, his expression somber, almost regretful. "There hasn't been a mating."

That told her. She tried to still that sharp little pain that drove a spike through her chest, but damn, it wasn't easy. And it made her question her own mind. Because she could have sworn she heard that faint little rumble. And now she wondered if she had just needed to hear it.

"Well." She stiffened her shoulders and her upper lip. Because if she wasn't careful it was going to start trembling. "That puts me in my place, doesn't it?"

"Dammit it, Ria." He reached for her, scowling.

"I have to shower, as you said. You expect company soon, and parading around naked isn't my favorite pastime anyway."

She turned away from him and moved quickly for her bedroom.

"Straighten the couch up if you don't mind." She paused at the doorway and looked back.

He hadn't moved. He still stood there, watching her, his expression arrogantly impassive. The couch cushions were in disarray, and God only knew what *his* company would catch scent of when they walked into the room. Probably her complete humiliation.

"And there's room freshener in the kitchen cabinet," she told him. "Make use of it please. I'd prefer your *company* not know exactly what happened in here."

His lips parted to speak, and she couldn't bear to hear anything he had to say. She didn't care what it was. She slipped into her bedroom, closed the door behind her then leaned against it with a hitching, silent sob.

Only mated Breeds purred. They only purred for their mates, not for women who were too stupid to steel their hearts against the need to hear it. And she was one of those stupid women.

✦   ✦   ✦

Mercury watched the bedroom door close, his fists curling, the need to punch something riding so hard inside him it was nearly impossible to deny.

She didn't know what he would have given to purr for her. To know that all that wild courage and passion was his alone.

Before he could help it, he ran his tongue over his teeth again and snarled in fury. Nothing. Not an itch, not the slightest swelling of the glands, not even a vague sensitivity to give him hope.

He pushed his fingers through his hair and did as she'd asked. He straightened the couch, he sprayed her detestable air freshener. But unknown to her, that wasn't going to do anything to cover the scent of their sex. And he refused to wash her scent from his body.

He needed her scent on him, soft, delicate, merging with his to create something that, when he breathed it in, seemed to comfort the rage building inside him.

Belonging. It was something it seemed would be forever

denied him. Callan had revoked his rank within the enforcer hierarchy when his weapon and uniform had been confiscated. He had backed the safe path rather than an individual Breed, and logically, Mercury couldn't even blame him for it. The Breed community as a whole was of more importance than a single Breed. Even one whose need to belong was like a hunger in his soul.

He sat down on the couch, close to Ria's scent, and breathed her in, knowing she was in that shower, washing his scent from her body. It infuriated him, knowing that it took no more than soap and water to wash the smell of him from her flesh.

Mating changed the scent of each mate. Their scents combined, created something unique that couldn't be washed away. It wasn't like the scents that mingled on his flesh now, both of the them together, because he could still distinguish between her scent and his.

He paused, staring down at his hands in confusion. His sense of smell was sharper than it had been. That knowledge sent a pulse of wariness tearing through him as he inhaled, and frowned again. Perhaps it was. He shook his head. What he thought he had smelled moments ago was gone. There was no combined scent, just the smell of sex, of the pleasure they had shared.

He had lost the ability to distinguish smells as other Breeds could in the labs. When the drugs killed the feral rage inside him, they had killed the animal that lurked beneath his senses as well.

Once, he had known himself as two halves. The man and the animal. They existed together, complete, until the animal had fought for supremacy. A form of madness that normally meant instant death when it showed itself in an adult Breed.

The scientists in the labs he had been created within had developed a drug instead. One that killed the animal instinct to dominate the human. But he had also lost those extraordinary powers to see in the darkness, to smell the slightest scent, to touch, to taste. He had become more merciless, more cunning, but he had lost the animal instincts inside him to the point that he was only slightly better than a non-Breed.

The Breed with the face of a lion, and the instincts of a normal man. It was laughable.

He pushed himself from the couch and paced to the kitchen.

Opening her cabinets, her refrigerator, he found nothing more than coffee and beer and a few old Danishes. Good God, how did that woman survive eating as she did?

He shook his head and moved to the phone. Five minutes later he had an order in to the local grocery store, whose owner he often went hunting with.

He couldn't fix coffee worth shit, but he was a mean cook. He was tired of starving to death in this dark little cabin where she existed after work. And he grew tired of pizza fast.

Ria wasn't his mate, but his mate was dead. She was taken from him before he had even had a chance to realize what being mated meant. It didn't mean he was dead. It sure as hell didn't mean there were no emotions lurking beneath his odd appearance.

He had emotions, and those emotions were tightening, building within him and centering on one contrary little woman. A woman with an intelligence that often amazed him as she stood back and watched people. She watched and she listened. And what she saw, he sensed, was often much more than others did.

Such as her determination that there was a power play being orchestrated in Sanctuary. The more Mercury thought about it, the more it concerned him, and the more he realized how incredibly difficult it would be for him to investigate it.

He wasn't an enforcer any longer. He couldn't just walk into the secured areas of Sanctuary and begin investigating the oddities he was beginning to put together for himself.

Something wasn't as it should be. He could feel it, he could sense it, but he couldn't put his finger on what it was.

He moved to the front door and stepped outside, ignoring the Jaguar female that hissed at him as he stepped out the door.

"It's damned cold out here," Shiloh grumbled. "And listening to you have fun in there is not fun out here. Do you realize I had to spend the better part of the damned hour in the woods, to escape the sound of her caterwauling?"

He turned and arched his brow. Most Jaguars possessed darker skin tones and black, silky hair. This Jaguar Breed was an anomaly. The rich auburn highlights in her black hair and her creamy complexion gave her a unique look that never failed to draw stares.

She was a bit shorter than most Breed females, barely five-five, and for some odd reason the scientists that created her had allowed her to have a temper.

"Shi, you're going to piss me off," he warned her, hiding his smile, knowing she wouldn't, unless she really wanted to.

"Do you hear my knees shaking?" she growled as she pulled her jacket tighter around her.

He grunted at that. "The grocery from town will be delivering supplies soon. I need to talk to Rule and Lawe. Make certain when the owner arrives that he doesn't enter the house. Take the bill and I'll collect it when I come back."

"You're going to cook!" She accused him with a hint of disbelief. "While I'm stuck outside? Mercury, that's not fair."

"Take it up with Jonas." He shrugged as he left the small porch and headed toward the tree line. "Maybe he'll send you back to Sanctuary."

Mercury doubted it. Once he had a chance to talk to Jonas and lay out his suspicions, he knew the director would begin shifting his own people, keeping those in place that he trusted and shifting back those he didn't.

Most would have suspected Jonas of heading a revolt against Callan and the Ruling Cabinet, but Mercury couldn't see it happening. Jonas was a sneaky, manipulative son of a bitch, but Sanctuary and the Breed community were his primary concerns. And Mercury had spent enough time as the man's personal bodyguard to know Jonas didn't have revolt in mind. Driving everyone insane with his games, yeah, Mercury could see that one coming where Jonas was concerned. But a strike against the security of the community? That wasn't going to come from Jonas.

Jonas had no desire to rule. He liked playing puppet master, and he loved poking his nose in where it wasn't involved, but he didn't have the temperament to play the games it took to weave such a play for power.

Jonas would challenge outright. He would never allow a breakdown in authority. And that was what was happening. Someone had waited, watched, and while Callan was occupied with staying alive and then healing from his wounds, they were moving in to disable the power structure the Ruling Cabinet had in place.

He could sense it. He could feel it, but with his rank stripped now, he had no idea how to identify who or what.

As he entered the thick forest growth, Lawe and Rule fell in place beside him. They turned to face the cabin, all three silent for long moments.

"She's not my mate." He answered the question he had seen in their eyes.

Lawe grunted at that.

"Whatever," Rule snorted. "I don't know about this mating bullshit, Mercury. Seems to me there aren't any rules to it. You act mated."

And there had been a few odd moments that he had felt a bond, an unbreakable *something* that he couldn't put his finger on.

"Jonas contacted me ten minutes ago," Lawe murmured. "He's pulling Shiloh back to Sanctuary before he arrives here. It seems there's a problem at home base."

"What kind of problem?" Mercury swung his gaze to his friend, watching as Lawe leaned against a tree, his expression implacable, his eyes burning with a hard, savage light.

"He's going to explain things when he gets here, but notice had gone out that Callan has reinstated your rank. He'll be bringing your uniform and weapon when he arrives."

Mercury shook his head. He didn't want the rank, he realized. Jonas would have found a way to force Callan to reinstate it. It meant nothing to him that way.

"There's something going on," he said quietly. "There are too many anomalies."

"Meaning?" Rule gripped his weapon, his gaze sharper now.

Mercury shook his head. "I can see the threads of it, sense them, but I can't put my finger on where they're going. Ely has targeted me, though, and she's never done that with another Breed. She needs me out of the way. Or someone does." It just didn't work for him that Ely would be in on any kind of deception, but he knew it was possible. It was even probable.

"Ely?" Lawe straightened and started back at him in disbelief before he shook his head and suspicion began to fill his eyes as well.

"We need to be careful." Mercury stared back at the cabin, and thought of the woman inside. "Ria's not here just to decide whether or not to stop Vanderale funding. The files she's going through have nothing to do with funding, and everything to do with outgoing transmissions. Ely's managed to separate me from Sanctuary, but not as far as she could have without Jonas standing in her way. When Jonas arrives, I want you at the meeting."

"And Ria?" Lawe asked. "Will she be in on it?"

He turned back to Lawe. "She'll be there, or there will be no meeting."

She wasn't his mate. But he didn't have to mate her to know she belonged to him.

✦   ✦   ✦

Ely stared at the test results as she sipped at a bottle of water and felt the anger burning in her mind. She was sitting here, putting together the proof for what she was trying to convince the Ruling Cabinet of, and a part of her already knew they weren't going to listen to her.

Mercury was a strong enforcer, and not just in physical strength. His animal qualities were more a part of him than anyone suspected. The Council drugs may have recessed the more violent qualities of his animal, and the senses he had once possessed, but he was still intelligent, and cunning. That animalistic intelligence was by far his most dangerous trait, because it was stronger than other Breeds' she had run across since the rescues.

If it hadn't been for the feral fever, he would have been trained to lead and to command. He could have possibly been a stronger alpha than even Callan. As hard it was to believe that there could be a stronger alpha.

She pushed her fingers through her hair and fought the rage burning behind her eyelids, fought the screaming warning her own animal was sending through her head. She had never felt like this, and she knew the pressure was beginning to get to her.

Reaching around, she rubbed at the back of her neck, fighting the headache that seemed to spread there.

Shaking her head, she opened a bottle of over-the-counter pain medication and washed two down with the water before turning back to her computer.

She put a tight hold on the anger, forced it back and forced her mind to work on the analysis of the fluids she had taken from Mercury.

There was something in the semen that she knew was off, something odd. The saliva as well. His blood was corroded with the feral adrenaline, and that terrified her. The images of the videos taken in the labs where he had killed so horrifically continued to run through her mind.

His hands, the nails thick and curved like claws, had punched right through a man's chest. The bloody mess of the man's heart had still been in Mercury's clenched fist when he drew back. That heart had been ground into the trainer's face before Mercury ripped his head from his shoulders.

That shouldn't have been possible. To just rip flesh and muscle, cartilage and spine away in such a brief span of time and toss the head away.

She shuddered, imagining Callan or, God forbid, Jonas taken apart in such a way.

Jonas was her nemesis, but there had always been a sense of fondness between the two of them, until now. He had respected her opinion even if he didn't always want to believe what she had to say. He pushed her to find other answers, and because of that she had run these tests until her head was about to explode.

"You bastard!" The snarl surprised her as she jumped from her stool and began to pace the room. "Damn you, Jonas, I can't find any other answer."

And why should she care what she found for him? This was the man who had had his own sister captured. The man who had blackmailed that sister, laid her head on the chopping block of Breed Law, and he would have gone through with it. He would have killed Harmony if she hadn't done as he ordered.

Just as he killed others.

He thought she didn't know the things he had done. The trips the Breed heli-jet made to an active volcano, one that bubbled and churned and waited with greedy anticipation for the sacrifices he fed to it.

The bodies he had dropped into it. Council scientists who had been wiped away within the boiling mass of molten stone. He and his pilot, the wild-eyed Jackal.

Jackal. Damn him. He was protecting Mercury as well, and he was furious with her. And he was just as much a killer as Jonas was himself. Everyone knew it. Even Kane, head of Sanctuary's security, knew it. Jackal was a murderer. He should have been born a Breed rather than a human.

She dug her fingers into her neck, trying to rub away the pain there. There had to be a way to convince the Ruling Cabinet that Mercury had to be confined and forced to undergo the testing

Ria was surprised when Mercury submitted to her need that he lie back. He moved until he was in the middle of the bed, his savage features wicked, sensual. His tilted eyes, the flicker of blue in them, and the sexy quirk of his lips were enough to make any woman wet.

But his approval at her touch sent her juices spilling from her. That sexy grumbling little growl as she stroked her hands up his legs, moving between them, coming over him, made her heart race.

And his body. That body was definitely the talk of many a woman that had glimpsed it. The online blogs and Breed sighting websites were filled with talk of this body. Six-four and broad. Proportional. Legs that were muscular and strong, the strength and power beneath his flesh would bring out any woman's more feminine instincts.

The instinct to submit beneath him. To have him cover her, take her, draw screams of pleasure from her.

But she hadn't expected him to be willing to lie beneath her touch so easily. The male animal inside him was stronger than most men; she knew that just from the time she had spent with him. And he was hungry. Hard and aroused. The thick length of his cock rose from the heavy sac between his thighs, along the hard planes of his muscular abdomen.

Thickly veined, the flesh a golden bronze, matching the rest of his skin. But that heavy shaft was absent the fine pelt of body hair that covered the rest of his flesh.

It was silk over iron, the broad head throbbing, damp with pre-cum. And with a Breed, there was no need to worry about birth control or STDs. They were the perfect lovers. He would break her heart and she knew it.

But until then, she could enjoy. She lowered her head and stroked her tongue along the length of his erection, licking and stroking. She tasted the thick crest, drew the essence of him onto her tongue and moaned at the taste. It was like midnight. Like a fire burning in the hearth as a cold wind blew outside. Earthy. Not sweet, not tart, but clean and completely male. And she wanted more of it.

Her tongue flickered over the tiny slit, aware as she did so that his hands clenched in the comforter as he arched to her.

So much power. She could feel it throbbing in the air around them and beneath the broad head of his erection. And it filled her. The power of one woman over the sleek animalistic male beneath it. It was heady. An aphrodisiac all its own. And when she filled her mouth with him, that power intensified. His body tightened, his hips jerking as though he wanted to do nothing more than thrust into her mouth as he had taken her body earlier.

"Damn you," his voice rumbled. "That's so damned good, Ria."

She licked as she sucked at the broad cock head. Teased and stroked and let her senses fill with him. The taste of him, the heat of him.

One hand lifted from the blankets, cupped the side of her face, and he watched her. As though the experience were special, as though he had never had a woman suck him into her mouth.

How could any woman resist? The sight of the blue intensifying in his eyes made her crazy with lust. The small taste she'd had of his semen had her craving more, as though it were addictive. As though the taste of him were all she needed to survive.

She worked her mouth over his straining cock head, sucked it to the back of her mouth, flicked her tongue against the sensitive underside and moaned at the dark arousal filling her when his hands clenched in her hair.

She had never liked the power games men played in bed. The pain that they believed would force submission of her sexuality to them. The calculation in each act. With Mercury, there was none of that, but each hard tug at her hair had her moaning with pleasure. She liked it with him. It wasn't calculated. It was pleasure. It was the man following her into that shadowed realm of hungers that she knew had never been sated until his touch. And then, it had only been satisfied until he touched her again.

"Beautiful," he groaned. "The feel of your mouth, Ria. Damn." He arched, pressing more into her mouth as she retreated.

She wrapped her fingers around the heavy stalk of flesh, with no hope of surrounding it completely, and stroked. Her lips slid from the head, caressed down the shaft, and she licked and sucked at the tight sac below, as his hands deepened the fire in her scalp.

She felt the scrape of his nails against her head. Those blunted claws, the physical representation of the animal inside him, and she nearly came from the feel of it.

Her clit was swollen, throbbing. Need was knifing through her body, and the hunger for more of him was driving her mouth.

"Keep this up, Ria, I'll come." His voice was thick, almost a purr itself, with a growl throbbing beneath it. "I'm going to fill that pretty mouth if you don't stop."

She sucked him deeper, tightening her lips and her mouth around the broad head and working it with her tongue, with the roof of her mouth. She loved it, laved it; she moaned around it.

His hand tightened more and she whimpered with the ecstatic pleasure. She sucked him more, needing his taste. She needed it, ached for it.

"Ria. Damn you." He pulled at her hair again.

Moving one hand from his cock, she raked her nails down his thighs and would have cried out at the force with which his hips jerked.

His hands held her still then; a snarl left his lips and his seed spurted hard, hot, filling her mouth with that wild taste as she fought to consume each heated pulse.

She was almost coming herself from the sheer excitement of it, the taste of him. The taste was like fire, burning through her cells and filling her with something just as wild as the lust burning between them.

When she had taken all he had to give her, he surprised her again. Shocked her. He pulled her along his body, gripped her hips, and before she realized his intention he'd buried several hard inches inside the weeping depths of her pussy.

He was still aroused. Still iron-hard and hungry.

Resisting the force of his hands, she lifted, opening her eyes to stare down at him before she took those inches again, working herself on the thick intrusion and loving every second of it.

She had never had a lover take her after finding his own release. Hell, she had never been with a man who could find his release more than once in a forty-eight-hour period.

"Take me." Mercury stared back at her.

She smiled into the fierce set of his features. Savage lust gleamed in his eyes, in the hard, sharp angles of his face.

"Make me."

Challenge. Defiance.

Mercury stared into Ria's eyes and saw the things he had never seen in another woman's. Acceptance.

The animal lust was rising inside him, something he had always fought before, something he had no ability to fight with Ria. And he saw her acceptance of it.

He'd never had a woman go down on him. They feared his release, the infection of his semen. He'd never had one take him. His Ria was taking him. Struggling against him, challenging him to take her, begging him to.

"You don't want me to do that, Ria," he groaned, his hands clenching on her hips. "Take me, baby. Don't do this to both of us."

He didn't want to hurt her. He didn't want to release the primal lust pounding in his veins and demanding that he fuck her as he wanted to.

She gave him a sexy little pout, lifted her hips, wiggled against his hold and teased him more. Her tight pussy, so fucking tight it burned into his flesh, clenched and milked at the engorged head of his cock. But just the head. She was tormenting him with the hold she had on him. She was tempting a part of him he had never allowed to rise inside him.

"Maybe that's exactly what I want, Mercury." She leaned forward and nipped his lips.

When he tried to catch her kiss, she shook her head and a light, sexy laugh left her.

"Ria." The warning was ignored as she lifted again, nearly freeing her body of him before he slammed his hips upward, taking more of her, but not enough. "This is the wrong time to tease, sweetheart."

"Take me again, Mercury," she whispered, her nails digging into his chest. "I dare you."

He could feel the sweat building on his chest as he tried to force more into her and she fought him further. She was in a position of control, slippery and wet, and tempting him. Tempting something he didn't recognize within his own lust.

He tried to breathe in, to clear his head of the red tide of lust sweeping over him, but all he could smell was her challenge, her need ripping through his senses.

He strained against her and she lifted again. His hands tightened on her hips to slam her down on him, and she wiggled, fought until she was free of him.

It was the final straw.

"I dare you," she groaned.

With a surge of power, he lifted her, flipped her to her stomach and rose over her. He wrapped an arm beneath her hips, lifted her, held her and buried himself inside her.

She took part of him in the first thrust with a strangled cry. She took more with the second; on the third powerful stroke of his hips, he was buried full-length inside her and almost roaring out his triumph as she screamed out her pleasure.

It *was* pleasure. Her sheath convulsed around him, her juices spilled along his shaft, and her body writhed with impending release.

"Taken." He rose over her, locked his teeth on her shoulder to hold her in place and began thrusting inside her with all the raging lust and hunger that had been inside him for a lifetime.

It didn't take either of them long. The hard, powerful strokes of his cock inside her sent them both hurtling into ecstasy. Mercury felt her tighten, felt her pussy spasm and heard her release in the strangled scream that filled his head. Her cries mingled with his growls as he felt his own release begin spilling from him. And still he thrust, stroked, snarled with the power of the pleasure. Until he had given her all he had, more than he had ever thought he could give a woman, and collapsed over her.

Hell, he hadn't even taken her gown off. He hadn't stroked or sucked her pretty breasts. He hadn't tasted the sweet flesh between her thighs again. He had just taken her. Savagely. And never had completion been so deep, so satisfying.

He still lay over her, hating the thought of pulling free of her, of releasing her from his possession and once again facing reality.

She had no idea the power of her hold on him, and it wasn't

just physical. It went deeper. It called something from him that made no sense, something he knew he should be wary of, and yet couldn't find the strength to search for answers to.

"If you move I'm gonna kill you," she sighed drowsily.

"I'm heavy." He kissed her shoulder.

He had bit her. A smear of blood stained her shoulder now; the print of four sharp canines were indented into her flesh.

"You're so warm," she sighed, and he could hear the exhaustion in her voice. "I'm so tired of being cold, Mercury. Keep me warm, just for a few more minutes. Inside and out. Let me stay warm."

He stilled against her, looked at her profile. Her lashes covered her eyes, and he swore she was but seconds from sleep. And she wanted only to be warm for a little while longer.

Could he deny her that? He knew what the cold felt like, that feeling that there was nothing to warm him, that the loneliness had dug its way so deep inside him that he would never know what true warmth was.

Yet she had warmed him.

He realized that. Something frozen inside him had been warmed the moment he glimpsed her, and right now, holding her just like this, there wasn't even the slightest chill inside him or outside of him.

He wouldn't deny her that, when she had given it to him.

He held her, let her slip into sleep, then pushed the forgotten laptop to the corner of the headboard before jerking the comforter around them and easing beside her.

She moaned at the loss, but only until he wrapped himself around her. He surrounded her with his arms, embraced her legs with his and let her head tuck against his neck, the feel of her breath against him there comforting.

And he felt the need for sleep himself. Just a nap. Just something to restore his sense of balance. Because somehow, somewhere, Ria had shaken his life up as nothing else ever had.

◆　　◆　　◆

The animal watched from eyes that were wary of detection. It forced the sleeping man's eyes open, looked around and saw only the darkness of the room where they slept.

It looked down and saw the woman. Into its ragged, pain-

ravaged soul it felt the first sliver of peace arise. That little bit of light that gave it hope.

The woman had made the man's control weak, made him less diligent, less suspicious when the animal came to awareness.

The man's emotions were finally breaking free, and with that, the animal could feel freedom just at the edges of its mind.

How tired it was. How it hurt, locked so deep within the man's mind that its captivity was like hell filled with its own roars.

Sweet Ria. The man thought of her as Sweet Ria. The animal saw more. So much more. As the man slept, it stretched out slowly and touched her hair. Emotion clenched its weary mind, gave it strength. She gave the man and the animal strength.

Her hair was soft, so soft. The animal let itself experience the feel of it through the man's hand. The man slept deeply wrapped around her, but still the animal moved cautiously, so cautiously. It couldn't allow this woman to escape it. The man believed she would try to leave. He was preparing himself for it. The animal refused to allow it.

The mark the man had made on her shoulder was just below the man's mouth. Slowly, edging closer, the animal let its power seep into the man. Just a little bit. Just enough.

Seconds later, the animal rumbled its soft purr as the man licked at that wound. The taste of primal hunger filled the man's mouth, the animal's being. Its tongue felt thick, aching. He lapped at the woman's shoulder, probed at the tiny wounds that sharp canines had made and spilled itself inside her body.

Not enough, just a bit. The taste of her was true warmth. The ice encasing the animal weakened, and as it licked at the soft flesh of her shoulder, it was as though that warmth sparked its strength.

Strength. It could be free now. It could struggle free of the bonds holding it, but if it did, if it moved too quickly, the man would fight.

The animal stepped back, aching, but stronger. It wasn't enough. It wasn't strong enough for the battle the man might wage. And the man was ever diligent. Even now he was struggling past sleep, aware that something was different. That something moved inside him.

The animal hid in the cold darkness, the warmth of the

*woman so close. Its eyes closed. It forced itself to sleep. Because
the woman was so close. And still, the animal was so weak . . .
And danger was approaching.*

◆   ◆   ◆

Mercury came awake quickly. For a moment, he felt something
he hadn't felt inside himself for so many years that at first, he
simply didn't recognize it. That surge of feral adrenaline, rage
tearing a hole through his mind as his claws flexed, but gentle,
very gently because the soft flesh beneath them belonged to Ria.

And he didn't dare move. Not yet.

The shadows were slipping past the door. There was no
scent. Not the scent of human or the scent of Breed. There was
the scent of clothing, of danger.

A silent snarl tugged at his lips; rage pumped through his
system. He didn't stop to think about feral displacement or the
animal instincts suddenly rising to the fore.

He could smell the weapons they carried; that was enough
for him. He could taste the danger surrounding the shadows
stealing through the night.

He tracked them, his night vision no longer clouded as it usually was, but still it wasn't perfect. Not quite as clear as it had
been before the feral displacement. He couldn't make out their
faces, but he could track their bodies, watch them move.

They paused as they entered the room. The taller, broader
form motioned the other to the side of the bed and indicated he
would round it.

Not likely. If they separated, taking them down would be
harder. Just another second.

He waited, muscles bunching, and then with a snarl of rage
he was out of the bed.

He didn't question the adrenaline rushing through him; the
burst of power or the surge of strength that burned through his
body.

They were there, in Ria's room, too close to her. Too close to
his woman. Too close to endangering her. And that was intolerable.

He slammed the first against the wall as Ria screamed. Beneath a well-placed powerful kick to his kidneys the second
went down and rolled in pain.

The enemy should have been dead. Only a last-second thought saved him from it as the first shadow flew at Mercury.

It had to be a Breed. Nothing else could be so fucking strong.

Light flared in the room, momentarily blinding Mercury's sight but not his senses.

His arm snaked out, throwing the Breed back, slamming into the dresser with enough force that wood cracked as he felt the second coming for his head.

His arm flashed out, his hand wrapping around a throat, the other knocking the weapon from the other's hand. Slamming into the wall, his sight still fuzzy, adjusting from dark to light, Mercury snarled in the intruder's face.

"You want to let him go, mate," a hard voice informed him as the barrel of a gun pressed into his neck.

Mercury froze.

"Mercury." The sound of Ria's voice inflamed him.

Instinct had his hand flashing up, jerking the gun to the side as it discharged and his elbow slammed back at the same moment the voice penetrated his mind.

"Dane!" Ria screamed the name as Mercury's vision cleared, his eyes locking on the pale blue gaze, the bulging eyes of Ryan DeSalvo, the bodyguard who traveled with Dane Vanderale.

Mercury loosened his grip only enough to keep from killing the other man before turning, his eyes falling to Dane himself as Ria bent over him, her gaze locked on Mercury in horror.

He loosened DeSalvo slowly, watching as the other man sort of slid down the wall, choking on the oxygen pouring back into his system.

Dane was also breathing.

Mercury snarled again as Ria lifted Dane's head to her lap. He couldn't stop himself. Naked, enraged, he gripped her arm, dragging her to the side of the bed as she fought him.

Her fists struck his chest, tears fell from eyes.

"Do you want him to live?" he snarled into her face, the feral adrenaline still surging through his body as he gripped her shoulders and shook her just enough to force her to stare up at him. "Touch him, and he dies." He didn't recognize his own voice. "Do you understand me?"

"You're crazy!" she screamed. "He wasn't here to hurt me."

"And I knew this how?" He meant only to yell, but it came out as a primal roar. "How did I know? No scent, Ria. No warning." He shook her again. "How did I know?"

"I have to help him." She was crying. Crying for another man and she had never shed tears for him.

He lowered his face until they were nose to nose.

"Touch him, and he dies."

If she could have paled further, she did. Her face was stark white as he released her, growling. He was growling like a rabid animal. Releasing her slowly, his finger pointing at her as he stepped back for his clothes, warning her.

A movement from behind him had him turning and snarling furiously again. Half roar, half enraged growl. Ryan DeSalvo halted, his hand within touching distance of the weapon he had carried.

Behind Mercury, Ria's sobs were wrenching, tearing him apart.

He kicked the gun beneath the bed, spared a glance for the still living Vanderale and jerked his pants from the floor.

As the zipper locked he jumped across the bed, ignoring Ria's scream, and pressed her to the wall as the door slammed open and Breeds raced in.

Lawe and Rule, Jonas and Callan. They came to a jerking stop, staring in horrified shock at the tableau that met their eyes. Then swung to Mercury as he growled back at them warningly.

"Easy, Merc." Jonas was breathing harshly as he jerked the silken robe Ria had worn earlier from the floor and tossed it to him. "Take care of your woman. We have this."

Merc caught the robe, feeling his blood pounding in fury at the thought of anyone seeing Ria naked. Seeing her bend over Dane, naked, her long silken hair flowing around her, he had wanted to kill Dane. Rip his throat out. Had Dane been conscious, Mercury wondered if he wouldn't have done just that.

He turned back to her, helping her into the robe as the tears continued to fall from her eyes.

"Keep crying for that bastard and I'm going to lose my mind," he bit out, that hard, violent rasp of his voice causing her to flinch.

"You've already lost your mind." She slapped his shoulder, hard. She could have punched him in the face and he knew it. The fact that she pulled back was a testament to her fear.

He tied her robe around her waist gently.

"Get dressed." He was fighting the surge of adrenaline now. "Get enough clothes on that I don't go crazy. Do it now."

Ria stared up at him, swallowing tightly as the blue burned in his eyes now, mixing so deeply with the hammered gold that it was hard to tell the true color of his eyes. They glowed in the savage features of his face. Feral rage tightened every plane and angle and warned her that he hadn't yet gotten control of the fury raging through him.

She slid around him, casting a look toward Dane despite Mercury's growl of protest. He was alive. Bloody, but Callan and Jonas and the two Breeds surrounded him, as did Ryan. Or Rye, as Dane had a habit of calling him.

Rye was battered, bloodied, his shirt nearly torn from him and his throat bruised. Dane looked worse. Blood matted his tawny hair, smeared across his face, and his lips were bleeding, his nose.

She glanced back at Mercury. He had his back to her, his hands braced against the wall, ignoring all of it as he obviously fought to get hold of himself.

What the hell had happened?

She gathered her clothes together. Jeans and socks, a bulky sweater. Enough clothes that he wouldn't lose his mind, he had warned her.

She slipped into the bathroom, uncertain what to think, what to feel. Uncertain who or what the animal was that her lover had turned into.

◆   ◆   ◆

"Fuck." Dane came around with a slow, slurred curse as Mercury dropped his hands from the wall and turned back to the room.

He stalked across the room, jerked a clean shirt from the dresser that had had its top cracked clean through, and tugged it on over his head.

It was tighter than normal. His jaw clenched. Feral displacement.

He pushed his fingers through his hair and fought it back. The need to kill was like a hunger burning inside him. He turned and focused on Ryan DeSalvo and Dane Vanderale, and his lips tugged into a primal, silent snarl.

"They slipped into the fucking room," he bit out. "Nothing but shadow and they thought I wouldn't attack?"

Ryan lifted his gaze from his boss, and Mercury saw the suspicion in his eyes. Just as he saw it in everyone else's.

"He's right." Ryan shook his head and breathed out roughly. "Dane slipped in. He likes to play games with Ria. Hell, he thought it would be funny to scare the hell out of her. We didn't know she had company until we were already in the room."

"Li'l witch never has company." Dane chose that moment to cough out the accusation. "She's so damned grouchy no one can put up with her long enough to stay in a bed all night beside her." He cracked his eyes opened and focused on Mercury. "Figures it's you."

Callan's growl was intimidating, furious. "You slipped past her guards, broke into her cabin and thought for one damned minute that you could sneak up on the Breed sleeping with her?" He jerked to his feet, his long tawny hair unrestrained and flowing around his shoulders. "Son of a bitch. Do you know what? Vanderale can shove its fucking money because I'm sick of your games." He jabbed his finger toward Dane. "Obviously genetics fucked up with you, Dane, because anyone of the first Leo would have better sense."

"Hybrid," Ryan snorted. "Just wait, Lyons, you'll find out what fun raising a hybrid is."

"He tries to slip up on me again and he'll find out how a hybrid dies," Mercury snapped, barely in control, but hanging on to it as Dane sat up slowly.

"Get him out of here." Jonas rose to his feet, his gaze meeting Mercury's, his silver eyes flat and hard. "Out to the living room and patch his ass up before I finish it off for him."

He ran his hands over his short hair, and Mercury's jaw bunched as they helped the other Breed to his feet.

"Dane." That growl was still in his voice.

Dane turned his head painfully, wincing at the movement.

"Invade our bedroom again without warning, and I'll kill you."

"You're not killing anyone. If you were, you would have done it tonight." Ria stepped from the bathroom.

Mercury swung around, and something inside him stilled instantly.

She wasn't pale or crying. Her eyes glittered with irritation, and a flush of anger mounted her cheeks. She was dressed in jeans and a bulky sweater and there was nothing to threaten whatever primal rage had built inside him at the thought of her nakedness being revealed in front of the others.

But she wasn't happy with him either. He could hear it in her voice, seeing it in the look she shot him.

"Hell," Dane muttered. "Rye, did we bring the knapsack?"

Rye grimaced. "It's in the living room."

"Don't worry." Dane was limping as they helped him from the room. "I have your fucking bribe."

Ria laid her bling on the cabinet. It was quite a nice haul: several nearly perfect diamonds, emeralds so brilliant they were nearly blinding and a tiger's-eye stone that swirled with magic and majesty.

She slid the stones into a velvet bag, tied it off and tucked it into the pocket of her jeans, then flipped her sat phone closed and erased the speed dial set to go straight to Leo's emergency number. Her threat to Dane. Had the bribe not pleased her, she would have called and tattled to hell and back.

She wasn't mercenary. It wasn't the worth of the stones or even the stones themselves. It was the fact that they seemed to keep Dane from involving her in games that were too messy to consider allowing Leo to catch them in. She was a sucker for the games herself, but she did have a bit of caution. Dane had none.

To say Mercury was upset over the payment was putting things mildly. There were still tiny, rumbling growls echoing in his throat. And those tiny sparks of blue hadn't completely left his eyes.

Feral displacement was a phenomenon that Breeds couldn't control, though, and he had all the signs of it, but it was firmly under control. Dane still had his heart in his chest, and Rye still had his head on his shoulders. Ria was contenting herself with that even though she suspected Dane might have lost more blood than was wise.

"Look at her, Rye." His tone was amused despite the pain in it. "I'm surprised she didn't pull her jeweler's glass out."

She turned to face him, her insides still shaking, the knowledge of how close Dane had actually come to dying horrified her.

"You have a trip scheduled to Asia next week," she told him. "I expect natural pearls when you return."

He gave her a hooded look and glanced at the velvet bag. "I just paid you a fortune."

"Two fortunes aren't enough for what you put me through tonight," she snapped, feeling the tears clog her throat again. "You've lost your mind, Dane." She couldn't control the accent that slipped into her voice either, and she knew every man in the room could smell her pain and her fear.

Dane grimaced at that, his gaze sliding to where Mercury attempted to place her behind him once again.

"I'd say you've slipped the path a bit yourself, love," he drawled. "Why doesn't it surprise me that you've mated a feral?"

"There's no mating." Mercury snarled the denial, and Ria thought her heart was going to break.

Hell, he could have just remained silent.

Dane stared between them, his golden brown eyes thoughtful for long moments.

"My mistake," he finally said slowly as he glanced to Rye. "She can't do anything the easy way, can she?"

Rye laid his head back on the couch and stared at the ceiling while Dane settled into the corner and stared back at the other Breeds in the room. Especially his brothers.

"Don't start," she warned him as she slid around Mercury once again, certain Dane was going to begin baiting Callan and Jonas. "This has gone too far."

Dane shrugged. "Very well. You called for extraction. Pack your bags and I'll have the limo sent from the private airfield we landed at. Rye and I hiked in. I doubt you want to take that path out, though. We'll have you safe and sound in your own bed within hours. Wouldn't that be nice?"

Her lonely, cold bed. Without Mercury's hard, warm body.

She turned back to the others, her gaze moving over Callan and Jonas's suspicious, savage expressions. They weren't pleased, and they knew something was going on.

"It's gone too far," she told Dane.

He stared back at her coolly. "You're going to get your heart broke, love. You know what that does to you. Makes Leo damned growly. And Elizabeth will try to fuss over you. You know how you hate that."

His voice was gentle, a reminder of how easily she could be

hurt, and a warning. The warning came a second before Mercury's arms surrounded her, warm and strong, and he pulled her close against his chest.

His head lowered, his lips at her ear. "You're not leaving." He nipped the shell of her ear after growling the demand against it.

Ria's gaze remained locked with Dane's, and she knew he saw what she was trying to hide even from herself.

"We have to finish this, Dane." She let her hands grip Mercury's wrists, aware of the suspicion directed on her now. "It can't go any further."

Mercury tensed behind her; Callan and Jonas watched her with hard, implacable expressions.

"Well then, I guess that's that." He relaxed farther back into the couch, a mocking smile crossing his lips. "If I don't make it out of here alive, be sure to tell the Leo I did him proud," he chuckled.

Ria shook her head and turned to Callan. "Pride Leader Lyons, it is my sincerest regret to inform you that I wasn't sent here in any way to track expenditures by Sanctuary from the Vanderale support funds. As always, those have been given by the Leo, your father, and they have no strings attached."

Callan rose slowly to his feet, power humming through him, his amber eyes brightening, glowing as animalistic anger began to surge inside him.

"What the hell have you two been doing in my fucking home?" He glared between them.

"Protecting it." Dane surged to his feet as well, drawing Callan's focus from Ria to him. "Remember, mate, she's my employee. You have a problem with that, you'll take it up with me."

Callan swung back to Ria, the look on his face so filled with anger that for a moment she swore she was facing the Leo.

"Back down, Callan," Mercury growled, trying to push her behind his larger body again. "Let's see what she has to say first."

"What she has to say?" Callan's voice boomed through the cabin as Jonas moved warily to his feet. "You want me to hear what she has to say? She came into my home on a lie? Under this little bastard's orders." He shoved his finger toward Dane.

"I should point out, Leo and Elizabeth *were* wed before my conception."

Callan turned and snarled in his face. Nose to nose. The rage emanating from him was a terrible thing to see.

"See why he brings me bribes," Ria murmured to Callan. "This is what I have to put up with when Leo finds out I've helped him in one of his games. But it's usually my face Leo's screaming into."

She moved to Mercury's side, pushing at his restraining arm to no avail as Callan swung on her. He took one look at Mercury's face before growling furiously and pacing to the other side of the room.

"That's what Leo does when Elizabeth gets in front of him," she whispered to Mercury. Almost amused. If it had been Leo, she might have been amused, but who knew which way Callan's genetics had actually swung?

He turned back to them and glared at her. "I can hear every word out of your mouth," he snapped.

"Keep snarling at me." She watched him warily though her tone was airy. "I'll get half a dozen perfect pearls next week rather than the few scrawny ones he would have brought me otherwise." She shrugged, burying her fear. When one dealt with Breeds, one never admitted to fear. Even to oneself.

"What have you been doing in my home?" His tone sliced through the room, and Ria swallowed tightly. Even Dane appeared a bit wary.

"Tracking the person or persons responsible for slipping information about Breed mating heat and age depression to a pharmaceutical company researching a drug to exploit its ability to work on the human body. Three non-Breeds have already died and one is missing due to that research, and scientific information regarding it is leaking from your home, Pride Leader Lyons."

"Impossible," he snarled furiously. "Every transmission, every fax, every breath taken in that compound is monitored. There's no way to slip that information out. Not without being caught."

"There is, though," she told him softly. "If you're trained in creating a code to carry it, then you can slip anything out. Unless someone trained to break that code finds it. I found the code, Mr. Lyons; now I just have to break it."

Silence filled the room. Jonas, Callan and Dane all stared at her in suspended disbelief.

"You can pay up when we get back to the office," Rye commented to Dane from his position on the couch. "I told you she'd do it in less than a month."

"Are you telling me someone within the estate house has been giving secrets to some fucking bastard Council researchers? And he knew about it?" His finger pointed imperiously to Dane.

She breathed in slowly. "No, Pride Leader. Someone is selling secrets concerning mating heat to a drug manufacturer who is now experimenting on non-Breeds. And they're doing it for money."

The roar of rage that shook the cabin had her flinching, and this time she stepped behind Mercury willingly. Because in over twenty years of dealing with the Leo, she had never, not even once, seen the rage in him that now filled his son.

And Leo had never, in all the years Dane had been an adult, jumped for Dane as Callan did. It took Jonas, Rye and Mercury to pull him back, as Dane rose slowly to his feet and Ria watched the compassion flicker across his features.

The moment he was pulled back, Callan jerked from the others' hold, stalked to the other side of the room and fought for control.

She watched his shoulders bunching, tensing, as Mercury moved back to her, obviously protecting her.

"Perhaps we should have been a bit more delicate," Dane commented with a snort. "It seems the pride leader has a bit of a temper."

"Ms. Rodriquez, is the Leo's number on your speed dial?" Jonas asked carefully.

Ria remained silent.

"He's on mine, whelp," Dane grunted. "Would you like to call him and tell him what we're investigating? Go ahead, split his loyalties between Sanctuary and the twins my mother just gave birth to before flying out to save her older son. I'm certain those babes don't need her, even if they do appear to be ill at the moment." Disgust laced his voice. "Why the bloody hell do you think he doesn't know about it now?"

That wouldn't stop Leo from blasting her and Dane both with his anger, though, once he learned about it.

"Callan." Ria stepped forward, ignoring Mercury's warning growl as Callan turned, his head lowered, those dangerous eyes watching her closely, the rage burning in him so close to the surface that it washed from him in waves. "Any coup needs an event to give it momentum. You were nearly killed and you've been recovering from it. Your senses aren't back to peak, Sanctuary is ripe for a takeover. Someone is moving to destroy you from the inside out. If the information Dane uncovered is correct, then it's only a matter of weeks before those secrets are completely shifted to the researchers. We can't risk that. My job was to uncover the culprit or culprits. And there were very few people we were certain weren't involved in this, until I had spent some time with those files myself."

"We knew you weren't involved," Dane told him, his voice harsh. "But other than that, we couldn't be certain. Whoever is moving on you and getting this information out is a strong enough force that other Breeds, enough of them, may back him."

"There are very few Breeds strong enough to do that," Callan snapped.

"Exactly," Dane agreed. "We couldn't risk the information being leaked, and you trust your inner circle with your life. We had to make certain no one in that inner circle was involved before coming to you."

Callan turned to Mercury then. "There was no order to relieve you of your rank," he told him. "And there was no order to confiscate your weapon, your uniform or to force you into testing."

"You have interoffice memos being falsified?" Dane's eyes narrowed. "Are you using the tracking equipment we sent you last year?

The caustic look Callan shot him was thick with disgust.

"So you are." Dane grimaced. "Have you traced them yet?"

"We're still working on it."

"Many of the memos coming from Sanctuary to the research institute and subsidiary contacts have come from one office," Ria informed them then. "I've traced the information piggybacking memos as well as scientific purchases to three locations directly connected to Brandenmore Research."

"Who?" Callan's voice was dangerous, savage, the enraged primal male just beneath the surface rising to the fore once more.

"From the Breed labs," she said softly. "Dr. Elyiana Morrey's office. And from Pride Leader Lyons's personal computer."

◆   ◆   ◆

Mercury braced his hands on the table and stared at the proof Ria had managed to slip from the files and electronic messages she had duplicated from the office she worked in at Sanctuary. Proof that their safeguards weren't worth shit, because under the watchful eye of the security cameras she had managed to slip the most incriminating evidence against Ely from the labs. The evidence was pretty damned incriminating against Callan as well.

"I'm not entirely convinced, either way in regards to Dr. Morrey's involvement," she stated. "But my suspicions against her have risen by the day. Her aggression when I refused to submit myself to her testing procedures upon my arrival. Her determination to induce the feral adrenaline in Mercury's system, and her insistence that he be confined. Mercury was trained in a variety of highly sensitive and exacting areas before the feral displacement showed itself. And even after, many of the areas he excelled in still carried high ratings."

"How the hell do you know that?" Jonas snapped. "Most of the Breed records from his lab were destroyed."

"Vanderale Industries was hacking labs while you were still in nappies," Dane sneered back at him. "We've had those files for years. Leo was arranging an op against that particular lab to rescue several of the Breeds when news hit that the labs were being hit. Mercury was one of the Breeds he was most concerned about."

Mercury glanced up at him silently.

Dane sighed. "You're trained in code, Mercury. Don't bother denying it. We've seen your files. You're trained to both create and crack sensitive coding. It was part of several of your missions."

"Not like this." Mercury waved his hands to the printouts of the information spread out over the kitchen table. I was trained in military code, not in whatever they're doing here."

But he could see the threads of it. If he had been going through the transmissions himself, he would have caught it, even if he couldn't decipher it.

"You were one of the most successful creations the Council had attained. You're the strongest of the enforcers and you command incredible loyalty. The only reason you don't head your own command is because you turned it down." Dane shook his head. "Humble doesn't become you."

Mercury shot him a scorching glare. "Humble has never been a concern of mine either. I don't command because what I do is better served working alone. It's that simple."

"And it hides from those who may tell the tale the fact that you've been experiencing the feral adrenaline," Dane pointed out mockingly. "You've known the feral displacement could be returning."

"I handle it." He shrugged. He had been handling it for years, and he had informed Jonas of his suspicions. That was all he had been required to do.

"Mercury's loyalty or his ability to handle himself has never come under question," Callan informed them, his voice cold now.

The rage had solidified to icy determination. Mercury glanced up at his pride leader, meeting his gaze across the table, and felt the certainty of Callan's trust. It eased the anger that had built at the thought that his pride leader, the man he had sworn his loyalty to, could have distrusted him.

"How many know you didn't send those communiqués out?" Dane asked him.

Callan's nostrils flared. "Kane and Jonas. Kane's running the diagnostics on the orders that went out, using Vanderale equipment. Neither Ely nor the security tech is aware I didn't send those orders."

Dane nodded at that as he crossed his arms over his chest and stared down at the various information Ria had slipped from her office.

"The information was piggybacked on these electronic memos and purchases." She slid them free and lined them up. "I ran a diagnostic on each message, and you can see the code that was inserted within it. It was attached to individual letters within words. That technology is so new that Vanderale is even still playing with it. Brandenmore Research has their own electronics branch, though, and they could have refined the program for limited use such as this." She tapped her fingers against the code that had generated once she printed out the messages using the program Vanderale had invented to display it. "It's taken most of a week to track this down, and from the looks of it, the rumors that the information is being sent in stages with a deadline appear correct."

"This came from my office." Callan slid one of the messages free. "An order for office electronics. It's an order I sent," he snarled.

"It is. And it's a duplicate." She slid free of the pile another memo that included the coding. "This one is from your computer." She tapped his. "This one is the one that actually went out in transmission."

He looked up at her slowly. "Someone is managing to intercept the transmissions before they go out and attach this coding?"

She inhaled slowly as she nodded. "That's the beauty of this particular technology, and the danger of it."

Callan's fists clenched, his expression tightening further.

"How many departments at Sanctuary have been compromised?"

"So far, I've found it in nearly every department," she told him quietly. "The main deliveries are coming from the labs though. Part of my transmission to Dane earlier in the day was a request for the beta program to detect the coding as it goes out. When I asked for the heli-jet, it was actually a request for that."

Mercury glanced at her, pride filling him at the thought of just how intelligent she truly was. He was still uncertain of the anger he could feel pulsing just below the surface, and he had no idea how she was going to handle what she had seen when Dane slipped into the bedroom.

But she stood beside him now, allowing him the ease he needed in knowing she was safe.

Damn the Council scientists. This woman should have been his, completely his. Not just his woman but his mate. Every instinct inside him reached out to her, held on to her. And he knew the lack of mating heat hurt her.

She had no idea how much it hurt him as well.

"How soon can it be installed?" Callan questioned her.

"How well do you trust the people overseeing the outgoing transmissions?" she asked him. "This can't be used or installed without their knowledge, Callan."

"All communications, outbound as well as in, go through one secured office in the communications bunker," Callan informed her. "That office is overseen by my sister Sherra. She has four Lionesses working beneath her, each that she's trained herself."

"How well can she trust her assistants then?" Ria asked.

Mercury glanced at her. Her attitude had always been respectful toward Callan, not once had she shown so much as a shred of disrespect. But she wasn't backing down in what she knew, or in her suspicions.

"Ely can't be behind any of this, nor is she involved." Jonas had finally spoken up, and Mercury heard the certainty in his voice. It was a certainty he didn't share.

"Ely's running scared," Ria said softly, compassion lacing her voice because, Mercury knew, she was aware that Ely was more than just a friend to all of them.

"Ely's kept us sane." Lawe moved in behind Jonas, staring at the evidence on the table before staring back at Ria bitterly. "She's not capable of this."

"How secure are the labs?" she asked then.

Jonas grimaced. "No one in or out without clearance, retinal scan and fingerprint authorization. They then pass the security post. Even Breeds coming in for testing are escorted in by the enforcer on duty."

"Do you trust the enforcers on duty?" Ria asked.

"Fuck, are we allowed to trust anyone now?" Callan growled. "They're Breeds. They're men and women who survived hell and know the consequences should we ever lose public approval. I can't imagine anyone in Sanctuary capable of this." His finger stabbed into the papers lying before him.

"Yet you know yourself that even your most trusted personnel can be compromised," she pointed out gently. "Taber proved that."

Mercury looked back to Callan. They all remembered that. When Callan's brother Tanner had brought his mate to Sanctuary, she had also brought with her information that an attempted kidnapping of Callan's son was in the works. Taber, a Lioness entrusted with David's care, had been the one to attempt to kidnap the child, as well as Tanner's mate, Scheme.

"Yeah, Taber proved that." Callan wiped his hand over his face and glanced at the watch on his wrist. "My mate and my children are alone at Sanctuary, and we have a greater risk now than we did then."

"I contacted Jackal, Callan," Jonas told him quietly. "He informed Kane, to let the others know to be on guard with their mates and their children. They're safe."

But for how much longer? Mercury lifted his gaze to Lawe and Rule before turning to Jonas.

"We need Rule and Lawe back at Sanctuary. The main family is of prime importance and only God knows what could happen if someone actually decided to attempt a coup right now. We have the party tomorrow night, as well as visiting dignitaries arriving the night after. We can't take any chances with David or the unborn child's life. We all know just how badly both Council and non-Council scientists would love to get their hands on a mate or child born of those matings."

"It's too late to cancel the parties," Jonas murmured.

"And you don't want to cancel them," Ria said. "Horace Engalls of Engalls Pharmaceuticals will be there if I remember the guest list correctly. As well as the CEO of Brandenmore Research. Let's see what we can detect during these parties. They have no idea we're onto them," she stated. "Let's play them right back."

"How?" Mercury could feel her mind working; he could feel the confidence and certainty pouring out of her.

"Put Lawe on Horace Engalls. Rule on Phillip Brandenmore. Close quarters. Have Lionesses on their guests. Make certain there's no way to transfer information while they're here."

"Whoever's transferring information will know we're onto them," Mercury pointed out before Jonas or Callan could. But he was thinking, moving through the security that had been designed for both parties and working it out in his head. "They'll have to use the transmissions," he said then. "We'll have the program installed and ready to use. If they can't transfer information face-to-face, they'll have to use the transmissions quickly."

"Exactly. We pinpoint the computers these memos originated from. The Vanderale program can do that, and it can intercept and toss the emails, personal chat messages or memos back to Callan's program with no one being the wiser. Callan,

Kane, Dane and Rye can set a schedule to monitor it without causing suspicion."

"True." Dane spoke up then. "We were invited to the party after all."

Mercury couldn't halt the growl that came to his throat as Dane moved closer to Ria. Dane grinned at the sound and backed away once again.

"You're going to have to let me get back in her good graces, Mercury," he told him with a chuckle. "Otherwise, she'll end up costing me a fortune in jewels."

"That's okay," Ria murmured absently as she continued to spread the papers around the table. "Bling is always nice."

She didn't sound particularly concerned about letting Dane back into her good graces or allowing him to distract her from whatever she was putting together.

Mercury moved behind her, staring over her shoulder, watching as she moved the pages, studied them, then moved them again. When she was finished, the code laid out began to look more familiar.

"Do you see it?" she asked him, shifting a page before turning it upside down. Another right side up.

"It's a Council code," Mercury realized as he narrowed his eyes at it. "Son of a bitch."

Jonas and Callan both moved in closer.

"What are you looking at?" Jonas bit out.

Mercury looked down at Ria as she turned her head and stared at him.

"This is why they wanted you out of the way," she whispered.

"I don't see a damned thing that looks familiar, Mercury," Jonas snapped. "And I know Council code as well as you."

"It's not just mating heat they're after," Mercury breathed out roughly. "This code was developed in one place only. The labs I was created in. This code," Mercury tapped several lines of the attached transmissions, "it's the code for feral displacement. They're attempting to duplicate it."

As he stared at the code, bits and pieces began to show a pattern. Numbers, glyphs, scientific formulas began to come together. He shook his head. Hell, it had been too damned long since he had done this. "It would take months to piece all this information together without the key to the code."

"We don't need the key to the code to stop them," Ria told

him, turning back to the papers before glancing back at Callan and Jonas. "Whoever's behind this knows Mercury's lab history, the tests he excelled in as well as the experimentation done on him in regards to the feral displacement. Adult Breeds were killed when they began showing it. Mercury is one of the few they allowed to live. Whoever's doing this knows that."

"And Ely knows it," Mercury said dispassionately.

Like Jonas, he found it hard to believe the doctor they had depended on would be the one to betray them. But unlike Jonas, he had firsthand experience in just how far Ely would go to prove he should be locked up, confined, drugged.

The drugs for the feral displacement had made him easier to control, had turned him into an automaton. By time the drug therapy had taken hold, he hadn't even been certain which world he existed within, or rather which one he fought within. It was a world she would have returned him to.

"Can you slip Dane into the estate tonight to install the program?" Ria asked Callan. "He'll also need access to the main security terminal in the communications bunker."

"I can get him in," Jonas stated.

"We have about eighteen hours to get installed and running," she added.

Mercury was there when she turned to him. He backed up just enough to meet her eyes, to watch as her gaze moved from his just as quickly as she'd met it, then moved away again.

"You behave." She pointed to Dane as she moved quickly from the living room back to the bedroom. Mercury let his gaze slide to Dane's then.

Dane arched a tawny brow mockingly. "Feral displacement," he murmured. "Interesting."

Mercury glared back at him. "She's not in any danger."

"I never imagined she was." He grinned. "You know, I have to admit, life has livened up a bit since the Leo revealed himself to this pride. I can see I'm going to have to pace the amusements or I may burn myself out."

"Shut up, Vanderale," Jonas ordered him as Mercury stared back at Dane, refusing to be baited by him.

"Invade her bedroom again and you'll be more than burned out, you'll be bled out," he told him.

"Hmm," Dane murmured. "Too bad you can't mate though. She would have made a fine mate. A wonderful mother."

Mercury's chest clenched. He stared back at Dane, wishing he had killed him when he had the chance.

"Dane," Jonas growled. "That's enough."

"Yes, it is." Dane shot Mercury a caustic look. "No worries, my friend. When she's had enough of the hardheaded Breeds here, she'll return home." His smile was smug, confident. "And when she does, I'll be waiting."

Mercury closed the bedroom door, locked it, then attached the small, rectangular temporary alarm over the crevice between the door and the frame.

He moved to the window, attached another alarm and then turned to face her.

Ria resisted the urge to rub her hands over her arms as she stepped from the bathroom, once again in her gown, weariness dragging at her as she caught a glimpse of his face.

Primal and wild just didn't do his expression justice. It was suffused with sensual lust, his eyes glowing with it, the flesh stretched taut over the hard planes and angles of his face.

The clean white silk gown she wore might as well not have been on her body. The way he was looking at her stripped it from her, revealed the hardened tips of her breasts and the dew she knew was accumulating on the curls between her thighs.

"Has Vanderale been your lover?" he asked her, his voice rough, grating with animalistic fervor.

Ria swallowed tightly. "Not in this lifetime. I grew up watching that man play more games than a chess master."

She had no intentions of allowing him to play games with her heart or her emotions. And Dane wasn't above it. He was a good man, but his focus was set on the protection of his parents and the Breeds rapidly making their mark in society. He would do whatever it took to protect both. And if that meant breaking her heart, he would apologize, he would regret it, but he would do it over and over again.

"And when you leave here?" He stripped his T-shirt off his body, before sitting down in the chair in the corner and unlacing his boots efficiently. "Will you take him to your bed after being with me?"

When she left here. She turned her back on him, straightening the laptop and files she had placed on the small table by the bed, trying not to let herself feel hurt at his easy acceptance that she would leave him. That things wouldn't last between them.

She finally shrugged and said, "I have no intentions of going to bed with Dane."

Could she allow any man in her bed now that she had been with Mercury? The thought of it sent a sharp, painful spike of denial racing through her mind.

She straightened and turned back to him, breathing in roughly at the sight of him naked, aroused. Damn, were all Breeds this sexual?

He moved to her, muscles rippling beneath the dark bronze flesh, the light in the room picking up the shimmer of that fine, silken pelt that covered them.

She loved the feel of those tiny hairs against her flesh, stroking over her, caressing her.

"Are you ready for me to leave already?" she whispered, trying to hold back the hurt as she couldn't hold back the question.

She didn't want to leave him. She never wanted to be without him.

"Can I kidnap you?" he asked her as his hands stroked over her shoulders, her fingers curling against his chest. "When this is over, I want to tie you to my bed and make certain Dane Vanderale can never bribe you away from my side."

She stared up at him, feeling her heart melt. His eyes softened, filled with hunger and desire, and truth.

"You don't want me to leave?"

"I want you in my bed, by my side, for as long as I can keep you, Ria." His hand cupped her cheek. "But after what you saw tonight, can you stand to be there?"

Her lips parted.

"You were crying for him," he growled down at her. "Tears were falling from your eyes and you knelt over him, naked, your hair stroking him."

Jealousy throbbed in his voice. Complete primal male Breed jealousy. They were completely territorial over their women. Ria knew that, had seen it with Leo and Elizabeth several times over the years.

Ria felt herself tremble at the memory.

"I thought he was dead." A frown snapped between her brows

as she moved back from him. "He may not be my lover but he is my friend."

"A friend that slipped into your bedroom while you lay naked in my arms. A friend that knew I lay there with you," he pointed out. "The same friend who informed me that when this was over he would be waiting for you when you returned home."

Surprise had her turning back to him, watching him closely. He was completely comfortable being aroused and nude.

"Dane is as adept at his little games as Jonas is." She shrugged as she moved to straighten the bed. "But I'll not defend myself over something that hasn't happened or whether or not it will happen if you're no longer a part of my life."

"I will always be a part of your life."

The sound of his voice, the large body suddenly behind her, the erection pressing between her thighs, rubbing against the slick, heated cleft there had the breath catching in his throat.

Just as he had over the desk in the office, he bent her over the bed now, his palms flat against the mattress, his larger, harder body holding her in place as her head snapped up in surprise.

"Will you, Mercury?" she asked him, uncertainty filling her voice. "Breeds mate. They mate their other half."

He tensed against her, a violent tension; it poured out of him and whipped in the air, tightening around her chest with spiked bonds that she thought would break her heart.

"I could not want another woman the way I want you." He nipped her neck. "Mating heat be damned. There are enough anomalies in it that it can get fucked as far as I'm concerned."

Tears filled her eyes as he turned her, stretched her out beneath him and held her trapped to the bed despite her struggles.

"Let me go, Mercury." She shook her head, pressing her hands against his chest as she fought to be free.

She wasn't going to let him see her tears. She wasn't going to cry about something she had no hope of fighting, no way of changing. She had learned better than that years ago.

"I can't let you go."

His voice, the guttural roughness of it, the spike of need and emotion that filled her, had her fighting hope. And she had never been good at fighting hope.

"Mercury." Her breathing hitched, the emotion nearly strangling her now. "You'll mate, someone, sometime."

"That time is past," he ground out.

"And she *was* your mate," she flashed back at him, the anger at that tearing through her. "You loved her so desperately you nearly went insane when you lost her. I'll always be second."

"You'll always be first," he snarled in her face, silencing her, the blue highlights in his eyes increasing, glowing, as his voice thickened with his hunger. "Always, Ria. Always first."

He pushed his hips between her thighs, spread her thighs, and before she could do more than gasp, he tore her gown down the center with strong, powerful hands.

"Tell me you don't want me," he demanded, the thick head of his cock pressing against dampened folds between her thighs. "Tell me now, Ria, that you could want another man as desperately as you need me right now."

She couldn't possibly desire anything in life as much as she desired Mercury. She couldn't ache, need or dream of anything as much as she did a life in his arms.

As she stared into his eyes earlier, while the feral rage consumed him and he fought to shield her nakedness from the others, she had known that nothing mattered but Mercury.

"I wasn't crying for Dane," she admitted. "I was crying because I was afraid."

He paused. "Of me?"

The first tear slipped free. "That they would try to steal you again. That they would see your protectiveness as the feral displacement. That I would lose you, Mercury. And I couldn't bear losing you."

Silence stretched between them, his hard body covering hers, his cock throbbing at the entrance to her body.

His hips shifted, parting her folds further, pushing inside her, slowly, until her flesh surrounded the thick, throbbing crown.

"I need you more than I need freedom." He lowered his head and whispered the words at her ear.

And more tears fell. Because she knew the Breeds' need for freedom, and she suspected his need for it was fiercer, stronger than any others'.

"You are my mate, Ria," he growled at her ear. "In my soul. You are my mate."

He moved inside her, burying himself deeper into the desperately clenching flesh awaiting him. She surrounded him, arched to him and let a cry fall from her lips.

"This is freedom." His growl was tight, thick with hunger. "Right here, buried inside you, racing through pleasure with you. This is my freedom."

Ria wrapped her arms around his shoulders and held on to him. Once he was deep inside her, she wanted nothing more than to feel him moving, thrusting.

He stilled instead, buried full-length, stretching her, burning her.

"Look at me, my sweet Ria." His lips brushed over hers. "Look at me, baby. See how much I need you. How much I want you."

She opened her eyes, her gaze blurring with the tears that ran from the corners of her eyes.

"No tears." He kissed them away. "Just you and me, Ria. Would you deny us both this? Would you walk away and return to the cold, when I could be right beside you, warming you?"

She couldn't. She could never return to the cold and she knew it. Not willingly. Not without hurting, without feeling the parts of her that Mercury owned now crying out in agony.

"You'll miss your mate," she whispered.

"How can I miss my mate?" He kissed the corner of her lips, licked at the lower curve. "She's right here, in my arms. I won't miss you, Ria, because I won't let you go."

He kissed her. His lips covered hers, his tongue slid inside and she tasted something wild, untamed, in his hunger. A subtle flavor that was there and gone just as quickly.

Her arms wrapped around his neck as she held on to him, feeling him move, feeling the heavy width of his erection stroking her slow and easy.

"There, baby," he groaned, his lips moving to her neck. "Hold me, nice and hot, just like that."

Milking him. She could feel her vagina milking his flesh, contracting around him, stroking him and being stroked as she flew in his arms.

The need built, consuming her, creating a flame unlike any sensation she had yet experienced with him. She writhed and twisted beneath him as his hips slammed against hers, burying his cock inside her as they groaned, moaned, cried out with each forward motion.

There was a tightening in her womb, stronger, deeper than before. A need for his taste that had her begging for his kiss, searching for his lips.

His tongue speared past them as his cock plunged inside her. They were racing with the pleasure, flames whipping through her, burning her as his tongue pumped into her mouth.

Closing her lips on it, she suckled as he pulled back, then reached in again. Instinct drove her to hold on to him, to lock him so deep inside her that there was never a risk of losing him.

"Hold me," she cried out, even as he did just that. Wrapping his arms around her, holding her close and taking her, pushing her, throwing her over the edge of madness as orgasm tore through her.

She exploded, fragmenting and melting around him as she arched and felt her womb contracting, her clit releasing the agony of need inside it as her sex clenched and pulsed.

His release drenched her, pumped into her with hard, heated blasts, and when his canines scraped her shoulder, she swore she came again.

She was flying with him. He was a part of her, spilling himself inside her, marking her with his teeth, his touch and his hunger. She would never be free of him. Yet she knew, as he had said earlier, that freedom existed in this. Just in being with him.

It was long moments before he lifted her to her pillows, dragged the sheet over them and turned off the lights. He didn't give her a chance to get cold, because his large, warm body wrapped around her.

"I don't know if I could keep from killing another man who touched you. Even Dane," he told her as he kissed the bite mark on her shoulder gently.

He always did that. Locked his teeth in her flesh as he growled his release, and that minute pain always sent fire streaking through her body and her orgasm tearing through her system.

Ria stared into the darkness then, feeling him inside her where he shouldn't have been able to invade her. He had broken down the shields surrounding her heart and stolen it more completely than any other ever had.

"I hate losing when I love," she whispered into the darkness.

Each time she did, she remembered being a child, only six, rocking herself in her mother's bed when night came and her mother hadn't returned to their small apartment.

She remembered being hungry and cold and being too frightened of the darkness to venture from the bed. She remembered crying for her mother, and knowing she wasn't coming back to her.

That same pain filled her each time she had allowed herself to feel security, or to feel love. Because each time she had done so, it had been taken from her. And she had never cared for anyone as she did Mercury.

"I won't leave you, Ria." The rumble of certainty in his voice had her relaxing in his arms. "I promise you. I'll keep you warm."

His mate was dead, she reminded herself. Gone forever. And Breeds only mated once. It wasn't as though someone could walk in and take him away from her.

He could belong to her. She could let herself belong.

She let the fear and anxiety seep from her until sleep stole over her. If she dreamed she heard her Breed purr behind her as she slept, then she marked it down to her own need to know, to belong to him as fully as she felt she was meant to.

If she felt his lips touch hers, and tasted something so wild and primitive that it drew a moan from her lips, filled her mouth, then she let herself sink deeper into the dream. Because she knew nothing could be this easy. Something or someone would take him from her. After all, now that she was playing with the ultimate fire, there was no way not to get burned.

◆   ◆   ◆

The animal waited until the man slept. Only when he slept was it safe to emerge. The man was watching, on guard, strengthening his control against the animal's freedom.

But here in sleep, with his defenses lowered for the woman, the animal found that smallest hint of freedom.

It stepped forward slowly, opened the man's eyes and stared at the woman. She slept curled against the man's chest, her expression at peace. There was a part of her that wasn't at peace, though.

The animal could feel her pain, even in her sleep, and it sought to comfort her. It let a soft rumble of a purr free, let it vibrate against her cheek as it reached out and felt her hair against the man's fingers.

She relaxed, a little. A little smile touched her lips, lips that parted to take the man's pleasure, the animal's pleasure. During those moments the animal could ease closer, feel more, and the man was unaware.

But still, the woman wasn't bound to him enough. The man feared her leaving. The Breed, the hybrid that had invaded their lair earlier, thought to take her from him later. The animal had felt the strength of that man's inner animal. There was no threat of a mating, but there was the threat that the man could touch her, mark her, possess her.

The animal couldn't allow it. It feared what the man feared, and no other could possess its mate. It slipped further from its cell, let itself stretch, just enough, just enough that the glands in the man's tongue began to thicken the slightest bit.

And the man searched for his woman, laid his lips against hers and slid his tongue inside.

The animal snarled silently, and made certain there was more of the taste that would bind the woman to him. Enough to feed into her system, to make certain no other could take her, no other would be allowed to claim her.

As the kiss aroused both man and animal, it retreated once again. The man sighed and tucked his head against her shoulder, his tongue licking over the primal bite he had left on her once again.

The remainder of the hormone fed into that bite, into her flesh.

The power it took for the animal to slip so silently, to control itself with such exacting precision was wearying. If only the man did not regard the animal with horror. If only the man didn't reinforce the chains surrounding the animal each time he awoke, it wouldn't have been so hard.

The animal would merge with the man if he would allow it. It would protect that man and the female. It would pour its strength into the man and allow him to be the Breed he had been created to be.

For now, weariness flowed over it. It collapsed within its chains once again and let itself rest. Not a true sleep, for there was fear of the darkness and the eternal night it had known for so many years.

◆　　◆　　◆

The next morning dawned cold. There was a hint of snow in the air, and as Ria and Mercury stepped from the cabin to the limo waiting outside the door, she realized winter was definitely on for the mountains where the Breeds made their home.

She was bundled tight in a long leather coat Mercury had produced for her. She wore another skirt, but only because he had taken her jeans away from her when she went to dress.

Not that Ria was a jeans person; she wasn't. Even her casual wear was mostly dresses. Jeans were only used where a skirt or a dress couldn't or wouldn't apply. She had to admit the skirt outfits and dresses she had brought with her were the worst she owned, though. They were her "persona" clothes, not her preferred attire.

Today she wore one of the better outfits she had brought, however. The skirt wasn't bulky; it was soft cotton with a little flare at the knees, and the drab gray color didn't detract from the attractive cut of the cloth. The matching long-sleeved light sweater made her brown eyes seem darker, maybe a little bit prettier.

Ria wasn't big on her own looks. She knew she was rather plain. Her eyes were her best feature; they were thickly lashed and dark and matched her darker flesh, compliments of her father's Puerto Rican–American roots.

As she slid into the warmth of the limo and Mercury moved in snugly against her, Ria couldn't help but think about the mother she barely remembered, the father she hadn't known since his death while she was still an infant.

She had been so alone that sometimes, over the years, she had ached at that loneliness. Until Mercury. Until he stepped forward and filled all those cold, empty places, and made her wonder how she had survived without him.

But you couldn't fully appreciate, or fully miss, what you had never had, she reminded herself silently. Until Mercury, she'd had no idea the depth to which she could belong to another person. She hadn't known how easily she could lose in a man's arms the core element of exactly who and what she was.

And she had done that last night. When he had whispered that she was the mate of his soul. That she was his soul. When he had wrapped her in his arms, sheltered her with his body and eased her to sleep with his vows.

"You worry too much."

Ria looked up at her lover as his hand slid past the opening of her coat and smoothed beneath her skirt.

She had been off balance since waking. She couldn't seem to decide if she needed to cry or to throw his body to the ground and rub herself against it. Take him. Explode with him in ways she hadn't exploded with him yet.

He had taken her in the shower. He had taken her after that first cup of coffee, and still she burned inside for him.

"It's going to be difficult to make certain we have everything in place once we manage to trap the traitor in Sanctuary." She spoke low, even though Mercury had raised the window, and the driver, the Breed Lawe, had been present during the meeting the night before.

"Oh, he'll be caught. And he'll be dealt with." The underlying growl in his voice was one of retribution.

Ria shook her head. "There's more than one. Just one person couldn't pull this off."

"It doesn't matter how many there are." His hand slipped higher, causing her breath to catch as his fingers touched the damp material of her panties.

This time, his growl was sexy, sensual.

"You're still wet for me."

He lifted her into his arms, staring down at her, approval and arousal building in his eyes now.

"You're addictive, even without the mating heat." She pushed the fingers of one hand into his hair and drew his lips to hers.

She loved his kiss. The feel of his lips moving over hers, his hands holding her to him as his tongue twined with hers, and she swore there was just a hint, the slightest flavor from her dreams.

"That camera's coming out of that office today," he muttered against her lips. "Crowl can shove it up his ass if he wants to. There's no way I can wait all day to have you again."

Her heart raced at the knowledge that he hadn't had enough of her. And she was woman enough to admit that it fed that small little part of her ego that was completely female.

"Crowl might shake in his little shoes if you try to choke him again." She smiled against his lips, loving the feel of being this close to him. So close that they kissed as they spoke. That she could hear his heart beat against the side of her breast and the warmth of his body wrapping around her, stealing through the leather coat.

He pushed the leather from her shoulder, nudged her

sweater to the side and stole her breath as he licked over the mark he had left on her.

"I've never marked another woman," he told her, kissing the small bite gently. "Only you, Ria."

She hadn't known she needed that information, but she had. The vague fear rising inside her stilled at the knowledge that no one else, not even the girl who should have been his mate, had carried his mark.

Her head tilted farther to the side, and for the few moments of privacy that they had left, she luxuriated in his touch.

And Mercury liked to touch her. Stroke her hair. He'd refused to allow her to pin it up that morning. It flowed around her now, the thick, heavy length perfect for him to run his hands through and fill her with pleasure.

She kept her hair long for very specific reasons. The old maid look didn't go very well with short hair. Besides, short hair had a tendency to make her face look a bit chubby, not quite studious or severe enough. She had needed the studious look.

But she knew she would never cut it again now. Because of this. Her eyes fluttered closed in pleasure as his hands stroked through her hair and his tongue lapped at the wound on her neck.

"We're almost there," he growled.

She didn't want to be *there*. She wanted to be right here forever.

Suddenly, Ria had a very bad feeling about Sanctuary, one that went far deeper than the conspiracy she knew was building there. That female part of her was rising inside her, warning her. She had given too much of herself, and now she risked losing it all.

· C H A P T E R 1 5 ·

Callan and the others were taking care of adding the ghost program to the compound's server and systems, and within the office, camera covered, Ria took care of sending the various files
and information through the independent program she had attached to a ghost drive she was now able to use on the computer
system she had been given to work with.

There were no outside lines on the computer; it was completely self-contained. It wasn't even attached to the main compound server. There was no way out of it, no way inside it
except from the seat she was sitting in.

The ghost drive was simple. It attached to the computer as
another hard drive, but once it disconnected, all signs of it were
wiped completely from the computer it was attached to. There
was no way to tell it had ever been there.

Efficient for her, because it allowed her to go through the
files she needed to decrypt to reveal the code; very bad for Dr.
Elyiana Morrey, though. Because many of the transmissions Ria
had questioned had come from her office.

As she worked, she was very much aware of Mercury sitting
across from her. He did as he always did, read one of the magazines lying on the table beside the chair, but unlike always, her
skin prickled with the need to rub against him.

Rubbing against him was a pleasure in and of itself. The
fine, supersoft hair that covered Mercury's body was—unique.
The sensation was—oh, she really shouldn't go there.

"The look on your face is going to get you fucked."

Her head jerked up and she felt a flush suffuse her face at the
look he was giving her.

"Locking the door is easy." He glanced to that lock. "And
very simple."

She shook her head and turned back to her work. This part of her job was child's play. It was simply gathering the suspected files, sending them through the program, then saving to the ghost drive those that needed decrypting. The real job came when it was time to decrypt them.

"How close are you and Dane?" he asked a few minutes later.

Ria lifted her head slowly and stared back at him. He had laid the magazine aside and watched her, slouched in that chair, one ankle lying on the opposite knee, his elbow propped on the chair arm as he rubbed at his chin with his index finger. The pose was so sexy, so virile, she wanted to come from the sight of it alone. But the question, posed with just the right amount of serious interest, warned her there was more beneath the surface than a sexy, brooding male.

"Haven't we been through this?" she asked.

"No, we have satisfactorily answered whether or not you've slept with him or intend to sleep with him," he said to refute her. "That doesn't answer the question why he felt he could invade your bedroom or why he displays such an air of protectiveness toward you."

She shook her head at that.

"My mother worked for Vanderale. In the main office. When a neighbor heard of my mother's death, she contacted Dane to find out if I was in the car with her, because she hadn't heard one way or the other about a child. Dane was the one who found me in our apartment three days later."

She had been hungry, though there had been food in the kitchen. She had been thirsty, and there was water available. But her mother hadn't been there, and she had been a good girl. She didn't climb and she didn't try to cook. And her mother hadn't contacted the neighbor to watch Ria that weekend because the neighbor had been ill. Ria's mother had had secrets, and she had taught Ria how to stay alone if she needed to.

"Mom was just supposed to be gone for a few hours," she said softly. "I was to be good until she returned."

"And she didn't return?"

Ria shook her head. "Dane arrived. He stepped into the bedroom, and the moment I saw him, I knew my fears that my mother wasn't returning were true."

She remembered that as clearly as she remembered yesterday.

Staring back at him as he stepped into the room, his expression lined with sorrow as he moved to the bed, picked her up and carried her from the apartment.

She shook her head. "I'd drank water from the bathroom tap. I could reach it." She shrugged. "There had been some cheese, a bit of fruit in the fridge and I'd eaten it. And I slept. Huddled in my mother's bed."

For three days, alone. Mercury stared back at her, hearing a child's horror in the too calm words that the adult spoke.

"The Vanderales took good care of me." She cleared her throat. "They found a foster family to take me in. And when that didn't work out, they found a better one. We finally struck it lucky the third time, but I was already in my teens. They compensated the families for taking care of me. Dane would often take me shopping for the clothes I needed and school supplies. He brought me Christmas presents, and sometimes, I'd spend an odd weekend here and there on the Vanderale estate when they were there."

But she had never had a family of her own. She'd been shuttled from one place to the other, and he had a feeling a few of those places hadn't been happy ones.

"How did you come to work for them?" He watched her, piecing the information Jonas had on her together with what she said.

She shrugged. "I was on the estate one weekend when I was sixteen. I'd been driving Leo insane. I was always being a brat." She lowered her head. Mercury guessed she had always been looking for attention, looking for a place to fit in. "Anyway, he pushed me into his office, sat me down at a desk and told me that if I could find the puzzle in the papers there, then he would teach me to ride one of the horses on the estate. That was what I was begging for." She smiled. "I thought he didn't think I could do it. Five minutes later, I found the code he had me looking for, but I had also broken the code."

"And did he teach you to ride?"

Her gaze slid away from his. "Eventually, yes. Leo always keeps his word."

But he hadn't taught her to ride that day, he guessed.

"I went back to my foster family that week and I was placed in special classes. When I turned eighteen, Leo had my own apartment waiting for me, and a job, as well as training. I've been there ever since."

And she had always been alone.

"That was when Dane started sneaking into my bedroom," she sighed. "He would leave things on my pillow. A trinket. Tickets to a movie or concert. Vouchers to a clothing store. But it was usually about the same time that I caught the evidence of his recklessness." She flashed a smile, one that told him she had enjoyed the game as much as Dane had. "He bribes me now, to keep me from going to the Leo. Leo likes to rage at him for endangering himself. And he rages at me for not telling on him," she finished mockingly.

Leo wouldn't be raging at her again, Mercury promised himself. He would make certain Dane, as well as Leo, clearly understood that Ria was no longer the other man's keeper.

"You never married?"

She shook her head, lowering it once more, letting her hair hide her expression as she worked. Or pretended to work. He could sense her uncertainty flowing around her now.

"Did you have many lovers?"

She shrugged. "A few," she answered, still not looking at him.

"No one that stayed?" he asked gently.

Her chin lifted. Pride glittered in her eyes now, her expression tightening as she glared back at him.

"I don't need a man to complete me," she informed him as she moved to her feet and walked around the desk to the file table. "I had dates for whatever functions required one, and if I decided I wanted a lover, I knew how to find one."

"I don't doubt that for a moment, Ria," he murmured. "I wonder though why you rarely wanted one."

She frowned. "And what makes you draw that conclusion?"

He flicked his fingers to her outfit. "You have a gorgeous body but you dress like someone's maiden aunt. You pin your hair up in that tight little bun and whenever you work you wear glasses that come from the last century rather than having corrective surgery done. You dress to hide."

And the light of battle glittered in her eyes.

"I dress to work," she told him stiffly. "This," she waved her hand down the outfit, "is safe. Unassuming. And completes the image of the poor little orphan child the Vanderales felt sorry for. It gets results. I'm not seen as a threat, nor am I seen as someone who needs to be suspected of searching for secrets."

"And you didn't risk your heart, because you made certain you wore a shield that screamed *keep away*," he told her.

He could see it now. He had seen it the moment she stepped off the plane, those sharp eyes taking everything in, that homely bun in place and those dowdy clothes covering her body.

She was silent. She crossed her arms over her breasts and stared back at him impassively.

That look made something rise inside him that had him cautiously probing for the feral displacement he was so wary of. It was like a primal stretching, an arch of challenge to an inner part of him that he hadn't felt in so long it gave him pause.

As though the animal the scientists thought they had killed inside him were reaching out, demanding that he push her, to bring out the woman he knew hid behind those eyes.

"What would you wear for me, Ria?" he asked her, letting his eyes rove over her body. "You have gorgeous legs. High heels instead of those thick heels you're wearing?"

Her lips pressed together tightly.

"You wear silk to sleep in, gowns that make my mouth water to chew off your pretty body. I know your breasts are perfect, perfect for my hands, for my lips. Would you wear silk that hinted at those curves? Skirts that bared your pretty legs?"

"Trying to change me already, Mercury?" she asked with false sweetness. "You actually lasted longer than I expected."

He grinned at that. He was pushing her, daring her, and pricking at needs he knew she had. She had been Vanderale's paper pusher for so damned long she didn't know how to be anything else. He wanted her to be herself. He wanted that wild woman he could glimpse within her. The one who scratched at his shoulders, who bit his arm when she came, just as he bit her shoulder.

"I dare you." He voiced what he knew she didn't want to hear. "Just one day. Just with me. Show the woman you hide, Ria. Show me how she dresses, how she laughs. Show me how she lives."

Her eyes darkened, regret and pain, want and need flickering within them.

She shook her head and looked down at her clothes. "What you see is what you get, Mercury."

He shook his head to that. "What I see is the shell of the woman who opens up and screams beneath me every night. I want all of you, Ria. Everything."

"What you see is what you get!" she repeated as she straightened from where she leaned against the table. She jerked the files that she needed from the table and stalked back to the desk.

He was waiting on her.

As she moved past him, Mercury reached out, catching her around her hips and dragging her to his lap. He caught the files before she could drop them and placed them safely on the table beside him as he stilled her struggles by the simple means of kissing her.

He kissed her wild and hard, the sudden need to fill her with all the lust riding him causing a growl to tear from his throat.

Damn her. She made him crazy to kiss her. It was like sinking into pure fire, being enveloped by it and loving every second of it.

He wanted her naked; he wanted to be naked with her. He wanted to feel her rubbing against him, stroking his flesh and pleading with those desperate little moans for him to make her come.

"Mercury." She sighed his name as his lips parted from hers and he opened his eyes, staring into her face, seeing the beauty she tried to hide from the world.

Delicate cheekbones, such beautiful hair. Long and thick and sensual. He could bury his hands in it and never have to worry about not having enough of the thick, silken strands to caress.

That stubborn chin. Perfectly arched brows. And beneath those clothes, created to drive men mad with their own fantasies of what she might be attempting to hide, was a gorgeous body.

"Be wild with me, Ria," he crooned softly as he let his lips trail over that stubborn little chin. "Stop hiding on me. Don't hide from me."

He wanted the woman he had sensed in her from the moment he met her. The woman straining beneath her flesh to emerge.

"Who could hide from you?" she whispered nervously. "You don't even give a girl a chance to think before you start pulling her out of her safety zone."

"You don't need a safety zone, Ria," he promised her, lifting his head to stare down at her, feeling the hard, intense drive rising inside him, to take her as he felt her buttocks clench against the rise of his erection beneath his mission uniform. "You never needed one. All you need is all that wild passion inside you." He grinned at the thought of it. "And you'll make me crazy with it, even while I'll love watching the woman you are."

Ria forced herself to struggle from his grip, to come to her feet and push her hair back over her shoulders as she stared at Mercury in confusion.

He wanted something from her that no one ever had. Hell, he was seeing things in her she thought she had kept hidden, even from herself.

She thought of the clothing she had at home, outfits she only wore for herself, that she rarely allowed those who knew her to see. The shorter skirts, the ultrafeminine clothes. The shoes that made her legs look longer, made her feel sexier.

She shook her head at the thought of it and moved away from him, ignoring the wicked, knowing glint in his eyes.

"You're scared." His voice was a deep rumble of certainty. "What are you so frightened of, Ria?"

The things she had always been frightened of. Watching someone else leave her without the safety nets she had built for herself.

"You're asking for too much too soon."

"I'm only asking for the woman I know you're hiding from me. I told you, I won't accept that. I want it all."

He wanted it all. He wanted all of her, but she couldn't have all of him? Somehow, despite his inability to control that, she couldn't see the fairness in what he wanted.

Shaking her head, she turned away from him, only to still a second later as she felt him behind her, pressing against her back. Lifting her skirt.

She couldn't move. As though his hands had the power to shackle her in place with no more than the lightest touch, she stood still.

"What do you want from me?" he asked, his voice moving through her as his lips stroked the shell of her ear.

She shook her head. She couldn't have what she needed from him. Or at least, she found herself fearing what she wanted the most.

His hands shaped and cupped the bare curves of her butt then. The thongs she wore left her bare, left the tender globes naked beneath his hands.

Ria could feel her body responding to him, felt his touch in places she knew she should have never felt it. She felt that core of long forgotten defiance welling inside her. The one that demanded action, that demanded she claim what she knew was hers.

"I just want you," she finally whispered.

"Drive me crazy, Ria." He smiled against her neck as his fingers slid beneath the material of her panties, followed the small strap between the cleft of her rear until he came to the aching center of her body. "You have my permission."

"You're already crazy," she panted.

She couldn't seem to draw in enough air, couldn't seem to find her balance as she felt him work the tip of his finger inside her.

Ria gasped, arched her back and felt her juices building between her thighs with his touch. She couldn't get enough of him. No matter how hard she tried, she couldn't sate herself with his touch.

"Only you have ever made me this kind of crazy, Ria."

But another woman had made him another kind of crazy. The kind of crazy that had nearly destroyed him. The kind that had made him kill with his bare hands when he had lost her.

"Do you think I'd be any different if I lost you?" His voice was suddenly savage at her ear, anger pulsing in his voice. "I can feel your pain, Ria, and I know what the hell you're thinking." He released her, letting her go so quickly she nearly swayed without the support of his body.

"You don't know what I'm thinking." She shook her head, keeping her back to him as she fought to clear her expression.

"I can feel how bad you hurt," he snarled behind her. "I can smell your pain and it tears through me like a blade."

She turned back to him, watching him as he pushed his fingers through his hair before glaring back at her.

"I'll get a handle on it." She moved back to her chair shakily. "It's not you, Mercury, it's me."

It was that vague feeling of panic moving inside her. The panic she had felt as a child when her mother was late. The panic she had felt before Dane arrived to take her from a foster family, to move her to another. It was the panic she felt each time someone walked away from her.

She knew what was coming. She was going to lose him.

She looked back at him, watching as his features tightened, making him look more powerful, more sensually dangerous.

A second later he was moving behind her desk. He pulled her chair around and knelt before her. She didn't know what she'd expected, but she hadn't expected his hands to grip her hips, and she hadn't expected to find her skirt around her hips so quickly she couldn't combat it.

And then she didn't want to combat it.

She drew in a harsh breath as he kissed the sensitive mound beneath her panties, as she stared at his large body bending to her, lifting her legs to his shoulders while his lips moved over the wet silk of her panties.

"The smell of your need is driving me crazy. I've never smelled another woman's lust like this. Subtle and wild, reaching into me and shredding my control."

She stared down at him in shock as he lifted her leg, his eyes staring back at her from beneath lowered lashes, as he pulled her shoe from her foot, tossed it to the side and propped her foot on the edge of the desk beside her.

"I love these stockings." He kissed the bare flesh above the lacy top of the silk stockings.

"You're depraved." She sighed, and it wasn't a protest. It was a sigh of complete approval.

She didn't think she had ever felt naughtier, or more female than she did right now. She should have been embarrassed. She should have felt at least a hint of hesitancy, spread open for him like this, her foot on the desk, blatantly wet and eager.

"The door." She swallowed tightly.

"Locked," he growled, lifting her other leg over the padded arm of the chair. "Camera's covered, and you're sweet and wet for me. I'm going to eat you like candy, Ria. Right here. Just like my own little treat."

He pulled her panties to the side, growled and licked through the saturated slit, with a slow, easy stroke of his tongue that was just a little bit raspy, a whole lot exciting.

"I love these curls." He rubbed his lips against the damp curls, blew against them, and Ria had to bite back the moan threatening to fall from her lips. "They're so wet, so soft against my lips."

He blew against them again, creating a subtle caress that had her clit swelling, aching. When he moved again, it was to lick her again. A slow stroke of his tongue from her entrance to the swollen bud, her clit. A rasp of extrasensory pleasure from his

tongue as her hands gripped his hair and that moan she was trying so hard to hold back whispered from her lips.

She had to be careful. Oh Lord, if she started screaming
here, then every Breed in the house was going to hear her.

Did she care if every Breed in the house heard her? It felt so
good. Her head rolled against the back of the chair as she fought
back a cry. She couldn't cry out.

She whimpered. She bit her lip. She slapped her hands to the
arms of the chair and clenched, then slid her fingers back into
his hair and clenched again.

His tongue was wicked. Wicked and sensual and lapping at
her as though he loved the taste of her. As though nothing mattered as much, nothing was as important as making her insane
with the pleasure rising hard and sharp inside her.

She was an inferno. She was gasping, desperate and oh so
very close to coming. Spread out in the office chair, taking his
licks as though she had demanded them. Rising to him, perspiration building on her skin as she felt a finger slide inside her.
Then two. Then he was pumping them into the gripping depths
of her vagina, twisting and stroking as his lips covered her clit.

He suckled the little bud inside his mouth. He kissed it,
laved it with his tongue, then drew on it with gentle pulls of his
lips, creating a friction that finally, devastatingly sent her exploding into complete ecstasy.

Her legs lifted, wrapped around his shoulders as she shuddered, shaking, and bit her lips to hold back the cries that refused to stay silent.

There was no staying silent in Mercury's arms. It just
couldn't happen. Her wail was muffled, but it shook her body,
seemed to echo around her and to gain in momentum as the
pleasure exploded through her again and again.

Gentle licks for long moments eased her from the incredible
heights. Tender hands pulled her legs free of his shoulders and
he straightened, his fingers gripping his cock as he pressed it
against her.

"Take all of me," he demanded, his expression intense, fierce.
"Everything I have."

"I'll scream," she moaned hoarsely, feeling the broad head
of his cock pressing into her, possessing. "Oh, Mercury, I'm
going to scream."

His lips covered hers as he pierced her, impaling her with

tight, heavy strokes. Working into her. Stretching her. He covered her screams, gripped her rear and lifted her closer before he began pounding into her.

This wasn't slow and easy. It wasn't careful and gentle. It was taking and giving; it was marking each other, sharing breaths, touches and ultimately a release that tore through her mind and left her shuddering in his arms.

Arms that held her tight against him. Sheltered her. And when it was over, stroked the last of the tremors away.

CHAPTER 16

Ria had never had office sex in her life. She knew Dane had, quite often. She had covered for him several times, rolling her eyes at the habit he seemed to have acquired. But she had never seen the benefits of it.

Until Mercury.

And if she was smug over the pleasure to be found, the wicked naughtiness it filled her with, then Mercury was down-right cocky about it as he sat in the chair across from her hours later.

Pretending to read that damned magazine. He would watch her over the top of it, his lashes lowered over his eyes, his expression sensual.

Ria controlled her need to experience the sensations again, though. She copied the work she needed, removed the ghost drive, and as he watched, she tucked it carefully in her bra, beneath her breast.

His tongue touched his lower lip and her nipple hardened.

"Stop that." She tried not to laugh. "The first chance I get, I'm informing Jonas how little he knows his Breeds. You're the quiet, calm Breed. Remember?"

His brows lifted. "Sorry, sweetheart, his chest doesn't hold the appeal your breasts do."

She rolled her eyes as she stood to go.

She pulled over her arms the leather coat he had managed to have waiting on her this morning, and shrugged into it before wrapping it around her and picking up her purse.

She looked up at the camera above them as Mercury snagged his own jacket from it. He grinned at her as he did so, then looked back at the camera and snarled.

She could just imagine Austin Crowl jerking back in alarm.

"I thought Breeds were all tough and hard and merciless," she commented as he pulled the lighter jacket on.

"The scientists experimented with advanced intelligence in Breeds like Austin." He shook his head. "They didn't program in the genetics for strength and predatory awareness because they felt it would give those particular Breeds the power to overthrow them."

She arched her brow. "You could do his job with your hands tied behind your back. I've seen your file."

"But I wouldn't have the patience." He shrugged. "Austin is good at what he does, or at least he used to be. He's always been a little superior, a little bullish, but he was damned stupid the other day."

"No, he was certain of himself," she stated. "He thought he had power backing him."

Mercury nodded as they left the office and started down the deserted hallway toward the main section of the house.

"He thought he had Callan's backing." His voice was lower. "We're going to let him believe that for the time being."

Mercury wanted to believe Austin was somehow involved in what was going on, but Ria had her doubts. Austin Crowl was an irritant, but neither his files nor the information she had pulled in so far indicated he was a traitor to his people.

As they turned the corner, they both came to a slow stop. Ely stepped from another office. She stood poised at the side of the hall, her expression somber, her gaze concerned.

Mercury moved to Ria's side, placing himself between her and the doctor before urging Ria forward.

"Mercury." Ely stepped forward slowly, looking between them. "Please. Talk to me for a moment."

Her voice trembled, causing Ria to watch her cautiously as Mercury drew to a halt once again.

Elyiana Morrey had been specifically created against emotion. She had been trained in the hellish conditions of the Breed labs and had experimented on her own people.

"Ely, I don't have time for games," Mercury told her tiredly. "There's a lot to do today."

Ely glanced at Ria again, inhaling slowly.

"Your scents are changing," she said, her voice low. "I need to test—"

"No tests, Ely." His voice was firm. It wasn't unkind; he wasn't angry, but his tone brooked no refusal.

Ely's hands were shoved in the pockets of her white lab coat, and they were clenched, tight.

Ria paid attention to the doctor's demeanor, and it wasn't nearly as calm as she was attempting to appear.

"Mercury, are you willing to risk all your friends this way?" the doctor asked him then. "Don't you remember how horrible it was to lose control and to kill without thought?"

"Enough, Ely." He stiffened as Ria watched the pain in the doctor's eyes.

"Mercury, you could kill her." She nodded to Ria. "You know how easily it could be done. Do you want to rip her heart from her chest?"

His hand tensed at Ria's back.

"I didn't kill friends in those labs." His voice was deadly. "You know that as well as I do."

"But you could kill friends now," she whispered urgently. "I have the confinement cell ready. You have to let me test—"

Ria had had enough.

"Have you lost possession of your senses, Dr. Morrey?" she asked the other woman. "A confinement cell? For what reason?"

"Because small, closed-in places will force me further into feral displacement if its already begun," Mercury said, his voice cold, emotionless. "It won't ease. In the labs, it kept me in a state of rage, and allowed them to research the phenomenon and create a drug for it."

"It's the only way, Mercury." The doctor's voice hitched and broke.

"I think perhaps your good doctor needs to be confined instead," Ria stated. "I'm ready to leave now."

She started forward.

"Damn you!" Ely stepped forward, rage contorting her face now. "You're the reason it's happening. I warned Jonas it would happen. That increased exposure to whatever pheromone is in your system would cause this. If he kills, the guilt lies on your shoulders."

Mercury snarled and stepped between them. "Back off, Ely. You don't want the confrontation this is going to turn into."

Her expression twisted, anger and fear warring in her eyes as she stared back at Mercury.

"You know you'll destroy Sanctuary if the feral qualities in your adrenaline continue to strengthen and you end up killing." Ely's voice roughened, became harsh and growling. "I thought better of you, Mercury. I thought you cared more for your people than this. And I thought Callan did as well."

"Do you think Callan can force me into that cell, Ely?" Mercury asked her, the guttural sound of his voice causing the doctor and Ria to flinch. "There aren't enough Breeds in this compound to force me back into that cell. You'd have to kill me first."

Ria watched the doctor's expression. She watched the maddening fear glitter bright and hot in Ely's eyes.

"I'm petitioning the Ruling Cabinet when they convene," she told Mercury then. "You deserve to know that, Mercury. You have to see these tests through. It's the only way to save us all. As a member of that cabinet, it's my place to tell you you are no longer permitted off the boundaries of Sanctuary."

Ria froze. She reached out slowly, her hand gripping Mercury's arm as danger seemed to sizzle around him.

"Council-trained, weren't you, Ely?" he sneered. "Have you noticed how easily you fall back on Council tactics when you don't get your way?"

Ely paled.

"And according to Breed Law, you cannot order me confined anywhere without due cause."

"Initial tests show due cause." Ely's voice trembled as tears filled her eyes. "I didn't want to do this, Mercury."

Ria tightened her grip on Mercury's wrist. The tension filling him now was incredible, the anger and fury building inside his muscles.

"Initial tests are not enough, Ely."

They swung around to face Callan, Kane and Jonas where they stood at the end of the hallway.

In her peripheral vision Ria watched Ely's face. It tightened into a mask of pained betrayal as she faced her pride leader.

"Respectfully, Pride Leader Lyons, you can't make that determination."

"No," Jonas answered for him. "Breed Law has made that determination. As a member of the Ruling Cabinet, Ely, it's your place to uphold 'due process,' not to accuse or attempt to confine one of our own. Until Mercury shows the inability to control his anger or otherwise destructive behavior, then he cannot and will not be held against his will, nor will he be ordered to undergo any testing until he's deemed a danger to Breeds or humans. The Ruling Cabinet will be convening, Ely, and a protest against your abuse of your position will be lodged instead."

"You and your rules," Ely sneered. "We both know, don't we, Jonas, exactly what you think of Breed Law. You use it to suit your own means and purposes. How will the Ruling Cabinet feel to learn how far you'll go to manipulate us all to get your way?"

Jonas smiled at that. "Ely, sweetheart," he said gently. "Do you think you know anything that could harm me or my job? If you do, you're welcome to list it in your petition of complaints."

His voice was smooth. There was no warning, no sense of worry or nerves. It was like watching Dane work. Of course, Jonas had enough secrets to sink Sanctuary, the Breeds and himself. But like his brother, he would never give one person enough information to do more than irritate him if it were ever revealed.

"You think so little of me?" Ely was staring back at him, hurt. The conflicting emotions surging through her were reflected in her expression, and in her scent, Ria assumed.

The Breeds were all tense, watching her closely, the smallest hint of confusion in their eyes.

"I think something's wrong, Ely," Jonas finally said gently. "I believe perhaps we've allowed you to be under too much stress, or you've overstressed yourself. I think you need to rest, and think about the steps you're taking. How many Breeds will ever trust you should the knowledge of what you're attempting to do become known?"

"You think you're so damned smart." Her hands slid from the pockets of her lab coat, the fingers clenched in fury as a flush rose to her cheekbones. "You're risking everything. Not just Sanctuary and the Breeds, but Mercury himself, and you know it."

"Enough, Ely." Callan's voice was as sharp, as demanding, as the lash of a whip, causing the doctor to flinch in response. "Return to your office or to your quarters. That's an order."

"Pride Leader—"

"That's an order, Ely!" His voice never rose, but something in it, some primal growl, had the doctor jerking in reaction.

Ely shuddered then turned on her heel and stalked past them, moving through the hall and away from them as something rumbled in Mercury's throat.

He turned back to Callan. "There's something wrong here," he finally admitted. "That's not the Ely I know."

Jonas shook his head, watching the doorway the doctor had slipped through. "It's not the Ely I know either, but just as with you, until we can deem her a hazard, we can't force her into testing."

"Why try to force her?" Ria asked. "Do to her as she did to Mercury. Trick her."

"We would first need a scientist with the ability to run the tests."

Ria crossed her arms over her breasts. "You kidnapped a Council scientist just last month, didn't you? Jeffery Amburg? He was never released from your custody despite repeated attempts by several governments to learn what happened to him."

Jonas's brow lifted. "We released him. We have proof of it. What happened to him after he left Sanctuary isn't our concern."

Ria stared back at him mockingly. "Give that line to someone who doesn't know better. I know about the cells beneath the labs here, and I'm betting Amburg is resting quite uncomfortably there. Put his ass to work."

"And ensure the safety of this facility, how?" Callan asked her coldly. "He's a Council scientist, Ms. Rodriquez, not an ally."

Mercury watched the exchange quietly before turning to Jonas.

"Put Blade on him. Blade has enough medical experience and strong enough senses to keep an eye on him. If Ely's sincere, then she'll agree to her own testing first. Tell her if she'll do it, then I'll submit to one more round of samples taken."

He felt Ria's shock, watched Jonas's eyes narrow. "Are you sure you want to do that, Mercury?" he asked.

No, he wasn't.

"Something isn't right here, Jonas. Ely's not a traitor. I'll take the risk if she will."

"And what makes either of you think Ely needs testing?" Kane bit out. "She's scared. She's running scared and panicking."

The head of Sanctuary security was less trusting than most Breeds when it came to the internal security of the estate.

"We can't lock her in her rooms, Kane," Jonas growled. "Ely's emotions are raging too strong beneath the surface, and her scent is altered just enough to concern me."

It was something Mercury had caught as well, though he'd kept silent. His sense of smell was growing marginally stronger, and the proof of that concerned even him. He'd lost those senses when the feral displacement had been "cured" in the labs. That it was returning was further proof that he had cause to keep a careful check on his anger and his emotions.

"Is there any way she could have been compromised?" Mercury asked then.

Jonas shook his head. "The Council never managed to develop a drug that could control us, Mercury, not to that extent. Even the one used on you for the feral displacement didn't completely control you. And one of us would have scented any biological or chemical imbalance in Ely by now."

"Have her restricted to quarters for twenty-four hours," Callan ordered. "We can't risk her confronting Mercury during the party tonight."

Mercury stared at him in surprise. "I wasn't assigned to security for the party."

"No, you're ordered to attend the party in full dress uniform," Callan growled. "You and Ms. Rodriquez. Both Engalls and Brandenmore will be in attendance. I want all eyes on them, and I want Ms. Rodriquez there in case any transmissions are suddenly logged as incoming or outgoing. I want this stopped, Mercury. Now. Before I have to ignore Breed Law myself and kill the bastards."

With that, he turned and stalked from the hallway, leaving Kane and Jonas both to breathe out in surprise.

Callan never disregarded Breed Law. He had helped to fashion it, to lay in the framework for the rules that would govern the Breeds and allow them to work within society. To even hint that he would ignore one of those rules . . .

"I wasn't anticipating a party." Ria sighed, but Mercury could hear the acceptance in her voice. "Dane is always doing this to me."

"Dane didn't request your presence, I did," Jonas bit out.

Mercury caught Ria's smile, though he smothered his own.

"There's a difference?" she asked with false innocence as she moved past Jonas and headed for the front of the house. "Strange. I haven't found one yet."

Ria pulled her coat around her and stepped into the limo, keeping her expression composed until the door closed and the window rose between them and the driver.

"One of these days, someone is going to kill Jonas," she told Mercury.

Mercury snorted. "Yeah, someone's been trying for months now. Those windows in his apartment you mentioned when you first arrived?"

"Were shot out." She nodded. "I can understand the need, I truly can. I wanted to shoot him myself. Why hasn't he forced Ely's testing by now? My investigation into her lab files as well as her Sanctuary files doesn't even hint at the irrationality she's showing. The woman is obviously on the edge of some sort of breakdown."

"It isn't that easy." Mercury shook his head as he moved to the seat across from her, then leaned forward. "Breed Law, everything in it, every value Callan and Jonas have attempted to see put in effect for Breeds, is based on one simple ideal, Ria. Breed freedom. You wouldn't force a non-Breed into testing for acting irrational. If we allowed a Breed to be forced into it, then Breed Law would become null and void, and we'd be animals again in the sight of the world."

Ria crossed her legs and stared back at him, folding her hands carefully in her lap as she let herself consider that.

"Breeds and humans are different sides of the same coin," she reminded him. "You are not fully human, Mercury. You are extrordinarily human. And you're still learning what your bodies, your hormones, are capable of. In such instances, there should be a safeguard put in place."

"There is." He nodded. "But only if we show ourselves to be a danger to ourselves or to others. It doesn't matter which side of the coin our humanity places us on, we're still entitled to the same rights and privileges of freedom. We can't ignore an anomaly in my case and force testing on Ely in hers."

Dane would have, easily, even it meant kidnapping the Breed in question. But Ria had disagreed with many of the decisions she knew Dane had made, for whatever reason.

"She's too focused on you," she finally told him, concerned

at the doctor's continued erratic behavior. "Fanaticism is possible in Breeds, just as it is in humans. And it's just as destructive, perhaps more so. She's intent on pulling you into confinement, no matter what it takes. No matter what she has to do to achieve it."

Mercury stared back at her, knowing the truth in her words. He knew that was exactly Ely's aim, and the betrayal that filled him at that thought bothered him.

"Did you smell anything that could indicate she was drugged?" Ria frowned back at him, her gaze direct.

"What makes you think I could smell it if she were?" he asked. "The drugs for the displacement wiped out those senses, remember?"

She regarded him with haughty amusement. "Really, Mercury, you should try a little harder to lie. That one was so easy to see through it may as well have been cellophane."

His lips twitched.

"I felt you inhaling. Very slowly, very deeply," she informed him. "What did you scent?"

He finally shook his head. "Anger. Fear. And it was very heightened, more than it should have been. She believes in what she's saying. She believes the feral displacement is returning, and it's impossible to control."

Ely believed he would suddenly lose his mind and destroy the very people he had lived to protect for over eleven years now.

"And what do you think?" She tilted her head and watched him, her gaze soft. There was no fear there, no suspicion, almost as though she had formed her own trust in him, and had no intention of backing down on it.

He reached out and touched her cheek with his fingertips then cupped it with his palm. The need to touch her was overwhelming. As he did so, her fingers curled over his wrist, holding him to her. Trust. Complete trust. Something he had never felt with anyone else. Not even long ago with the Breed that could have been his mate.

"I think I would rip apart anyone who dared harm you," he finally told her softly. "There would be nothing on the face of this earth, short of death, that could control me."

Ria stared back at him, seeing the truth in his expression, in the savage light of his hammered gold eyes and the flecks of blue that materialized in them. Whatever that phenomenon was that changed the color of his eyes, that made him appear stronger, more savage, it was only frightening to the enemy.

He wasn't her enemy. He was her lover, in every sense of the word. In ways no other man had ever been.

"Then it's under control," she said softly. "And I have no doubt it will stay there."

If he hadn't already lost his heart to her, then Mercury would have sworn he lost it to her then.

"That still leaves a problem, though," she told him as he pulled her to him, lifting her into his lap even though they were too close to her cabin to do more than just this. Just hold each other.

"There are more problems?" he growled. "They're piling up here, Ria."

Her laughter, soft and light—he swore it warmed his soul.

"I forgot to mention how much I absolutely detest parties," she told him. "And Dane knows it. I might have to kick him for this one. Or tell Leo on him. I don't think this sort of maneuvering can be fixed with bling."

His lips kicked up in a grin. His mind was on her hand, though. The one that had pushed beneath his jacket so her fingers could play against his neck.

"I'll take care of Dane's maneuverings," he promised her. "But the party's a small one."

"Visiting VIPs and dignitaries? Three hundred at best."

"Three hundred and fifty." He smiled as she groaned and buried her face in his chest.

"Too many."

"No, too many is the Christmas party," he promised. "The guest list, so far, is at a full thousand. They're predicting snow, and Callan is pulling his hair out as he and Kane work out the logistics of security for the children and mates. Every available Breed is being rescreened for clearance and those that pass are on twenty-four-hour duty shifts. The party is held on the fifteenth. That allows for a private party on Christmas Day. Four hundred, I believe."

She groaned again and he stroked her hair soothingly as he grinned. She made him grin. She made him happy. She made him want to pick her up and hide her from all eyes, to experience the joy of her with no distractions.

"We could hibernate in the winter," she finally suggested.

"We're not bears," he chuckled, enjoying the play.

"We could go on vacation." Soft lips kissed his neck; her tongue stroked over it. "I know several secluded beaches. No cold. We could bask in the sun. Lie at the water's edge and allow the waves to lap over us."

His cock, already engorged, still hard and eager to pleasure her, throbbed at the thought. Ria naked, her nut brown body laid out on soft white sand as water washed over her and the sun heated her flesh.

If it had the chance to touch her. He'd have a hell of a time allowing to sun to caress her, because he'd be too damned busy touching her himself.

She lifted closer then, her teeth raking over the lobe of his ear, her warm breath caressing his neck. "I want you," she whispered. "Again. Why am I burning so hot and deep for you after I've already had you?"

"Why am I?" He gripped her hair, pulled her head in place and let himself take her kiss.

It wasn't gentle, and he wanted to be gentle. It was hot and fierce, fiery and consuming, and burned through him with the force of wildfire.

It was pleasure, it was the agony of arousal that was never sated for long, and it was the breath of life. A breath he feared he couldn't live without now.

· CHAPTER I 7 ·

Mercury made it into the house with her. He even managed to growl at Lawe and Rule to clear out of the house after they checked it thoroughly. The second the door closed—and locked—he was on her.

Ria was so enflamed, so desperate for his touch, that she was tearing at his shirt, clawing at him as he shredded her sweater with those blunted clawlike nails of his and jerked her skirt over her hips.

He didn't bother with the bedroom, or the couch. He lifted her, shoving her against the wall as she managed to get his pants open and his erection free.

He tore the panties from her hips and in one hard lunge he was buried inside her. Buried so deep inside her he swore he was losing himself in her.

Her legs wrapped around his back; the liquid heat of her sex wrapped around him like a slick, tight fist and had him clenching his teeth. Had him aching for that tight fullness he'd heard filled the tongue when mating heat was devouring a Breed.

He wanted that with her. Wanted it with her until he swore he could feel his tongue itching and a wild subtle taste teasing at his mouth.

His lips took hers, his tongue spearing into her mouth as his thighs bunched and he began moving. His cock ached, throbbed to the point of madness as he tried to fuck her hard enough, deep enough to ease the agonizing pleasure filling him.

Her sheath gripped him, milked him. Her hips writhed against his, her lips moved beneath his, suckling at his tongue, moaning as though the taste of him was as much pleasure as the penetration of her body by his.

"I can't get enough." He tore his lips from hers, his head tilting back on his shoulders as he slammed his hips against her.

His hands clenched on her ass, and the needs assailing him were richer, deeper than any he had known before. He wanted to bend her over, take her as he knew she had never been taken. Put his mark on her as irrevocably as possible. Until she knew, beneath her skin, clear to her soul, who she belonged to.

Who belonged to her.

"Harder." Her hands clawed at his shoulders, her lips were on his neck, her teeth scraping. Biting.

"Ah hell. Fuck yes, Ria. Bite me, baby. Bite me hard."

But she already was. Her teeth were locked in the tough flesh at the base of the side of his neck, sending fire and ecstatic pleasure racing through him.

His head lowered, his teeth seeking her shoulder. He growled. He snarled. He bit her as he felt her erupting, exploding around him, the tight grip of her vagina increasing, milking his release from him until the snarls coming from his lips were nearly enraged and the ache of the furious blasts of semen jetting from him had him wanting, needing, to roar.

It was exquisite. The agony and the pleasure of filling her, and the rage. Because there was no mating. And yet Mercury knew in his soul she *was* his mate. This woman. She held on to him, her tears dampening his neck, his knowledge that she felt that missing part of him eating inside him.

As the tremors of release eased and he could think, could find balance again, he held her to him, placed his own back to the wall and slid to the floor.

There, he held her against him, his head still buried against her neck, his eyes closed.

"You're my mate," he whispered against her neck, against the mark he hadn't allowed to heal. Because he kept biting it, kept wounding her in ways that went far beyond those tiny marks at her shoulder.

She shook her head. "It doesn't matter, Mercury." She lifted her head and stared back at him, causing his heart to tear in half.

There was no recrimination there. Her eyes were damp, but languorous pleasure filled them, and emotion. She was open to him now. He could smell the sweet scent of desire that could renew with his lightest touch, and emotions he hadn't smelled in so many years. He could sense them now, swirling through him, digging into his soul.

"I love you anyway." She touched his jaw, smoothed her hand down his neck. "Just as you are, just as we are now. I love you."

"I love you," he repeated, the words comfortable, easy on his lips. She wasn't just his mate, no matter the lack of mating heat. She was his heart.

She laid her head against his shoulder and breathed out with a little sigh of completion, and of weariness.

"We could hibernate tonight," she finally suggested with a grin he felt against his neck. "Just hide."

And he chuckled. Despite the pain, the betrayal he felt, by his own genetics and the body that refused to produce the mating heat, he had to laugh at the amusement in her voice.

"You call Dane and I'll call Callan," he told her, and he meant it. If she didn't want to go, they wouldn't go. It was that simple.

But she sighed. "Dane would pout. He's not nice when he pouts."

"Callan doesn't pout," Mercury laughed. "Games aren't his style. He would understand." He touched her hair, smoothed his hands down it. "But I'd probably lose vacation time. That fun in the sun you were talking about."

"Hell. Figures. Dane just gets stingy with the bribes. He doesn't bother revoking my vacation time."

"Do you ever take vacation time? Somehow I doubt you do." He helped her to her feet before dragging himself from the floor.

He looked at her then—her messed hair, torn clothes—and couldn't believe the hunger that had swept through him as they entered the cabin.

She wrinkled her nose mockingly. "Know-it-all."

He stared back at her, knowing he was totally besotted with her. "You will be now. I promise you, Ria. You're going to be begging for vacation time now."

If she stayed with Vanderale Industries. Sanctuary needed her more than Dane or Leo Vanderale. And Mercury needed her with him. He would do what she needed to do, what she wanted to do, but he didn't think she was as happy working for Dane as she would be here.

"Damn parties," she muttered, turning away from him and walking toward the bedroom before casting him a heated little look over her shoulder. "Want to shower with me?"

"Wrong question," he growled. "Because you keep me from it."

He followed after as she laughed, the thought of playing with Ria in the shower again causing his cock to jerk in anticipation.

Hell, it might not be mating heat, but it was damned close. For now, for tonight, he would content himself with that. But he was going to have to stop rubbing his tongue against his teeth, hoping. Because he swore he was making it raw.

✦   ✦   ✦

Later that evening, as Ria stepped from the bathroom, clipping the pearl earrings to her ears that she had chosen to wear, her hair pinned behind her head, it was all Mercury could do to hold back his growl.

He was in his dress uniform. The severe black pants and jacket were confining enough. The dress boots were a pain in the ass, but he tolerated them when he had to. He wore the insignia of his rank, that of second commander, a narrow golden bar attached to the left shoulder of his jacket. On the right was the gold lion's head denoting his genetic ranking, and below it the brass Bureau of Breed Affairs pin, a simple brass pin with the initials BBA.

The dress uniform was a necessary evil. Ria's hair pinned up wasn't.

"Take your hair down." He'd meant to make it a request as his gaze swept over the simple black gown she wore. The long sleeves covered her arms, while the material reached to the base of her neck in back.

The front was cut lower, scooped and rounded over her breasts, leaving the barest hint of cleavage.

She wore pearls around her neck to match the earrings, and nothing more.

"I'm not taking down my hair." She moved to sit on the bureau and checked her earrings. "It would be . . . Mercury."

As she talked, he had moved behind her, pulled the anchoring pins and watched that thick, silken mass of hair as it unraveled down her back.

"You did not do that." She turned on him, incredulous. "Damn you!"

His eyes narrowed back at her. "Get as mad as you like. I want it down."

Her eyes narrowed back at him. "I want that damned cheesecake I mentioned before. Doesn't mean I'm going to get it."

He growled. "There will be four different kinds of cheesecake on the buffet. I requested it. Just for you. All chocolate."

For a second he could have sworn her eyes glazed with something akin to approaching ecstasy.

"I'm going to revise my opinion of you." She pouted with charming irritation. "You're a cruel, evil man. Teasing me with cheesecake. I'll get you back. You watch."

He smiled back at her, his brows arching as he pushed his fingers through her hair and restrained the need to kiss her. If he kissed her, he would never get out of that cabin with her.

He let his gaze go over her again, noticing as he did so that the cut of her dress hid the bite he had placed on her shoulder. For some reason, that bothered him.

"Leave the hair down," he told her. "We'll discuss the dress later."

"Yeah, with a whip and a chair in my hand," she informed him archly. "Don't start giving orders, Mercury. I don't obey so well."

Ria allowed him to get away with the hair, simply because she was learning how much he enjoyed it down. But her clothes, as much as she sometimes disliked them herself, were imperative.

Clothing style, makeup and presence were a hazard in her job, and at parties such as the one Sanctuary was hosting tonight she met many of the people she was sent to investigate.

"You should be able to dress as you like," he growled. "I swear, Ria, I can feel your dissatisfaction with that dress."

She looked at him sharply. She hated this dress. It was simple, the cut and design elegant enough. And it was unassuming. She had never hated unassuming as much as she did tonight.

"The dress is like your dress uniform, less threatening and more civilized in ways than the uniform you work in. My line of work requires that I appear unthreatening at all times. No matter the job or the event."

She moved to the closet and pulled a pair of low heels from

the shelf inside. She had to keep herself from staring at them in regret. As with the dress. Simple. Unassuming.

She put them on anyway and turned back to Mercury.

He was staring at her, his expression somber, his eyes that odd color once more, as though something lived inside him that he wasn't always aware of.

"I won't tolerate it," he suddenly bit out.

"Tolerate what?" she retorted. "My refusal to do as you order?"

If he turned arrogant Breed on her now, she was going to get violent herself.

"Your refusal to do as you wish," he snapped. "That dress. Those shoes. I didn't even have to see your face to feel how much you hated those damned things. Where are the pretty clothes, Ria?" He stalked to the closet and looked in, growling at the sight of more of the same. Simple clothes. Dowdy skirts. "Where are the clothes you want to wear?"

"In the stores." Her voice was clipped, her own anger rising now. "Where they belong. If they're here, I'll wear them. That simple. I told you, Mercury, I can't risk the people I investigate suspecting that there's more to me than they've always believed. The Vanderales' poor orphan employee could never afford those clothes. A paper pusher? Really! How long do you think they would believe that if they saw me dressed in the clothes you're talking about?"

"Who put that in your head?" He raged, stalking from the closet, stomping from it actually. "Dane? The Leo? I'll be damned if it will continue. You're a beautiful woman and you love pretty things. Why shouldn't you have them?"

"Because it's detrimental to my job," she pointed out, her voice rising. "My job, Mercury. Remember? Would you have believed I was no more than a paper pusher researching your damned accounts if I had arrived dressed in silk and heels?"

He stared back at her, the blue lights in his eyes firing deeper, darker. "I wouldn't have had the brainpower to think," he finally muttered. "I'd have been too busy fucking you before you ever arrived at Sanctuary."

She wanted to roll her eyes at him. "Neither you nor Jonas would have ever taken me seriously."

He pushed his fingers through his hair, his gaze raking over her. "That's a cop-out," he informed her. "One look at you, Ria,

and anyone knows better than that. Do you think the reason
the companies you investigate aren't suspicious of you is your
clothes? That's not true, Ria. They're not suspicious of you because they're arrogant and too certain of their own intelligence to
believe anyone could be smarter than they are."

She shook her head. She didn't want to hear this. It wasn't
true. It was the job, and it was that simple. She owed the Vanderales. They had kept her safe until she was grown, they had
given her a job, they had given her a life when she was alone,
deserted.

"You hide, Ria," he stated. "Those clothes aren't because of
your job. Those clothes, your demeanor, the way you dress—it's
so you can hide."

She shot him a scathing glare before pulling away from him
and jerking her wrap from the end of the bed.

"Are you ready to go?" She pulled the heavy cape over the
dress and latched the closure at her throat.

"It didn't keep me away, did it, Ria?" he asked her as he continued to watch her.

"I don't know what you're talking about."

"The dowdy clothes. Your hair twisted into that perfect, tight
little bun. It keeps everyone at a distance. It shouts *Go away*.
But I didn't go away."

Not yet he hadn't.

"No, you haven't gone away," she finally whispered. And
she wondered what she would do when he did.

That small warning instinct inside her wouldn't stop. It continued to echo caution, and she continued to ignore it.

But she hated the dress and the shoes more than she had
when she put them on. His arguments had made her remember
the few dresses she owned that made her feel alive. The ones
she longed to dress in, the ones that fit the makeup she preferred, the heels she loved. And she was reminded each time she
"dressed up" that she was alone. There was no one to see her.
Because she had always been safer alone.

She couldn't be broken, if no one knew her well enough to
break her.

Until now.

Through the ride back to Sanctuary, and their entrance into
the secured glittering beauty of the mansion, Mercury's accusa-
tions played within her mind.

She glimpsed Dane across the ballroom, immersed in talks with several of the high-level corporate shareholders she had investigated in the past. Dane moved among the crowd, his silver eyes watching everything, the blond lawyer he was rumored to be involved with at his side.

Breeds filled the mansion in dress uniform, as did Kane Tyler's personal security force, the men he had brought with him when he came to Sanctuary in those first steps the Breeds had taken into the world.

She moved through the room with Mercury, watching the gazes that slid over her, dismissing her. They always dismissed her, and until now she had never realized how much she hated dressing down to allow for it.

Mercury saw something completely different. As they moved around the room and he introduced her to the men and women present for the party, he saw how many recognized her name or her.

He saw how easily her cool, stark beauty intimidated others. The women saw the simplicity of her clothes and the regal grace that showed through, and they moved on. The men took one look at her on Mercury's arm, and most knew fear at the thought of tempting a Breed's anger over his woman. It wasn't done. To become forward with a Breed mate was to take one's life in one's own hands.

And he felt her dissatisfaction. Her need to let all that wildfire inside her free. She only let herself go when he was taking her, loving her. But that fire burned inside her eternally.

He could see her in reds—garnets and the vivid scarlet. She would light up the night with her long hair, high heels and the dresses he knew she would love. And she would light up everyone around her.

But she was frightened. He could feel her fear, and it pricked at the animal he could feel stretching inside himself, called free by that primal response in the woman he loved.

He hadn't felt that instinct in over eleven years. Until her fear. Until the smell of it as they entered Sanctuary drifted around him and he felt it come awake inside him, stretching past the bonds of control, easing into his mind. Watching. Waiting.

And more. He felt something *more*, and it made no sense.

As they mingled and talked, she sipped at her champagne

and watched the CEO of Engalls Pharmaceuticals as closely as decorum allowed.

She could feel Mercury's tension beside her, increasing as they chatted, working closer to Horace Engalls, one of the men information was flowing to, and his snobbish wife, Cara Brandenmore Engalls.

Ria ran the information she had on the woman through her head quickly. There was nothing significantly important about Cara. She was on the board of both Engalls Pharmaceuticals and Brandenmore Research, of which Engalls was a division.

She was the daughter of Phillip Brandenmore, married to the man her father had chosen for her. She was younger than Engalls by ten years and her voice had risen against Breed law when it came up for vote several years before. She was a powerful figure in her own little set, regarded with wariness and considered a formidable enemy.

Horace Engalls had begun courting Sanctuary years ago in the hopes of acquiring Breeds to strengthen his security on his labs. He'd been turned down repeatedly. But he and Brandenmore both were associates of a very powerful senator that Sanctuary liked to keep happy. Which meant the two men had the invitations the senator requested for them.

Ria knew Cara well, just as she had known Cara's mother before Phillip Brandenmore divorced her.

"Ria, my dear, what are you doing here?" Cara's cool, superior smile hid the heart of a viper as she glanced at where Ria's hand rested on Mercury's arm. "And with a . . . man." The pause had Ria's eyes narrowing. "I'm surprised Dane allowed it."

Ria arched her brow. "Dane's my employer, Cara, not my brother."

"I always assumed much more." Cara's laughter was light, vicious. "Perhaps I was wrong?"

"Perhaps you were," Ria told her. "I haven't seen Phillip tonight, though." She glanced around the room, looking for Cara's father. "I'd hoped to say hello to him."

"He had an unexpected stop to make at the airport on the way." Cara's lips curved in smug satisfaction. "His newest little playmate, I believe, was delayed. He should be here momentarily."

"I hope to see him before I leave then." Ria smiled tightly, nodding to her as well as Horace. "Perhaps we can get a chance to talk later."

"Oh, I'm sure we will, dear." Cara's tinkling laughter grated on Ria's nerves. "I'll make certain of it."

Ria's gaze sharpened on the other woman before moving away. The feeling of panic sweeping through her intensified.

"How is security holding?" she asked Mercury, keeping her voice low as they moved through the ballroom and he drew her onto the dance floor.

He danced as well as he made love, she thought, restraining her sigh, waiting as he checked the security points.

"Everything's holding," he murmured in her ear. "What's wrong, baby?"

The endearment weakened her knees. Which was silly. Dane called her sweetheart or baby often. He always had. Yet the effect had never been the same.

She shook her head, lowering it as she let him draw her closer.

"Ria, we need to talk soon," he told her softly, his voice deepening, almost a growl as she flicked her earlobe with his tongue. "Very soon."

She closed her eyes and smiled. She could feel his erection beneath his dress jacket. She could feel *him*, warm and aroused, holding her as close as convention allowed.

"Do we have to stay very long?"

"Longer than we're going to stay. Damn," he cursed, his head lifting. "Let's go. Jonas has just ordered us to Callan's office."

As he released her, she glanced at the minute receiver barely visible at his ear.

"What's wrong?"

His hand settled in the small of her back, pressing her forward toward the ballroom doors.

"Hell if I know," he muttered. "He's not saying."

The panic intensified. Ria couldn't explain it; she couldn't force him not to go to that office, but every feminine instinct she possessed was screaming out at her, demanding that she run, that she escape.

That instinct was a part of her. She always heeded it. The few times she hadn't had seen her heart broken, her pride in shambles. And she had seen the pity for her weakness in Leo and Dane's eyes. Always the sad, poor little orphan.

"Ria?" Mercury questioned her as they entered the foyer and moved to the back of the hall. "Are you okay?"

"Fine." She sent him a smile she hoped wasn't as brittle as she felt. "I think the shoes are pinching my feet or something."

Or something. The closer they moved to that office, the more she had to restrain herself not to turn and run.

"I hate it when you lie to me," he snarled softly.

"I hate it when you ask me questions I don't know how to answer," she hissed back. "I've had a bad feeling all day."

She clutched the side of her dress, lifting the long skirt as they moved closer to their destination. She could run now, she told herself.

Like hell. She wasn't a coward. And it wasn't physical danger she could feel awaiting her. She couldn't explain the premonition. She had never been able to explain them.

"Jonas, Callan and Dane are waiting in Jonas's office," he told her. "Dane wouldn't allow you to walk into danger."

She shook her head. "It's not danger."

She could see the door. It was closed. They moved closer and she wanted to scream. She licked her lips nervously, ignored her sweating palms and waited as Mercury knocked on the door.

It opened, but only partially. Dane stepped outside.

"Mercury, I'll stand outside with Ria." His expression was livid.

"The hell you will." Mercury tugged her closer to his side. "She doesn't need a babysitter."

The door swung open.

"Mercury." The soft, feminine sigh shattered her as she stared back at the other woman in horror.

Shoulder-length golden hair, hazel brown eyes shadowed with a light dusting of bronze over the lids. High cheekbones, exotic eyes and a smile that trembled. And a face Ria had seen in her nightmares over the past weeks. Except that face had been younger, softer—and death had taken her years ago. Or it was supposed to have.

"Alaiya?" Shock filled Mercury's voice, and seared Ria's heart.

She stood still. Frozen.

Another woman's arms touched his face, caressed it, though he almost pulled back. Another woman's arms wrapped around his neck, and another woman snuggled against his chest.

"Oh, Mercury. It's been so long."

Those eyes blinked back at Ria, and for a moment she could have sworn she glimpsed malicious pleasure in the eyes of Mercury's mate.

· CHAPTER 18 ·

She was going to disintegrate into a million pieces. Shards and fragments of her soul would be found on worlds light-years from Earth before the pain completed its journey.

She had been so certain she was his. So certain she had finally found a place to belong, because he owned her soul, and no one else ever had.

She felt Mercury pull away from her. His hand slid from the small of her back, and she heard a growl. An angry sound of pain that she wondered if she might have made herself.

She wanted to smash her fist into that perfect face. She wanted to tear all those perfect hairs from the woman's head. She wanted to howl in rage, fear and pain.

"Ria, sweetheart." Dane's voice was at her ear. She could have sworn it was thick with grief. "Darling. Hold on. You don't want to break here."

She shook her head and stepped back, pulling her arm from his grip. She didn't want him touching her. She couldn't bear to be touched, not right now. Not while the pain was exploding in her brain, shattering her heart, nearly stopping it.

The slow, sluggish beat reminded her. It had done that the moment she realized her mother was never returning to her. That she would always be alone. She should have remembered, should have known it couldn't be real.

"If you break here, you'll never forgive yourself." Dane's voice lashed at her, a quiet male hiss of fury as Alaiya tilted her head up to Mercury and spoke.

"I knew when I read the tabloid stories what happened." She sighed against Mercury. "Mates. That's what we are, aren't we? That's why I never forgot you, Mercury."

Ria couldn't breathe. Oh God. It hurt. It was knifing through her chest, shredding flesh and bone, and she was going to scream with the rage and the pain of it.

Don't touch him!

The words were whipping through her mind as Mercury gripped the other woman's wrists and pushed her back. Just a little. Just enough to keep Ria from collapsing, from begging him not to hold her.

"Alaiya?" There was a wealth of surprise, shock and perhaps anger.

Of course he would be angry. Eleven years they had been separated and here she was, mere hours after he had pledged himself to another woman. To some stupid human that just couldn't understand where her place was.

"Ria." Dane's arm was around her shoulders.

He was trying to shelter her. He had done that when she was a little girl, every time he saw her. He would wrap his arm around her shoulder and try to shelter her from whatever had hurt her while he was away. There was no way to shelter her from this.

Ragged, gaping wounds tore through her soul. She could feel herself bleeding from the inside out, ripping apart and not a sound was made.

"What the fucking hell is going on here?" Guttural, ragged and filled with fury, Mercury's voice echoed around her. Sliced into her. She looked into his eyes, and they were nearly blue. They weren't amber. They weren't hammered gold. They were blue, the color they had been when he showed the first signs of mating Alaiya in the labs.

Alaiya was back. And, it appeared, so was Mercury's animal.

"You need to take care of this," she whispered to him, glancing at Alaiya. "I know it's been a long time." She backed away from him. "You'll need to"—she waved her hand helplessly—"talk." She couldn't imagine anything else. If she did, she would die. Right there, she would lose her will to live.

She couldn't bear it. It hurt. Nothing—no desertion, no vicious words from cold, cutting lips—had ever hurt as this hurt.

"Mercury, could you step into the office please?" Jonas's voice was like a whip slicing through the tension. "Dane, Ms. Rodriquez might be more comfortable in the receiving room across the hall."

She stared back at Jonas. His silver eyes seemed alive, an entity separate from the rest of him, swirling and clashing with tempestuous anger as he watched her.

Of course, he would be angry. He would believe this could affect her job. That it would affect Sanctuary's relationship with the Vanderales.

She shook her head. She was the poor little orphan to the family, not really family at all. She had always known that.

She backed away, feeling Dane's hand on her arm like a live current, painful, unwanted.

"The hell she will."

Before the words were out of Mercury's lips he had hold of her, jerking her to his side, his arm curved around her back, pulling her to him.

"Don't do this to me." The sound of her voice shocked her. It was barely passable, so thick and rough it was hardly understandable. "Don't make me see this."

His eyes were almost pure blue; now the gold flickered in tiny pinpoints rather than the opposite.

"This isn't what you think." He glared into the room before pulling her outside it, out of sight of the others, pressing her against the wall as he stared down at her, his eyes raging.

And the pain was raging inside her. She had to get away from him. Before she begged him. Before she pleaded with him, *Please don't leave me alone.*

She pressed her hands against his chest. "Take care of this. I'll wait with Dane." She shook her head, knowing he wouldn't be returning to her.

Mating heat was like a drug, an addiction. He wouldn't be able to leave his mate's side until it eased. And Ria would be long gone by then. Long gone and far away.

"Like bloody fucking hell." He snarled the words into her face. "Not happening."

"Mercury, listen to her," Dane urged quietly from behind him. "Do you want to hurt her like this, man? I could smell the mating heat on you the moment Alaiya flung herself into your arms. Denying it isn't going to keep Ria from hurting."

Her knees turned to rubber.

Oh God. She couldn't fall. She stared up at Mercury in horror.

"It's not like that. Ria, listen to me." His hands gripped her face, his expression twisted in agony. "Baby, you have to listen to me. It's not like that."

His head lowered, and she knew what was coming. He was going to kiss her. Let her taste what she couldn't have. Let her know what belonged to another woman. And he would destroy her with it.

"No!" Her hand jerked up, covered his mouth. "Let me go, Mercury. Let me go."

"You're my mate." He shook her hand away. "Damn you, you will listen to me."

"Let her fucking go."

Dane spun him around, away from her, but none of them could have expected what happened next.

A roar tore from Mercury's chest and Dane went flying. He slid across the waxed floor, ending up in a pile against the wall before he shook his head and came to his feet with a snarl of rage.

"Touch my mate and you die." Mercury placed himself between her and Dane. "Do you hear me Vanderale? I'll gut you like I did that fucking bastard in the labs and I'll shove it down your throat."

His voice—wasn't his voice.

Ria backed away from him, shaking her head as Callan, Kane and Jonas rushed from the office, putting themselves between Mercury and Dane as Jonas held his brother back, snarling in anger as Dane fought him.

"Mercury?" Alaiya stepped from the office. Sensuous silk hissed as she moved, like a serpent's whisper. Her voice was almost childishly soft, confused, but her eyes—Ria stared into Alaiya's eyes, and she saw the smug satisfaction there. "Mr. Vanderale hasn't touched me."

She touched his arm as Mercury's gaze swung to Ria.

"Don't you walk away from me." He shoved a finger in Ria's direction, fighting for control, obviously fighting against the rage tearing through him with mating heat.

Mating heat. For her. Ria looked at the other woman and felt like screaming in her own rage.

"Looks like the party's over," she whispered, staring back at him, aching to the depths of her soul. "Take care of your mate, Mr. Warrant. I'll take care of myself."

She felt the ice building, though she knew it wouldn't last

long. It was forming in her veins, covering her flesh, washing through her mind. The shield was as brittle as frost, and just as cold.

Mercury's lips pulled back from his teeth in a silent, warning snarl as he started for her. And he might have reached her, he might have actually touched her, if Alaiya hadn't been there. If she hadn't reached up, her hands sliding over his shoulders, her lips pressing to his before he could push her from him.

And Mercury stilled, silent as death, against her.

Ria couldn't bear any more. She turned and ran, aware of Dane behind her, calling out her name, catching up with her. He stopped her at the entrance to the foyer, forced her to slow down before wrapping his arm around her and leading her quickly for the door.

The doorman was waiting with her cape.

Dane grabbed it. Ria would have kept going. She had to run. She had to escape. She had to get away from the pain. It was splintering inside her so sharp and deep she didn't think she could survive it.

The first sob tore from her throat as she rushed down the steps, ignoring the echo of a roar behind her.

Dane's limo was waiting outside. Rye rushed to open the door and slammed it behind them as Dane rushed her into the back. A second later, the car was pulling away from the mansion, slicing a path through the fallen snow as Dane wrapped her cloak around her.

"It's okay, little mink," he whispered, drawing her into his arms, rocking her.

He had done that too, when he found her at the apartment, all alone. Called her a little mink and took her in his arms.

"This too shall pass, Ria," he murmured against her hair.

And her heart kept breaking. Her chest was one live, brutal wound that tore open over and over again. Breathing hurt. Living hurt. She could feel the pain sweeping over her body, like barbed agony, ripping and shredding at her.

"She was supposed to be dead," she whispered. "She wasn't supposed to be here."

She could speak. As bad as it hurt, she was still breathing.

"I know, sweetheart." His arms tightened around her. "God, Ria, I'll kill him for doing this to you. I swear to you."

And he meant it. She knew the ice in his voice, the rage echoing in it. And she stilled.

"I'll die with him."

His curse rent the air.

"You're dying without him." His voice was hoarse. Dane's voice was never hoarse. He never really let himself care enough about anything or anyone, except family, to become that angry. And she wasn't family. She never had been.

She moved away from him, hating the feel of him holding her. Hating the feel of anything against her flesh now.

"We're going to the airport," he informed her. "I'm taking you home."

She shook her head. "I have a job to do."

There was the job. Her word. She owed. She owed the Vanderales. This one last job.

"Ria." He leaned forward as she moved into the opposite corner and huddled against the door. "God, sweetheart, I can't let you do this to yourself."

"You can't stop me," she said tonelessly.

Toneless. There was no emotion in her voice, but it was shredding her insides, over and over again. Like the vultures from hell that forever tore at flesh that grew back. That was the pain ripping her apart.

She stared straight ahead, watching the snow come down, the wipers beating at it.

"Take me to the cabin, Rye."

"Boss said the heli-jet, darlin'," Rye told her gently as Dane glared at her.

She didn't look at him. She watched the snow.

"Take me to the cabin."

"No."

She turned and looked at him. "It's over, Dane."

He stared back at her, his brown eyes hard, furious.

"Meaning?"

"If you don't take me back to the cabin, don't let me finish this job, then I'll go to the Leo and demand it. It's my job. I'll finish it."

He wiped his hand over his face, his jaw clenching, and she could see him thinking, fighting for an answer.

"We'll go to Asia." He suddenly smiled, the curve of his lips gentle, sad. "I heard of black pearls, Ria. Natural black pearls. I'll buy them for you. As many as we can find, mink."

She shook her head. No more jewels. No more pearls. Nothing could compensate for what she had lost tonight.

"Please," she whispered. "I need to go to the cabin."

"So you can fucking torture yourself? God's sake, Ria, I know what you'll do, baby. I've been there. You're going to curl in that bed and pretend it didn't happen. That he's coming back, that he's not mating that bitch cat that showed up tonight." He gripped her shoulders. Shook them. "I'll kill him, Ria. Do you hear me?"

"Take me back." She stared back at him. "Touch him and the Leo learns everything, Dane. All of it. Can you kill me to silence me?"

He stared back at her in shock. "You don't mean that, Ria." He shook his head bitterly. "You wouldn't do that, even in rage."

"I've never asked you for anything." Her voice broke. "The bribes were your idea. I had fun with it. Hurting Mercury is off bounds."

Because he was right. She needed to curl up in the bed that still held Mercury's scent. She needed to burrow beneath the blankets and oh God. Oh God. She needed to pretend.

She wrapped her arms over her stomach.

"Please," she finally sobbed. "Oh God, Dane, please take me back to our cabin. Please."

The first tear fell, and she fought it. She fought it valiantly. She buried her head against the door and shuddered, and another sob tore from her.

"Take her to the cabin, Rye." Dane's voice was tortured. "Just for tonight. Let her have tonight."

She rocked herself because she couldn't bear to allow Dane to do it. She shook and bit off the sobs. Her face burned, her throat hurt from the ragged need to scream, and as they took her to the place she had begun to think of as home, Ria shattered inside.

◆   ◆   ◆

She entered the cabin alone, aware of Rule and Lawe driving in behind them, spreading out around the cabin. They didn't speak. Dane had stayed in the car when she held a restraining hand out to him.

She entered the cabin and felt it. She could smell him on the air. The scent of their passion that day, the feel of him against her, between her thighs as he pressed her into the wall and called her "mate." And everything she had thought she could hold back came tumbling from her. Tearing from her. It gouged holes into her spirit, and as the door closed, she had to force herself through the house. To the bedroom.

"Mercury." She whispered his name, a sobbing, agonizing sound as she dropped the cape on the floor and stumbled to the bed and dragged herself to his pillow.

And she howled. The doors holding back the rage and the pain opened and she screamed in agony. Her hands locked in her hair as she curled against herself and the tears poured from her eyes.

"Mercury!" She screamed his name into the darkness and she sobbed, dying inside, so broken she felt as though she could never put herself together again, as though the world had just dissolved around her.

Heaving sobs tore from her, his name was a prayer on her lips, and she lay there, surrounded by his scent, by his memory, by everything she knew could never be hers. She felt herself die inside.

She pulled his pillow to her, smelled him, and her flesh ached. The pain, physical and emotional, ripped at her, left her twisting against the blankets as the tears poured and the pain raged.

He was supposed to love her.

You're my mate. Heat be damned. You're my soul, Ria.

He had kissed her as he said it. As the shower washed over them earlier. As the water slickened their flesh and poured over their passion.

My mate. I love you, Ria. My heart.

She screamed his name, buried her head in his pillow and curled into the agony. He wasn't her mate.

❖　　❖　　❖

Dane stood against the car, his head down, snow falling around him, aware of Rule and Lawe approaching slowly as Ria's screams echoed outside. As the sound of her agony, carried on the silent breeze, filled with grief, echoed through the night.

He lifted his head as they neared, silent, their gazes somber.

"Someone should go in there," Lawe said softly. "She shouldn't be alone."

Dane hunched his shoulders. "She needs to be alone now. She needs to accept it."

Rule snorted at that. "Mercury's going to kill you, you son of a bitch. You should have never taken her out of there."

Dane shook his head. "If dying would make Mercury her mate, then I would take my own life." He looked back at the cabin. "She deserved what she found with him. And she deserved it to last far longer than it did."

"Merc isn't going to let her go," Lawe told him. "When you hear that Harley prowling this way, you better run, Vanderale. Because hell doesn't describe what he's going to bring down on you."

His name echoed in the air again, the agonized feminine scream of pain causing them all to flinch. But Dane didn't hear a Harley prowling. He heard a lion's roar. One of the natural lions that roamed Sanctuary's boundaries. Drawn by the screams, roaring its own anger.

He shook his head again, opened the door to the limo and stepped inside.

He had listened to those screams once before. When she was a child, barely more than a baby, screaming for a mother who had been taken from her. Screaming at the pain tearing through her.

And even in the limo he couldn't block her cries. He stared into the night, watched the snow pile up and listened, and he ached. Because this time, he couldn't spare her. There was no way to ease it.

He reached into the pocket of his evening jacket and drew out the sat phone. He stared at it for long moments before pushing "speed dial."

"Where the hell are you?" His father's voice came over the line. Equal parts exasperation and concern filled it.

"Sanctuary. The party, remember?" he answered.

The Leo grunted. "How's everyone?" His sons. Dane knew who he was talking about.

"Just like you," he chuckled. "Arrogant as hell and making me crazy."

"More like you then," Leo stated.

"How are the girls?" His mother had given birth to twin

girls. They had been ill for a while, though Leo had reported the day before that they seemed to be doing better.

"Healthy as they were before they took that cold." He could hear the relief in Leo's voice. "Get home. You can babysit."

Dane grimaced. "Try the nanny, she's better at it."

Silence filled the line.

"What have you done, Dane?" Leo finally asked.

Dane stared out at the snow and heard Ria's cries as they echoed through the night.

He sighed wearily. "Ria's here."

"Why is my girl there, Dane?" Leo asked him.

Dane watched the snow. "Cracking code. Someone's slipping secrets to Engalls and Brandenmore," he said quietly. "I put her on it."

Leo was silent. "Good choice," he finally commented. "So why do I feel the but?"

That was his father. Sometimes Dane wondered if Leo wasn't aware of every damned game he was involved in.

He sighed wearily, spoke heavily and told his father the situation. Leo listened, for once without exploding in the middle of the story. Leo liked to explode. It made him feel better. When Dane finished, he remained silent and watched that damned snow pile up. At least Ria wasn't screaming any longer.

"Have you identified the traitor yet?" Leo's voice was hard, furious.

"Not yet. She was working on it when Alaiya showed up."

"I'm having the jet prepared. Meet us at the airfield in Buffalo Gap. Your mother, the girls and I will be there ASAP."

"Not good, Leo," he sighed. He hadn't expected that. "We can't risk it yet. And we sure as hell can't risk the girls."

"Leo Vanderale is arriving in Sanctuary to check the status of how his fucking money is being spent," his father snarled. "The Leo doesn't have to advertise who the hell he is. Arrange it. And I want that whelp Jonas ready to account for himself. Tell Callan to make room for me in the estate. I'll bring my security with me as well."

Dane rubbed at his forehead. "I'm bringing her home tomorrow. She'll be ready to go."

Leo waited. Listened.

"You don't want to see her like this, Dad." He rarely called Leo dad. "Let me bring her home. We'll heal her there."

Leo snorted. "If you're not on that jet by afternoon, I'm heading out. Count on it."

"I'll count on it," he answered.

"Did you get her nice baubles for risking her ass against my anger when I found out what you two were up to?" Leo finally snarled.

"Yeah. I did." But they weren't enough. There weren't enough baubles to ease her now.

"Hell," Leo sighed. "Take care of her Dane."

"I always do." Dane disconnected the line and continued to stare into the night. He always did, yet he hadn't this time.

And as he watched, the first powerful four-legged lion stepped into the clearing. The male animal shook the snow from its dark, flowing mane, tilted its head and roared into the night.

Another call followed, and yet another. And as Dane watched, Lawe and Rule moved warily from their positions, edging back to the limo as he threw the doors open and allowed the two Breeds to slide inside the warmth of the car.

Rye didn't bother to get out and enter the back through a door. He slid over the seat positioned behind the driver's area and stared back at Dane in surprise.

"There's a lot of fucking lions out there," he commented uncomfortably.

They were screaming into the night now, spurred by the animal Dane could swear he could feel heading this way.

Another animal stepped in. A lioness, her scream echoing through the night as the lions surrounded the cabin.

A dozen fully grown, enraged creatures, following one simple command. To protect Mercury's mate.

Dane let a smile tip his lips as he opened the small bar set in the center of the seat and pulled free the whiskey and glasses.

"Looks like the night just got interesting, my friends," he drawled, pouring the alcohol. "I say we enjoy the show while we can."

Ria's mate was coming for her. He had feared the mating was for the bitch that arrived that night, and his instincts had been infuriated by that. He'd have to call the Leo back.

He saluted his companions as another lion appeared. Damn, those bastards were big.

"I say, when Mercury arrives, we just pretend we're not

here." Lawe tipped back his whiskey and swallowed in a single drink. "Stay real quiet. Don't make eye contact."

They all nodded.

"Damned good idea," Rule muttered as one lion roared a challenge to the limo. "Yeah. Damned good idea."

As Alaiya's lips pressed against his, Mercury froze. He went completely still, completely silent, all his energy, all his consciousness focused on the animal that broke free of the mental chains he now realized had held it, roaring out in rage.

The sensation was like having a piece of his brain ripped from his skull. Animal instinct poured into him, breaking through his consciousness with the force of a blast ripping through concrete. It disintegrated the chains Mercury hadn't been aware of.

He felt power pouring into him, strength surging through his body and the adrenaline they called feral displacement overtaking him with such violent force that even the Breeds watching him growled at the threat he could become.

He was a threat. At the moment he was pure power and rage, man and beast, and the beast was strong. It was screaming out, roaring, and from his own throat came the rumble of danger. Of death.

He could smell Ria, Dane. Another man was taking his mate from his presence. Another male's scent surrounded her now, that male enclosing her in his strength. Only one thing was saving Dane Vanderale. There was no lust in his scent. Only protectiveness. Only pain. But he was taking Mercury's mate, and for that he would have to pay.

And Mercury felt the animal. It was free. Adrenaline was spiking through him now in crashing waves, the feral displacement threatening as the animal clawed at his mind in rage.

He felt his muscles thicken, blood pumping into them. He felt the strength he had once known pouring into him. His senses became sharper, brighter. Suddenly, Mercury knew every shift of every body around him, each individual smell, each ounce of anger that was filling the hallway. And the suspicion, the knowledge, that the woman that pressed herself so tightly against him was no more than an elite player.

Calculating. Manipulating. A woman who was there for much more than what she claimed.

As Alaiya's lips pressed harder to his, her tongue against the closed seam of his lips, his hand released her arm, shot out and gripped the wrist of another hand nearing him. He tightened his hold on Alaiya's other arm and peeled her from him easily, despite her struggles.

She had been attempting to gain access to the hormone filling his tongue now, his mouth. The hormone that had begun racing through him as he danced with his mate earlier, the scent of her panic and fear jerking at the animal until it stretched, paced and reached for her.

That had been the first moment Mercury knew his animal wasn't dead. The first moment he had known that everything his soul had told him was true. Ria was his mate.

He drew Alaiya away, ignoring the scent of her desperation, the scent of her anger, and turned his head to see Jonas, the extraction vial in one hand, the determination to take blood filling his silver eyes. But there was no threat—only concern, only a need to know.

He stared into the other man's eyes, swirling silver with power, and knew the reasons why he would attempt to take rather than ask. Because they knew the animal screaming inside him now. Jonas knew. And he might not fear it, but he did fear for it.

Mercury smiled. A baring of canines as he took the vial, shoved the needle in his vein and watched the blood, brilliant red, fill the small attached canister.

"Is this what you need?" He pulled the needle free and looked around.

He knew Ria was gone, but he could still feel her. Her agony was reaching out to him, causing the animal inside him to roar in rage, to shred his control with the overwhelming fury within it.

He tipped his head back and roared. Anger was a living, breathing entity inside him now. He was no longer half a Breed; parts of him weren't even human. More parts of him than ever before.

He slapped the vial into Jonas's hand, a small part of him realizing that the community as a whole would need the answers within it. They couldn't confine him simply because the animal was back. And if they tried, they would die.

He moved to follow his mate.

"Mercury, where are you going?" Alaiya was on him again, blocking his path, her body slithering against him as he snarled in distaste.

"Mercury, she's safe." Jonas's assurances behind him did nothing to ease the fury tearing at him. "Let's take care of this first. Dane, Lawe and Rule are watching over her. You can go to her soon."

"The hell he can." Alaiya's hands were digging into his shoulders, her expression twisting in anger. "Do you think I'll lose you to that weak little human?"

A hiss of silk at her movements and she rubbed against him as he inhaled her scent. The smell of other men clung to her body, the scent of anger and jealous rage. The smell of a woman who wanted things, simply because they weren't hers.

He remembered that about her. He remembered a time when it had been a challenge to him, the thought of taming that part of her. She had pricked the animal's sense of fairness, and he would have taken her to mate because she was the strongest female, the most defiant and, at the time, the one he felt the most need to fuck once her body matured.

But that was no longer true. Now her scent was an affront to him. It was nothing compared to the sweet scent of his Ria. With all her little contradictions, her honor and her fears. It didn't compare to Ria's warmth, her gentleness or the pleasure he found in each smile that he drew from her.

The scent of his mate was an elixir. It was nectar to his senses. And the scent wrapping around him now was waste and blood. It was death and disease.

He allowed her touch. Allowing her, for only moments, to cling to him again, staring down at her, letting her realize there was nothing here for her. Her touch was an abomination to him. And the only way her animal would realize it was to sense the feeling of it.

Then he gripped her arms, ignoring the discomfort in his palms at touching her. His tongue was thick and swollen, the hormone pumping furiously into his mouth now, and he swallowed. He swallowed and snarled in triumph.

The animal that had slept, that he had feared would return, was merging with his mind, tearing its way to that cold, empty place that had only been filled when Ria touched him.

And he realized it was because Ria had allowed the animal to awaken from whatever isolation those drugs had forced it into. That cold, empty place inside his mind had been a result of the drugs, and Ria had saved the animal now filling it.

"You're my mate." Alaiya's claws dug into his forearms, pricking him with anger rather than with desire, as she refused to acknowledge every instinct he knew she felt, that she was touching something that could kill her for the insult she was dealing to his mate.

"So where have you been then?" he asked her, his voice dark, fury pouring through him.

The need to get to Ria twisted inside him. He reined back the animal, just for the moment. Ria's turn would come, and he would make certain she never walked away from him again.

Alaiya's eyes dilated and he felt the lie before it ever passed her lips. He scented it, a dark, acrid smell that offended him.

"I was kept from you," she whispered.

"You lie." He shrugged from her touch. "You've played as you always played. You've done as you wished and given little thought to those you left behind in those labs. You were fucking your trainer, Alaiya. I knew it then. You killed him and you escaped, and you hid like the coward you've always been. And I ask you again, why come here now?"

Her lips thinned.

"You heard of Ria," he answered for her. "Which means you have ties into Sanctuary. Ties you shouldn't have."

Her gaze flickered over his shoulder, to Jonas.

"She turned herself into the Bureau six months ago, Mercury," Jonas told him. "I've had her working as an undercover agent in certain sectors since then."

That was Jonas. Always making use of a tool, no matter how flawed it was.

"And you didn't tell me she had been found?" He didn't take his eyes off her. He watched her, as he would a snake, while he watched the lies darken and lighten her eyes.

"She's not your mate." He heard the shrug in Jonas's voice. "Her scent isn't a part of you, and when I had Ely run the mating tests, they showed nothing. There was no reason to inform you."

Mercury nodded slowly. Reining in the fury, pulsing, pounding in his head, wasn't an easy thing. The animal was roaring in his head, demanding that he go to his mate. His true mate.

"That isn't true," Alaiya snapped. "The mating was there in the labs."

Mercury pushed her away. "The need to fuck was in the labs," he snarled back at her. "The lust was there, for the only female of any strength."

"Then explain the tests," she cried out, fists clenched, jealous fury pouring off her like body odor. "The tests they did. The same ones the tabloids are screaming over. Everyone else may think those rags are full of crap, but I remember the test results, Mercury. I remember them and I remember how possessive you were each time they allowed you near me. It was mating heat. The same as the matings I've read about since working with Jonas."

He shook his head. "I don't care about those tests, Alaiya. This heat is for one woman. My mate. For Ria."

"Breeds only mate once," she hissed, her face flushed in anger.

"We didn't mate," he reminded her before turning to Jonas. "I want her secured for further questioning." His gaze locked with that of his commander. He recognized the animal in Jonas as well now. And he smiled. The secrets Jonas held weren't that far beneath the skin, and animal sense met animal sense in an acknowledgment of strength.

Jonas nodded slowly. "I'd already decided that when she arrived tonight claiming to be your mate."

The timing was perfect. At the moment, the three strongest Breed males were not at that party. They were distracted, and Mercury was in full feral displacement. He could feel it. Under any other circumstances blood might have flowed.

But the animal was more experienced now, more mature, more intelligent. And the man knew freedom. A freedom the animal hungered for.

"Secured?" Alaiya growled. "I will not be secured. I came here for you, Mercury. You went insane when you thought you had lost me. How can you say I don't matter?"

He turned back to her, his eyes going over the perfect figure dressed in the perfect clothes, and she didn't hold a candle to Ria.

"How do you know what happened in those labs?" he asked her softly. "It's top-level information, Alaiya. You couldn't have gotten it unless you had a contact within those labs."

The battle to stay sane now was one he was going to lose soon if he didn't leave her. If he didn't get to his mate.

He swallowed, his knees nearly weakening with the taste of the mating hormone. It reminded him of Ria, tasted as though it were infused with her scent, with the sweet desire he'd licked from her body more than once.

The thought of sharing it with her, of watching her burn with him, was making his cock thicker, harder than it had ever been.

As he spoke, a Breed unit stepped into the corridor. Four silent Breeds, their eyes on Alaiya, knowledge of their orders in their eyes. They would make certain she was held until she could be questioned.

He moved to pass Alaiya, nothing more imperative than getting to Ria.

Damn her, she had dared to walk away from him. To leave her mate with another woman. He'd show her the error of that quickly.

But even as that thought passed through his mind, still his heart melted for her. She had loved him enough to let him go without recriminations when she thought his mate had returned. When she thought the mating heat Dane had smelled on him was for another woman.

She was stronger than he. He would have never let her go.

"Mercury." Alaiya's hand gripped his arm, over the material of the jacket he wore. "I never forgot you. Never."

He stared down at her, and for once he saw the truth in her eyes. For all her weaknesses, there had been parts of Alaiya that had been funny, intense, that had once given him hope that she would be a worthy mate to walk by his side. But he had found a woman that called to both the animal as well as the man. Ria had saved the most elemental part of him. She had called it forth. And she controlled the beast.

He pulled his arm from Alaiya's grip. "Don't let me catch you in the presence of my mate, ever again," he warned her. "The pain you dealt her tonight, deliberately, was uncalled for.

You touched what you knew, what the animal inside you warned you was not yours to touch. Do it again, Alaiya, harm my mate in such a way, ever again, and what I did in those labs the day when they told me, in exacting detail, how you supposedly died, will look like fun and games. Do we understand each other?"

She paled, staring back at him with eyes that flickered with fear now.

"You were part of my pride," he reminded her. "And admittedly, the woman I would have taken as my lover once you matured. Whatever mating hormone was showing up must have an error. Or some anomaly. You are not my mate."

"How can you say that?" she whispered.

Mercury could feel the animal clawing harder, screaming out in rage in his head. The hormone was pumping into his tongue, making it hard to think past the haze of lust consuming him now.

This had to be dealt with. No matter the distaste that filled him.

"I say it very easily," he growled. "I was pride leader then. In those labs, you were my responsibility. You were my woman, just as the other female was mine as well. I was an animal there. The animal ruled me and it guided me, and the animal needed to mate. It was that simple." He turned and stared back at Callan, recognizing the animal there. Powerful. Honorable. The animal inside Callan blended perfectly with the man, in accord, strong and enduring. And Callan ruled.

As powerful as Mercury knew himself to be now, knew his animal to be, he had no desire for the responsibilities that came with the pride leader position.

"You're Callan's responsibility now. Perhaps he can deal with you."

"I won't let that bitch take you."

The words were no sooner out of her mouth than the animal struck. His hand was around her neck, not bruising, but definitely threatening.

She gasped, fear finally contorting her expression as Mercury leaned close to her and inhaled. "The smell of the men you've lain with permeate your pores. The scent of your jealousy and your greed, the maliciousness of who and what you are, sicken me. Your calculation to steal what you know belongs to another enrages me. Come near my mate again, and

I'll not be able to help myself, Alaiya. I will kill you. No one, neither man nor woman, threatens what's mine. Do you comprehend me?"

Her eyes locked with his, the need to challenge his power flickering within her gaze as his hand tightened around her throat and he growled in warning.

"Yes." Her eyes lowered, went to his shoulder. Acknowledgment of his strength filled her scent now, as did her submission to it. The animal inside her, that part of her genetics, the strength he knew she held, the qualities that had made her survive, he respected. The woman, he would never trust.

He jerked his hand back from her and turned back to Callan and Jonas. The two men he followed into battle, respected and fought for.

"We'll talk later," he growled back at them. It wasn't a request. As much as he respected them, as much as he owed them, his mate came above them.

Callan nodded as Jonas glanced at the vial of blood in his hand.

"Run the fucking tests," Mercury snarled. "Perhaps we all need to see exactly what we're dealing with now."

He knew what they were dealing with. Pure animal genetics. Inside and out. Mercury was indeed a lion walking on two legs, and that blood would prove it.

"Blade," he told the Wolf enforcer at the head of the unit. "Inform them outside to have my Harley brought around."

"It's snowing, Merc," the Breed Enforcer informed him carefully. "Hard."

The Harley would go through a blizzard. Mercury had made damned certain of it.

"Tell them now." He turned back to Alaiya.

She stood against the wall, watching him carefully, calculation filling her eyes before she jerked them away from his gaze.

"Fuck with me, Alaiya, and it will be the last mistake you make."

He walked away from them all then and allowed the animal driving him freedom. It had been confined, so deeply hidden within him that even he hadn't known it still lived.

It wasn't confined any longer, and it was going for its mate.

As he stepped outside the mansion and moved for the Harley, he inhaled deeply.

He could smell them now. Knew where they were. Each living, four-legged lion that wandered the grounds, protecting its two-legged cousins, following them.

He roared out into the night, the animal and the man announcing their presence, their strength. And the calls came back to him. A symphony of animal screams, roars that filled the mountain, the acknowledgment from the animals that all moved to be near him, in triumph.

He was aware of the Breeds guarding outside, watching him warily now. The sounds of the lions called back to him, roaring out their greeting, their challenge, the echo of the fury they heard inside him.

He roared out again, filling the night with a sound he'd never known he possessed. His head tipped back, rage and triumph and the call for his mate tearing from vocal cords that were now more animal than human.

And the animals answered. He felt their response, felt them moving toward his destination. They were his pride and they would protect what was his. His woman. His mate. Their alpha female by choice and by nature.

The Breed that brought him the Harley stood back, wariness and respect filling his gaze as Mercury strode to him.

The Breed was awed by the sight of him. Eyes so blue they could rival a summer sky, the thick mane of hair flowing back from his savage features, his shoulders appearing broader, his body larger, than ever before.

The Lion Breed male saw something that both terrified and awed him, because this vision was a true Breed. The pure merging of lion and human. And he was enraged. That roar had been one of pure fury, and in it, it had held a message. A message so primal, so demanding, that the Breed himself nearly followed it.

Protect Mercury's mate.

✦   ✦   ✦

Ria heard the roars in the exhaustion of her sobs. They still tore from her, but the screams were no longer ripping through her. They were trapped inside her now, flowing out with the tears that had swollen her eyes and left her wrecked, clinging to Mercury's pillow, his scent the only solace she could find.

The memory of his smile flitted through her mind. The knowledge in his eyes when he stared at her. He knew her.

There were things she hadn't had to tell him. He knew who she was, when no one else ever had, even the Vanderales.

She hadn't wanted others to see who she was, so she had hidden it. But Mercury had seen her. He had felt her. And now she was losing him.

She had walked away. Should she have fought for him? Her sobs became deeper at the thought. Oh God, she wanted to fight for him. She wanted to claw that woman's eyes out. Tear her away from Mercury and rip at that perfect hair that had framed those perfect features.

And what good would it have done? Where did love fall into place within mating heat? She had done her homework. She knew there was no denying the heat. And the heat hadn't been between her and Mercury. At least, not with Mercury.

She was bleeding agony through every pore of her body at the thought of another woman touching him. How would she survive it? How was she going to do her job then walk away?

She curled tighter around the pillow she held to her. She couldn't stay here. Dane was right. There was no way she could survive it, but she couldn't survive returning to South Africa either. Where Elizabeth would fuss over her and Leo would watch her with sad disappointment. Because she had messed up and let herself care again.

No, that wasn't it, she realized. It was because he knew her. He knew she refused to share her hurt, and he'd always been disappointed in her because she didn't fight when she hurt. She hid, and she tried to heal. And Leo only knew how to fight.

And Dane? Dane always brought her baubles, trinkets and bling when she hurt. As though he knew no other way to try to ease her pain. And she had always taken them, because she had always known it comforted him. Even if it didn't comfort her.

She was the poor orphan relation because she had allowed herself to become one. Because, as Mercury had accused her, it allowed her to hide. It kept men at a distance, and it kept her heart safe. Because she didn't want to hurt. Because that six-year-old child still existed within her. The one who knew that life could so easily take the center of her world.

She heard the lions roar outside again, just outside the cabin.

Did animals feel the death of a soul? A heart? Were they moving in like scavengers to partake of the destruction? She had seen the lions on Leo's estate. Large and powerful, they al-

ways attacked the weakest in a group first. The ones that were
injured. That couldn't fight.

For the first time in her life she was willing to fight for something or someone, and she knew the battle was hopeless. A
woman couldn't defeat mating heat.

But he had made her promises. He had called her his mate.
He loved her. Love could fight biology, chemistry. It could
move mountains.

She shook her head. She would destroy both of them in the
process, wouldn't she?

"From all evidence I've gained, as well as the tests I've conducted on myself and Leo, I have to say mating heat always
comes with emotion." Elizabeth had stood before her more than
a year ago, frowning as she worked, while Ria went through
Leo's transmissions and updated the security of his encryption.
"What do you think, Ria? Does love conquer all?"

Ria had looked up from the computer to meet Elizabeth's
gaze.

"How would I know? I've never been in love." She had
smiled back at the other woman.

"But you've helped me with many of these tests," Elizabeth
pointed out. "The matings are strengthening in the American
Breeds, though we've had rare matings among Leo's pride."

Ria snorted. "Leo's pride rarely leaves the plains. What are
they supposed to mate? The zebras?"

And Elizabeth had laughed at that one, agreeing with her.

"Look at this. Devotion, Ria." She laid out pictures that had
been taken of the mated couples. "Look at their eyes, their expressions as they watch each other. These are more than biological, chemical or pheromonal. That's why the mating tests are
not always conclusive. Sometimes they're right, sometimes they
aren't." Ria knew Elizabeth often worked secretly with the
Breed scientist Ely Morrey. "This is love. Love, the predisposi-
tion for it, or the animal sense that that woman is somehow more
perfect, more worthy than others. It begins the mating heat."

Ria had stared at the pictures. The pride leader Callan Lyons
and his wife at a news conference after they announced to the
world what the Breeds were. Taber Williams and his mate,
Roni. Tanner and Scheme. An enforcer, Tarek, and his mate,
Lyra. In their expressions that extra something that had always

fascinated Ria. It was love. It was always love. Mating heat had managed, in every instance, to combine the chemical, biological and pheromonal with love.

Mercury loved her.

She heard the roar outside. Closer, throbbing with rage, reminding her of Mercury.

He loved her. She knew he did. Her soul was being ripped from her body without him.

He didn't love Alaiya. Mating heat came with love. Mercury had shown signs of the mating hormone in those labs. Not mating heat.

She buried her head deeper into his pillow, drew in his scent.

He was hers. He was meant to be hers. Yet what should have been hers had come alive for another woman. The scent of mating heat that Dane had smelled. The moment Mercury saw Alaiya.

She was tensing to move, to force herself from the bed, when the slam of a door had her stiffening. A snarl filled the cabin and the bedroom door burst open, thrown into the wall with a force that shook the room.

She jerked up in the bed. The light from the bathroom speared over him.

Mercury. Savage. Enraged.

"You ran from me, mate." Buttons ripped from his jacket as he tore it from his body.

She watched in shock as he undressed. Boots thudded to the floor. His pants slid from his powerful hips. His erection was thicker, throbbing, his eyes pure blue as she stared back at the apparition prowling to her bed.

"Mercury . . ."

"Mate," he snarled, his canines flashing as he moved to the bed.

She watched, entranced as he paused at the foot of the bed. He looked bigger, his muscles more powerful, the strength in his body amplified.

She swallowed tightly. "You didn't mate me, Mercury." Her breath hitched on a sob. She was going to cry again, and she couldn't bear crying in front of him. She wanted to be strong, wanted to give him the chance to choose without being burdened by promises made to her.

"There's no heat for me." The tears dripped from her eyes anyway, the pain scoured her soul.

His eyes flashed with rage. Blue eyes, pinpoints of gold flaring in them like fire. As they had been in the labs. As they had been for another woman.

She reached out to him, then drew her hand back, fighting her sobs.

"Why are you here?" she whispered. "Why? Oh God, Mercury. I can't bear this. I can't stand losing you twice. Don't do this to me."

The roar that filled the room had her flinching. It was animalistic, it wasn't Breed. It was filled with all the power and the rage of genetics that had somehow been increased with him, that poured through him. That sound was pure animal.

When his head lowered again, the expression on his face terrified her. Because she knew he wasn't letting her go. She knew he would ignore mating heat and it would destroy them both.

She moved to jump from the bed, to rush from the room. He caught her before she did more than tense. He was on her, pushing her down, snarling. His fingers tangled in her hair, held her in place, and the enraged lust that filled his face had her heart tripping in fear.

"My fucking mate." The growl was savage.

"No . . ." Because he was going to kiss her. Give her something that belonged to another woman. Not to her.

And she couldn't evade him.

His lips came down on her, slanted over hers, and his tongue passed into her mouth with determined hunger. Greed. With a desperation that surged through her senses and a taste that had her going still inside.

Wild. Primal. Heat and lightning, power and dark hunger. It filled her mouth. It covered her tongue, and it was so good. Like nectar.

She fought it. She bit at his tongue, but not hard. Because when she did, more of that taste filled her mouth.

"Suck my tongue," he snarled against her lips. "Take it."

"It's not mine!" she screamed back at him, her own fury growing now. "Damn you." Her fists struck his shoulders. "It's not mine!"

His lips came to hers again; he pumped his tongue into her mouth, forced the taste into her senses, and oh God, it was so good. It was everything she'd dreamed it would be. It was impossible to resist.

She whimpered. She begged him with her tears as her lips closed over his hesitantly. She drew it from him. She tasted him. And within seconds, she was consumed by him.

· C H A P T E R   2 0 ·

She was his mate. Nothing else mattered. No other thought
filled Mercury's head as he felt her lips surround his tongue, felt
the hesitant, suckling movements, milking the hormone from
him.

He felt her pleasure, sensed the desire rising eagerly inside
her even if she was hesitant in this. He was giving to her, taking
what belonged to him, giving what belonged to her. What he
had dreamed of giving her.

Heat flashed through him, a burning wave of searing pleasure and ecstatic agony. The animal and the man merged here,
with her. There was no battle, no fight for supremacy between
the two. For Ria, they were one.

He growled into the kiss. His fingers kneaded her scalp and
he drew the scent of her into his very being. His mate. He had
needed this. Ached for it. From the moment he had first caught
sight of her, he had prayed for it. And he had never realized that
he was the reason he hadn't mated her.

That the control he had forced on himself after coming off
the feral displacement drugs had blocked his ability to mate her.

He hadn't realized it until the animal inside him had sensed
her panic and her fear, her premonition of danger.

She had drawn the animal free. From the first scent of her,
the first time he had seen her, spoken to her, the animal had refused to sleep any longer. It had awakened, drawn as Mercury
had been drawn, by her scent, her honor, by the fact that she
was created to live inside his soul.

Now, as she drew the dark, potent hormone from his tongue,
and he knew it was potent, the growls that came from his chest
echoed inside his head.

At the moment, he was more animal than man. She had run

from him. She had left, refusing to see who she belonged to, refusing to allow him, *him, her mate*, to protect her.

Protecting her was his pleasure. Protecting her, ensuring she survived at all costs, was what he had been born for. He had been born for this woman. Born to fill the cold places inside her, just as she filled them within him. She eased the cold, dark loneliness inside him. She vanquished it, brought warmth, laughter, brought the sweet knowledge that the animal and the man he was truly belonged.

She had run from him. She had allowed another woman to come between them, stepped aside, no matter the reason. She would never step aside again.

She would never dare consider it, even if she might suspect his happiness lay elsewhere, she would never think to turn from him. She would hold on to him with talons as deep, as sharp as any animal's.

He would show her. Her pleasure was his. Her security was his. His Ria was going to learn to take what belonged to her.

"You dared to leave me." He tore his lips from her, glaring down at her, watching the flush that suffused her tear-swollen face, watched the hunger that began to fill her chocolate eyes.

She shook her head slowly. "What have you done to me?"

"Taken you." He fingered the cloth of that detestable dress. "And I will take you more. And more. Until you realize, Ria, nothing can tear you from me."

He had to touch her. The lion inside him needed to spread its mark across her entire body. The fine hairs along his body tingled, the mating hormone that infused his kiss beginning to seep along those hairs. He wanted to stroke against her. Fill her pores with his scent, and his scent alone.

Never would another Breed, male or female, attempt to encroach upon what belonged solely to him.

"You'll destroy me," she sobbed.

That sound, the sight of her tears and the smell of her pain were destroying him. He stared down at her, seeing the conflict in her gaze, the emotions that had torn her apart, that still tore at her, and he wanted nothing more than to ease her. Everything inside him demanded he ease her, and he knew of only one way.

The only way. He would draw the animal inside Ria free, if it killed them both. It was the only way.

"You are my mate." He touched her face, leaned forward and

kissed her gently. To apologize now for what he knew her anger would be later.

Mercury rubbed his lips against hers, heard the catch of her breath from the hunger filling her, and the rumble of pleasure in him was like a deep-throated, growling purr.

Then he speared his tongue inside her mouth again, forced her to take more of the heat, even as a part of him ached. His proud mate. So proud, so frightened of the emotions clawing between them.

"Mercury." Her broken sigh had him pulling back, his hands gripping the material of her dress before he ripped it.

He wanted that ugly fucking dress off her body. No later than next evening her closets would be filled with clothes that suited his Ria. That suited the feminine animal he knew paced and prowled within her.

She wasn't Breed, yet. But the animal in him recognized the primal core of her. And he would bring it out. He was created with the strength, the arrogance, to ensure it.

"What are you doing?" Her cry was one of shock, but not one of fear.

He tore the shreds from her, ripped the delicate material until there was no way it would ever cover her body again, and then he stilled.

Crouched over her, he could see what she wore beneath it now. The sexy, lacy, black garter and stockings. French-cut silk-and-lace matching panties. And a bra that was only barely there, pushing her breasts high, revealing her stiffened nipples. Rose-colored peaks surrounded by dusky temptation.

The sight of them made him hunger, make him growl. It made his erection throb in painful hunger and had him licking his lips at the thought of tasting them.

Once his lips covered those hard peaks, the hormone in his mouth would sink inside them, burn them, fill her with the need to have him suckle from her until they both expired with the ecstasy of it.

Then his lips would move lower. He let his eyes lower to her panties. He didn't want to remove them. They were sexy as hell, drove him insane with hunger at the sight of them.

He pushed her legs apart with his own, inhaling, smelling her arousal and the heat beginning to infuse it.

Her back arched off the bed. His head lowered, his lips covering a nipple and drawing it into his mouth as she whimpered in pleasure.

For a moment, there was enough sanity left inside him to wonder how it felt for her.

Ria was sinking in a whirlpool of sensation. Mercury had always pleasured her. She had never known anything but pleasure from his touch. But this—she arched her back, ground her head against the pillows and fought to make sense of what she was feeling now.

Her mouth was filled with the taste of dark, primitive lust. Primal lust. There was no other description for it. A deep flavor of male pleasure, like a mountain storm. Crisp. Clean. Yet tinged with fire. And it enflamed her.

She could feel it pulsing through her veins as the taste of his kiss fueled a hunger she couldn't have imagined feeling.

She couldn't fight him. She wanted to claw and scratch and demand he take her now, but the pleasure, oh God, the pleasure held her bound, watching as he lifted his head and pushed himself between her thighs. A second later her panties were torn from her body.

And it was erotic. It was so sexual that she wasn't prepared for what he did next.

Her back arched and a whimper tore from her as she felt his finger plunge inside her. It wasn't a slow, easy thrust. It was a penetration. An impalement, as his head lowered and his lips covered the too-sensitive, distended peak of one nipple.

What was he doing to her? His tongue rasped over the hard tip, and it flamed. It tingled and burned, and as he drew on it, lashing it with his tongue, she began to writhe beneath him.

It was too much. His finger pumping into the tight, slick confines of her sex, his tongue destroying her with the pleasure that filled her nipple. The sensations tore through the tip, raced along nerve endings and sliced into her womb with the power to steal her breath with the ecstasy of it.

"Mercury." She gasped his name, barely realizing her nails were piercing the tough skin of his shoulders rather than the blankets they had been latched onto. "What are you doing to me?"

Her head tossed. Fear and pleasure, agony and terror were streaking through her. She didn't know if she should pray for release or beg for death it was so intense.

"Mating you. Mate." His head lifted, his eyes crystal blue, the gold pinpoints flickering within the gemlike color.

His head lowered and his lips covered the other nipple. And it was the same. She was twisting, clawing at him. Needing him. Her pussy was pulsing around his finger as it moved inside her, stroking her, caressing her as she cried out his name again.

"Mercury. I can't stand this," she panted. She fought to hold on to him as the fear began to rise inside her.

She had read the reports on mating heat—the list of sensations felt, the intensity of it—and it hadn't prepared her for this. Not this. The wildness rising inside her, crashing over her and obliterating any control she could have thought to possess.

All she could do was feel.

His lips drawing on her nipple, heating it, his tongue rasping it. Spreading that hormone over her. It was sinking into her pores. The rasp of his tongue was opening the tiny pores farther, allowing that hormone inside her.

"You can't do this to me!" She tried to scream, but all she could manage was a sharp, smothered cry. "Damn you, Mercury. You can't do this to me!"

He was filling her with that hormone. Licking her, spilling it into her very flesh as he growled against the mound of her breast and began to inch lower. A kiss, a lick. Pausing to suck at her flesh, to rake it with those wicked canines of his, rasp it with his tongue. He was destroying her, one lick at a time, and edging lower by the second.

She knew where he was going. Where the heat of her arousal was burning so deep, torturing her, twisting through her.

His finger plunged inside her, his wrist twisted, stroking her inside, and it still wasn't enough.

"You'll never run from me again." His voice was tortured, thick, primal. "You tore my soul out, Ria. Running from me. Leaving with that bastard!"

He nipped at her flesh and she arched. The tiny bite was too much pleasure.

"I can't do this." Her head thrashed on the bed. "Oh God, Mercury. You'll destroy me. This isn't for me. You know it isn't for me. It's for her."

His head jerked up. "Do you burn, Ria?"

She whimpered at the question. Burning didn't describe the sensations tearing through her.

"It's killing me." She wanted to scream, but she could barely gasp.

"Do you need my taste again, baby?" He came over her, his lips lowering to hers, and her mouth watered for him. Her need for his taste consumed her. "Answer me, sweet Ria. Do you need my taste?"

"Please. Please." She lifted, touched his lips with her own and took his kiss.

Her lips parted for his tongue, closed on it, and she drew the storm into her again. She knew better. A distant, sane part of her mind knew better than to allow this to happen. She knew her own life was over if he ever left her. Her soul would shatter knowing he had regretted this night, this moment, when his need for his true mate began to burn inside him.

Death would be easy compared to the hell she would endure.

And yet, paradise was here. The taste of his kiss seeping into her, filling her, making her hunger. She could feel every inch of his flesh that touched her. The tiny hairs, so silken, so soft brushing against her flesh.

His hand between her thighs, his finger pressing inside her, the calloused tip finding a place deep inside her that had her clit screaming for relief.

It was swollen and hard, and it needed. Needed as much as her lips needed his kiss, her nipples needed his mouth. She needed.

And he gave.

He suckled at the tender tips, sending flash points of agonizing pleasure streaking through her until she was writhing, twisting beneath him. Broken cries filled the room as he finally began to lower himself again.

Kisses, licks against her flesh. Tasting her, moving down her body until he was stretched between her thighs, his fingers parting the material he had ripped, baring the engorged bud of her clit.

Ria stared down her body, watching. Her mouth dried out, her senses became dazed, as she watched his tongue part his lips, distend, stiffen. Then his head lowered, his eyes still on hers, and she watched as he nudged at the glistening knot of flesh.

Ria jerked, flinched; her upper body came off the bed, only to have his hand flatten against her stomach, pressing her back as his lips covered her clit.

She screamed out as electricity seared the little knot of nerves. She felt herself coming, clenching around the finger invading her as her clit spasmed, convulsed and throbbed against his torturous tongue.

And still, it wasn't enough. Nothing was enough. She was dying with the need and it wasn't enough.

"Please!" she cried out, trying to draw him to her as his tongue went lower. "Please, Mercury. Now. Take me. Please take me."

Her thighs spread farther for him and she whimpered as his finger slid free of her grip. Only to have his hands slide beneath her rear, lift her. His head lowered farther and his tongue plunged inside her. Licking, stroking, he didn't let up. He thrust inside her, filling her with that hormone, burning her flesh alive as she began to twist beneath him.

Oh God, if he didn't fuck her, she was going to die. She was going to combust into flames and be gone forever.

"Please," she whimpered. She begged. She screamed his name until she came again, arching and jerking against him as she felt her juices flowing from her vagina to his tongue.

The growl that came from him was harsh, spiked with ravenous hunger as he straightened, jerking to his knees and dragging her thighs over his.

Mercury could smell the heat on her now. Inside her. It infused him with the taste of her sweet syrup and stroked his lust to a boiling point.

His cock throbbed like an open wound now. And the cure for it was but a breath away from the engorged, flushed crest beaded with the hormone-infused pre-cum.

"You know what will happen," he growled down at her as she stared back at him, her eyes wide, her face dazed with pleasure.

"When I take you, Ria. When I come inside you, you know what will happen."

She shook her head, but the knowledge was in her eyes. She knew. She knew what he would give her, that when he released inside her, the extension he could feel throbbing beneath the head of his cock would become engorged. It would lock him inside her. It would spill the hormone that would begin preparing her body, changing her, making her receptive to the altered semen that could—and how he prayed it would—give her his child.

"Please," she whispered again, her voice ragged, filled with her need as he pressed his cock against her.

She was so tight, and he was larger than before. Thicker. Anticipation built inside him, satisfaction glowing in him. This was his woman. His mate. He clenched his teeth and began to fill her.

He watched as his cock began to sink inside the velvet heat of her body. Her panties, black lace and erotic, framed the penetration. Lightly tanned thighs strained, bunched as she arched and her pussy gripped him, milked him in until he was snarling with the pleasure, feeling the sweat pour from his body as he fought to hold back.

Ria was dying from the pleasure/pain of the penetration. Everything about Mercury seemed larger now. His shoulders, his muscular body, the engorged length and width of his erection.

She arched and writhed beneath him, moaning, begging as he took her. And she felt more than the penetration of his body into hers. More than the impalement of his cock. She felt a feral hunger driving inside her now. Her blood was fire. The perspiration covering her body was lava. Each nerve ending was pressing too close to her flesh, and she needed more.

"My Ria." He rose over her with a groan as he lodged his heavy flesh into her to the hilt. She could feel the press of his balls below, the throb of his cock inside her and his body covering her.

She felt ecstasy and agony and could do nothing but hold on to him as he began to move. Slowly at first. So slowly. Easing into her, thrusting deep and slow, working inside her as her flesh clenched and convulsed around him.

"Put your legs around me, Ria." The deep, rough rumble in his voice sent a shiver down her spine.

She shook her head. She couldn't bear it. He was so large inside her, filling her so completely now.

His teeth nipped her shoulder warningly. "Do it. Wrap around me, Ria. All the way."

She whimpered, but lifted her knees and wrapped her legs around his thighs.

"God! Mercury." Her hands clawed at his shoulders, as the pleasure seemed to radiate inside her, brighter, hotter.

"You're so tight. Like a hot, slick fist. Better. So much better than anything I could imagine."

Mercury was hanging on to his control by the most fragile thread. The mating hormone had sensitized his flesh to a degree that he could barely breathe for the pleasure consuming him now.

He could feel the hot press of delicate muscles surrounding his cock, every ripple, every little milking spasm that worked through the too tight channel of her pussy.

Agonizing pleasure. The head of his cock throbbed. He could feel the barb pulsing just under the flesh. *He felt it.* It was for her. All of it for her. Rising inside him like a tide of insanity and possessing with a hunger that went far beyond lust.

His sweat coated them now. Making them slick as he slid against her. Hard, hot little nipples poked against his chest. Tight and hot, they drew his mouth as he began to thrust harder against her, working his erection in and out as violent need began to break through that last measure of control.

"You won't leave me again." He nipped the upper curve of her breast. "You will never run from me again."

Where would she run? How could she run? She could never live without knowing this pleasure again, without feeling it rising inside her with such ecstasy.

Ria bit her lip, twisting against him as the need began growing, burning brighter, hotter. She rose to meet each thrust, whimpering, dying for more.

And he was giving her more. Hard, powerful lunges buried his cock inside her, stroked her internally as the need for his taste began to overwhelm everything else.

Her lips turned to his shoulder. Panting breaths, ragged cries left her throat, and as his thrusts increased, as they pounded inside, she licked the flesh of his shoulder, moaned, cried out, and before she could help herself, she bit him.

As he had bitten her so many times. She latched onto the hard flesh of his shoulder, held it tight, licked it, sucked at the taste of him.

Mercury froze against her. His entire body tightened, shuddered, then with a snarling growl of hunger his teeth pierced her shoulder like a brand and his hips surged against hers.

Ria would have screamed, but the pleasure, the need for his taste, the driving, furious stroke of his body inside hers, was tightening her womb, throbbing in her clit.

Tears spilled from her eyes at the incredible power and

beauty of what he was doing to her. The pleasure—it wasn't just pleasure. It was ravenous. Shameless. It was pure sensation, blinding-hot and reaching inside her to places where she'd never known could know pleasure.

Her womb tightened furiously. Her clit exploded in ecstasy, and rapture erupted through her entire consciousness.

She had to let go of him to scream. To buck against the furious thrusts powering the whipping sensations racing from nerve ending to nerve ending.

Her head ground into the pillow. She knew she was clawing his shoulders and she couldn't stop. She couldn't breathe. She couldn't scream. A starburst of color exploded before her eyes as she felt him give one last, hard lunge, and then his release spilled into her.

His release and something more. She felt the barb. Felt it extend, engorge, press into flesh convulsing, tightening around his cock, locking him inside her. Her upper body jerked forward, but his hard chest held her in place, his strong teeth tightened on her, his tongue licked, and this time, she did scream. The pleasure was too much to contain. The sheer violence of another orgasm tearing through her, stealing control of her responses, her body. She jerked and shuddered, writhed and arched, desperate to escape, to get closer.

The barb was blunted, like the tip of a thick, heavy thumb pressing into her, oh God, stroking her, pulsing as though it were coming as well.

She could feel his semen blasting inside her, and from that extension, the barb male Lions possessed, she felt a burning ejaculation to add to her pleasure.

Mercury jerked above her, his head lifting from her shoulder, a roar of triumph leaving his lips, filling the room as he bucked against her again, driving his cock and the barb deeper inside her.

The animal was free, and she should have been terrified. She knew what this meant. She knew it wasn't for her. But she couldn't let go of him. She held on to his arms with desperate hands, his hips with enclosing legs. She let the pleasure take her like a tidal wave sweeping across the land. She was helpless before it. Rocked to her soul by it. And now bound by chains that would never allow her to walk away from him.

She was mated to him. His mate, whether it was meant for

her or not, and satisfaction should have filled her. It should have blazed inside her. She had won the man and the beast. He was hers. He loved her. He had mated her. But nothing could over-shadow the fact that it had been another woman that called the animal free inside him.

Mercury eased slowly from Ria's exhausted body, grimacing as the overly sensitive flesh of his cock was stroked by the snug grip of her pussy.

Damn, he was still hard. Still hard and so fucking aroused it was painful. But he had his senses back, his sanity.

He pushed her hair back from her face, watching as her lips pouted and she burrowed against his chest as though she were cold.

A little moan passed her lips as her hard nipples raked the pelt over his skin. They were still engorged, reddened. And he wanted to suck them. He wanted them against his tongue, the sweet taste of her flesh in his mouth.

He inhaled harshly and pulled the blankets over her, coming down beside her as she stretched against his body and let him wrap himself around her. His hands played in her hair, touching it, petting it. Loving the feel of it.

He loved the feel of her.

He frowned, thinking back to the confrontation with Alaiya. Distaste had clotted his senses when she touched him. And when her lips had pressed to his, he'd had to freeze, to force himself not to kill her. She knew; the moment she saw him, smelled him, Alaiya had known he belonged to another. And still, she had pretended to play the wounded mate.

What game was she involved in here? Definitely one he knew he wanted no part of, but one he knew had the potential to destroy Ria.

Alaiya was a perceptive creature. She was as cold and calculating as Jonas in many ways. Though the director of Breed Affairs didn't have the cold-blooded maliciousness Alaiya possessed.

He rubbed a heavy strand of Ria's hair between his fingers

as he considered this problem. His Ria. She was confident, powerful, a force to be reckoned with when it came to what she knew. Codes. Tracking threads of deception. She was the best he had ever seen, even within the Breed community.

It was the woman she hid that concerned him. The one he could see in her, feel in her, the one she refused to release. That woman would be wild, powerful, a mate who could endure the years it seemed mated Breeds were being allowed.

She kept that part of herself vanquished, refused it freedom just as Mercury had refused his beast freedom. Because a woman's confidence was so easily shattered. That woman had never been free because Ria was terrified of losing the one last part of herself that gave her strength.

She was a contradiction, there was no doubt. The woman inside hid, while the logic and business sense of the woman faced the world. The woman who faced the world hid the one that longed to wear sexy dresses and high heels. To be vivid and wild.

Because vivid and wild drew attention. They made such a woman an object of speculation, of gossip, of men who wanted nothing more than her name notched into their bedpost.

And Ria couldn't afford that shame, that hurt. Just as she couldn't afford to appear to be more than the employee the Vanderales depended so highly upon.

There it was. He frowned at the thought. Ria couldn't afford to become visible, because she feared losing the advantage she had in her job. Wallflowers faded among the crowd. No one noticed them. No one feared them, she had told him. But it was more than that. She held an advantage. One the Leo approved of, needed. She was a tool he used quite effectively. And the Vanderales were the only enduring thing in Ria's life.

She feared losing that one certainty. The family that had saved her. They hadn't raised her, but they had overseen her raising. They had educated her. They employed her. She was the poor orphan child everyone thought the powerful family felt sorry for.

The inner woman had no confidence in herself, in her ability to command the attention and power Mercury knew was her due.

He growled at the thought of it, his eyes narrowing into the dusky light of the room as he considered each avenue open for him to proceed.

He was her mate. It was his job to protect her, to assure her security, her happiness.

She was never going to believe he had mated *her*. That part of her that refused to allow her to accept anything as her own would always pull back. Because the mating heat hadn't made itself fully known until Alaiya's appearance.

He couldn't fully blame her, and yet he did. And he knew when she awoke, the fury of a woman terrified that she had something that didn't belong to her would blaze as high and as hot as the mating heat.

Simply telling her would never be enough. And it wasn't enough for him. She had enraged him when she ran from him. Torn at his own pride and sense of worth. This was his mate. She would fight for him. She would fight for him or there would be no fury greater than his own.

He lifted his head and focused on the open closet door. Within it were those ugly clothes she insisted on wearing. He looked at the clock, and a hard, determined smile pulled his lips back from his teeth.

He eased away from her, tucked the blankets around her and moved for that closet. He had a few hours before the heat would awaken her. Before the need would begin clawing through her.

He stepped into the large closet, closed the door behind him and switched on the light. He turned, and his eyes narrowed on the clothing before he looked down at his hands.

The clawlike nails were blunted, but they were still dangerous. He took the first skirt from its rack silently, and only the rending of cloth whispered through the night as he began the destruction. Every shred of dowdy, miserable clothing she had in her possession was dropped to the floor of the closet, shredded. Skirts, tops and slacks. Sweaters and blouses. They were all rent beyond repair.

The shoes came next. Excellent quality, perfect workmanship. They were no hindrance to the silent rage working through him. His mate hid, even from him, and he would allow it no longer.

When he finished with the closet, he moved to the dresser and chest. He left nothing but the sexiest underwear, the lightest, skimpiest gowns. He dropped each item to the floor as he finished with it. Ripping it, tearing it, destroying every last article that she had brought with her.

Except one outfit. One pair of jeans. One shirt. A pair of leather ankle boots. She would need something to wear when he took her into Buffalo Gap and bought her new clothes. Clothes that befit the woman he knew she was.

Arrogance surged through him. He had an abundance of it, there was no doubt. And he knew that the fury he would face tomorrow would be one he might wish he had avoided. But there was more at stake here than her anger, her pride. Her confidence and belief in him were at stake, and he'd be damned if he would lose any of that.

He was her mate. Damn her for thinking she could so easily give him to another. That she would simply walk away. He knew, had sensed and felt and been rocked by, the complete love that surrounded him when she stared at him. She was devoted to him. He knew this. And still, she had walked away.

Her selflessness went far deeper than his ever could. Because he would kill the man that tried to take her. Even before the mating, he would have torn any competitor for her heart, limb from limb. Shredded him just as he shredded her clothing.

Then, as though those shreds of fabric were no more important than the sigh of satisfaction he gave, he returned to the bed.

He curled around her once again, and as sleep came over him, he smiled. Ria was right, he could purr.

✦   ✦   ✦

She was burning. Ria could feel the blistering arousal dragging her from sleep, imperative, tearing at her body and at her mind as she fought awareness. She didn't want to wake up. She wasn't ready to face reality.

She wasn't ready to face her own emotions. The ones that clawed at her far deeper than the arousal did. The satisfaction, because he had chosen her. Willingly, though she hadn't believed it was possible for a Breed to make such a choice. According to Elizabeth Vanderale, it wasn't possible. But Mercury had made that choice.

He had walked away from the woman whom nature had chosen for him years ago, and he had come to her. He had loosed the full force of all that savage hunger on her and she had taken it eagerly. Not just physically, but emotionally.

Something inside her had eased, while another part of her

tensed. He chose her, for now. She was terrified the other shoe
would drop later.

God, this was why she didn't involve herself in relationships. She had been terrified of caring to this depth about anyone. Scared of loving to the point that she didn't know how to
walk away. And that was how she loved Mercury. When she did
walk away from him, she didn't know how to go any further
than the bed they shared.

His touch fed a part of her soul that had always been closed
off from others.

But her body was ready to be fed now. It was hungry for the
taste of Mercury. For the feel of him. His possession and his
kiss.

She moved against him, feeling his erection pressing against
her stomach, his hand petting her hair. Her own hands were
pressed against him, the feel of his flesh warming them, exciting them.

He was awake, so why didn't he just take her? He could
smell her need, she knew he could. She had watched him inhaling her scent last night, pulling it into his nostrils and growling
with pleasure.

So why was he waiting? Her fingers curled against him as
she fought to restrain herself. To keep from attacking him. Devouring him.

"If you want it, then you'll have to take it yourself, mate."
The hard growl in his voice assured her he wasn't asleep. Assured her he was still as volatile, still as wild as he had been the
night before.

She struggled to open her eyes, feeling her heart pounding in
her chest as he stared down at her with those arctic blue eyes.
Eyes that sank inside her and reminded her of the lab photos
she had studied before coming to Sanctuary.

"Your eyes changed colors," she whispered, remembering
that from the night before. The color was even more vivid now.

"My eyes were blue until they tried to destroy what I was," he
informed her, a flash of anger sending sparks of gold through the
blue. "It's not my eye color you need to worry about, though."

The tone of his voice was just on the edge of pissing her off.
The storm, the emotional upheaval from the night before, had
passed. Thinking was still a delicate process, but she was get-

ting there. Her emotions were volatile, though. She could feel them rising inside her, pushing her, straining to break free of her control. She would have to deal with them later, though. As soon as he put out the fire blazing in her body.

"What do I need to worry about then?" She pulled the sheet over her swollen breasts as his gaze flicked to the covering.

"Do you want me, Ria?" he crooned, his voice heating with his own arousal.

Nervousness rose inside her as she tried to fight it back.

"That's a stupid question, Mercury."

He grinned as she pointed that out.

"Then come to me," he told her. "It's my pleasure to relieve your heat. All you have to do is take what's yours."

She flinched. He had to say it like that. And he knew what he was doing; she saw it in the narrowing of his eyes, the tightening of his features.

She lifted her chin, staring back at him furiously. It hurt. He couldn't realize how much it hurt, fearing that she would eventually lose him to a woman who didn't deserve him, who hadn't come to him when he needed her. Instead, she had waited until someone else loved him, needed him.

"You were supposed to be the nice Breed," she stated, trying for cold, but her voice trembled with need.

"Oh, I was very nice," he assured her. "I still am. Notice if you will, I haven't yet paddled your ass for running out on me last night. Though, the option still remains."

She needed to protest that. She really did. But as he spoke, he shifted the sheet from his hard body and she lost her breath, her will to fight.

His cock was thick, reaching nearly to his navel, the thick, engorged head throbbing dark and powerful.

She licked her lips. She felt dazed, so hungry, suddenly so desperate for that hard, heated flesh inside her body that she whimpered.

She reached out, touched the hard plane of his chest, stroked her hand to the middle of his stomach and stopped. She wanted to go lower, wanted to touch and taste and take everything she longed to claim as her own.

"Mercury." She lifted her gaze to him. Imploring.

"It's so easy, Ria," he whispered. "To take what you need. It's always my pleasure to give it to you, you know that."

"Take what isn't mine," she bit out, anger rising inside her at the thought, the affront that the mating heat hadn't shown up for her. She hadn't drawn its force. Another woman had.

The dark, warning growl that rumbled from his throat had her flinching.

He kept his arms behind his head, but they bunched, the veins beneath the flesh bulging as the muscles did.

"Don't push me this morning, Ria," he warned her. "This is no place for it, and my patience is raw enough as it is. If you need me, I'm here. If you don't, then I'll suffer through the hell of it, shower and get on with the day's business."

"Damn you!" she cried, aching, bleeding inside from the emotional storm rising inside her.

"Damn you for your stubbornness!" he bit back. "You're my mate. You will accept that fact or we'll both suffer for it. Now make up your mind. Are you going to fuck me or fight with me?"

She had every intention of doing both, but she had her priorities. He wanted to torment her? Torture her? Then she would play his game as well, for as long as she could stand it.

She swung one leg over his waist, above the heavily engorged head of his erection, and leaned forward as his hands shot from beneath his head and spread into her hair.

Her lips came down on his.

"Give it to me," she demanded, nearly panting for the taste of him now. "Give it to me now."

All if it. His touch, his possession, his heart as fully as he claimed hers.

His head lifted, his lips slanting over hers and his tongue in her mouth. The glands beneath it were swollen and heavy, spilling the electric taste of lust into her mouth. It was addictive. She needed it. Needed it even as it made her writhe. She pressed her mound against his hard abs and whimpered at the feel of her swollen clit caressing the taut muscles there.

She reveled in the pleasure, in his touch, in the knowledge, that for now, this moment, he was all hers.

She sucked at his tongue, tangled her own with it and felt his kiss rock her soul. It was as deep, as hungry, as her own. A growl rumbled in his chest, caressed the hard tips of her breasts and sent a vibration of pleasure streaking through her.

She was too needy, too hungry to wait. He said to take what

she needed. And she needed desperately. Needed all of him, physically, emotionally.

Her hips lifted, slid down until the engorged crest met the slick, swollen folds of her sex.

Mercury pulled his tongue back, nipped at her lips and then returned that spicy taste to her as she began to work herself on his hard cock.

Excitement exploded inside her. She controlled this. Her nails bit into his shoulders as she felt the hormone from his tongue invading her system. She devoured every taste of it as her hips worked against his cock. She eased down the length of it, crying out into his mouth as his hands cupped the swollen mounds of her breasts.

His fingers flicked over her nipples. His tongue pumped into her mouth as she fought to hold on to it. But she controlled the erection—the depth she took with each movement of her hips, the length of the stroke, how it stroked her, how it stretched her.

She controlled the powerful, primal force of the male below her, and she could feel it. She gloried in it. He growled beneath her, but he didn't attempt to stop her.

When her head drew back, she stared down at him, watching the sweat bead on his forehead, the grimace that revealed the wicked canines at the side of his mouth.

"Do you love me, Ria?" he groaned. "Give me that, baby. Love me."

She stared down at him, loving him with everything in her soul.

"I love you past sanity," she finally whispered, and cried out in pleasure as his hips jerked beneath her.

She barely had half the length inside her. He was stretching her; she swore that damned hormone either made him larger or her smaller, because the pleasure/pain of the entry already had her on the verge of coming.

"God, you're so thick," she moaned.

"You're so tight," he growled back, his head grinding into the pillow. "Take me, Ria. I'm going to have a fucking stroke waiting."

She paused. A slash of red stained his cheekbones; gold glittered in those artic blue eyes and arousal twisted his expression.

He had the look of a man hanging on to his control by only the thinnest grip. But the fingers that plucked at her nipples didn't hurt her. Each touch was primed for her pleasure. For her excitement. For her needs. His gaze filled with tenderness, loving her just as he had before another woman had destroyed her world. She had no choice but to love him the same, to love him more, because she was desperate to fill herself as deeply with him as possible.

"Ria. Move dammit," he growled. "Fuck me."

She moved slowly, lifting and lowering her hips as she watched him. Was this how she looked when he took her? Demented with pleasure? Dazed with the need ricocheting through her?

Hunger, need and desperation filled his expression. It throbbed in his cock, pounded inside her pussy and had her twisting her hips against him and moaning at the effect.

His teeth clenched, jaw bunching with tension.

"You're killing me," he groaned, his eyes narrow slivers of blue as he stared back at her.

He was killing *her*.

She lifted and took more of him, her back arching, thrusting her breasts out to his hands as she braced herself against the hard planes of his stomach.

This was exquisite. Taking him an inch at a time, feeling him stretching her at her pace, experiencing sensations she had never known before.

"Ria, sweet Ria," he groaned desperately, his hands sliding from her breasts to her hips as she worked more of him inside her. "Ah, baby. Take all of me."

"Not yet," she panted, shaking her head, feeling his hands grip her hips though he did nothing to force her farther onto the erection impaling her.

"When?" His voice was tortured, half laugh, half growl.

She tightened around him and moaned as an animalistic snarl filled the air.

"You're torturing me," he accused her, but she heard something akin to joy in his voice as she moved against him, tightening, working him inside her, milking him and easing farther down on him.

Moments later, he was buried fully inside her, every throbbing inch burning her as she felt her control disintegrate.

Need was a lash of furious pleasure building to ecstasy. It was Mercury's hands tight on her hips, his head thrown back in pleasure as he lifted his hips and gave himself to her. Remaining still otherwise, letting her find her pleasure as well as his.

It was riding him while he was stallion-hard, thick, throbbing with his own need to release, yet holding back for her. It was watching the rivulet of sweat trail from his forehead to the thick strands of his hair. Another down his powerful, corded neck as her orgasm began to tighten inside her.

Her body was a pulsing mass of need. Lightning flickered over her nerve endings, every nerve ending. Pleasure was cell-deep, soul-deep, and taking him was fueling something wild and powerful inside her as well.

"Mercury." Her head tilted back as she cried out his name. "Oh God. Mercury!"

She tried to keep moving as she came, tried to plunge him into his own release, but it was tearing her apart. She was shaking, shuddering, feeling it exploding inside her, and he gave it to her then. Took her. His hands tightened on her hips as his moved beneath her, thrusting hard and deep, impaling her with the thick intrusion of his flesh, until his hoarse shout, then a primal, smothered roar, tore from his throat and his release joined hers.

That didn't mean it was over. She collapsed to his chest, barely aware of her nails digging into his forearms as she felt the barb extend, felt it throw her higher, deeper, into a release that stripped her bare and left her begging him. Begging him for mercy, because the pleasure was tearing her apart and remaking her, and she didn't know how to live with being remade.

It was a long time later before she could lift her head, before she could drag her sated body from his and roll to the side of the mattress.

Sitting up, she pushed her hair from her face, her gaze on the floor, and she froze.

Those weren't her sturdy winter boots, in shreds? That wasn't her gray wool skirt? Her panty hose? Her shoes?

Oh God.

She turned and stared at the closet. The door was open, the light was on, and she felt herself pale. She felt Mercury tense as he lay still beside her, his gaze on her, watching her carefully.

She couldn't look at him. All she could see was her clothes. Shredded. As though someone had taken shears to them. Her sturdy shoes and boots, plain socks and panty hose. The only thing she didn't see was the delicate silk-and-lace underwear sets she had brought with her. There were no push-up bras torn to shreds. No stockings. Like the ones she still wore and hadn't even realized.

Shock slowly bled to fury. She stared at the mess, the deliberate calculation in each carelessly dropped shred of fabric, and she turned back to him slowly.

He was watching her with those icy blue eyes that still seemed wicked, burning with greedy flames. His expression was controlled. His look arrogant. Confident.

"What the bloody fucking hell have you done here?"

He grinned. "Have I mentioned how much I love it when that very proper, very precise accent of yours shows up? It means there's a party on the way. Be careful, Ria, it's not just coffee that makes you hotter. But also anger."

She stared at him, incredulous. The arrogance, primal self-confidence and complete calm in his expression enraged her.

"You destroyed my clothes," she clipped out.

His eyes narrowed. "Yes, I believe I might have done just that."

"Why?" She could barely form the word, could barely form a thought.

He lifted up then and leaned toward her, nose to nose.

"I'm sick of fucking a stranger. Of sensing the woman I mated and never seeing her. Those," he snarled, pointing to the clothes, "hide my mate and I will no longer allow it."

She edged back and moved to her feet, staring at him, shaking, and it wasn't from arousal. It was from complete, overriding disbelief and anger.

"You are insane," she sneered back. "Your mate, my arse. Your mate is back at Sanctuary slinking around like a damned cat in heat. Waiting on you. Waiting on you while you fed me that fucking hormone and made certain I couldn't leave you. What's wrong, Mercury? Couldn't you handle the fact that you didn't have it the way you wanted it? Now you have to turn me into something you can bear to touch?"

He came out of the bed with a snarl heavy enough, primal enough that something inside her rebelled. Did he think she would back down in the face of his anger? That she would flinch?

Before he could take the first step she was in his face.

"I can have those clothes back, this fast." She lifted her hand and snapped her fingers imperiously. "A Vanderale Breed will deliver them and a Vanderale Breed will follow any request I make of him. And you can take these shreds," she sneered, "and shove them."

"You want a Vanderale Breed to die?" he drawled, his nose almost touching hers, anger a live thing in his eyes now, a living, breathing entity within her as well. "Let one deliver more of those mockeries of what you should wear and I'll rip him apart and send him running and crying to the imperious Leo he follows. You're my mate and I'll be damned if you'll hide from me any longer."

"Alaiya is your mate," she screamed in his face. "With what you did to me, you've mocked everything nature intended mating heat to be. What, Mercury, do you need a fucking harem instead of one woman?"

He smiled. A cold, quiet smile that penetrated her fury, that left her staring back at him warily as he straightened.

"We can go shopping this morning. I saved you an outfit."

"Excuse me!" Her fists were clenched; violence was ripping her apart inside. "What did you just say to me?"

The look on his face had her stepping back. Not in fear, but in caution. Those eyes narrowed, flickered a heavy gold, and his expression tightened with such primal arrogance that she had no idea how to fight it.

"I said, we will go shopping. This morning. After we shower, eat and, if you need me again, have me. We'll replace your clothing."

"The clothing you ripped apart?" Her voice was hoarse, strained with anger and disbelief.

His brow arched. "I hardly think so. But you can try to convince me if you like. You are my mate, and Breeds have been known to spoil their mates atrociously. Want to see how far I'll spoil you?"

She ached to.

"You bastard!" she breathed out, incredulous, certain one of them had lost his or her mind, and she was pretty damned certain it wasn't her.

"It was just a suggestion." He shrugged.

"You dirty, arrogant, egomaniacal Breed," she screamed. "You're worse than Dane. Worse than Jonas. You're worse than the Leo." And that was the highest arrogance insult she could deal anyone.

"Compliments help." He smiled and moved past her, his hand caressing her butt as he passed, and drawing an enraged squeal from her lungs.

"I'll kill you."

"Damned if you won't if we keep going at each other the way we did this morning," he called back to her. "I'll die happy."

The bathroom door closed. She stared around her, still in shock, certain she was dreaming. The tightly clenched, furious snarl that left her lips would have rivaled his best. And the bastard laughed at her. She heard it. Heard his chuckle, and before she could stop herself, the small clock on the bedside table was in her hands, then flying across the room to shatter against the door.

She stood there, breathing roughly, then groaned and sat back down on the bed, and stared at the ruins of her detestable clothes. What the hell was she going to do now?

CHAPTER 22

"Whew." Mercury was very, very careful to keep the sharp expulsion of breath quiet as silence filled the bedroom.

He braced his hands against the sink and waited. She stayed in the bedroom. She wasn't running. Damn if it wouldn't suck running out into the snow naked to catch up with her.

He could smell the sweet scent of her arousal, the sharp tang of her fury, and had to admit, damn, she was a challenge when she was pissed off.

Not that he would want to chance this one again soon. As he'd said, Breed males generally spoiled their mates, especially during mating heat, when their emotions and sense of balance were so off-kilter.

Male Breeds were highly sexual during mating heat, but they didn't experience the painful, agonizing arousal that a mated female felt, especially one that wasn't Breed. They didn't experience the sharp spikes of anger because they couldn't control their emotions or their needs. Females were dependent on their mates, and for an independent woman, that was a hell of an adjustment to make.

Ria was one of the most independent women he had ever run across. On the outside, she was so self-sufficient, so contained, that others moved uneasily around her. Humans needed to be needed, just as Breeds did. They weren't comfortable around those they sensed didn't want or need such entanglements.

That's how Ria affected others. They shied away from her, watched her warily, unconsciously aware that she was pushing them away.

That wasn't going to work in Sanctuary, or anywhere within the Breed world. If she didn't claim him as her mate, herself, then she would never be happy. And making a place for herself in his life would be agonizing for her, no matter how easy he tried to make it, or how he spoiled that. Her fears would always be there. And other Breeds would always sense them.

He tensed as he heard the bedroom door close. Frowning, he moved quickly from the bathroom.

The one outfit he had left her was missing. Damn her if she had run from him again.

He heard another door close, but not the outside door. Moving through the house, he paused at the closed door to the guest room and sighed in relief.

She was there. Showering without him. He had hoped to shower with her, to ease her.

He frowned and entered the bedroom, drawn by something, a sensation, a scent that tore at him. The scent of her tears mixed with the water. The scent of her confusion, so bleak and unfamiliar to her.

And it broke his heart. Tore at his soul.

The shower was running in the bathroom and Ria was there. He pushed aside the shower curtain to see her, her head against the wall, her hands covering her face, her shoulders shaking with tears.

"Ria," he whispered.

"Don't." She shook her head, her voice hoarse. "I don't scream. I don't cry. I don't hurt like this." Her voice became ragged, angry. "Leave me alone. Please. Let me control this. I have to control this."

He stepped in behind her, enclosed them in the steamy warmth and pulled her to his chest. Where she belonged, and he let her cry. He bent his head over hers and closed his eyes, knowing how hard this was for her. Feeling it. Sensing it.

"I love you, Ria," he whispered against her hair. "I can't give you any more assurances than that." He wouldn't give them to her, because he knew right now she wouldn't hear them.

She sobbed harshly, her arms going around his waist, holding on to him as her tears branded his chest.

"I didn't want to love you," she cried brokenly. "I didn't want to hurt like this."

"I know, baby." He kissed her hair, stroked her back. "I know."

He let the storm rage inside her, and he stroked her as it

eased. When she stood silent against him, he moved back, snagged a washcloth and he washed her. Gently. He cleaned the tears from her face and touched her lips with his, holding back the need that thickened his tongue, that burned inside him. For the comfort.

He gave her the only comfort he knew how to give her. His love.

◆   ◆   ◆

Sanctuary's heli-jet whisked them to Buffalo Gap hours later, after Mercury slung her over his shoulder and deposited her in the back area, beneath the pilot's amused gaze.

She was furious. So mad she could barely breathe, and once they landed at the mall, she had no choice but to behave with decorum. She wasn't about to get into a screaming match with an arrogant Breed for the press to get hold of.

And Mercury capitalized on it. He even went so far as to allow her to choose an outfit and try it on. She had no sooner undressed than he jerked open the door and stole the clothing she had worn into the store.

And she heard him—he was a dead man—she heard him tell the salesclerk to get rid of her jeans and sweater. He was dead. She was killing him.

She stepped out in the clothes she had chosen. Black slacks and a gray sweater. He took one look at them, flexed his fingers and growled in disaproval as he asked her, very quietly, "Do you want to leave this store naked?"

She left the store dressed in butt-hugging, leg-caressing blue jeans that drew more male eyes than she had drawn in her life, and he dared to snarl at the men watching her. Paired with the jeans was a crimson—*crimson* for God's sake—figure-hugging, boob-conforming shirt that she hid beneath the leather coat he'd allowed her to keep for some reason.

He did the same thing at the shoe store. She left in a pair of flat, leg-flattering ankle boots that in no way resembled the ones he had trashed. And shoes. So many shoes the store was having them delivered that afternoon to the cabin. High heels, shoes so expensive even she winced; high-heeled boots, leather boots, shapely, sexy boots that sent a surge of panic inside her as he stood over her, intimidating her, all but forcing her to try them on and stand up. To walk in them. To feel the pure erotic feel of footwear designed not just for comfort, but for wicked sensuality.

Store after store. The exclusive mall, attached to the even more exclusive hotel built for Sanctuary guests, held every conceivable store. They were there for hours. From store to store, as Mercury shoved clothes into the dressing room, growled, threatened a scene and pushed her farther into the dark little corner where the feminine woman she hid shouted out in glee.

She wasn't pleased. When he forced her into the makeup salon, she dug her heels in, only to have him whisper insidiously that he had no problem giving the press a story that would keep them talking for months.

And the press was there. Mercury was a known figure with the Bureau of Breed Affairs. One of their top enforcers. He might not be dressed for duty, but the leather pants and black T-shirt he wore did nothing to hide the powerful male animal he was.

Black leather for God's sake. Displaying those powerful legs and the heavy boots on his feet. A T-shirt that stretched across his chest and forearms. His hair was tied back at his nape, showing off the proud, lionlike features that had other shoppers watching him warily.

She came out with makeup, hair accessories and a perfume so sinful she wanted to try it now. This instant.

He forced short dresses on her. Leather pants. A leather vest. Who knew he was so damned wild? Leather?

She should have known. She had known. There were infrequent pictures of Mercury out of uniform, and those pictures had made her wet, long before she met him.

There were simple business dresses and skirt outfits, but short ones, figure-flattering ones. Silks and soft cottons, sweaters that stretched over her breasts and displayed cleavage, and so many damned pairs of stockings, push-up bras and matching panties that she wanted to faint at the thought of the cost. He was spending a fortune and wasn't even wincing.

"I hate you," she muttered as they left another store. He had let her keep her simple leather coat until there. He pulled it from her shoulders, tossed it to the clerk with an order to burn it, then pulled a shorter, hip-hugging black leather jacket with a thin advanced insulate over her arms.

The soft interior felt like heaven. The leather conformed to her body, as the other clothes did, and drew the gaze to her ass in the back, her thighs in the front. Another damned reason for him to growl.

She wished she could protest his taste. She wanted to. But she would have had to lie, because he had exquisite taste in everything he chose.

"You'll love me again in a few hours," he promised her, inhaling slowly, grinning at the proof he found of her arousal. "Perhaps sooner."

"I really hate you," she hissed.

"I hear love in your voice, Ria." He kissed her quickly. "Come on, one more stop to make."

One more stop. At an exclusive dress designer who whisked her right in, measured her, hemmed and hawed and cackled gleefully as Mercury chose several dresses for her. Because she refused. She was horrified. Outraged at the price. And the sheer beauty of the party gowns he chose.

"Thanksgiving, several Christmas parties and New Year's," he told her. "You'll be attending with me."

"My job is almost finished," she informed him, striving for a calm she didn't feel as they stepped from the boutique.

Mercury came to a hard stop and glared down at her.

"Would you go back now?" he demanded then. "Would you leave me, Ria?"

She paused, staring back at him silently. He could come to South Africa with her, but she knew the same thing he did. Leo's pride was already established, the hierarchy formed, just as it was here. There was no place for him there, whereas here . . .

She shook her head slowly. No, there was no returning ever again to what she was. And she couldn't leave Mercury. She had proved that the night before. Dane had offered her escape, and she had refused it.

"No," she finally whispered. "Not yet."

"Not ever." His voice hardened.

"Not yet." Not until he asked her to. Not until he could no longer deny the pull Alaiya would have on him.

And then, she was terribly afraid, there would be no place to escape the pain.

"You love me, Ria." He stared into her eyes. "I can smell it pouring from you, reaching around me, inside me. You can't deny it."

"I don't deny it," she admitted.

"But you regret it?" Anger flared in his eyes.

And she had to shake her head. No, she wouldn't regret it. She would die from it, walk in sorrow when it was over, but she wouldn't regret it.

"I don't regret what I walk into with my eyes open," she finally told him. "But I don't have to like it. And when you realize the mistake you made, what you've done to both of us, Mercury, I have a very bad feeling you might regret it."

She walked ahead of him again, and Mercury let the smile tug at his lips as he watched her move. She owned the clothes she was wearing. Not just physically, but he could also see that her attitude, her demeanor were cracking.

He had to clench his teeth as he watched her walk, though. Those jeans hugged her ass like nobody's business, and that light black leather jacket called attention to her hips and slender thighs. She was a wet dream walking, and if he didn't get inside her, he was going to go crazy.

He checked his watch and grimaced. The small green indicator on it informed him of Jonas's need for contact. Not imperative; it wasn't an emergency, but he needed to finish up here soon and get her back to Sanctuary.

Mating was taking time. Time he didn't want to give up, to catch a traitorous bastard that he just might have to kill for interfering in his plans this way.

Shaking his head at the thought, he followed his woman, watching her mood, casting silent snarls at the men that ate her with their eyes. But pride filled him at the looks she was getting.

All that gorgeous, thick hair flowed down her back, her hips swayed, her ass bunched deliciously, and every man who saw her wanted her. He had a woman to be proud of, not just because she moved like sex itself, but because she was smart, honorable and loved him enough that she had tried to let him go.

Silly woman. She had no idea that he had no intention of ever escaping her delicate hold.

"One more stop," he announced as he caught up with her.

She sighed as though put out. As though the thought of one more shop was abhorrent. But he'd seen her eyes while they shopped, watched her try to hide her mounting excitement, her pleasure in the clothes and her inability to deny them.

If she truly didn't want them, she would have let him make a dozen scenes and watched each one coolly. But she did want them, maybe almost as much as she wanted him.

The stop surprised Ria. The shop exclusively carried apparel suited to riding motorcycles, in any season of the year. Mercury bought boots, leather pants, gloves and a jacket that made his eyes heat when he held them up to her and all but growled the order for her to try them on.

And Ria had to admit she loved them. Perhaps too much.

As they flew back to Sanctuary, she couldn't help but wonder if she would have a chance to use them. And when they stepped through the entrance of the mansion, she couldn't help the spike of anger that shot through her.

Alaiya stood on the other side of the foyer, leaning against the wall, watching as they entered. Her multihued tawny gold hair feathered around her face in attractive, designed disarray. Her hazel brown eyes narrowed, sweeping over Ria's new clothes with a sneer.

For a second, Ria was amused. She wasn't a stranger to pretty clothes; she just never let anyone she knew see her wearing them. This woman, she didn't know. She didn't matter where the clothes were concerned.

But when Alaiya's gaze lit on Mercury with lascivious hunger, Ria had to clench her fists inside her new jacket to hold back her rage.

"Jonas is waiting on us in your office," Mercury said softly as he placed his hand at the small of Ria's back and they moved toward the other woman. "He's getting impatient."

"That seems to be a Breed fault," Ria muttered.

"I consider it a strength," he told her, amusement lacing his voice as Alaiya straightened and smiled back at Mercury tentatively.

"Mercury, could I have a moment?" She stepped forward, reaching out, then drawing her hand back, her fingers trembling, the false nervousness causing Ria to nearly roll her eyes.

"Not right now, Alaiya." His voice roughened as they moved past her.

Perhaps later. He didn't say the words, but Ria felt them. She parted her lips to speak.

"Watch what you say, Ria," he warned her suddenly, his

voice low. "Remember how little control I have when you're so hot you're sparking. And, baby, you're definitely sparking."

She closed her lips quickly and cast him a fulminating glare as they turned into the hallway and moved for the offices set at the back of the mansion.

Just for spite, just because she was an inferno from the inside out, she added a little extra sway to her hips, a little sensuality to her stride. Oh, she *knew* how to do it. She had done it often when she was younger, before she had learned better. And she heard his sharp, quick inhalation behind her, a second before the door to the office she had been assigned jerked open and Jonas stepped outside.

He came to a hard stop, stared at her, inhaled slowly, then stared behind her at Mercury.

"I hate men," she muttered, brushing past him, careful not to touch him.

The few times the clerks or salespeople had brushed against her at the mall, it had been horrifyingly uncomfortable.

"Well, at least she doesn't just hate Breeds," Jonas replied cautiously as Mercury came up behind her.

"I hate them too," she informed him a little peevishly as she stared around at the disarray that had been made of the files she had placed in such careful piles weeks ago. "What did you do to my office?"

He and Mercury stepped inside as he closed the door behind them.

"Blame Dane," Jonas snapped. "He was making himself right at home in here earlier."

Ria closed her eyes and counted to five. She added another five just to be certain before she turned back to Jonas.

"Never, ever, allow Dane Vanderale to have access to anything in your office," she informed him with studied politeness, as she battled the anger that still wanted to fire inside her. "He does okay in his own little space, but he wrecks anyone else's."

She shed her jacket and tossed it over the back of the chair before propping her hands on her hips and staring at the mess.

Shaking her head, she tugged out the hair band she had stuck in her front pocket that day, pulled her hair back to her neck and secured it before bending over the table and restacking her files.

Behind her, Mercury narrowed his eyes at Jonas. Normally, the director was smooth as silk, but if he was looking where Mercury thought he was . . . Hell yes, he was.

Mercury moved behind her and turned to face his commander, lifting his lip in a snarl he couldn't quite control.

Jonas pursed his lips and blew out in surprise, shaking his head before turning away. Mercury caught the smile on the other man's face, though.

"These files need to be left alone," Ria informed them, a snap to her voice that had Mercury's cock jerking in his pants. Defiance and challenge filled her tone.

"Talk to Dane about it." Jonas shrugged. "I just finished uploading some information that came through after the party. We had a transmission go out across the secured server that didn't come from any of the computers. We haven't been able to track its destination as of yet. And there was code in it. Dane, Callan and Kane are in Callan's office working on that."

"Good place for them," Ria said impatiently. "You should help them."

Jonas grimaced as he shot Mercury an amused glance. The smell of Ria's heat, the sweet scent of hunger and need, filled the small office space, and Jonas's presence, his ability to smell it, rankled Mercury's possessiveness.

When she turned back to them, Jonas's gaze shot to her breasts. Mercury gave a small, almost silent growl of warning before Jonas turned away again, grinning.

Mercury turned back to look at her and nearly groaned. That damned crimson top he just had to see her wearing. It cupped her breasts like a lover's hand, and beneath the material, beneath the bra she wore under it, the imprint of hard little nipples could be clearly seen.

He turned back to Jonas. "I'll be here with her."

"You're out of uniform." Jonas cleared his throat before turning back.

Ria gave a delicate, mocking sniff to that comment.

"Mercury decided he didn't like my clothes last night," she drawled sarcastically. "He shredded everything I owned. So I shredded his."

Both uniforms actually. Mercury would have been enraged at the sight of his uniform in pieces like that only weeks before.

His uniform, his position, had defined him. Now he'd found something much more interesting to involve himself in than the uniform that proclaimed his rank.

"I'm sure I could find an article in Breed Law to make that grounds for some kind of punitive measure," Jonas grunted. "Could you two refrain from destroying each other's clothes? At least until we have things figured out here."

Ria gave them both a dark glare.

"Why don't both of you find something else to do and let me work here?" She gave Mercury a pointed stare.

"I'm sure I can keep from bothering you," he promised her.

Jonas sighed. "Damned mating heat. Lawe is threatening to join a monastery and Rule's threatening to quit. Why don't you two try to show the younger guys it can be fun instead of taking a note out of everyone else's books and letting it drive you insane?"

"I'm as sane as I ever was." Mercury shrugged.

"That's such a frightening thought," Ria muttered, and he almost chuckled. He would have, but he could tell her temper was rising with her heat.

"I'll leave you two to it then." Jonas cleared his throat again and opened the door to step out. "Have fun, kids."

The door closed behind him, leaving them confined, trapped within the scent of Ria's growing arousal, and her growing confusion.

She jerked several files from the table, stalked to her desk and slapped them on top of it before sitting down.

Mercury locked the door. Just in case she decided to get frisky. Or he did.

"Let her touch you in front of me again and I'll rip both your hands off." Her eyes shot chocolate fire across the desk.

Mercury arched his brow. "Who?"

"You know who," she told him, her voice clipped, precise. "Whatever you do, Mercury, however this turns out. Don't let me see her touch you, because I won't be responsible for my actions."

He kept his grin to himself. There she was. His woman. All attitude and fire and heated arousal. He nodded slowly, picked up his magazine and pretended to read it. He'd been reading the damned thing a month now. He still didn't know a single article in it.

"And it would help you to read that magazine if you turned it right side up," she said carefully. "If you're just going to pretend to read it, then pretend with at least a show of decorum."

He grinned behind the magazine. But he didn't turn it right side up. And here he'd thought she hadn't noticed.

CHAPTER 23

Ria hadn't imagined the agony of need Elizabeth Vanderale had once described to her as she explained mating heat. She couldn't have understood, she told herself later, feeling her womb spasming violently as a fire burned just under her flesh.

Sitting at her desk, her thighs clenched, her clit throbbing in heavy demand, Ria knew she was on the verge of screaming for relief.

She glanced through the screen of her lashes to where Mercury sat across from her. The comfortable easy chair that had been in the corner of the room for him held his large body easily. He was sprawled out in it, his long legs stretched out before him, the bulge between his legs thick and pressing against the black leather pants. His T-shirt conformed to the rippling muscles of his abs, and as she watched, those muscles bunched, his thighs shifted and she could have sworn his cock throbbed beneath the leather.

Moving up, her eyes finally met his. His eyes were brilliant with hunger. The sharp, crisp blue almost flamed within his dark face as he watched her. Yet he hadn't tried to touch her. Each time she walked by him to get more files, she prayed to find him against her, to have him reach out for her. She wanted him with a violence that was beginning to eat away at her nerves, but other than the bulge straining at his pants, he showed no signs of the same hunger eating him alive.

The need was like a steadily growing flame working over her nerve endings, building in her sex. The need, not just to fuck, but to rub against him, to have his arms around her, to stroke him and pet him, had her entire body heating like an inferno.

She forced herself to lower her gaze back to the transmission Jonas had loaded onto the computer. It was definitely coded, though the code was much shorter, more hurried. Ria rubbed at her forehead as she pulled up other transmissions from the night before and worked those alongside it.

There had been a pattern, until this one. The culprit leaking information had found a system that had managed to keep itself from detection by snagging outgoing transmissions already in the works, attaching the code and then freeing them to their destinations.

Each transmission had gone to a subsidiary of either Engalls Pharmaceuticals or Brandenmore Research. The majority of them went to a subsidiary company on the research arm, and one fairly popular within Sanctuary for ordering innocuous supplies such as aspirin. Breeds were prone to mild headaches as the seasons changed, and they used aspirin in vast quantities.

There was also an order for another headache medicine, though. One a bit stronger. Ria frowned, tracking the orders and the transmissions attached to them as she moved them through the ghost drive.

In the past year the orders for the drug had grown, and were all being delivered to the same Breed. Dr. Ely Morrey.

As she shifted in more files, frowning over the findings, a heavy knock landed on the door.

"It's Jonas," Mercury told her quietly as he unlocked the door and allowed the other Breed to enter the room.

Mercury moved to the side of her desk as she glanced at him suspiciously. Did he think Jonas was going to turn rabid and attack or something?

Nearly shaking her head, she lifted her gaze to Jonas as the door closed and locked behind them. At the faint click, Ria's eyes shot to the lock.

"Ely's called the Ruling Cabinet together," Jonas announced. "An emergency session. They're convening day after tomorrow."

"She's going to demand Mercury's confinement?" Ria knew that was the reason behind the emergency session.

Jonas nodded, his hard, arrogant expression tightening further.

"She's already begun calling the cabinet members, who in turn are calling Callan. She's not going to get the support she needs, but she could manage to force the tests for feral displacement and mating heat."

"What about the blood you took yesterday?" Mercury asked, drawing Ria's surprised gaze.

"What blood?" she asked.

Jonas's gaze met hers. "After you left yesterday, Mercury submitted a sample of his blood for feral displacement and mating heat. Which means we're going to need a sample of yours."

"For Dr. Morrey to screw with?" She stared back at him in disbelief. "I really don't think so, Jonas."

Jonas glanced at Mercury again, his expression questioning. At Mercury's slightest nod, Jonas turned back to her.

"We do have another scientist."

Ria smiled knowingly as she leaned back in her chair and stared at him mockingly. "You have Jeffery Amburg, don't you, Jonas?"

Jonas crossed his arms over his chest and turned his gaze to Mercury.

"Do you trust him to do the tests?" he asked.

Mercury shrugged. "He's a murdering bastard, but nothing matters to him but the tests and the results. He's a scientist, Jonas. The worse sort. But he'll follow through on whatever he finds."

Jeffery Amburg, Ria knew, had been one of the scientists assigned to Mercury's lab. He'd also been the scientist that helped develop the drug to control the feral displacement when Mercury had gone insane with rage at the news of Alaiya's death. He had also been the scientist researching the hormone that showed up in Mercury, which was known to be the precursor to mating heat.

She was surprised by the hard pinch of pain that brought to her chest. She should have grown accustomed to the situation as it stood by now.

"He doesn't touch her." Mercury jerked his head toward Ria. "A Breed can take the blood and saliva samples. Nothing more."

Jonas's jaw clenched.

"Wouldn't that be my decision, Mercury?" Not that she wanted those tests, but the arrogance in his voice raised the hairs at the back of her neck in both primal warning and irritation.

He shot her a glare. "Do you want Amburg to come out of there alive, Ria? If I saw his hands on you, knowing the blood that coats them, I wouldn't be able to restrain myself."

She ignored the declaration and turned back to Jonas.

"Is Alaiya being tested?"

His gaze moved to Mercury again.

"I didn't ask Mercury, I asked you."

He nodded shortly. "One of our enforcers escorted her to the lower-level labs we have Amburg in now. Her samples were taken several hours ago."

"And was she showing signs of mating heat?"

Jonas didn't speak. Ria felt her heart tighten, felt it burn like a live coal in her chest.

"I see." She leaned forward, straightened the papers on her desk and stared sightlessly at the screen. "Let me know when you need me to give you the blood and saliva. I'll be working until then."

Silence filled the room for long moments.

"I'll send Amburg's tech up when I leave. She's a young Breed; she worked in another of the labs, assisting the scientists there, before the rescues. She'll take care of you."

Ria nodded and moved another transmission into place.

She focused on work. She had always focused on work. It didn't betray, it didn't consume, it didn't eat away at her emotions. "By the way, your transmission last night came from the Breed barracks, rather than the estate house as you assumed. Low-level, it piggybacked on an outgoing transmission and ended at the hotel in Buffalo Gap."

She pushed her chair back from the computer as Jonas edged from the desk. Rising from it, she gave him the seat and moved around the desk as he sat down. He stared at the transmission display she'd had running within a tracking program she'd downloaded from the Breed satellite once the computer in the office had been linked directly to it.

"How did you find it?" Jonas's fingers were moving across the keyboard. "We don't have this program."

"Sanctuary's security level hasn't been raised sufficiently to allow use of the program," she told him. "I had clearance to use it personally, granted by Leo himself when I awoke this morning and checked my messages."

Which meant Dane had come clean with him. For some reason, that had made her feel less like an outsider. Dane had called Leo when the situation had grown out of her control. He had been ready to face Leo's rage to bring her back to South Africa.

She crossed her arms over her breasts, pushing that knowledge aside as she frowned at the other information she had found.

"Why is Ely ordering codeine from one of Brandenmore's subsidiaries?" she asked. "I would have thought all medications and research supplies ordered outside Vanderale or Lawrence Industries would go through Engalls."

Jonas paused and lifted his gaze, his eyes sharp, deadly.

"Breeds don't take codeine," he told her. "It doesn't work as well with our systems as it does with non-Breeds."

Ria shrugged. "Check her order transmissions, the ones with the attached coding on them. She's made several orders over the past six to eight months, with increasing frequency. She's also ordering pain medications of increasing strength. Morphine was added to the list last month."

"There haven't been any requisitions or payments for those drugs," he told her. "I'd know if there were."

"Then maybe she's paying for them another way."

The silence, the heavy, dangerous tension, that filled the room had the hairs along her arms and her neck lifting in response.

Jonas pulled a communicator from the side of his belt, attached it to his head and pulled the mic to his cheek.

"Jackal? Secure Dr. Morrey's office and place enforcers Blade, Noble and Mordecai within the labs until all computers can be confiscated. I want Ely confined to her quarters, and inform Callan and Dane I'm on my way to Callan's office for an emergency meeting."

He disconnected the link, pulled the headset off and stared at Ria, fury swirling in his eyes.

"When did you find this?"

"Just before you came in." She shrugged. "But I'd be careful, Jonas. It was too easy to find and I don't like that."

"Ely is no electronics wizard." He sighed heavily. "She hates computers just to begin with. If it's not scientific equipment, then she has no use for it. They would have to keep it simple."

His voice was heavy, filled with regret, as he rose to his feet. "Get this information printed out, pull the program here, and I want it installed on the personal network we're putting together for in-house use."

Ria smiled tightly. "Not without clearance, Jonas."

"We need this program, damn you!" His hands flattened on the desk as he growled back at her.

"Jonas." Mercury stepped between them, his large body tense, his voice warning. "Pull back."

Jonas jerked back from the desk and glared at Mercury.

"Fuck this shit! When this is over, I'm joining Lawe in the damned monastery. I've had enough of overly territorial Breeds and the mating heat bullshit that makes my job hell. Watch it, Mercury. I'll give *you* my job."

He pushed his hands over his short, dark hair and breathed out heavily before turning back to Ria. "Can you at least print out the information and bring it to Callan's office? I need proof, Ria. Not supposition or information on a program we're not allowed to have," he sneered.

"I can install the program on Callan's computer. It can ghost for up to seventy-two hours before it deletes itself and becomes inoperable and undetectable to the main network. Or any other private network."

He nodded sharply as he moved from the desk and allowed her back in her chair.

Sitting was agony. It clenched her thighs around her clit, reminding her of the emptiness inside her core, and tightened her womb spasmodically as the need for sex began to eat her alive.

She restrained the need to place her hand against her lower stomach in protest of the pain, and she feared that the next few hours were going to be impossible to get through.

She typed in the key to release the program from the computer, inserted another ghost program to clean it from the drive and the network, then pulled the small external drive that held the information they needed.

When she looked up, it was to see Mercury's gaze on her, that hard blue color of his eyes burning within his face. He needed too, and yet he did nothing to ease either one of them.

If she wanted him, she would have to take him.

She stared at him, almost feeling the sweet relief, the burning need as if she had forced his heavy erection inside her, taking him to the hilt and feeling all that heat and power at her control. That could become more addictive than the mating heat itself.

Her breasts became more swollen, her nipples painfully hard

beneath the lace of the bra she wore. She felt like panting. Like going to her knees and taking what she wanted.

"Today, children," Jonas cleared his throat, breaking the spell weaving around them. "Sometime today, if you don't mind."

Ria rose to her feet and forced her gaze back to the files she had laid aside to back up the information on the external drive.

She wanted to shake her head, to attempt to clear it and the emotions striking through her—anger and need, heartache and the certainty that living without him wasn't an option now.

He had done this to her, she argued inside. He had made the choice to take her rather than the woman that nature had meant for him.

And if that woman was suffering as a result?

She shook her head. It didn't work like that. Elizabeth's research proved that mating heat required an exchange of the hormone; a kiss, a sex act—more than just a desire. The hormone could only show up with mating heat in full force. The Breed tongue might itch, but the glands would swell only minutely at first unless further contact was initiated.

It took more than just the knowledge that mating heat could be an option. And obviously, it was possible for a Breed male to take another mate, if that exchange wasn't made. Because he had mated her. And mated her. And she needed him to mate her again before she melted into a puddle of need on the floor.

They left the office and Mercury came up beside her, his hand riding low on her back, fingers sliding beneath the short hem of her shirt as they headed to Callan's office on the other side of the mansion.

As they turned down the main hall once again, she was there. Avaricious eyes watched Mercury, sliding over his body as he and Ria moved toward her. Greed and lust flickered in the other woman's eyes as Ria clenched her fingers to fists to restrain the need to claw those eyes out.

She could feel the violence rising inside her. Something she detested, feared, within herself. There had always been a part of her psyche that she kept tightly restrained, that she never allowed free, for a reason.

She had dressed down, rarely worn makeup and stayed on the perimeter of everyone else, for protection. For herself. She hated the inner violence she felt whenever she lost something important to her.

She remembered the rage that had consumed her as a child when she realized, when it finally hit her, that her mother had left her forever. No matter the reasons, her mother had left her alone.

The foster family that she had been staying with had been forced to contact Dane. She had destroyed the pretty bedroom Dane had had decorated for her. She had smashed toys, ripped stuffed animals, and when that hadn't eased the hard knot of fury, she had tried to escape by running.

From that moment, once sanity had returned, Ria had fought to make certain it never happened again. And now she could feel that core—older, more mature, but knotted in rage at the thought of losing what she had claimed with her soul.

Mercury had made his choice. If he asked her for release, she would open her hands and let him go, though it would kill her inside. But this woman didn't have a chance of *taking* anything from her.

She let her gaze meet Alaiya's as Mercury moved beside her and Jonas moved up on the other side. As though protecting her. She didn't need their protection and she let Alaiya know it.

She held the Breed female's eyes, poured all that anger, frustration and determination into the look she gave her, and had the satisfaction of watching the other woman's eyes flicker.

Oh no, this battle wasn't going to be that easy. Ria knew it, and now Alaiya would know it as well.

"Jonas." Alaiya's lips suddenly curled. "I just received the results from the blood workup."

"Later, Alaiya," Jonas ordered as they moved to pass her.

"No, Jonas. Not later." Her voice stopped them all.

Jonas snarled back at her in anger. "You overstep your bounds, enforcer."

Alaiya smiled. "According to Breed Law, I'm establishing them. The mating hormone is in my blood workup, Jonas. And it matches Mercury's." She straightened from the walk, slid forward and stared back at Mercury with feral possessiveness. "He's my mate."

Ria felt herself shatter inside. But rather than the storm of last night, she felt a furious, burning core rage inside her instead.

"Breeds have only one mate," she stated through numbed lips as Mercury gripped her arm, pulling her forward.

"Exactly," Alaiya drawled. "And we matched."

"And we mated," she retorted coldly, watching as Alaiya's gaze suddenly narrowed. "You can smell it. You can sense it, can't you, Alaiya?"

The other woman's lips thinned as Mercury's rumbling growl became louder.

"Touch him, and you'll deal with me."

To that, Alaiya's lips curled in satisfaction. "Oh, I think I can take you, little mouse." Her laughter slid from her throat. "No contest."

"And I think, dear, if you attempted it, I might have to kill you myself." Dane stepped into the doorway at the same moment Mercury jerked Ria back and snarled in Alaiya's face.

"Remember my warning, Alaiya?" he snapped, his voice cold.

"Breed Law . . ."

"Don't you throw Breed Law at me." His voice was a powerful, dangerous rumble of violence. "Remember the warning. Heed it. Or you'll suffer the consequences."

"And I don't need either one of you to stand before me." Ria pushed by Mercury, coming back to his side, anger riding the arousal, like lava spewing its wrath from a volcano. "Let her find out for herself what she's dealing with. On her own terms."

"So confident," Alaiya sneered.

"So malicious," Ria retorted coldly. "There's nothing for you here. No matter your belief."

She let Mercury draw her away then. Not that she could have prevented him; he was all but dragging her through the hallway, passing Dane, heading for Callan's office, as anger washed off him in waves.

"This is fucking insane," he bit out as they pushed into Callan's office. "Get this taken care of before I lose patience entirely."

"Oh yes, let's not tempt your patience." She jerked her arm from his grip and cast him a furious look. "Especially considering the fact I've gone and lost mine period."

The door jerked open and slammed behind Dane as he stalked in. Within seconds he was in Mercury's face.

"Take care of that rabid little cat," Dane bit out furiously in

Mercury's face. "What the hell does she mean—her mating tests match yours? That's bullshit, I can smell you all over Ria, and her scent on you."

Mercury snarled back at him, pushing Ria behind him as male Breed genetics met hybrid fury and threatened to explode. Damned men. She turned and stared at Jonas as he leaned against the wall, shook his head and watched the scene with patient mockery.

"Let them get it out of their systems." He shrugged at her look. "Tell me, Ms. Rodriquez, is Dane your brother or your father?"

She sighed wearily. "I think he's my nemesis, but we won't go there."

"You could stop that woman from cutting her every chance she has," Dane was shouting in Mercury's face as Callan leaned back in his chair behind the desk and watched. Kane sat down, evidently more than amused at the confrontation.

Mercury remained silent. He crossed his arms over his chest and stared back at Dane broodingly. It was a look that made Ria intensely nervous.

"Amburg will run the tests on Mercury and Ria as soon we can get blood," Jonas inserted.

"Amburg!" Dane turned on him, disbelief tightening his features. "Jeffery Amburg? The butcher of the Breed labs? Have you lost your fucking mind, man?"

Jonas's browed arched. "We can't trust Ely's opinion at this point. Do you have a better alternative?"

Silence filled the room, but Ria saw Dane's expression.

"Don't do it, Dane," she whispered nervously. "It's not worth it."

Mercury's head swung around and pinned her with furious eyes.

"Do I have a better alternative?" Dane smiled. She hated it when a Breed smiled like that. All teeth and no amusement. "Oh, Jonas, you have no clue."

"Dane. I'm telling you. Don't do it. I mean it."

His gaze swung back to her, and what she saw had her hands trembling. "Please."

"I'll ask you one last time." Jonas tilted his head and watched them both. "Brother or father? The scent is there; it just took me a while to pick it up. Why didn't you tell us your perfect little paper pusher was a hybrid Breed?"

"Your Amburg will not touch her," Dane snarled then. "You'll await the arrival of her grandmother. Elizabeth can see to her tests, and no one else." He turned back to Ria then, his gaze heavy. "The information you give them is up to you. But these tests will not be conducted by unsecured sources. I'm sorry, Ria. I won't allow such a risk to you again."

With that, he jerked the door open and stormed from the office, leaving her with dead silence, three Breeds and one very curious human, Kane Tyler, watched her intently.

"Well." She breathed in roughly. "I guess that's that. Does anyone have a cup of coffee?"

"You know, I can tell they're related to you, Jonas," Callan chuckled.

Jonas glared back at him. "They're more related to you than they are to me, *Pride Leader*."

To which Callan grinned before narrowing his eyes on Ria. "Having Jonas for a brother isn't fun and games. Having him for an uncle could possibly be worse."

She swore Mercury paled. Evidently, having Jonas for a relative wasn't a comfortable prospect.

She smiled back at them all. All teeth.

"Gentlemen, if you don't mind, we have a traitor to catch, and I'd prefer to do it before the Leo and Elizabeth arrive. Shall we get busy?"

There wasn't a sound to be heard. And there was no coffee in the room. No coffee, no answers, no questions—nothing but the heat rising inside her, and her own animal stretching free.

Fuck it. She was tired of hiding.

CHAPTER 24

Mercury watched his mate, and pride filled him as never before. Pride and challenge. His little mate was someone to be reckoned with, obviously.

As he watched her working with Callan, her third cup of coffee empty beside her, her cheeks flushed, her eyes burning with arousal, he couldn't help but admire her strength. Her incredible tenacity. Any more than he could help the reaction her defiance and silence produced in him.

He had mated a Breed. A hybrid Breed. One with familial ties to the Leo, Dane, Jonas and Callan. A frightening thought.

Leo's granddaughter. Why didn't that surprise him?

"Look at the drug requisitions," Ria was explaining to Callan, Kane and Jonas, turning the screen to allow them to see it more clearly. "Codeine, morphine and here, this little puppy." She pointed to one of the longer names on the screen. "It's similar to a hallucinogenic. Bad, bad news for overworked, overstressed Breeds. The effect it has on our brain processes is similar to that of the drug the Council created to restrain the feral displacement in Mercury. We have a Breed mind-control drug coming into Sanctuary in minute quantities, right under your noses."

"And with no attempt to hide it," Jonas bit out. "Ely wouldn't drug us."

"Ely's being drugged, Jonas," she stated clearly.

"One of us would have scented it," Mercury pointed out then. "A few of the enforcers that guard the labs have the best sense of smell developed within the Council labs. Ely couldn't be drugged."

She shook her head. "It's nearly undetectable. The drug has a hold on the Breed; it's highly addictive to the brain, and it's not detectable until the effects it produces are at full strength. She's still fighting it. I don't have the sense of smell a Breed has, so I can't detect it at all."

"What are your talents?" Callan asked smoothly.

"Exceptional night sight and an ability to break code and detect patterns. I'm a logistical expert with a high rating in mental procedures. As a hybrid, naturally born of a Breed and mated human, my genetics are virtually impossible to detect without a deep-level genetic screening because they're recessed. Until mating heat. No hybrid can hide once mating heat begins. In my case, I needed the mating hormone Mercury produces to kick-start my hybrid genetics."

"You say that as though there are enough hybrids to detect the phenomena," Kane suggested. "How many are there?"

Her look was cool, composed; only her eyes burned.

"I'm a hybrid, you know that now. How many there are, where they could be or why they're hybrid is none of your business."

Kane's brows arched. "But you're Leo's granddaughter. That means Dane is your father."

"Or Callan or Jonas or any number of Breeds who were created using his sperm or any child born of mating with the Breeds who were created from them. You're asking the wrong person questions."

"Is Dane your father?" Callan growled. "Because if he is, then someone should point out parental responsibilities to him. You were in a series of foster families. The Vanderales didn't raise you. Leo and Dane both neglected your safety."

She rose from the desk and collected the external drive attached to it. "You have seventy-two hours to play with this program and find your traitor, Pride Leader Lyons. After that, it's gone. Don't bother trying to copy it, I created it. Trust me, I know my job. You don't have the time to figure it out."

"She's Dane's daughter," Jonas snapped. "Only he's that damned arrogant."

She simply smiled calmly, but Mercury knew what the others didn't. There was nothing calm about her.

"I'd prefer my status as hybrid remain a secret as long as possible. My Breed scent will become unmistakable before too much longer, but I'd prefer the true status of it remain between us," she stated.

"She places a lot of trust in us," Jonas growled.

"In you, Mr. Wyatt, I place about as much trust as I do in Dane. Both of you are going to end up strangling in your own webs one of these days." She turned to Mercury. "Are we ready to leave?"

"More than." He could feel the need pumping through him, adrenaline racing through his body, arousal tearing through his balls and hardening his cock further.

Every angle in her body was stiff with defiance. He could see it now, smell it. She had drunk her coffee against his advice. Caffiene only heightened mating-heat arousal. She had argued with Dane and pitted her wits against Kane and Callan's questions. And the animal inside her had been drawn into the open, the heat of her arousal pulsing through her, refusing to allow its captivity by that incredible will of hers.

Her animal was stretching free, and he could feel it reaching for him.

The scratches on his back and shoulders made sense now. Only a female Breed scratched with such force. And the bite that throbbed on his shoulder. He should have known. The moment her teeth sank into his skin, he should have realized what he was dealing with.

He rose from his chair as she moved from behind the desk, her body sliding with sensual power; the new clothes, the female animal growing in power inside her, gave her a smooth, erotic glide that had him clenching his teeth at the covert looks she received from the other men.

There was no lust there. All were fully mated, with the exception of Jonas. But curiosity, awareness of her, was evident.

No wonder she had hid that inner core of herself for so long. One look at her now, and there was no mistaking the female animal lurking beneath her flesh.

"I should warn you, Alaiya is still lurking around," Jonas stated.

Ria didn't speak, but her eyes flared with possessiveness when she looked at Mercury. He stared back at her silently, daring her rather than reassuring her. If she wanted to claim him, he was hers to claim. But she would claim him before one more assurance passed his lips.

The crimson top she wore, the snug jeans and flat boots emphasized the shift of power inside her at that moment, and anticipation roared inside him.

"Alaiya doesn't worry me." She shrugged. And Mercury

could tell she wasn't lying. Alaiya didn't worry her, but those mating tests sure as hell did.

"I'm ready." She moved to him, hips swaying, tempting, her hair flowing around her, teasing him; tight, swollen breasts pressing against her top, making his hands itch.

His tongue pulsed with the mating hormone as he laid his hand at the small of her back and drew her to the door.

No one spoke behind them. They wouldn't have been heard if they had. It was time to return to the cabin. It was time to see if the animal inside Ria was ready to fight for what was hers.

◆　　◆　　◆

The private airfield Dane had acquired before arriving at Sanctuary was filled with activity. Three Vanderale heli-jets landed as Rye pulled the limo into the clearing.

The heli-jets were spilling the Leo's security force, hardeyed, hard-trained, vicious Breeds with only one purpose in life, except for the few who were mated. The protection of the Leo and his family.

Thirty Breed security personnel arranged themselves in close-quarter protection before the Leo stepped out. And as always, Dane stood in awe of the power his father presented as he stepped into view.

His tawny mane of hair was darker in some places, streaks of black and red thrown in as he had grown older. It blew back from an imposing face whose strong bones and angles weren't for appearances only. The Leo was strong, he was imposing. He stood six-four, and the bone and muscle density in his body had made him nearly impossible to kill.

In comparison, the small, dark-haired woman that stepped from the heli-jet was incredibly fragile. Dane's mother was still a quiet beauty. With her shoulder-length brunette hair and gentle eyes, she ran the Vanderale pride with strength and feminine softness.

Keeping her close to his powerful body, the Leo turned and reach into the jet, accepting two small bundles swaddled in ultralight, ultrastrong bulletproof carriers.

Dane lowered his head at that point. His parents had raced to Ria's rescue, their infant twins secured in their arms, aware of the price of detection should they ever be revealed as who and what they were.

They had lost children before. Twin boys in infancy, murdered in an attack by Coyote Breeds that had managed to learn the location Leo and Elizabeth had been protecting their babes in.

His mother had nearly died in that attack, as had the Leo. Leo still carried the scars of the repeated rifle blasts to his chest, back and thighs as he covered his mate and children. And still the bullets had torn through his body, pierced his mate and his children before his then much smaller security force could rush to the rescue.

Years ago, Dane thought, wiping his hands over his face. So many years ago. Nearly a century. It had taken five decades before Elizabeth's body and the mating heat could again produce eggs the Breed sperm could fertilize. And Dane was born. Now, after another fifty years, his parents were still in prime physical condition, and twins had once again been born.

Heavily armed, the security force surrounded Leo, Elizabeth and the babes and rushed them to Dane's waiting limo, as the security force that had arrived with Dane finally arrived with vehicles to transport the Leo's security force to the property Dane had rented for the winter.

Or until they could clear out Sanctuary. He would much prefer to have his sisters and his mother protected within Sanctuary's walls.

"Dane." The Leo neared as Dane opened the door to the car. His mother reached up and touched his face as he bent to her, and he felt her quick kiss to his cheek before she entered the vehicle and the babes were passed to her.

"Son." Leo embraced him.

His father always embraced him, as though it had been years since he had seen him rather than a matter of a few weeks. "How's our girl doing?"

Leo moved into the limo, followed by Dane and two of the Breed personnel, their eyes and faces savagely hard.

Two others piled in the front with Rye as the others rushed to the waiting Hummers that had pulled around the limo.

"They know she's hybrid." He met his father's gaze worriedly. "We need tests done quickly, on the heat, Mercury's feral displacement and a Breed known as Alaiya, lab number six oh point three seven, lab designation Alpha Three."

Leo frowned. "She was thought to be a mate to Mercury," he

stated, his mind as quick, as competent as any computer running. "She was lost in a mission when she was fifteen, her and her trainer presumed dead."

Dane nodded. "She arrived at the Bureau of Breed Affairs six months ago and turned herself in to Jonas. He ran the required tests on her and Mercury; they came back showing no sign of mating anomalies or possibilities, so he never informed Mercury she was alive. She showed up at Sanctuary the other night, claiming Mercury as her mate. According to tests conducted on Mercury's blood last night, as well as hers, mating heat is showing in her and it matches Mercury's."

"But Mercury mated Ria," Elizabeth injected. "I ran her tests myself before sending Sanctuary the blood and saliva that I cut the Breed genetics from. My tests were conclusive, Dane; there was indeed the viability of mating heat. Breeds mate only once."

Ria's hybrid status was the reason Sanctuary had been given altered samples of her blood.

"But Mercury showed mating signs before Alaiya's disappearance," Leo mused.

Elizabeth shook her head as she opened the protective carriers to allow the girls more freedom of movement as well as to keep them from getting too warm. "I warned you both, his tests from those labs were not conclusive. Mating signs and the hormone showing up independent of physical contact cannot be relied upon. The scientists' tests weren't advanced at that time, and they had no idea what they were dealing with where mating heat was concerned."

"Ely's testing can't be trusted either." Dane sighed. "I suspect she's been comprised somehow. She's currently restricted to her quarters, and according to the human, Jackal, she's irate and suffering extreme agitation. I received a report from Ria, via Callan's personal network, as she used the secured program to track those transmissions, that there's a possibility Ely's being drugged with something similar to the drug used on Mercury in those labs." He named the medical designation of the drug and Elizabeth frowned.

"Undetectable by Breed senses until the subject has been well compromised," she murmured before turning to Leo. "It's a powerful mind-altering drug, especially where Breeds with certain weaknesses are concerned. I'll need equipment. Put one of our American contacts on alert for my requirements. This has to end here, Leo. We can't allow them to suffer like this. The right equipment, the knowledge I've gained . . ."

"Could destroy the Vanderale family, Mother," Dane urged her gently. "Think about this carefully. If you place yourself at Sanctuary's disposal, word is going to leak. Just as mating heat and the aging decrease has leaked."

Elizabeth stared down at her sleeping daughters. She brushed the back of her fingers against the nearest child's cheek before lifting her gaze to Leo.

"We've lost children," she whispered. "What will we do, Leo, if David is lost, Callan's child and heir? Callan is *our* son too. Not bred just from the semen the labs stole from you, but bred from both of us. Can we excuse ourselves, that our own safety was paramount?"

"If I must." Dane's father was harder, often more logical, and definitely less willing to take certain chances. But Dane knew what was coming anyway. "But in this, Elizabeth, I'm starting to agree with you. I don't want Sanctuary to suffer as we did. Perhaps, if Callan and Jonas, Dane and I can hammer out some agreements while we're here, then we'll see how much more we can accomplish."

"I want to be in Sanctuary first thing in the morning," she told her husband and son. "The girls will go with us; the compound is more secure than the house, especially with our force protecting them."

"Mother, Sanctuary is a time bomb right now," Dane said and groaned.

"We were invited to attend the pre-Thanksgiving celebration," Elizabeth reminded him. "What we do in private while visiting with the Lyons family is another matter."

"And when Vanderale suddenly donates advanced medical and research equipment?" he asked her. "Journalists are going to go crazy."

"There are ways to ensure silence," Leo told him. "I'll deal with this, Dane. You coordinate security and help Ria find out what the hell is going on here. I want this taken care of, then I want a team of our own Breeds in place. Permanently, Dane."

Dane winced. "Jonas isn't going to like that, Father."

Leo grinned. All teeth, his amber brown eyes filling with

amusement. "That young whelp. He'll find out exactly how he came by those manipulative instincts of his. I'm not an old man, Dane, despite my age. I still know what the hell I'm doing here."

That was true. Unfortunately, Callan and Sanctuary were becoming Leo's weaknesses. And Elizabeth's. Because Callan was one of the few children created using both their genetics. And he was a pride leader before his prime, just as Leo had been.

If Dane weren't fully confident of his place within the hierarchy of his father's pride, he might have been a shade jealous of his younger brother. Instead, he was very much worried. Unlike Dane, Callan hadn't yet realized, not clear to the bone, exactly how deceptive other Breeds could be. Especially traitors.

◆   ◆   ◆

"The Leo has landed," Ria said softly as she pulled the small, slender sat phone she carried at her hip free of its holster and read the coded message. "He'll be at Sanctuary in the morning."

As would Elizabeth. Ria forced herself to remain relaxed, calm, as the limo pulled into the lane that led to the cabin. Tomorrow, tests would begin being given by someone she knew she could trust. Elizabeth knew more about mating heat and Breed physiology than any other scientist could possibly understand. She had lived through the mating, the various phases of heat, the conception and birth of two sets of twins and Dane. She had tested herself, experimented on herself, and when Leo began forming his own personal army to rescue the children he knew were being created with his sperm and the eggs stolen from Elizabeth before their escape from the labs, she'd had other Breeds and other mates to compare her findings to.

And now she would have her granddaughter to test. Her granddaughter and the rabid little female cat determined to steal the mate Ria had taken.

◆   ◆   ◆

Ria stared at the back of the tinted glass as the limo drew to a stop in front of the cabin. The two Breeds from the front left vehicle approached the cabin and went through it for a security check before Ria and Mercury entered.

Did they know? she wondered. Lawe and Rule were exceptionally perceptive for Breeds, and they had Jonas's trust. Did they know what she was? She had no doubt they were aware by now that she was a Breed. It was becoming impossible to keep that animal contained. Before Mercury, it hadn't been a problem. Before the mating, she'd had no concerns that it could ever slip free, because her control was too ingrained.

"Why didn't you tell me?" He asked the question quietly as they waited for Lawe and Rule.

Ria stared into the forest, with its covering of snow, and the predators that were making their presence known. The lions seemed to follow Mercury. She had seen that in Africa, on the estate Leo had built deep within the Congo. There, were some Breeds, those like Mercury, who could control the fierce, wild creatures.

"I told someone once," she finally said quietly. "My first lover. A month later, Dane had to kill him. He was trying to find the Council, to connect with them and to sell me to them."

Dane had shown no mercy. The moment he learned what was going on, he had arrived at her new apartment, torn her lover from her bed and ordered Ria to the car. They had flown to the Congo. Twenty-four hours later she had watched as Dane put a bullet in her lover's brain. He was twenty. And she had thought she loved him.

She pushed her fingers through her loose hair, aware of his hand settling over her thigh, comforting, warm. She shook her head and refused to look at him.

"The Vanderales didn't raise you themselves?"

She shook her head. "They oversaw me, though. Dane was always about when I needed him. But they couldn't risk the questions it would raise if they took in an orphan and raised her. Especially an orphan tied to the victim of a violent act. My mother was in a vehicular accident with several other cars, but what no one knew was that she crashed the vehicle herself. She killed herself, the Coyote Breed that had taken her hostage and the occupants of two other cars, to protect the Vanderale secrets. Once the Vanderales learned about me, they were afraid the Coyote might have already reported his findings to the Council, and that I would be compromised as well. They protected me, but they protected themselves as well."

"Dane's your father?" he asked.

"No. Dane's my biological uncle. My mother was a Breed that Leo and his force rescued. She was created using the genetics stolen from the Leo and Elizabeth. I'm their natural granddaughter. My parents disappeared from Leo after their mating. When my father died, she returned, but never told them about me."

"They deserted you, Ria," he said, his voice quiet, but filled with anger. "They should have raised you."

"They should have done exactly as they did." She turned and faced him then. "Actually, they should have done much less, in order to fully protect themselves. I'm a hybrid, Mercury, and not even a particularly effective hybrid. My talents are simple, my instincts regressed. For all intents and purposes, I'm merely human. They risked themselves in what little they did, and I'm grateful for it."

"They didn't love you," he growled.

She smiled sadly at the accusation. "They loved me, Mercury. And they love me now. I didn't tell you what I was because I've never forgotten the value of silence. My lover died in front of me. Begging me for mercy. Begging me to stay Dane's wrath. Because my lover betrayed me. He risked my capture, as well as the Leo's, Elizabeth's and Dane's. My bad judgment could have destroyed us all. And it never will again."

The limo door opened as she finished speaking. Drawing her jacket closer around her, she never felt the cold as she stepped out into it. All she felt was the heat, clawing at her insides. She had waited too long and she knew it. Sating the horrific arousal tearing her apart wouldn't be easy. Nor would it be gentle.

Mercury escorted her to the cabin, stepped inside ahead of her and waited as she entered. He closed the door slowly, then locked it.

The sound of the click was like a bomb going off inside her mind. Her knees weakened, and her tongue began to itch. She closed her eyes. She didn't have the glands beneath her tongue that Mercury did; she didn't have the hormone needed to induce mating heat. But she could still feel the anomalies in her own body. She had felt them since the first time she had come in contact with him.

"What was his name?" Mercury asked her.

Ria knew who he meant. She shrugged out of the leather coat before sitting down and unlacing her boots.

"His name was Jason. He was the son of one of Leo's contractors. They never realized what happened to their son. Dane had his body flown back to Jo'burg and placed where he would be found. It appeared an act of random violence."

"He deserved it, Ria," Mercury growled.

She turned to face him slowly. "He didn't deserve it. I could have saved him. Dane looked back at me before he killed him. He gave me the choice and I remained silent. Because I knew if I stayed his hand, Leo, Dane and the Breeds they had rescued over the years would never be safe again."

The choices Dane had been forced to make broke her heart. The choice she had made that day had never broken her soul.

"Which doesn't explain why you didn't tell your Breed mate that you're a Breed," he pointed out, and though his voice was calm, she could feel his anger.

"Because I no longer consider myself a Breed, hybrid or otherwise," she said. "And I wouldn't have, as long as I could have kept that part of me in submission. There was no reason to tell you, simply because I had no intentions of allowing it to be free."

His lips lifted in a silent snarl as he paced to the other side of the room. He didn't try to touch her. She was burning, in agony; the pain that swept through the arousal was killing her.

"Are you regretting the mating?" she asked him then. She had expected this, but that didn't mean she welcomed it.

He turned back to her slowly. "Have I said I do?"

"You haven't touched me. All day."

His expression transformed. It became hard, savage, relentless.

"You want it, you'll take it. No excuses. Claim what's yours or you can suffer for it. Knowing what I know now, I'll have no mercy, Ria. You're a Breed, and whether you like it or not, the instincts of that animal are inside you. You can use them, by God, or we'll do without all that wild, hot sex we're both dying for."

She stared back at him in surprise. "You're not serious, Mercury. Breed males don't wait for their mates to make the first move. When did you lose your senses?"

"When you screwed up my mind and my soul with every emotion I swore I'd never feel for a woman," he snarled back at her. "When I realized you'll walk away before you'll fight for any damned thing you want. A man has his pride, and a Breed has even more. You want it, mate? Come and get it."

CHAPTER 25

Ria's eyes narrowed on Mercury. Those leather pants cupped and loved the erection straining beneath them. The heavy boots made his legs look more powerful, stronger than ever before. The T-shirt made her mouth water at the way it stretched across his chest.

Her mouth watered period. She needed his kiss. She needed the mating elixir filling her senses, taking her down that dark path of sexual hunger and need. It was a craving. A greedy addiction. Her nails curled at the thought of taking it, of tasting it, becoming gluttonous with the taste of him.

"Take your boots off," she warned him.

His brows arched, but he obliged her. He sat down on the couch, releasing the buckles and pulling the boots off before he leaned back and stretched his arms over the back cushions.

Ria's breathing became heavy, laborious.

"Anything else?"

She licked her lips nervously. "The shirt." She paced closer to him, her lips parting as she fought to breathe.

The shirt came off, teak flesh became available as she felt a moan rising in her chest. Dazed hunger began to assail her; the pain in her womb had her gasping, her hand pressing to her stomach as Mercury suddenly frowned, his eyes narrowing.

"You let yourself go until you hurt?" he asked her, his voice dark, heavy.

"Take the pants off. Now." Her voice strengthened as she gripped the hem of her shirt and all but ripped it as she tore it free of her body.

The red lace push-up bra framed her heavy, swollen breasts. Her nipples pressed into lace that barely topped them, did little to contain them. Her fingers tore at the snap of her jeans as Mercury shed the leather.

She shimmied out of the jeans, leaving them where they dropped as she crossed to him, straddled his lap and slammed her lips down on his.

"Gimme," she moaned, nipping at the lower curve, so hungry now, pain lancing through her as his flesh touched hers.

His lips slanted over hers, his tongue impaled her mouth, and she was waiting on it. Desperate for it. Wild lust filled her mouth, rose inside her mind like a haze of red and had her suckling at him, greedy. The glands beneath his tongue were heavy with the hormone now, and it spilled to her mouth. It infused her senses like a storm infuses the land, and had a smothered cry tearing from her chest.

She had waited too long. She had known she was waiting too long even as she pushed herself, refused to take what she needed. Because taking meant she was accepting. It meant she was allowing that careful hold on what she allowed herself to slip.

The animal took what belonged to it. It was the woman that had always held back. The woman who feared she belonged nowhere.

It was the woman and the animal that took now. The beast she had come to know as a child stretching indolently and hissing in hunger as the mating hormone began to rage through her.

Her hands stroked his shoulders; she wanted to lick his flesh, but not yet. Not until this need was sated.

Between her thighs she felt his erection where it rose between them, pressing into her mound. He was so thick, so hard. She needed him inside her. But not yet. She needed other things with greater desperation and she would have them.

The kiss inflamed her; the erotic images that swept through her mind, hungers she had never allowed herself to sate before, began to cascade through her imagination. If she was going to take, then she was going to take it all.

Mercury could feel the desperation in her kiss, and now that they were alone, and that incredible control she possessed was slipping, he could sense the physical pain brought on by the need to mate.

He'd wondered about it through the day. Why he hadn't sensed it. Because he would have never allowed her to hurt through her own foolishness. There had been no indication of it, no scent of it. Uncomfortable, yes. A bit angry sometimes. Frustration. But none of the pain he knew mated females felt if they didn't sate the need to be with their mates.

Damn her. He forced himself to leave his arms at the back of the couch, to let her take the lead, to let her take. He pumped his tongue into her mouth, feeling the liquid lust spilling from the glands beneath it, filling her mouth, her senses.

He could smell her heat now like an addictive drug, fueling his senses. He could smell her pain, her need, the emotions tearing free of her control, and sweeter than anything else, he could smell the luscious scent of a Breed female taking her mate.

There could be no more arousing scent in the world, he thought. It was more arousing than the scent of her burning for him just as his mate, and he had believed nothing could be hotter, sweeter than that. Until now.

A Breed female burned with a special scent. Equal parts of him and her, and a heated, underlying subtle scent that made him wild.

He clenched his fingers, fought to hold on to something, anything, rather than grabbing at her and ripping those pretty panties from her body before burying himself inside her.

He couldn't take her. This was for her. Her taking. Her claiming. She was far too strong to ever submit, to accept pretty phrases or reassurances that she was his. No, to claim her mate, this Breed female would have to establish her own, innate sense of strength.

And damn was she establishing. After the first frantic moments suckling at his tongue and the hormone that flowed from him, she slowed. The movements of her mouth became more sensual, more sensuous. She began to relish the taste, to draw it in, let it linger on her tongue before returning for more.

She twined her tongue with his, rubbed against it, stroked it and made him crazy. Growls were coming from his chest, deep rumbles of pure pleasure as she took him to the edge of madness before drawing back.

She licked her lips. Ran her tongue over them as her hooded, drowsy gaze had him clenching his jaw, wishing he had more to give her.

"I didn't think I would make it," she whispered, but the sound was more a feminine purr of pure pleasure as her hands stroked over his shoulders, her nails scratching at his tough hide.

"You waited too long." He tensed, pleasure racing down his spine to stab at his balls at the feel of her nails. "I should spank you for letting yourself hurt like that."

She undulated against him, rubbing the lace of her panties over the sensitive shaft of his cock and pressing her clit into the heat and hardness of him.

"I wanted to rub against you all day." She leaned forward, her nipples searing into his chest as she did just that, rubbed against him as he watched her eyes darken, the iris turning nearly black as her lips moved to his neck.

Mercury could have never imagined he had the self-control to sit there and be tortured like this. The damp heat of her pussy was like a brand through the sheer material of her panties as she rubbed against his cock.

Her touch was exquisite. Her lips over his shoulders, her hands stroking down the corded length of his arms as her hips undulated against him.

"Keep teasing me and I might not make it until you get to the taking part," he groaned.

She nipped his neck in retaliation.

"Damn you!" He tilted his neck to give her better access, cursing the pleasure that had his hips arching against her, his cock head pulsing in delicious torture.

She nipped him again, then laved the little pleasure/pain center before her lips went lower. Tilting his head, he watched her, watched her expressive face, so filled with pleasure as she licked at his flesh, raked her teeth over it.

When her hot little mouth covered the hard disc of his male nipple, he swore he was going to come. Every muscle in his body tensed to hold back. His balls ached. His cock flexed, throbbed, and a vicious groan tore from his throat.

That didn't stop her. He saw the smile that tugged at the corners of her mouth as she sucked the hard disc into there and flicked her tongue over it. Her expression was mesmerized, mesmerizing. Flushed and filled with sensuality. She was the most beautiful creature he had ever laid his eyes on.

"Are you ready to take me yet?" She kissed to the center of his chest, pulling back, going to her knees on the floor as he stared down at her, nearly helpless with anticipation.

"That wasn't the deal," he groaned.

"We had a deal?" She nipped his stomach, just above the throbbing crest of his erection.

"Understanding?" He gasped.

"Maybe I don't understand why." She lifted her lashes and stared back at him, and he saw the vulnerability in her gaze, the hint of confusion.

"Then maybe you need to figure it out." He stared back at her, implacable. He wouldn't be moved from this. No matter how much either of them hurt for it. No matter the stubbornness he could see raging inside her. She had to understand whom he had mated. Whom his soul belonged to. To do that, she had to choose to accept, to take what was hers. Just as he had taken what was his.

"Breeds are stubborn." She lowered her head and blew a damp breath of air over the too-sensitive crest of his cock.

"You should know," he said hoarsely, then nearly gave a shout of agonizing pleasure when her mouth covered the flared, engorged crest and drew it into her mouth.

"Ah hell," he snarled as his hips jerked, plunging his flesh deeper into her mouth. "Ah God, Ria. You're killing me."

She was drawing on him, her mouth hungry, her tongue a lash of heated pleasure against the overly sensitive head. His nails dug into the couch cushions. He was certain fabric tore. His thighs bunched, and he felt consumed by her. He was consumed by her. His heart, his soul, the heat of his cock, and he wasn't going to last long if she kept this up.

"Ria," he groaned. "Baby. I'm too fucking close."

He pressed his head back along the couch, fighting for control. But she didn't ease up. She sucked and licked, her hands, sweet soft little hands, pumped the hard flesh of the shaft.

"Ria. Dammit. I'm going to fucking come." Yep, the cushions tore, the foam inside shredding beneath his nails. "Son of a bitch!"

A ragged yell tore from him as her mouth enclosed the head, only the head, sucked and drew the pulsing, streaming jets of release from him.

Agony pierced his balls, the underside of his cock heat. The barb throbbed beneath the flesh, the milking motion needed to draw it free absent as she consumed the wash of his semen. She sucked and licked and he was panting, a sweat sheen on his body as his cock seemed harder, more viciously aroused than ever before.

He was seconds from insanity. Adrenaline raced through him, his vision blurred, hunger tearing through him with a force he couldn't seem to control.

And he could smell her need. It filled his head, drawing deep-throated growls from his chest as his head jerked up, watching as she rose over him, straddling him, the head of his cock tucking against the soft, curl-shrouded folds of saturated flesh.

She began taking him. Her eyes locked with his as he felt her moving, liquid-tight heat surrounding the tortured flesh, working it inside her.

And her eyes. So dark. They were filled with pleasure, pain, with possessiveness. He snarled back at her, seeing that, pleasure and pride tearing through him as he saw what she still yet refused to admit. That she was claiming him the same as he had already claimed her.

"What do you do to me?" she whispered as she worked his flesh deeper inside her, her nails digging into his shoulders. "Mercury, what do you do to me?"

He couldn't move his hands from the cushions. If he touched her, if he dared allow himself to feel the heat of her skin, then he would take her.

"I fill you, Ria." In every way. In all ways. He would always fill her, fulfill her, hold her and warm her. With her permission or without it.

He was a Breed male. The game he played now, to force her admittance that he *was* her mate, he played only because he was certain of the outcome. Otherwise, she would never get out of his bed. Never step foot from his sight until she realized it.

"I'm filling me," she panted. "You're just sitting there, Mercury." Her moan was hoarse as she took more of him, working herself on the thick intrusion as he strained against thrusting.

God, he wasn't going to last much longer. The feel of her snug grip, the slick, wet glide of her sex over his erection, was killing him.

He could feel sweat trickling down his neck, and even that wasn't left alone. Her head lowered, her tongue licked, and his hips jerked when her teeth raked against him.

He buried himself an inch inside her before he could stop, but the whispery whimper of her pleasure at his neck was worth it.

Her lips increased in speed, working over him, sucking more and more of him into her as the heat began to surround them like flames.

The cushion shredded beneath his grip; control was lost as with one deep cry Ria impaled herself fully on the hard rise of his cock.

Okay, she had him. She took him. That was it.

The growl that tore from him was pure male animal. His hands clamped on her hips as he began thrusting, meeting her hard downward strokes and falling into a pit of such ecstasy that he never wanted to be free.

Ria was entranced by the sight of Mercury. She stared at him—the way his lashes brushed his cheeks, the complete sensuality that washed through his expression. Not that she had enough mind left to do anything but ride the hard length of his cock.

The pleasure was tearing through her. Need was like a vicious, ragged wound at her clit, in her womb. Her muscles clenched, and wildness shuddered through her.

But she had to watch him. She had to hold on to something because everything inside her was rushing along the roller-coaster ride that this pleasure was turning into.

Her hands moved desperately over his shoulders, her nails raked against it; the tough, heavy density of his skin didn't break, but the welts would be clear for hours. A testament, a brand. But not enough.

"Mercury!" She was crying out his name.

Her teeth clenched. She wouldn't bite. She wasn't going to bite. She had bitten once, but she had managed to restrain herself. Managed not to break the skin, not to place her brand on him.

She shook her head.

"Do it, damn you!" His eyes opened, artic blue flaming with gold pinpoints. "Do it!"

She cried out his name, impaling herself furiously on him, fighting the need, fighting the obsession, the compulsion.

"You're mine!" he snarled. "Another man touches what's mine and I'll kill him. I'll shred him, Ria. Anyone dares try to harm you, and insanity will be the least of my strengths. I'll destroy. You're mine."

"No!" She couldn't stop. She thrust harder against him, pleasure pouring into pain, pain pouring into pleasure, sensation building and compulsion growing.

"My mate!" His hands tightened on her hips as he took her hard, pounding into her and she lost the will to fight. No, she *gained* the will to fight, she felt it pouring out of her, heard the female hiss of animalistic ecstasy and her head lowered, and she bit.

She bit hard. Blunted canines latched onto him with a force that barely pierced the flesh. But it pierced. She tasted blood; she tasted her own saliva, wild, filled with the hormone he had fed into her, and she fed it back to him.

His head lowered to her shoulder; his teeth clamped tight to her, pierced her; he sucked and licked, taught her to mark and she marked. Marked as her orgasm tore through her, raced over her, and her nails raked down his arms.

With a roar Mercury surged inside her again, his release just as fierce the second time, pouring into her as the barb extended, caressed over her inner muscles, and the animal inside her responded in ways that had her screaming in shock and Mercury growling in rapture.

Internal muscles clenched, tightened, and there, where the barb pressed into her, spilled its shimmery release, she felt pleasure erupt again. Her flesh surrounded it, tightened around it, latching onto his cock harder, massaging it with a force that had them both crying out in response.

Another orgasm tore through her. She felt his release pulse inside her again, and their cries, his and hers, echoed through the cabin.

As the last agonizing bolt of sensation eased in her body, Ria collapsed against him. He was still hard inside her, still thick. The barb slowly receded, but the heat remained.

She had waited too long, much too long, and easing the overriding hunger for him would take hours. She had helped Elizabeth in the labs, she knew the signs, she knew the research, and she knew she wouldn't die if she lost Mercury now. She would kill.

◆　　◆　　◆

Ely paced her quarters. They were small; she had preferred small. Until now. Now the walls seemed to be closing in on her, and fear was driving spikes through her brain.

And she was crying. She wiped the tears away before wrapping her arms across her breasts and pacing the room again.

Jonas had taken blood. He had come to her himself, by himself; at least he had done that. He had said something about codeine. Breeds couldn't take codeine; she knew that. She would have never requisitioned codeine for any Breed. She didn't even give it to humans.

And something else. She shook her head, trying to remember the medical name for it. All she could remember was the lab tag name for it: They called it *Mental*. Simple. To the point. Because it messed with a Breed's mind. She would never order that either.

What had he said? She lifted her head, clenched her hands over it and snarled.

This was Mercury's fault. The feral displacement. Jonas's loyalty to Mercury was going to get them killed.

He had to be confined.

There was a cell beneath the labs, padded, where the Council had kept the Breeds they had experimented on when they owned the estate.

A cell and a special lab.

She stopped, staring into the past, sightless. That lab—the memories of another lab identical to it were horrifying. And she couldn't block them. Breeds strapped down on tables, their bodies paralyzed by the drugs pumped into them, their chests open, and she watched. The heart, the lungs, the internal organs protesting the agonizing pain each Breed was enduring.

Blood coated her hands as she stared at the scalpel she was holding, then into the eyes of the Breed staring back at her. Rage. Inhuman rage reflected in his icy blue eyes. Pinpoints of gold flared in them, like stars, ricocheting with rage.

A growl tore from her throat, then a throttled scream. No, she wouldn't do that to him. Just the cell. That was all. They could treat displacement. She knew how. She would treat him.

But first she had to get past the Breed stationed at her door.

She moved to the small kitchen, jerked a bottle of water from the fridge and popped back a handful of aspirin. Her head was splitting. It felt as though someone were digging it out with a blunt instrument.

She pressed her fingertips to her temple and fought the pain. She had to think. That was all. She was the smartest and the brightest of any Breed created in her lab. She was taught how to be covert, how to fight. How to kill.

She stilled slowly. Mercury was doing this. She knew he was. Somehow, he had managed to convince Jonas and Callan that he wasn't a danger to Sanctuary. And they were punishing her.

Her breath hitched on a sob. They were punishing her. That's what Jonas was doing. He was punishing her for trying to protect the others. He was manipulating everyone. Mercury's displacement was suiting some plan of his, that was the only thing that made sense. And this time, he was going to destroy Sanctuary.

Unless she did something to stop him.

CHAPTER 26

The animalistic part of a Breed had attitude. It was almost a requirement. An animal trapped inside a human, influencing the human's psyche, thought patterns, hormones, actions and reactions.

Ria had managed to keep her animal contained to a point. It had been there. Unlike Mercury, she had known it was there. She had just managed to control it, to keep it from stretching free. Until mating heat.

The mating heat phenomenon was still a mystery in many ways, even to her grandmother, Elizabeth Vanderale. Elizabeth had been studying it for over a century, in herself as well as in the few mated pairings that had resulted within Leo's pride. And even she didn't have all the answers.

Ria wished she had some of the answers the next afternoon, after she redressed in the labs. Her flesh still felt seared by the examination she'd been forced to endure. Silently. She hadn't even been able to bitch about it, because Mercury was pacing like an enraged lion on the other side of the curtain.

"He's intense," her grandmother Elizabeth commented lightly as Ria stepped out from the changing room, clad once again in the black leather pants, high-heeled black boots and white, soft-as-silk and conforming-as-hell sweater she had worn with them.

Elizabeth didn't look like anyone's mother. In over a century, she'd barely aged the ten years she should have.

"Yes, he's pretty intense." Ria glanced at the screen, watching his shadow as he paced, and Elizabeth's gaze swept over her clothes again.

"You've changed," Elizabeth said softly. "In the few short weeks you've been here, you've finally come out of your shell."

Ria shifted uncomfortably, trying to look everywhere but at Elizabeth.

"I didn't betray you," Ria finally whispered. "Jonas guessed."

"Jonas could smell the familial scent." Elizabeth nodded. "His sense of smell is exceptional, even for a Breed. Rather like Callan's son, David. But, Ria, you've never betrayed us, and we've never suspected you would."

Ria pushed her hands into the back pockets of the snug pants. "I did once." She lifted her eyes back to her grandmother.

"Is that what you believe we thought?" Elizabeth asked her. "No, dear, Jason betrayed you. You were a child, and we were so worried about protecting you, about making certain the pride as a whole was protected, that we didn't make allowances for your need for family. Which all Breeds have, you know."

Elizabeth was excusing her actions, and Ria had expected it of her. They had always excused them. She was young. She hadn't understood. They had tried to make her guilt over the choice she made easier.

"Dane would have killed him anyway, Ria," Elizabeth said softly, guessing the turn of her thoughts. "He was offering not to do it where you could see; he wasn't offering not to pull the trigger. When Jason attempted to gain money by betraying you to the Council, he signed his death warrant. There was no way Dane would have allowed him to live."

"Jason wouldn't have known if I hadn't told him."

"And he wouldn't have died if he'd had an ounce of humanity in him," Mercury snarled as he stepped around the curtain and glared at her. "It wasn't your fault."

Elizabeth's brow arched as Ria felt her teeth snap together.

"I'll let you know the test results when I have them," Elizabeth promised. "I took Alaiya's earlier, performed the examination."

Ria's head jerked back to her grandmother.

Elizabeth's expression was compassionate. "She's showing signs of mating heat, Ria. But that doesn't mean anything. It merely means she's been in contact with her mate."

"She kissed Mercury."

Elizabeth's gaze turned to him, almost accusatory.

"It was no more than a press of lips," he snapped. "Do you think I'd risk my mate by chancing another woman having that part of me?"

Elizabeth frowned. "In every mating I've researched, for heat to begin, there has to be an exchange of the hormone in some way and it has to be compatible."

"Trust me, there was no exchange," Mercury growled. "Except with Ria."

"An interesting mystery then." Elizabeth turned back to where the vials and samples waited on the lab counter, next to the equipment that had arrived that morning and been put in place. "Go on then. I'll get things started here before Leo brings the twins to me. We should know something soon."

"Don't forget the party tonight," Ria reminded her. "Dane has already ordered my attendance."

"I'll be there." Elizabeth nodded, though she didn't turn away from her samples. "Go on now, and we'll talk later."

The party wasn't one Ria was looking forward to. The pre-Thanksgiving buffet and ball had Sanctuary in an uproar already. Leo was stalking the upstairs halls, as were a dozen members of his security force, as they protected the twins and other Breed children confined there for the day. No one was allowed upstairs without authorization, including Breeds, whether they were enforcers or guests.

The room Ria and Mercury had been assigned was on the basement level, on the other side of the labs. Her dress and accessories waited there; the hairdresser assigned to Merinus and the other female mates of the ruling family would be attending her as well.

✦   ✦   ✦

It was a mess. This was why she didn't do parties, she told herself as they moved up the stairs that led to the first floor of the mansion. In her alternate persona, she didn't have to go through this. She didn't have to worry about dressing her hair, making up her face, smiling at all the surprised looks or dealing with the false friendliness.

Not that she felt that way about the ruling family. But this party was for the Breeds' benefactors—corporate CEOs, senators and political figures, billionaires and groupies. And all eyes would be on her because most of them knew the plain paper pusher, not the woman they would see tonight.

"I could help provide security for the party," she told Mercury as they stepped into the long hallway. "We could just find a dark corner and make out."

"You're not providing security. The dark corner is an option." She heard the smile in his voice. "And I'm not working security tonight, at least not in uniform. I'll be attending as a representative of the Breed Enforcers and one of Jonas's assistants. He palms off on me the fat, balding little guys who want to hear war stories."

She glanced at him from the corners of her eyes. "And you deal with this how?"

"I usually growl, flash the canines and watch them run for cover," he chuckled. "Even Jonas thinks it's funny."

"Jonas would."

She could feel her palms sweating. Engalls and Brandenmore would be at this party. It was obvious they hadn't gained what they were after at the last one. They had procured this invitation as they had the other, by pulling immeasurable strings at the last moment.

As they turned the hall corner, another door opened farther ahead, and Alaiya stepped from Jonas's office. Her cheeks were flushed in anger, her expression twisted with it, as she glared back at Ria.

"Hello again," Ria muttered.

If she hadn't otherwise felt Mercury's surprise, she would have smelled it as he glanced at her quickly.

She almost bit her lip. There was that Breed attitude surging inside again. She hadn't been this psyched by her Breed genetics since she was a teenager.

Alaiya froze when she saw her, though. Her gaze flicked over Ria's body, her nostrils flared as she inhaled, and rage glittered in her eyes.

"Breed!" she hissed.

"My, do you think she's referring to me?" Ria asked in false innocence as the feline in her rose to the challenge.

"Hell," Mercury muttered. "Alaiya, stand down."

The other woman took a classic challenging stance, feet spread apart, her fingers curling at her sides as though imitating claws.

Ria almost hissed, but it came out as a surprised squeak, as Mercury shoved her behind him, barked out into his mic an order for reinforcements and snarled back at Alaiya. "I gave you an order, Breed! Stand down."

"Do you actually believe I need you to protect me against her?" Ria leaned against the wall, peeking around his shoulder and flashing the other woman a triumphant smile. "I can take her."

She wrinkled her nose playfully back at Alaiya, though there was nothing playful rising inside her.

Mercury's expression tightened in disbelief as he shot her a quick look.

"Our mating tests matched," Alaiya hissed, pacing closer, her body tense, prepared. "You stink of her."

"I thought you smelled kind of nice myself," Ria felt compelled to point out to Mercury with a hint of laughter. "Eau de Ria goes well with your Breed scent."

"Would you stop!" Mercury bit out as Alaiya growled again.

"Take up for her and I'll kick *your* arse instead of hers." Uh-oh. There was that accent again.

She lounged against the wall, her head turned, making certain Alaiya had a clear view of her expression as three Breeds turned the corner and Jonas stepped out of his office, behind Alaiya.

They all seemed to freeze at the scents assailing them. Ria could smell it herself. Mercury's anger combined with her own, the scent of their mating, their hormones adjusting, the two of them blending into each other until they were nearly combined. And Alaiya. Pure rage and heat, a singular scent mixed with fury.

"What the hell is going on here?" Jonas asked carefully as Alaiya hissed again.

"Remove her from him!" Alaiya shoved her finger toward Ria. "I demand it. Until the mating tests come back, I demand she be separated from him."

Jonas's brows rose in surprise as Ria bared her teeth in a hiss and glared back at him. "Try it," she snarled. "You won't like the consequences, Jonas, and we both know it."

Because Dane and Leo would come down on him like a ton of bricks. Him, Alaiya and anyone else who stood between her and her mate.

She didn't bother snarling, growling or copying that continual asinine hiss coming from Alaiya's lips. She merely narrowed her eyes back at the other woman in confident challenge.

"Alaiya, report to the female barracks," Jonas barked. "Now."

"You're breaking Breed Law," the bitch screeched. "You cannot separate mates."

"It hasn't been established that you're anything to Mercury at this point besides a nuisance," Jonas snapped as Mercury growled for Ria. She liked how he did that.

"I won't leave her here, claiming what's mine!"

Rage was a bitter, feral scent now, acrid, singeing the senses as Ria slowly straightened. She had trained with feral Breeds, fought with them and beside them; she knew the signs of a Breed reaching critical. And Alaiya was reaching critical rage. The animal would break inside her and attack—attempt to attack, anyway.

"You will return to the barracks now!" Jonas snarled, his expression turning savage as his enforcer Alaiya defied him, hissing in his face in challenge.

Ria watched in interest as the director of Breed Affairs turned into the fierce, coldly efficient enforcer he had once been. Alpha steel, Elizabeth called it.

His hand jerked out, fingers wrapping around Alaiya's neck as he jerked open his office door and all but threw her inside before turning to Mercury.

"Get your mate back to her office," he ordered. "I'll let you know when this has been dealt with."

"I could have dealt with it fine," Ria announced, bored, the animal inside her retreating in disappointment as Jonas glowered back at her.

"I gave an order," he told her softly.

Ria stepped from behind Mercury, ignoring Jonas's surprise at how she was dressed.

"But I'm not one of your enforcers, Mr. Wyatt. You are not my pride leader, and you have no control over me, unless I dare to challenge you directly," she reminded him, strolling past Mercury as he snarled in warning. "And never doubt, I will deal with her if she challenges me again."

Jonas stared back at her broodingly. "What the hell happened to you?"

She smiled. "Your enforcer, my mate. Perhaps you should

discuss the problem with him. But before you attempt to give me any more orders where that feline clawing at your door is concerned, then I'd talk to the Leo if I were you. Because you're going to lose an enforcer if she challenges me again."

"And how will I do that?" he bit out. "Alaiya is well trained, Ria. She's not city raised," he told her with a hint of censure.

"And she's not Leo trained," she told him softly, confidently. "Ask him, Jonas. See what you're facing before you allow that woman to challenge me again. Because I'll kill her."

"Shall I tell him, love?" Dane joined the party. He leaned against the corner of the wall and arched his brows, his tawny hair falling rakishly over his brow as he clenched a thin cigar between his teeth.

"This place is turning into a fucking menagerie." Jonas grimaced before cracking the door and roaring, "Stand the fuck down before I have you confined."

The snarls, feminine feline roars and clawing at wood were beginning to get on all their nerves.

Dane watched her, his lips kicking up in a grin as all the sensual female power Ria possessed was displayed in her smooth walk, her long legs, clothes that showed off her exceptional Breed conditioning and training.

Here was the niece he had longed to see return. The one who had driven him crazy as he tried to keep her out of trouble when she was a teenager. She was mature now, and that maturity looked damned good on her.

"Jonas, my friend," he sighed. "Since when does the Leo employ ineffectual employees?"

"I don't care if they employ robot clones designed to scalp and skin," Jonas snapped. "I expect her to obey my commands while she's within Sanctuary. Period, Dane. Hierarchy here has been established, and your rules don't mean jack shit to me, any more than the Leo's do. She *will* stand down."

"She will not," Ria informed him calmly. "She's an enforcer, and a Breed. She understands the challenge she's making. I may have been a wallflower, *Uncle* Jonas," she snarled softly, "but I've never been frightened of a fight. Inform your enforcer of your rules and your hierarchy. Not me."

Mercury blew out a soundless breath, fierce, overwhelming pride rushing through him as he glanced at Jonas, lifted his brows and grinned. Hell yeah. This was his mate.

"Someone should shoot you," Jonas growled at him.

"Give me time," Ria said as she moved past him. "I may take care of it."

But the glance she shot Mercury was anything but murderous. Unless she intended to kill him with sex. Could a Breed die of happiness? In that case, he thought, hell yeah.

◆ ◆ ◆

Ria entered the office, held the door as her mate stalked in, then slammed it closed.

She attacked him. She was burning, blistering with need, and he met her, kiss for kiss, giving her the wild taste of his hunger as they tore at each other's clothes.

Nothing was ripped this time, thankfully, but within seconds she found herself bent over the file table, her mate's erection pushing demandingly inside her.

"Take it," he snarled at her ear. "Damn you to hell. You hot little cat. Challenge me, Ria. I dare you."

She bucked against him. He didn't have to dare her; she could feel it rising inside her as his hips slammed against hers, burying his cock fully within her as her head turned and she nipped his chin.

First chance, she was letting those canines regrow and sharpen. It was natural. They had to be ground down monthly. She had nice canines. She knew she did. Perfect for biting, nails perfect for scratching.

"Take me." He was buried in her to the hilt, grinding against her as her arm curled around his neck, her body twisting against him to take his kiss again. To burn brighter, hotter.

It was hard and fast, the pleasure brutal, spinning them out of control, tearing through her as the first orgasm clenched her womb, exploded in her clit. The second one ripped her mind, flamed through her and had Mercury roaring out his release, locking inside her as she clamped down on him, the barb extended from his cock and rapture racing through both of them.

She hissed his name. Feline, possessive. She felt that possession, and it terrified her. Took hold of her. And she knew she was lost to it.

"What the hell happened?" Mercury was panting behind her, his lips at her neck as they waited for the barb to ease, to retreat back into his flesh.

"Mating heat." She lay against the table, bent over it, wasted.

"I'm still in uniform," he grunted. "Hell, I didn't even get my pants to my ankles."

"Mine either." They were tucked around her thighs, and she didn't give a damn.

"So tell me, mate," he growled, nipping her neck, "do you really think you'll end up shooting me?"

She grinned at the male pique in his voice. "Probably with your own weapon."

She wasn't ready to move yet. She was sated, relaxed for now, the mating heat a low simmer inside of her rather than a hard burn.

He nipped her neck again, causing her lips to curl in satisfaction, her breath to pass her lips in a rush as he eased from her.

"Stay still." His hand pressed against her back.

There was no need for that, she didn't know if she could move yet anyway. A second later she felt the gentle movements of a small hand towel between her legs.

She stared at the wall, unfamiliar emotions sweeping over her as he cleaned the proof of their mating from her.

"Why are you doing that?" she asked him, frowning. "I can clean myself."

"Stay still, mate, I enjoy caring for you." He laid a kiss against one rounded cheek of her rear before nipping the other gently and straightening.

"You're very strange then." She rose, straightening her clothes without looking at him. She felt too vulnerable right now, too off balance.

The sex was one thing; the way he touched her, the way he had cleaned her—that was something else entirely.

"Independent little cat," he growled as he moved to the small attached bathroom.

Something caught her gaze then, had her eyes narrowing and a snarl pulling at her lips as she looked up.

Mercury reentered the room, looked up and froze. The covering they had placed over the camera, which had still been there when they left the office earlier, was gone.

"The door was secured when we entered." His voice was hard, vicious as he stared into the lens. "There were no unusual scents, nothing to indicate anyone else had been in here."

"Someone was obviously here," she murmured, moving around the desk, running her fingers along the edges and the drawers.

Narrowing his eyes on her, Mercury grabbed her jacket, tossed it over the monitor then pulled the small electronic detector from one of the pockets of his mission pants before flipping it on and beginning to run it over the room.

Ria continued to run her fingers under the desk, working from top to bottom.

"The room's clean," Mercury announced.

Ria paused. She had found what she was looking for.

"Is it?" She pulled the small device from beneath the bottom edge of the desk and held it up for his inspection. The indicator light was silent, the device deactivated, for the moment.

A growl rumbled from his throat.

"Stop growling," she muttered, looking over the tiny receiver carefully. "This isn't a Vanderale design, nor is it anything Lawrence has. Do you use any other companies' devices?" She knew Sanctuary had agreements, contracts, with Vanderale and Lawrence Industries only.

"Not to my knowledge." He moved to her, took the box, inhaling slowly, his eyes narrowing. "It has a scent overlay, but I can't pick it up."

"It's warm," she pointed out. "It was active."

"Until I covered the camera," he snapped. "Let's go."

She knew where they were going.

Ria quickly adjusted her top as Mercury stalked from the office, his hand on his weapon as he spoke softly into the link he had reactivated at his ear. The small mic lay along his cheek as they moved quickly through the hallways, heading for the security room.

As they neared the heavy steel door that protected the sensitive security monitoring equipment, Jonas moved quickly from the other end of the hall, a six-man enforcer unit following closely on his heels, weapons drawn.

Jonas swiped the secured pass card through the security lock, waited for the retinal scanner to engage, then pressed his palm to the palm plate and waited for the green light.

When it lit the panel, he jerked the door open. The scent that met their senses was unmistakable. Jonas bit out terse orders as he entered the room, moving slowly, carefully around the body spread out in the floor, intestines displayed, horrified eyes staring sightlessly up at the ceiling.

Austin Crowl. His blood stained the metal floor, congealing, the stink of death surrounding him as Ria stared at the sight.

"Where are his assistants?" Jonas moved through the room, paused at the door to another section of the room and opened it carefully.

They were there. One shot, the other with his throat sliced end to end.

"Contact Pride Leader Lyons. Initiate Alpha Direct, and begin placement. We've been compromised."

By one of their own.

Ria stared up at Mercury, watching as the mate and lover turned into the enforcer. Hard, cold eyes, savage features.

Jonas turned to Ria. "Can you work this equipment?"

She nodded. "I can."

"Get in here and pull up the security discs. I want to know what the hell they were looking at, who was here and how someone managed to kill my men."

She moved slowly into the room, staring down at Crowl with a sense of anger and sadness. He had been a nasty little bully, but he hadn't deserved this.

"Lyons is initiating Alpha Direct. Dane Vanderale is moving to our locations; Leo Vanderale, his wife and babes are secure in the labs, their security force moving in.

"Get to work." Jonas stabbed his finger in the direction of the monitors. "We have four hours before this fucking party, and I want to know what the hell is going on. Now!"

He wasn't the only one.

Alpha Direct would pull all the mates and children in the ruling family to one secured location, known only to Callan, Jonas, and the security force assigned to the initiative. If Jonas decided it was needed, he could force Callan into the same secured perimeter. The protection of the ruling family fell under his designation and he wouldn't hesitate to use it.

"This is Vanderale equipment," Ria murmured, her fingers racing over the keyboard, attempting to code in the special security protocols the equipment had established when it was first initiated. "I need Dane in here. This is one of his babies. You have a backup, but you also have a set of protocols set to maintain security, no matter what. Protocols the techs were unaware of. Only Callan knew what they were."

Jonas gave her a sharp, brooding look. "Why wasn't I aware of this?"

"Need to know." She shook her head and smiled tightly. "Whoever did this, they're caught, Jonas. Sanctuary is one of Leo's priorities. You have the best, all the way around, and this baby." She entered the commands into the system program, watching the coded display as it came up. "This baby rocks!"

And there it was. Level five security active, recording now. She just needed Dane to help her finish the final sweep.

The monitor flickered, images of the last sweep coming up. Her office, transmission recorded. Callan's office, showing Dane, Callan and the males of the ruling family heavily into conversation over his desk, as of an hour ago, displayed, recording received, though the rooms weren't set for recording.

And the children. There, the room where the children of the pride were secured was displayed.

"Move on Alpha secured three point seven," Jonas ordered as Ria worked furiously, pulling up present security.

"Children are accounted for. Leo, Elizabeth and the twins are currently there. I need Dane on the line immediately."

Mercury attached his headset to her ear.

"Report." Dane's voice was hard. "I'm on my way to your location. Alpha one and parties secured."

"I need you in here. No transmissions out, only in. The equipment has been tampered with, but security protocols are still in force. I need you to find out where the transmissions are set to go. They've been rerouted."

"Execute a full sweep of the system and it should be displayed as I arrive. We'll track it and burn the bastard responsible."

She entered the command, working furiously as she kept her eyes on the security monitors that began coming back online. Each room of the mansion was programmed in, except bedrooms and bathrooms. Sitting rooms were displayed, the ballroom, main grounds and hallways.

She saw Dane rushing for the security center, Leo's security force inside and outside the room where the Leo, Elizabeth and

the children were being held. Mates were being escorted into
that room now, the females mothers to the children and as much
in danger as the children themselves.

"This isn't about the children, its about information," she bit
out, speaking more to herself as she continued to tap into the alternate system the computers held. "Why take the children if
they have the information they need? Why take this risk? Why?
Patterns," she continued to mumble to herself, barely aware of
the silence in the room as she began to read the information racing across the computer screen. "Always patterns. Where are
you? You're here, baby, I feel you moving. Come on. Give it to
me."

Mercury listened to her, leaning close. The whisper of the
accent, the curiously sensual tone of her caressing voice as she
pounded out commands and worked the system, amazed him.

He had never heard anything like it. As she worked, caressed, cajoled, information began popping up on the screens—
transmissions, commands entered and, finally, display.

They watched as the Breed moved down the hallway, lab
coat hiding the weapons that were shoved beneath it.

The door to the security center opened.

"There you are, come in. We have the card table set up in the
back. I'm getting my cash back out of you tonight," Austin
crowed.

The Breed smiled, stepped inside, and the monitor showed
the bloodletting that began. Dane stepped into the room,
stepped over the body and sat down at the control center beside
Ria.

"Are you ready, love?" he asked her gently.

They paused. "One. Two. Go."

Their fingers hit the keys at once, in identical commands,
and then simultaneously hit "enter."

"Sweet God," Jonas whispered at the information set to send
in less than seconds. "Holy Mother of God."

Dane and Ria ignored him. They worked their keyboards,
fed in commands, rushed to delete information coded to be impossible to delete, transfer or intercept.

They weren't after the children. They weren't after the Leo.
This information was much more destructive. Source files fed
directly from the lab computers were set to process and feed to
another location: matings, testing protocols and results—every

file, every ounce of information dealing with mating heat, the aging decrease and findings on the hybrid children, including genetic workups and full genetic testing.

"Fucker!" Dane cursed.

"Watch your language," Ria muttered, and worked.

Their fingers flew through commands, and as they worked, information was deleted, page by page, wiped clean, *Transmission failed* displayed.

The ultimate betrayal, by one they'd all trusted.

Transmission failed. Please check network settings. The message displayed a second before the screen went blank.

"Your system has officially crashed," Dane drawled, though his voice was savagely hard as he pulled a cigar from his shirt pocket, lit it and narrowed his eyes against the monitor, where the face of the culprit was displayed. "Do I get to do the killing do you think? I'd enjoy it."

"So will I," Jonas snarled. "So will I."

CHAPTER 27

The guests at the party had no idea the undercurrents moving beneath the Breeds on duty, or those circulating through the large ballroom and buffet room. They had no idea the danger that stalked within them, or the treacherous games a few would play to destroy the many.

The plan to capture those few Breeds was simple, yet so much depended on the coordination of everyone involved. If they missed a suspect or conspirator, then the whole plan could be screwed. They couldn't afford that. They couldn't afford to allow so much as a single traitor to be left unaccounted for when it was over.

Leo and Dane had accounted for Council-trained traitors within the rescued Breeds. The Council was always big on placing traitors among the small packs and prides, Breeds specially trained, specially brainwashed and treated with care to ensure they did as they were programmed. As those now attempting to betray Sanctuary were doing.

Except it wasn't for the Council. It was for greed. For the money they believed they would gain, and the dishonor of having destroyed their own community without Council help.

Callan and Merinus stood at the only entrance into the ballroom, calm and to all appearances unaware of the deception brewing within Sanctuary. But they knew, and Callan had already passed sentence once the Breeds were caught. They would die. No exceptions, even for the woman.

Merinus Lyons was as graceful and gracious as always, her brown hair upswept, displaying her slender neck and the pearls that circled it. She wore a ball gown that managed to be both fanciful and elegant, the sweep of bronze material floating around her.

Roni Andrews was with her mate and husband, Taber. Taber was dressed in a black tux, but Ria knew the weapons concealed beneath it.

The entire ruling family was there, including Dawn Daniels and her fiancé Seth Lawrence. They moved through the guests, smiling, chatting, laughing, but the tension was there. The scent of it would have been detectable if it weren't for many of the guests being nervous, some of them meeting the Breed ruling family for the first time.

Ria curled her hand on Mercury's broad forearm, moving along the perimeter of the crowd in the emerald sweep of her velvet ball gown, her gaze spreading out over the room, finding several of the security personnel Leo had brought with him as well.

"You look too hot," Mercury complained with an amused growl as male eyes turned to her, glinted with interest and then flickered in fear when her Breed mate growled at them.

But she heard the pride in his voice. For some reason, it pleased him that the animal genetics she had tried so long to fight were impossible to suppress since he had mated her.

"It's your fault," she reminded him, her voice low as she almost laughed at the tiny, warning pat just above her rear.

"Don't remind me. I'm ready to explode the way it is."

And he was. He was hard beneath his new dress uniform, and ready for her. He was always ready for her, just as she was for him.

She smiled at the thought of that, warmed to it as she tried to concentrate on the security placed around the room.

There were Breed Enforcers in the expected places for such events, but she knew there were even more ready, heavily armed and waiting.

Horace Engalls was there with his wife, on the dance floor sweeping through the crowd, his expression smug, arrogant. Brandenmore was dancing with none other than Alaiya, the Breed determined to take what Ria had decided there wasn't a chance in hell she was taking.

Exactly when she had made that decision, Ria wasn't certain. She had been willing to walk away once, to let Mercury have the mate that had first been intended for him.

He hadn't let her walk away. He had torn into her heart and soul, and pulled free parts of herself she had sworn she would never allow out again.

He was hers. And once this was over, she would make certain Alaiya Jennings understood, completely, no matter what test results might show, that Mercury would never belong to her.

But this had to be taken care of first.

She and Mercury moved through the crowd, placing themselves close enough to cover Roni Andrews and Merinus Lyons in case shots were fired.

They weren't up against one Breed, but several. As Dane began to pull the ghosted backups, tracking movements and meetings, they'd found what they needed.

Patterns, there were always patterns, and this one had been a very simple one, based on complete arrogance and the certainty that they had managed to gain all the information they needed concerning Sanctuary's security. Technical experts, they were not. Otherwise, they would have realized there were always recovery protocols designed into any security system. Especially a Vanderale system. Technology was Vanderale's game, and they did it better than anyone in the world.

Jonas, Callan and Merinus stood near the entrance to the ballroom, and it was there Mercury and Ria ended up after they made a short round of the room to give the appearance of mingling.

Along with Taber and Roni, they were greeting guests, smiling, the perfect, consummate hosts.

As Ria and Mercury moved in behind the Lyons family, Ria tensed.

Ely Morrey had stepped into the entrance, dressed in a black gown, her hair brushed attractively around her face. She looked sociable and pleasant, until Ria saw her eyes.

"This is bad," she whispered as she watched Jackal slide away from Jonas toward the doctor. "She's here early."

They hadn't expected this. And if her appearance was anything to go by, she was more agitated than before. She wasn't to have arrived until later. Hopefully, not at all.

Jackal stopped beside Ely, his dark head bending as he whispered something in her ear. Requesting that she allow him to escort her back to her room.

Sorrow filled Ely's eyes. Betrayal, fear and tears as she turned and looked at Jackal. His expression was curiously gentle for a man Ria knew wasn't considered gentle.

"Please, Ely," he whispered. "For me."

They had only a second's warning. Before Jackal could react, Ely had one hand wrapped around his balls in a hard grip and a taser to his neck as she watched him fall. Releasing him, she jerked a handgun from behind her back, beneath the dark wrap she wore, and held it on Jonas.

Guests nearby screamed. A woman cursed and another declared that she knew Breeds couldn't be civilized.

Enforcers were moving in. Callan and Taber pushed their wives back; guests cried out, as the movement to clear the ballroom became hampered by the fact that the only entrance was now guarded by a hard-eyed, savage Breed scientist, and that left only the enclosed buffet room to find safety within.

"What are you doing, Ely?" Jonas stared back at her coldly. "Stand down and return to your quarters."

She sneered back at him, the lethal automatic handgun aimed at his heart. She looked ready to use it. Fanaticism gleamed in her eyes, and hatred seared her expression.

"Don't order me to my quarters, you fucking girl pussy," she hissed. "Fucking manipulator. You're going to destroy us all."

Guests were gasping; growls were rumbling from the Breeds moving in behind her.

"I'll blow your heart from your chest, Jonas," she snarled. "I won't let you do this to Sanctuary."

"Ely, you're out of control." His voice, for all its gentleness, vibrated with a hard, cold core of fury. "Give me the gun."

"I'll give you the bullet," she warned him as a syringe dropped from the wide sleeve of her gown. "Tell Mercury to inject this into his arm." She tossed the syringe. Jonas caught it easily and stared down at it.

"What is it, Ely?"

"Poison to the Breed system," she answered easily. "It will stop his heart immediately and leave the rest of his system uncorrupted. The feral displacement will never threaten Sanctuary again, and when I dissect him, I'll find the answers I need to make certain it never infects another Breed."

"You would kill Mercury?" he asked her.

Ria's hand tightened on Mercury's arm as she felt his shock. His pain. Ely was a friend, she knew. Once trusted. And trust didn't come easily to her mate.

"What about his woman, Ely? Would you take him from her?"

Behind them, Breeds were moving guests into the buffet room, carefully cutting Engalls and his wife and Brandenmore from the crowd. Isolating them. They had to stay isolated, contained.

Ely lifted the gun until it was level with Jonas's heart.

"Inject yourself, Mercury, or he dies."

Mercury moved to pull away from Ria.

"No," Ria hissed. "I won't lose you like this."

He would do it. She could see it in his face. If that was what it took to ensure the safety of Sanctuary, then he would do it.

"Your first duty is to me, not to him," she snarled.

His jaw tensed and he moved, his eyes connecting with Ria, warning her. She felt it then, that leap of connection, that bond she had never allowed herself to connect to before. As though, spirit to spirit, he was promising her that he had a plan.

By God, he better have a plan, and death wasn't an option.

She loosened her grip slowly, fear moving through her, terror filling her blood. She wouldn't let it happen. She wouldn't let him do this.

As she shifted, she caught activity from the corner of her eye. Two figures moving past the entrance, heading along the foyer to the main doors. All Breed Enforcers were busy, drawn to the ballroom to protect guests and the ruling family.

Mercury eased to Jonas's side. Alaiya Jennings moved slowly into place then caught Ria's eyes.

On three, Ria mouthed slowly, her gaze moving slowly to Ely.

Alaiya nodded with a slow, subtle movement.

Mercury took the syringe from Jonas.

One. Two. They jumped.

Alaiya drew Ely's attention as Ria moved to take the gun. Jonas beat her to it. He twisted the gun from the doctor's hand, grabbed her and threw her to another Breed as he barked, "Hold her."

They raced from the ballroom and came to a hard, surprised stop.

Two lab assistants, male and female, were unconscious on the floor of the foyer as Dane stood back, a cigar between his lips, his arms crossed over his chest, as he smiled back at them.

He lifted his hand, and in it, between his fingers, he held a small external chip drive.

"Decoder." He smiled. "Shall we inform the Engalls and Brandemore of the penalty for fucking with Sanctuary?"

"Son of a bitch," Jonas snapped.

Dane lifted his brow. "I hope you're not referring to me, brother. I may have to take exception."

Lawe and Rule materialized, restrained the lab assistants' hands, despite their unconscious states, and hefted them over their shoulders.

"What about Ely?" Mercury growled.

Jonas sighed. "Place her in the confinement cell." He shook his head sadly. "Hell, I was hoping a few days off that shit would clear her mind. It's only made her worse."

That shit. The drug she had been fed in the lab. Elizabeth had reported finding it in the over-the-counter painkillers and aspirin in Ely's desk just hours before. They had known it was being fed to her somehow; they just hadn't figured out how.

"Confinement will be easiest." Elizabeth moved into the foyer. "I'll take care of her, Jonas. I checked Jackal—when he wakes up, he'll have a hell of a headache from the taser, but he'll be fine."

Jonas nodded and turned back to Ria and Mercury, his gaze filled with weariness, his expression heavy with sorrow. "I let them get to her," he whispered. "Hell, I vetted those two myself. And still I managed to let those bastards from the Council get to her."

Ria felt Mercury's arms surround her, drawing her to his chest, his warmth and security wrapping around her.

"They were trained to deception, all Breeds were, Jonas," she said softly. "Vetting them isn't always enough. We're no different than those who don't have Breed genetics, just a little better at what we do sometimes."

"Hell!" he bit out again, pushing his hands over his dark hair before staring around the foyer.

He was proud, tall and disgusted. The black tux he wore was wrinkled; a smear of blood stained the cuff of his shirt, and his expression was lined with the heaviness in his heart.

"Losing Ely is going to hurt," Jonas finally whispered. "Pray to God, Elizabeth can fix this."

Pray, that was all any of them could do. Ria nodded, her hands closing over Mercury's as he pressed them against her stomach, holding her close. Secure. Warm.

God, she could have lost him. If Ely had turned that gun on Mercury instead, she might not have hesitated to pull the trigger. She was that determined to see him destroyed for a condition he had never truly suffered from.

"I think I'm ready to leave this party," he told her, his lips at her ear, caressing the shell as the heat and hardness of him filled her with strength. "The bad guys have been captured and the dress is driving me crazy."

She almost smiled. "Yes, I think we're ready to leave this party."

"I think we all are," Jonas breathed out roughly. "Unfortunately, we have guests."

"And I'm off duty and in mating heat," Mercury growled. "I'm taking my mate to our cabin."

Because the adrenaline was crashing inside her, combining with the mating heat now that the danger had passed, now that the Breeds determined to destroy their own society were in custody.

Jonas nodded as he turned away. Ria turned, watching as he moved to the ballroom entrance, coming to a stop as Callan carried Ely in his arms and moved for the hallway.

The doctor was unconscious, her face paper white, a smear of blood beneath her nose attesting to the fact that the drug she was on was attempting to destroy her exceptional mind.

Callan's face was carved from stone; his wife's was wet with tears as she followed behind him. Ely was a cherished part of the community; she was their hope for the answers to the questions about their own physiology, and she was a friend.

"Will she survive, Elizabeth?" Ria asked as her grandmother moved to her, Leo close on her heels, as he always was.

"If she's strong enough, Ria. If she's strong enough."

Elizabeth patted her arm and moved past her, Leo's arm wrapping around his wife to pull her close to his side as they followed Callan and Merinus.

Seconds later, Horace Engalls, his wife and Phillip Brandenmore were escorted from the ballroom under enforcer guard, their expressions both furious and terrified.

It was over, Ria thought. As Mercury turned her to the doors and they moved to leave the party, she let herself believe it was finally over.

"We have about eight hours," Mercury growled at her ear as they entered the limo and the enforcer assigned to the car whisked them from the ball that had nearly turned into a blood-bath. "Do you think that's enough time?"

He lifted her to his lap, bent his head to her lips and licked her, with heat, with gentleness.

"I won't let you go," she whispered. "I can't."

He touched her hair, her face. "Do you think I want to be free, Ria?"

"What if she's your mate? What if the first tests were right, and she was meant to be your mate?"

He shook his head. "She's not my mate, Ria. Ever. She never was. I'm holding my mate right here, in my arms."

"I love you, Mercury," she whispered on a soft, almost hidden sob. "I love you too much."

"Never too much, sweet Ria. Never too much."

❖   ❖   ❖

The animal didn't prowl. It didn't crouch and glare. It sighed in contentment, watched its mate through the man's eyes, feeling the animal that reached out to him from the woman as well.

The animal in the man purred, ignoring the man's surprise as the sound rumbled in his chest. But the woman purred right back, and she laughed with a hint of tears.

Behind her eyes, within the unconscious depths of her being, the mate of the animal in the man stared back at it.

They were animals contained. Hidden parts of the man and woman that were no longer forced to silence. Genetics, yes. They were a part of them, the spirits the man and woman contained, no longer separate, but connected fully. And mated.

Animal to animal. Man to woman.

And as the man carried his mate into their lair, laid her gently on their bed and completed the union their bodies needed, the animals connected.

They were as they were always meant to be. Soul to soul.

Heart to heart. Pulsing and alive. They were Breeds, and they were proud.

TWO DAYS LATER

The lab was cool to protect sensitive equipment that didn't require the warmth Ria did. She sat on the gurney, forcing herself to relax as Mercury leaned against the wall and watched her silently.

Alaiya had demanded that the mating tests be completed quickly, mostly because her tenure in the Bureau of Breed Affairs was being reconsidered. She knew she was on her way out. Not out of Sanctuary perhaps, but out of the upper levels of Breed hierarchy. She had ignored her commander's orders. Defied him. And she had lost control of herself during that last confrontation with Ria.

Breed Enforcers had to always maintain control, until the full phase of mating heat was established. Hers hadn't been established.

"You're mates." Elizabeth stepped from the office she was using while overseeing Ely's duties at Sanctuary.

Elizabeth Vanderale was in her element here. Working with Breeds, adding to her knowledge and experience as well as Ely's.

"And Alaiya?" Ria knew she was Mercury's mate, there was no doubt in her mind, and she had no intention of releasing him. No matter the outcome of these tests.

"Well, she's definitely mated someone, but hers doesn't match the heat in your and Mercury's systems." She frowned, shaking her head. "Someone altered the tests Ely had done. They've been altering them for months, in several Breeds she ran tests on. She didn't catch it because the drug had already begun infecting her mind. Charles, one of her lab assistants, would tell her not to look for the anomalies, and she didn't."

The information had been easy to find over the past two days. Months' worth of altered tests, coded transmissions and attempts to drug other Breeds.

The two lab assistants, Charles and the older nurse, Maydene, had been working for nearly a year for Engalls and Brandenmore. But they had been smart where selling the information was concerned. They slipped it out, but then refused to supply the code to unlock it until they'd received full payment.

Something they would never see now.

"Does Alaiya know?" Mercury asked.

"She knows," Elizabeth breathed out heavily. "But she isn't accepting it yet. She swears Mercury is her mate and that I'm the one altering the tests. She will be best avoided for a while."

"I don't have time to avoid her." Ria slid from the small cot and glanced at Mercury. "I've already told Leo. I'm not returning to the main offices when the two of you leave. I've taken a position here, with Sanctuary. They need someone they can trust in Security Control, someone who can understand the systems they have and how to monitor any further attempts to break them. Leo's going to turn one of the newer satellites over to Sanctuary control, and Dane will never rest if one of his babies isn't being watched over." She grinned at that. Dane loved technology. Especially Vanderale technology.

"I already assumed that." Elizabeth smiled gently. "Leo and I will be staying awhile anyway. I want to continue to watch over Ely. She's coming along nicely, but once the drugs are out of her system, she's going to have a hard patch to overcome." She glanced at Mercury. "You're her friend, you know. She's desolate over what she nearly did."

"She's still a friend." He nodded sharply. "I'll be assigned permanently to Sanctuary now. I'll be heading the security detail we're reworking for the labs and for Ely. She'll be taken care of from now on."

Elizabeth shook her head. "They may have destroyed her. Bringing her back from this won't be easy."

"We'll bring her back." Mercury was arrogant, certain of himself. Ria grinned in pride.

"So, mate, ready to go home?" she asked him. Their cabin was prepared, one within Sanctuary's secured walls, but also within the heavily forested mountain that surrounded the estate.

Mercury's gaze fired, artic blue eyes that burned. She loved those eyes.

She loved him.

With a smile, he escorted her from the labs and to the main floor, urging her to walk faster as he whispered in her ear exactly how he intended to please her.

"All night," he growled as she fought to restrain her laughter. "Couch. Chair. Floor."

"We have a bed," she reminded him.

"I was getting to that." He nipped her ear in retaliation as they entered the foyer.

And Alaiya stepped in from another room.

She wasn't in uniform. She wore cotton leggings, flat boots and a T-shirt. She was ready to fight.

"Keep going," Mercury growled when Ria came to a stop.

Running had never been the answer. Ria had run her all her life—from who she was, from what she was. She wasn't running any longer.

She read the challenge in the other woman's face, in her eyes. Alaiya hadn't accepted that she had lost Mercury. That he wasn't her mate, and that he never would be.

"You don't want to do this here, Alaiya," Ria warned her.

"Better here than anywhere else," Alaiya sneered, glancing back at Mercury as he growled his warning at her. "Is your false mate going to protect you? Does he fight your battles for you? Does he know you're nothing but Dane Vanderale's whore?"

Ria backed into Mercury as he moved to intercept Alaiya, anger tensing his body. Ria turned her head, glaring at him.

"It's my fight."

"The hell it is," he snarled. "I warned her."

"You warned her, but only I can convince her."

Animal to animal. She turned back to Alaiya, hissed, and they charged.

Ria was a Breed. She had trained with the strongest, the most merciless Breed ever created or trained, and she was fighting for everything that had ever belonged to her.

Mercury leaned against the wall, crossed his arms over his chest and fought against the overpowering urge to step in and shake the hell out of Alaiya.

He winced as Ria grabbed a handful of Alaiya's hair and gave her a hard shake for him.

Ria took a punch to her hip when she jerked to the side to avoid a midsection punch. The flat of her hand slammed beneath Alaiya's chin, driving her back before her leg sliced up in a kick that threw the other woman against the wall.

Alaiya came back snarling.

Mercury growled furiously as Ria caught a fist to her chin;

then he smiled in cold, hard satisfaction as Ria's elbow slammed into Alaiya's kidney and a kick sent her to the floor, sliding.

Alaiya was slower getting back up, but no less vicious as she came back at Ria with a hard kick.

"Mercury, your mate is fighting in my foyer," Callan told him as he stepped from the dining room.

"I think she's winning too," Kane stated.

"Shouldn't we stop them?" Jonas eased around, watching the display as Breeds were drawn to the foyer.

"Let her alone." Dane grinned from the doorway. "She's just playing with Alaiya right now. Just wait till she starts fighting dirty."

Alaiya snarled, her teeth sinking into Ria's arm. Time seemed to stand still. Dane and Jonas grabbed Mercury before he ripped Alaiya from his mate, about the same time Ria smiled.

Blood dripped down her arm. She lifted it, slammed Alaiya's head into the wall once, twice, and broke the bite; then she got dirty. A fist to the other woman's face had blood pouring from Alaiya's nose. A high, hard kick to the head, another to the knee, and Alaiya was down.

Ria tangled her fingers in the other woman's hair, bounced her head against the floor and then hissed.

"He's mine. Do we understand each other?"

Alaiya moaned.

"Answer me." Her head bounced against the floor again. "Do we understand each other?"

"Yes," Alaiya cried out, surrendering, submitting as she stared back at Mercury. "He's yours."

Ria jumped back from her. There was no triumph in her face, no smug satisfaction. There was a faint light of regret in her eyes, and one of compassion.

"Find your own mate, Alaiya." Then she turned and stared at the crowd watching her.

Her brow arched at the male Breeds, more than two dozen now, watching for the sheer satisfaction of watching women fight.

"Men." She shook her head. "Breed or human, you're all perverts."

"That makes me your pervert, I guess," Mercury laughed.

"Come on, mate, let's try that theory out. We'll see how you fight me."

He pulled her to the door, her laughter sliding through his senses, stroking them, reminding him that he was mated. And he was loved. And his mate was his greatest treasure.

· EPİLOGUE ·

THREE WEEKS LATER

Jonas opened the door to the confinement cell and entered it slowly, his chest aching as he stared at the huddled form of the doctor he had really grown quite fond of over the years.

Her hair was mussed and lay over her pale face. Her tiny body was curled on the mattress in the padded room, and she looked fragile, incredibly breakable, as he crouched down beside her and watched her for long, long moments.

"We were all played with in the labs," he finally said softly. "The drugs, for many of our females the raping of their minds and their bodies. Do you believe that what happened to them was their own fault? That they deserved such horror because they allowed it?"

She was silent for so long that he wondered if she was even going to answer him.

"No," she finally whispered, her voice hoarse as she continued to lie with her back turned to him.

She was dressed in clean clothing. He had made certain she was kept clean; she would have never forgiven him otherwise. Ely was particular about her appearance. Though she might never forgive him for the fact that they had sedated her to make certain she was bathed and dressed before the madness took her again.

"Then it isn't your fault, what happened," he told her as he sat down on the padded floor and leaned against the wall behind him. "It happened because we were all not diligent enough. We had grown complacent in areas we believed were secure. It won't happen again."

He would make damned certain of it. He would have nightmares for years to come of Ely's breakdown and the near loss the community as a whole had suffered when they thought they would lose her.

"It wasn't you," she whispered, still refusing to turn to him, but he could hear the tears. "They didn't do it to you. They didn't make you do those things."

She broke off, and Jonas had to blink back the burn in his eyes, swallow past the thickness of his throat. Ely was such a proud little creature. With her velvet dark eyes and her pointed little chin that held such stubbornness. Even her sometimes contrary nature was little more than a woman's pride as she fought to make decisions too heavy for her fragile shoulders.

"But it could have easily been me," he told her. "Or Callan. Or even Kane or Tanner. Would you have blamed them, Ely? Would you have turned your back on them and ever blamed them for something that you realized you shared the blame in? We were arrogant believing the labs so safe and our greatest treasure invincible. It was our fault you were touched by that evil, not yours. Your job is to protect us when we're brought to you. Ours is to make certain evil never invades your domain. The failure was ours, little cat, not yours."

She sniffed and shook her head.

Ely hadn't known the horrors of the labs. From birth, she had been the star child of the scientists who created her. The finest, most intelligent genetics had gone into her creation, and she had been treated with the utmost care to ensure she was never damaged.

She had seen the horrors. She had been horrified by them and fought to protect the Breeds she had been created to torture. But she had never experienced that pain herself. It had never been hers before now.

"You can't look me in the eye and allow me to apologize, yet you so easily punched me in the face and called me a 'fucking girl pussy,'" he chided her. "Really, Ely. Where's the fairness in that?"

A tearful laugh escaped her lips.

"And I'll never, as long as I live, forget the look on Jackal's face when you grabbed his crotch. You know, Ely, that man has seen everything, done everything, but I do believe you nearly brought him to his knees."

She moaned and covered her head with her hands. And perhaps others would call him cruel for reminding her of what he knew mortified her. But Ely was made of sterner stuff than that, he assured himself. Besides, others would never allow her to forget it, and preparing her now was for the best.

"Bastard," she whispered tearfully.

He sighed. "FGP," he told her. "Fucking girl pussy. You are aware that title is now being whispered behind my back, aren't you, Ely? You really need to drag your ass off that mattress and get back to work so I can get a little strip of your hide in return."

She almost laughed; he felt it.

"Ely." He said her name softly. "Look at me, just for a moment."

He waited patiently. Finally she pushed her hair back and lifted herself enough to turn and look at him. And he opened his arms to her. "Please, Ely. The guilt is killing me. I didn't protect my favorite girl. Forgive me. Please."

And her tears came now. From eyes bruised with fatigue and pain, as dry lips parted and the cries came. She burrowed into his arms, against his chest. She pulled her legs tight against him, and he wrapped her in his arms and fought his own tears.

Sweet Ely. How could he ever look himself in the mirror after what he had allowed to happen to her? If he couldn't protect her, how could he ever protect anyone else?

He rocked her; he crooned to her, kissed her forehead gently.

"Never again, little cat," he promised her tenderly. "Never again. I swear it."

Anya was where she was supposed to be, but things weren't going as planned. Nothing had gone as planned. When she returned to the labs that evening, within hours, the attack came.

There was no warning. There was no call. Security alarms were blaring, cell doors were opening as safeguards were overridden and locks on the weapons rooms deactivated.

She pushed the scientists into a secure, hidden wall she had found the month before. They hadn't been here long enough evidently to know all the secrets of the labs. Dr. Chernov had replaced the aging scientists ten years before and brought his protégé, Sobelova, a much younger female scientist, along with him.

"Don't leave. Don't move," she ordered them. "Stay here until you hear only silence."

Pale, shaking in shock, the two scientists did as they were told, huddling in the little room as Anya slid the secured door closed and rushed to the exits that led to the cold, desolate land above ground.

"Anya, get out of here." Sofia Ivanova, one of the administrative assistants gripped her arm and dragged her down another hall. "Go that way." She pointed to the stairs. "They're free. I'll cover you."

Cover her? Anya stared behind her as doctors raced from labs with weapons drawn. They were firing on personnel? Shock rushed through her, tore through her mind. She knew those men and women. Knew them well. And they were firing on the personnel attempting to escape?

"Run damn you!" Sofia pushed her to the exit. "Get out of here before I have to shoot you."

Anya ran. As she ran, fury fed the fear and the shock coursing through her adrenaline-laced mind. This was the exact plan she had given Del-Rey for the rescue. Had he not trusted her? He had attacked only hours after her return, giving her no time to ensure her father and cousins weren't here?

No, it had to be something else, she decided in desperation as she raced up the stairs. She gripped an older woman's arm, one of the secretaries, and pushed her ahead.

"Hurry, Marie," Anya urged the other woman as she sobbed and nearly fell. "We must hurry."

Other personnel were racing past them as Anya grabbed Marie's arm and all but dragged her up the steps. Marie had children, grandchildren. A husband that was ill. She was needed. And besides, she always brought the Breeds cookies. She was kind and gentle.

The door was broken from its hinges above, lying on its side as security forces were waving personnel through, urging them to hurry, to rush. Masks covered their faces to protect them from the cold. It was bitterly cold outside, and Marie had no jacket, no coat to wear.

"Run for the barracks," she told the other woman. "It will be warm there and safer. We'll hide there."

She ran into the cold, aware of the gunfire, the yelling voices, the clash of forces. Then she was only aware of the hard arm that wrapped around her waist, jerked her against a broad chest and the knife that lay at her throat.

She could feel the cold blade pressing into her throat, pinching the flesh, within a breath of actually cutting her skin.

"Kobrin, I have your daughter."

Loud, echoing through the valley, she knew that voice, knew the growl that sounded in it and felt the sob that tore from her throat.

Betrayal. He had betrayed her.

Agony tore through her with such pain she could only gasp at the reality of it.

The sound of gunfire faded away. Personnel were no longer rushing through the doors. She could hear them at the entrance though, feel the tension that thickened the air.

Del-Rey. She felt the first tear fall. Oh God, she had trusted him. She had trusted him so much.

"We're lowering our weapons," her father called out. "Take the Breeds. Go. We'll not stand in your way, but let Anya go."

She stared back at her father's pale face, at her cousins moving with him. All four of her cousins were on duty tonight. Her friends were here, those who would have helped her had she asked, but she hadn't.

A shot fired out and her first cousin fell, gripping his leg and screaming out in pain. Three more shots in rapid succession had the other three writhing on the ground.

"Stop it!" She screamed, her hands clawing at the arm wrapped around her waist. "No. No. Don't do this."

Fury and pain gripped her. She stared back at her father miserably, sobbing with the shame of what she had done.

"Transport's landing in sixty seconds, boss." That was the one Del-Rey called Brim. Sometimes he had called him Brimstone.

They had all betrayed her. The small team of men she had become friends with, that she had trusted her father's and her cousins' lives to.

"How can you do this?" She sobbed. "Damn you, how can you do this?"

"Anya, be still child," her father cried out. "Remember your control, daughter. Your cousins live."

"For now," Del-Rey called back in a lazy drawl. "Tell me, Kobrin, you've been here since the first Breed was created, did you ever think to aid them?"

"They live," her father called back. "I have killed none. This was not a slaughter house."

Del-Rey chuckled behind her. "I think I will take your daughter with me, Kobrin. Insurance, I believe. You will not notify your Russian air force; you will notify no one of what has happened here for six hours. Or she will die. Are we understood?"

"Leave her here," her father called out desperately. "I swear to you no one will follow you."

Del-Rey laughed. "No, they won't follow me. I have the prize of the Genetics Council's young protégés. Your daughter, Kobrin. Don't make me kill her."

Another shot fired and her father stumbled, falling as Anya screamed out for him. Her hands reach out, her fingers curling as she was lifted off her feet and the sound of a heli-transport arriving could be heard.

She screamed out for her father, clawed and slapped at the arm securing her. She kicked, she cursed, and she sobbed.

Rage ate her insides as the betrayal that filled her burned

into her mind. He had lied. From the first moment, he had lied, and she would never forgive him.

"Move out!" Del-Rey ordered as he raced into the back of the transport behind the other men that converged on the huge black craft. "Cavalier, get this bastard off the ground."

Cavalier. She had arranged his transport the year before. How many others were here? How many of those she had trusted had betrayed her?

"Stop fighting me, Anya." Del-Rey held her in place as he settled onto the metal bench, holding her secure, and the transport lifted off.

She couldn't see outside it. She had lost sight of her father. Lost sight of her family.

"You bastard!" she screamed, struggling harder as her fists struck back at his face. "You son of a bitch. You fucking bastard. How could you? How could you?"

"How could they?" He snarled, jerking her around to face him, his black eyes blazing in fury as his lips drew back from his lethal canines. "How dared they leave a child to arrange this? How dare they endanger you as they have? They have a bullet in their legs rather than their heads. They should be fucking thankful."

She slapped his face. Her hand slammed into his cheek with enough force to burn her palm before she slapped him again. Furious, enraged screams were strangled in her throat as he jerked her arms to her sides, holding her in place as a growl tore from his throat.

Then his lips pressed into hers. She tried to scream again, but he stole the opportunity to push his tongue past her lips. Spice filled her mouth. She swallowed and sobbed into the kiss, because it was good. Because his lips stroked over hers as she had always imagined they would. Because he tasted like warmth and passion, and because he had lied to her. He had betrayed her. And now he was stealing her mind.

She was still sobbing as his head lifted and his arms locked her to his chest. His hand covered her head, holding her against him as her fists clenched and beat at his shoulders.

She hated him. She hated him. Oh God, she hated him. And she loved him. And she felt as though her soul had been shredded. Her Coyote warrior had betrayed her. He had lied, over and over again, betrayed every vow he had made to her. He had stolen her innocence before he ever kissed her, and she wondered if she could ever forgive him for that.

Del-Rey stared over her head at the Coyotes that now joined him. Breeds, their gazes flat and hard as they watched him. They were a threat, he could smell it in the air; his men could feel it as they surrounded him.

"Mine," he told them all, his voice cold, commanding. "This woman is mine."

The five female Coyotes stared back at him. They were the most dangerous he thought, especially the oldest, Sharone.

Her gaze flicked to Anya's sobbing form.

"You were wrong," she told him flatly. "You should have left her family alone."

"They put her in danger. They are lucky they live."

"No, my friend." She shook her head. "You will be lucky if you live. You betrayed her, and she won't forget it. She won't forgive it. We see the wisdom of what you did. The retribution we all felt was needed. But we stayed our hand, because she's ours as well." She indicated the Breeds that had come out of the underground facilities. "And what you have done this night, she will make certain you pay for."

Tender Anya? She would rage, might hate for a while, but he had left her family alive. He would make her understand.

"Stay out of my way," he told her, and he meant all of them. "You swore loyalty to me and to my packs. Not to this girl. Where she's concerned, you will not interfere."

"Then you will ensure she is not harmed, in any way," Sharone told him fiercely. "We follow you, Alpha, but that one"—she nodded to Anya—"that one, is one of us. Mistreat her, and you mistreat us all. Remember that."

Mistreat her? He had no intentions of mistreating her. Loving her, perhaps. Easing her from her anger, definitely. Fucking her until they were both screaming with the pleasure, that was a given. She would forgive him. He would ensure it. After all, he hadn't killed her father or her cousins. They lived. They would merely hurt. A lot. And it was pain they deserved. Much more than they received.

He smoothed his hand over Anya's loose hair. Without the braid it hung well past her shoulders. He cupped the back of her head to him and leaned his own against the wall of the transport.

He was aware of his own men watching him, questioning his

decision. They had questioned the wisdom of it when he had first told them what he planned. He has sent half his men six months ago to Colorado to secretly secure the caverns that overlooked Haven, the Wolf Breed compound. They were preparing things there for his arrival. Arriving in secrecy was paramount though. That meant ditching the transport and going in, in small groups. That was easily handled.

Anya might not be as easily controlled, just as he was finding his own response to her was by far less easy to handle than he had imagined.

His head lowered again, his lips touching hers. His tongue was burning for the taste of her. Desperate for another of those hot, passionate kisses, the feel of her mouth sucking at him, drawing the tightness from his tongue.

He was aware of the eyes that watched, yet he couldn't draw back.

"They should have protected you better, little one," he whispered against her lush lips. "They well deserved my vengeance."

Her lashes lifted. Her eyes were dark with misery, with pain, as an exhausted sob tore from her throat.

"You betrayed me. You lied to me," she cried again. "I'll never trust you again, Del-Rey. I can never trust you."

He stole the words. He couldn't bear to hear them, couldn't bear the pain or the anger in her eyes or her voice. He took his kiss. Her lips parted for him helplessly. He could feel her fighting the need, felt her giving in to it even as she cried out in surrender. And even as he kissed her, he realized there was something not quite as it had once been within him. A hunger, a need, a driving inferno of lust building inside him that made no sense, that defied description.

He needed this woman to survive it though. And Del-Rey always ensured he had what he needed to survive. He blamed it on the Coyote side of his genetics. Blood will tell and so, evidently, would DNA. At least in some part. Maybe he should blame it on the human side, he thought wearily. Anya might have accepted that easier.

THREE DAYS LATER

Three days. She burned. Flames licked over her flesh. Fury, confusion, betrayal and pain ate at her mind while the most horrible arousal she could have ever imagined ate at her body.

It had to be the taste of his kiss, she thought. She was craving it. It was killing her, the need for that kiss. And he kept forcing it on her, as though she actually wanted his kiss now.

She paced the bedroom of the cabin she was locked in. She was dressed in the soft cotton pants and T-shirt Sharone had brought her earlier.

She had begged Sharone to help her escape. She had it all worked out. All she had to do was get to a town and contact the embassy, they would take care of everything. They would contact her father; she could go home. She could forget Del-Rey Delgado ever existed.

And Sharone had been going for it. Anya had seen it in her eyes until Del-Rey had stepped into the room, furious, and pulled Sharone from it.

Now, she was alone. Alone to think, to worry. God, her father was lying in the snow bleeding, her cousins with him. Her cousins had family, children. Who would support them now? Times weren't good in Russia right now; the economy was weak all over. They would lose their homes. They would be in the cold. Her father.

She sniffed. Who would bring him his vodka when he was tired and worn from trying to manipulate the Council scientists and members? Who would bandage his leg?

The tears were flowing from her eyes again. She should have more control than this. Her father had berated her for her loss of control. But that was something he did. She had red hair, he told her often, like her mother. And her mother had learned that holding her temper always helped herself and others more than losing it did.

She couldn't control her emotions now. She hadn't been able to since those shots had been fired. Since Del-Rey had kissed her. Since her world had exploded around her. Since something had exploded within her.

She pressed her hands into her stomach. Her abdomen rippled and she could feel the pulse of dampness between her thighs. Her nipples were so sensitive the rasp of the T-shirt was torture. Her clitoris was engorged and aching. Even when she had touched herself she had never been this aroused.

What had he done to her? He had to have done something to her. There was no other explanation.

She paced the room, she cursed. She would rage and then

she would cry. She reviled Del-Rey Delgado. "Of the king" her ass. There was nothing kingly about that bastard.

"What did you do to me?" She screamed, picked up one of the few objects still in the bedroom, a wooden bowl, and threw it at the door.

It didn't shatter. It hit the door with a resounding bang and then fell to the carpet as she collapsed on the end of the bed, curling into herself, moaning at the need rippling through her.

Her eyes closed, and she swore she tasted his kiss, felt his hands on her flesh. One touch, she told herself. She could allow one touch, just to still the demand raging through her body. Maybe one more kiss.

"No!" She gritted out between her teeth. Not even one touch. One touch would lead to another, and she would be begging. God help her if he even kissed her. She wouldn't survive it.

And she didn't want that liar's kisses. Lies. Six years of lies. Promises he had broken one right after the other. She would be warned before the rescue. She would have time to make certain her father and cousins were safe. She would have time to ensure that personnel were able to get out safely rather than being murdered in the stampede to escape.

She had seen those doctors wielding automatic rifles and turning them on the innocent administrative personnel and lab techs trying to escape.

She hoped the doctors were dead. She hoped they were roasting in hell. Unlike Del-Rey. Oh, she didn't want him dead. She wanted him alive. Alive and well so she could kill him herself.

She whimpered as another punch of sensation slammed into her stomach, her vagina, her clitoris. It was like a racking blow of electricity being shoved inside her. It sizzled and burned and left her gasping in need as the bedroom door opened.

She rolled to her feet, stumbling, staring at the man watching her with the devil's black eyes.

"What did you do to me?" Her fists clenched at her side.

"I don't know." He shook his head wearily. "Whatever it is, I did it to myself as well."

"You bastard!" There was nothing left to throw at him. She had thrown everything she could find over the past three days and the final object, that damned bowl, now lay at his feet. "You're lying. Just like you lied to me all these years, you're lying to me now."

"No, Anya."

The sound of her name on his lips was too much. She snarled, her fingers clawed as she jumped for him. She was going to claw his lying eyes out of his face. She was going to make him hurt the same way he was making her hurt.

He caught her hands an inch from his face.

"Stop this, Anya, it isn't helping."

"Do you think I don't know that?" she cried out, struggling against him, mind and body torn apart by conflicting emotions and needs. "You betrayed me, Del-Rey. You lied."

"I know, baby." He held her hands with one hand, the other touched her cheek, his thumb moving over her lips. "We'll deal with that, I promise. But I need your kiss. Now."

"No," she moaned, a long, drawn-out sob of need and despair as she pressed her cheek into his palm, bit his thumb.

Oh God, he tasted good. So good. Her tongue licked over the pad and her lashes fluttered.

"One more kiss," he growled. "Then we'll figure this out. I promise."

"One more kiss," she gasped. "One more."

She was reaching for him, needing him. Her lips opened beneath his, accepting his tongue and that taste she craved so desperately. She sucked it into her mouth and heard his groan of pleasure. She arched into his arms and begged silently for more.

One more kiss wasn't enough. She needed him to touch her. So bad. So bad that she gripped his hand and shoved it under her shirt. Then her hands were burrowing beneath his shirt, touching hot, hard flesh as she felt his hand cup the swollen mound of her breast.

Oh, that was good. His thumb raked over her nipple and it was even better. He lifted her into his arms, and a second later she was stretching back on the bed as he whipped the shirt over her head.

Her hands buried in his hair as his lips covered her nipple. She tore at his shirt until he lifted his head, ripped it off and moved to her other nipple.

His skin covered hard, corded muscle. It flexed beneath her palms, her nails, as she felt his hands pushing at the cotton pants she wore.

It was desperate. She could feel the enraged lust traveling between them, as though electricity connected them, one feeding from the other until she was burning inside and she knew she wasn't going to get enough of him. She needed more of him.

A second later she found herself flipped to her stomach. Her fingers curled into the blankets as she opened her eyes and stared in dazed confusion at the bed. Her hips were jerked up. Calloused fingers ran through the sensitive folds between her thighs, and she was wet. So slick and wet and hot. And it felt so delicious she stretched into the caress.

"Tell me you want me," he growled behind her.

"I want you," she sobbed the answer into the bed, tears falling from her eyes again as she felt him behind her. "I want you."

Broad and hot, the crest of his cock tucked between the wet folds.

Not like this. She pressed her head into the bed. Not like this, where she couldn't hold on to him, where she couldn't find a sense of control or focus.

Why like this?

He pressed inside and she went crazy from the pleasure. Her back arched at the stretching heat, a cry falling from her lips, part protest, part hunger.

She felt a pulse of heated fluid filling her, burning her further. She felt her sex flex and ripple and draw him in. With each heated spurt she became more sensitive, hungrier, needier.

She should tell him she was a virgin. She should tell him she hadn't done this before.

A scream ripped from her throat as he tunneled inside in three hard strokes. Every inch. And he was so thick, invading her, stretching her, tearing through her virginity without the pain she had expected, but with more impact than she could have imagined.

Her thighs parted more, her hips tilted back farther and he was coming over her, his powerful arms braced by her head as he began thrusting into her. His lips were at her shoulder. Sharp little kisses, heated and fierce just below her neck.

She was filled with him. She could feel every heavy vein in his cock, every pulse of blood through it, and it was killing her. She needed more, wanted more.

And he was giving her more. Surging inside her as she felt her body tighten. The muscles wrapped around his erection tightened, her clit throbbed, pulsed, and then everything inside her exploded in a cataclysm of light and color that had her screaming his name.

She shuddered through her orgasm, jerking beneath him as he continued to thrust hard and fast, gaining speed, pushing into her as she felt more of those pulses of heated fluid.

A second later, she heard him snarl, and felt something shocking. Something she knew couldn't be natural. This couldn't be real. His cock was swelling in one place. Getting larger, separating her farther as she felt his semen begin to spurt inside her.

Animal genetics, she thought distantly. He was locking inside her. Held tight and sure inside the heavy muscles of her vagina. He suddenly snarled with animalistic fervor, and she felt his teeth pierce her upper shoulder.

She should be screaming in pain. She was screaming in pleasure. Another, harder orgasm ripped through her, shook her, wrenched her senses from her and left her lost. She was so lost, with nothing, no one to hold on to. Thrown into a pleasure so violent, so brutal, she wondered if she could survive it.

Behind her, Del-Rey was growling. His teeth still gripped her flesh, his cock still locked inside her. She sobbed out his name. She wanted to beg him to hold her, but the last shreds of her pride held her back.

He had taken her like this, impersonally, and he had to have done it for a reason. She didn't matter. The same reason he had shot her family: the same reason he had lied to her for so many years. Because Anya Kobrin and the fragile love that had been building inside her for him, didn't matter.

Which left her alone, at the mercy of a man that she now knew had no mercy.

◆　　◆　　◆

He had made a grave tactical error and Del-Rey knew it. The anger that had festered inside him over the years had overlooked the intense, all-abiding loyalty Anya felt for her family and friends. Del-Rey was a man who believed in retribution. He had been such a man all his life, until he sat here now, staring into the darkness of his own soul, and realized he had wounded a treasure he hadn't known he'd held.

He had known from the moment he met her that he was going to betray her. It was the way of the world. He couldn't fully trust. He never gave complete control or complete trust to another person outside of Brim. Just as he had known that retribution would be dealt to the guards' leaders, as he had always dealt it. He had always killed before. He'd pulled his punches because of Anya. He hadn't killed; he had only wounded. Her father and her cousins would know they had been dealt with fairly. They were men of war. War had different rules than the fairy tales young women such as Anya lived within.

She was sleeping. Finally. Del-Rey sat in the chair beside her bed, dressed, his head in his hands as his elbows rested on his knees. He had sat down there the minute he withdrew from her, as soon as the knot that had been swollen in his cock had receded enough to pull away from her. He had jerked his jeans back to his hips and sat. To keep from falling to the floor.

And he had remained there as she silently folded herself onto her side, tugged the blanket over her shoulders and cried silently until she went to sleep.

She hadn't sobbed again. She hadn't cursed him or railed at him. She had retreated into herself, and he had no idea how to pull her back.

He lowered his hands and stared at them. Large hands. The hands of a warrior. A killer. These hands had held her beneath him. His teeth had held her in place. His cock had knotted hard and deep inside her.

He had never done that. In his entire sexual life, he had never done that to a woman. Why this woman?

He rose to his feet and fixed his jeans before jerking his T-shirt on. He could hear Brim, his second-in-command moving up the steps to the second-floor bedroom. Del-Rey opened the door as the other man reach it.

Concerned light blue eyes stared back at him.

"Vehicles are here," Brim reported. "Those women downstairs are pissed off though. Watch your back."

He didn't blame them. Hell, someone should shoot him.

"Have you contacted Haven?"

"Messages have gone out, no answer," Brim reported before inhaling with narrowed eyes. "Something isn't right here, Del-Rey. You took the girl?"

Del-Rey growled. Anya was none of Brim's business.

Brim shook his head. "Her scent has changed, shifted, and yours has as well. Something whacked is going on here."

That was the understatement of the century. He looked back at Anya.

"Get ready to move out," he told his second-in-command. "Have them send Haven another message. I need their doctor. Now. This can't happen again, Brim. I don't know what the hell happened in here, but it can't happen again."

He closed the door and moved back to the bed.

"Anya," he whispered her name, and she flinched.

Was it so horrendous, his touch? The greatest pleasure he had known in his life, and now, she flinched from him.

"Get dressed. The vehicles are here and we're moving out. Now. I don't think you want to risk any attempt I would make to try to dress you myself."

He tried to make her angry. It didn't work. She pushed the blankets from her as though the exhaustion that gripped her was painful. He watched as she found her clothes and went to the bathroom, closing the door behind her.

He didn't hear her sobbing, didn't hear her crying. But he could smell her, and what he scented clawed at his chest. Somehow, he had managed to douse that fiery flame that was so much a part of her. At this moment, his Anya smelled of defeat. And Del-Rey felt it. For the first time in his life, he knew the taste of defeat.